MW01036571

THE CHILDREN OF EVE

ALSO BY JOHN CONNOLLY

THE CHARLIE PARKER STORIES

EVERY DEAD THING

DARK HOLLOW

THE KILLING KIND

THE WHITE ROAD

THE REFLECTING EYE
(NOVELLA IN THE NOCTURNES COLLECTION)

THE BLACK ANGEL

THE UNQUIET

THE REAPERS

THE LOVERS

THE WHISPERERS

THE BURNING SOUL

THE WRATH OF ANGELS

THE WOLF IN WINTER

A SONG OF SHADOWS

A TIME OF TORMENT

A GAME OF GHOSTS

THE WOMAN IN THE WOODS

A BOOK OF BONES

THE DIRTY SOUTH

THE NAMELESS ONES

THE FURIES

THE INSTRUMENTS OF DARKNESS

OTHER WORKS

BAD MEN

THE BOOK OF LOST THINGS

THE LAND OF LOST THINGS

he: A NOVEL

SHORT STORIES

NOCTURNES

NIGHT MUSIC: NOCTURNES VOLUME 2

NIGHT & DAY

THE SAMUEL JOHNSON STORIES (FOR YOUNG ADULTS)

THE GATES

THE INFERNALS

THE CREEPS

THE CHRONICLES OF THE INVADERS (WITH JENNIFER RIDYARD)

CONQUEST

EMPIRE

DOMINION

NONFICTION

BOOKS TO DIE FOR:
THE WORLD'S GREATEST MYSTERY WRITERS ON THE WORLD'S GREATEST MYSTERY NOVELS
(AS EDITOR, WITH DECLAN BURKE)

SHADOW VOICES: 300 YEARS OF IRISH GENRE FICTION: A HISTORY IN STORIES (EDITOR)

PARKER: A MISCELLANY

MIDNIGHT MOVIE MONOGRAPHS: HORROR EXPRESS

THE CHILDREN OF EVE

John Connolly

EMILY BESTLER BOOKS

ATRIA

NEW YORK AMSTERDAM/ANTWERP LONDON

TORONTO SYDNEY/MELBOURNE NEW DELHI

An Imprint of Simon & Schuster, LLC
1230 Avenue of the Americas
New York, NY 10020

First Emily Bestler Books/Atria Books hardcover edition May 2025

EMILY BESTLER BOOKS/ATRIA BOOKS and colophon are trademarks of Simon & Schuster, LLC

Manufactured in the United States of America

1 3 5 7 9 10 8 6 4 2

Library of Congress Cataloging-in-Publication Data has been applied for.

ISBN 978-1-6680-8394-9
ISBN 978-1-6680-8396-3 (ebook)

For Cliona O'Neill

1

To thee do we cry, poor banished children of Eve.
To thee do we send up our sighs . . .

"Salve Regina," Catholic prayer

CHAPTER I

The antiques store owned by Antonio Elizalde and inherited, like his name, from his father, stood on Calle Del Beso, close to the intersection of Avenida San Luis, in the Mexican town of Santa Ana Tlachiahualpa. The store didn't look promising from the outside, its windows dusty, its frontage dilapidated, and its displays of furniture, paintings, and craquelure plates seemingly untroubled for years by the interest of customers. Its opening hours, in common with its owner, were eccentric and unpredictable despite Elizalde residing on the floor above. Those opening hours had once been posted on a handwritten piece of card jammed in the left-hand corner of the window, but years of sunlight had faded them to illegibility, if they had ever been anything more than aspirational to begin with.

Elizalde, in his late sixties, was a single man and likely to remain so. Cadaverously thin, his complexion yellow, and his dress sense favoring gray flannel pants, mutedly striped shirts, and shabby cardigans, irrespective of the temperature or time of year, he attracted few admiring looks from even the most desperate of the town's widows and spinsters. His universe appeared to be a small one, even by the standards of that place. It was bounded by his place of business, the Iglesia de Santa Maria, the Abarrotes Polo convenience store, and the Zitala restaurant and bar, in the latter of which he would smoke Marlboro cigarettes (until the ban on smoking in public places forced him, like so many others, to indulge his vice in secret, like a criminal) and drink no more than two palomas a night. Twice yearly, he left the town to embark on buying trips, vanishing without fanfare and returning similarly unannounced. He was once spotted at Mexico City International Airport by an elderly local woman returning from a trip to visit her grandchildren in El Norte, who was so shocked to encounter Elizalde outside his natural environment that she had to sit for a moment to recover herself. Elizalde had simply raised his hat to her and proceeded to his gate, passport in hand, quietly amused at the effect he had created.

Elizalde was not unsociable, but his sociability was almost as limited as his orbit, rarely extending beyond polite comments on the weather, football, or the failings of politicians, both national and local. Nobody resented Elizalde for his reserve because he was courteous and paid his bills on time, both qualities rarer in society than one might wish. He was understood to have money—he would otherwise have been a poor advertisement for his trade—but not so much as to make him a target for theft or extortion. His enterprise might have been more successful had he advertised his wares on the internet or found premises closer to Mexico City, but on those occasions when he could be drawn on the matter, he declared the internet to be too noisy—*demasiado ruidoso*, whatever that meant—and Mexico City to be louder still. And who could fault him for this? That he preferred to keep Santa Ana Tlachiahualpa as his base and let the *norteamericanos*, *chinos*, and *europeos* come to him if they wished to buy—because come to him they did, if not in any great numbers, and always by prior arrangement—was something to be celebrated, not condemned.

Elizalde's clients would often be accompanied by the local guides who had led them to his door, although some buyers arrived from Mexico City with their own drivers, security experts who made no effort to hide the guns they wore. The customers had nothing to fear from Elizalde, who was an honest, if costly, broker, but Mexico suffered from a surfeit of bad publicity, even if foreign visitors were at greater risk of being kidnapped in New Zealand or Canada than Nuevo León or Chiapas. As for being shot, well, that was a different matter, although the Bahamas were more dangerous than Baja when it came to stray gunfire, and nobody really wanted to see *turistas* hit by bullets. It attracted too much attention, and anyway, the *cholos* preferred to prey on their own people, *pendejos* that they were.

So moneyed men and women would enter Elizalde's cool, dark store, where they would be offered bottled water, soda, a beer, even whiskey or tequila if they preferred. Tea and coffee were also available, but most opted for something cooler after the journey. On rare occasions, Elizalde's hospitality would be declined outright, not even an *ahorita* or a *después de un poco más tiempo, por favor*, a breach of etiquette that would, in the event of a sale, result in the customer receiving a smaller discount than might otherwise have been available. After such negotiations, assuming they were mutually satisfactory, Elizalde would buy a round of drinks at Zitala that evening, where his neighbors would toast his good health and fortune.

Unspoken—by Elizalde and the community in general, even if the *metiches* inevitably whispered among themselves—was the precise nature of what he was selling, because offloading junk paintings and scuffed art deco furniture salvaged from the more distressed residences of Coyoacán would not be sufficient to support Elizalde's modest existence, even allowing for the fact that he owned the building in which he lived and worked. Also, while his loyalty to the town was admirable, might his decision to remain there not also have been linked to its proximity to the ancient city of Teotihuacan? The great archaeological site covered about eight square miles, its massive pyramids, its Avenue of the Dead, and its history of human sacrifice attracting more than four million tourists a year, some of them eager to return home with more than photographs of ruins or replica figurines of the Old God, the Fat God, and the Flayed God.

True, some said that Mexico should not permit its treasures to be sold so easily (if not cheaply) by unscrupulous men. Others argued that the country had more than enough ancient pots and figurines already, most of them gathering dust in museum basements or university attics. What did it matter if a handful went to the United States, Europe, or the Far East? Señor Elizalde paid his taxes, contributed to the Church, and shared some of his bounty when a sale, legal or otherwise, was concluded. If one were to search even a handful of the houses in the locality, one might find similar items on shelves or by doors, discovered in the dirt by someone's grandfather or uncle and kept for the family instead of being surrendered to the state. Let he who was without sin cast the first stone; if one was a thief, all might be thieves.

So Elizalde went about his business undisturbed. He sold items of value not only from Mexico but also from Peru, Chile, Colombia, and Ecuador. They did not always come with paperwork, but their authenticity was unquestionable. Among collectors of a particular stripe, the name of Antonio Elizalde was a guarantee of quality and probity. His years in the trade had provided him with reliable contacts in shipping companies and ANAM, the Mexican National Customs Agency, but he could also arrange for purchases to be ferried across the border with the United States by car or truck, which avoided the kind of closer inspection that negotiating airports was wont to involve.

All might have continued as it was—regular sales of primarily small and easily transportable pieces, yielding an income designed to support a comfortable but unostentatious lifestyle—had those Marlboro cigarettes not caught up with Elizalde: first as a cough, then as chest pains, and finally, having ignored the early warning signs, as a tumor the size of a baby's fist. Elizalde had never been seriously ill before, his family boasting a happy history of long lives followed by relatively quick deaths, and he had never seen any reason to invest in health insurance.

That apart, he was also superstitious and regarded insuring his health, like writing a will, as a prelude to inevitable decline, an invitation to Death to take a seat at one's table. Only when a brush with COVID had left him fighting for breath, convinced he was going to suffocate, and he found himself queuing with others at least as unwell at a local clinic, did he decide that some form of coverage might be wise, even if he kept it to the cheapest option. Now Elizalde was being forced to face the consequences of his parsimony. The quality of private healthcare in Mexico was excellent, and the hospitals in Mexico City, Guadalajara, and Monterrey were among the best, but the treatment he required was expensive, and even a lifetime of illicit dealing in Mesoamerican antiquities would not be sufficient to settle his bills while leaving him financially positioned to enjoy life afterward.

And so, immersion in various miracle waters having failed to heal him, Elizalde had instead involved himself in an act of theft and smuggling unprecedented in his history, one that had brought with it a payday large enough to cover the bulk of his treatment, albeit at considerable personal risk should his complicity become known. Then again, if he hadn't agreed to take part, he would have been forced to take his chances with another bunch of crooks, namely his insurers. They had already made it clear that whatever they were prepared to offer would be enough to deal with perhaps only one of the fingers on that malignant fist, leaving the rest to be tackled by the public system. The choice, then, was between slow, painful treatment for cancer—which, with his natural tendency toward the pessimistic, Elizalde felt would lead only to a slow, agonizing demise and the prospect of another decade or more of survival after the best medical treatment money could buy. The downside to the latter was the possibility of a differently agonizing death—slow by the standards of, say, a heart attack, but over with in the blink of an eye compared to cancer—should the victim of the crime connect Elizalde to its commission.

Elizalde took the second option, because only a fool would not, and all had proceeded without a hitch, because good things still sometimes happened to moderately good people. The payment was released upon safe receipt of the cargo in the United States, and Elizalde requested that the funds be forwarded directly to his oncologist, who knew better than to ask any questions about their source. Nevertheless, in case the Mexican tax authorities should take an interest, the money was funneled via a private nonprofit foundation registered under Section 501(c)(3) of the Internal Revenue Code as a health charity, set up in 2022 through an online legal filing service and registered in Delaware, USA. On the advice of an anonymous client, Elizalde, poor and frightened, had written to the charity shortly after receiving his diagnosis, and in his possession was a copy of his original email, as well as the encouraging response he had received. God bless America.

Thus, as the sun was setting, Antonio Elizalde walked back from what would be his final trip to Zitala for a while. The following day, he would take a plane to Monterrey, there to commence a course of therapy he had been warned would be unpleasant but was also likely to be successful. He had enjoyed a final paloma and bought a round of the bar's best tequila for all present, who wished him good luck in the struggle to come. He had sold off—at knockdown prices, though still at a profit—whatever items of dubious provenance remained in his store and arranged for a local family to take care of the building while he was away. In a brown paper bag from his favorite bakery, he was carrying three sweet breads, two of which he planned to eat for breakfast the next morning and the third on the plane, consuming a piece of sweet bread being a known remedy for fear.

In flagrant breach of both the law and his doctor's advice, Elizalde was also smoking the remaining cigarettes in his final packet of Marlboros on the grounds that the damage had been done and a few more weren't going to kill him. As though by divine providence, he finished the last cigarette just as he reached the Iglesia de Santa Maria. He entered the church and offered a prayer for himself. Later, at home, he planned to burn incense and make an offering to the Great Goddess of Teotihuacan, deity of the underworld, mother of creation, because one couldn't be too careful, and the Great Goddess had probably been around for at least as long as Santa Maria.

Elizalde paused at the church door to button his coat before stepping outside. Ever since his diagnosis, he'd been feeling the cold more, which he ascribed to Death's proximity. The town was silent; no children, no dogs, not even a bird pecking at the dirt. It was as though the rest of humanity had faded away, leaving Elizalde as the last man extant. He tried not to take it as a bad omen, a premonition of some future state of being in which he was reduced to a specter haunting the places he had known in life, invisible to others just as they were rendered unseen to him. A melody came to him, one beloved of his father, Antonio Aguilar, singing "Nadie Es Eterno":

Todo lo acaban los años
Dime, ¿qué te llevas tú?
Si con el tiempo no queda
Ni la tumba, ni la cruz.

Everything ends with the years
Tell me, what do you take with you?
If nothing remains after time
Not even a tomb, or a cross.

It was a song of suffering and loss, the kind, Elizalde reflected, that only a Mexican would find consoling. He decided to embrace the solitude and enjoy the emptiness of the streets as he made his way home. Upon reaching his store, he paused by the window and took in his reflection, almost relieved to find confirmation of his continued substantiality. A shape descended on his face, causing him instinctively to try to brush it away until he realized it was a spider spinning a thread on the other side of the glass, rappeling across Elizalde's likeness. He watched it reach the bottom of a display case, where it landed on a bayonet that had been used at the Battle of San Jacinto in 1836; there the arachnid joined more of its kin. To his disgust, Elizalde noticed that the window was crawling with small black spiders. He could only assume that an unnoticed egg sac had recently burst, freeing the young, even if these were unexpectedly large for newborns. If only he'd spotted the sac in time, he could have sprayed it with bleach and water and killed the babies before they could hatch. Now he'd have to turn on all the lights, take a vacuum cleaner, and try to suck up as many of the little *cabrones* as possible before they overran the showroom.

(But had he looked closer, Elizalde might also have spotted other insects alongside the arachnids: beetles, centipedes, wood lice, earwigs, and more. And while some were preyed upon by the spiders, most were ignored because the spiders, like the rest, were too busy trying to escape . . .)

Elizalde hurried to the front door, unlocked it, and stepped into the dark, where he felt small bodies crunch beneath the soles of his feet. He hit the light switch and saw that the floor was alive with spiders: house spiders, thankfully, and not widows, recluses, or hobos, which would have been a very different matter, requiring him to exchange his last night at home for the safety of a hotel room until the exterminators could take care of the infestation. Nevertheless, the spiders were revolting in such numbers and might require him to spend the night at a hotel anyway: he wasn't convinced that his vacuum cleaner would be capable of dealing with all of them, and he couldn't start throwing around buckets of watery bleach without damaging his floorboards, his walls, and—not least—his stock. However difficult to shift some of his inventory might be, it would be harder still to offload if stained with streaks of white. But where had the damned spiders come from? Indeed, where had the other bugs come from, because now he observed them, too, even as they scuttled by him to vanish into the night through the open door. Could it be a fire? Yet he smelled no smoke.

Elizalde heard movement from the store, accessed from the main hallway via a doorway to his left. The door opened into his office, which was little more than a nook in a corner filled with dusty paperwork. If there was an intruder, they'd gained access through the rear of the building, since the front door had been locked and undamaged, and the alarm had not been activated. Elizalde could see the glow of the lamp in his office, which remained lit day and night. Natural illumination did not extend far into the showroom, and his shins were already scarred enough from miscalculating the distances between objects without adding further darkness to the equation. His neighbor Señora Cárdeñas or one of her sons might have dropped by to check on him. If so, what were they doing stumbling around among the antiques unless they, too, were trying to discover the reason for the swarm?

Curiously, while the spiders were climbing the walls and crawling over the floor, they showed no interest in Elizalde and were leaving a clear area around his shoes, such that his clothing might have been treated with repellent. As he progressed toward the inner door, they continued to avoid him, perhaps having learned from the fate of their brothers and sisters crushed upon his return. Elizalde slipped his mini revolver from his jacket pocket. He'd had the gun for years and rarely went anywhere without it, as an aging merchant operating out of a small town might offer a tempting target for some *pinche narco* with a habit to feed. The NAA weighed only eight ounces, but it held five .22 rounds that would leave holes not easily filled.

Elizalde didn't announce himself before entering, since that was an excellent way to get killed. The door was slightly ajar, and the hinges were well-oiled, so he made no sound as he opened it wider. The office nook beyond was empty—unless one counted the spiders and insects. The glow from the lamp, combined with the moonlight filtering through the muddle of stock in the window, served to render regions of the store semi-visible while leaving others in shadow. The lamp was angled away from the door, and Elizalde stayed behind it to avoid making himself too much of a target. However, he could pick up no trace of an intruder and heard no further movement.

His attention was distracted by an object on the floor, gilded by the lamplight. It was a figurine: the representation of the Great Goddess to whom he had intended to make an offering before going to bed. He kept it on a shelf in his office, hidden by files, pens, and stationery because he didn't want prospective customers with the proper knowledge to espy it and begin making offers. The Great Goddess had been handed down from his great-grandfather, who found it at Teotihuacan long before the city became a UNESCO site. The beautifully preserved statue, which had been wrapped in cloth and placed in a stony hollow, more correctly belonged in a museum. But Elizalde, like his forebears, took the view that its heritage was as much familial as national, and as long as it was looked after and did not leave the country, he was doing his duty toward it. It could even be argued that the statue was performing its designated function as a household deity to be respected and worshipped, not trapped behind glass to be gawped at for a few seconds by the ignorant before quickly being forgotten. The Great Goddess wore a feathered headdress and her face was masked. From her nosepiece hung three fangs, while she held seeds in one hand and a pitcher of water in the other. Traces of red and yellow pigment were still visible on her.

And all around the Great Goddess spiders scuttled, these ones larger than the rest, but they gave her a wide berth. Now Elizalde began to understand, even if it was an understanding born of a recognition of the numinous. The Great Goddess was frequently depicted in the company of night creatures—jaguars or owls, but oftentimes spiders, because they, like her, preferred the dark. Was it a sign, an augury on the eve of the commencement of his treatment? If so, did it mean he was blessed or cursed? And how had the statue come to be on the floor? It might have transported itself—if it could summon spiders, who could say what else it was capable of?—but Elizalde was more inclined to believe that someone had placed it there. This was confirmed when a throat was cleared and a man's voice spoke from the shadows.

"That's quite the show with those spiders," he said. "She's calling them for protection, the ones that haven't tried to get away out of fear. I wouldn't have believed it if I hadn't witnessed it for myself."

The accent was Anglo-American, but Elizalde couldn't place it precisely. He'd dealt with gringos from across the United States and Canada, and this man sounded like all of them rolled into one; not neutral, but an assemblage of cadences, as of one who had traveled much, absorbing into his speech elements of what he heard along the way. Elizalde squinted into the ordered clutter of the store and thought he could pick out a shape seated on one of a pair of early twentieth-century hacienda armchairs in cocobolo wood, their glossy finish apparent even in the dimness. It struck him that the man was small for an adult, more like a *duende* or an imp.

"What are you doing here?" Elizalde asked, adding: "I have a gun."

"Oh, I'm sure you do," came the reply. "You'd be unwise not to, what with all the valuables that pass through your hands. I don't see much sign of them here, though. I'm no expert, but a lot of this looks like junk to me, and junk won't keep a man in gravy. By the way, you can tilt that lamp some in my direction if it makes you feel better. I'd appreciate your keeping it more down than up, though. I don't care to be blinded."

Elizalde moved the light, but he stayed to one side of the lamp and made sure that the frame of the office nook offered him cover. The beam revealed a slight man, possibly no more than five feet in height, wearing a red-and-white-spotted shirt with its top button undone and a blue tie at half-mast. His navy trousers were held in place by suspenders, and he wore red-and-white two-tone shoes. He looked, to Elizalde, like a character who had strayed from a *norteamericano* Fourth of July parade and never found his way back again. His hands were folded in his lap, and Elizalde saw no gun within his reach. Relaxing slightly, Elizalde stepped from the nook. The man smiled encouragingly.

"That's it, I won't bite. I can't swear to these little critters on the floor, but they've behaved themselves so far."

"They're house spiders," said Elizalde. "If they bit you, you'd barely notice."

"I might, if all of them took a nibble at the same time, but I'll accept your word on them as individuals. And in answer to your question—and those to come, like who I am—let's begin with the first two, the what and the who, which may be the easiest to answer. I'm here, naturally enough, to speak with you, Mr. Elizalde. Forgive me for not addressing you as 'Señor,' but I don't speak Spanish very well and wouldn't want to set up any false expectations in that regard. But from my inquiries, I guessed that you'd have good English, considering the business you've conducted with speakers of that tongue over the years.

"As for who I am, my name is Seeley, and I'm a fixer. I help solve problems." He crossed his legs and leaned back. "I have to say, this is one comfortable armchair. It's nice and low but not too deep. I've been known to struggle with chairs because of my stature—beds and tables also. I always thought Goldilocks erred on the smaller side, which may be why I like that story so much. The world takes the path of least resistance, or so I find. To those of us who deviate from the average, it's unforgiving."

Seeley caught the look of bewilderment on Elizalde's face.

"There I go again," said Seeley. "I've been advised that I have a predilection for garrulity. I used to think it made people relax, but I appreciate that's not always the case. Call my loquaciousness a trick of the trade. I come out of sales, and the only quiet salesman is a dead one."

Elizalde was happy he had a gun. The more he heard from Seeley, the more convinced he became that the man meant him ill.

"And what are you trying to sell here, Mr. Seeley?"

Seeley smiled sadly.

"Why, Mr. Elizalde, I'm trying to sell you an easy death."

CHAPTER

II

To the north now: cold, and bitter to boot because of the wind, but with an end to winter in sight at last. A thaw promised in the week ahead, and spring to advance gingerly in its wake, sidestepping puddles of foul water, all dark and oily, and mounds of compacted snow and ice, more black than white, that might linger until April, like the vestiges of some defeated army skulking in the aftermath of capitulation.

But that was to come. For the present, the dying season was making its final stand: a fresh freeze, with black ice on the minor roads, thin skeins of it on the water where the Nonesuch skirted the banks, and a mist obscuring the Scarborough marshes, as of the smoke of musket and cannon after a fusillade. Such stillness, broken only by a car driving along Black Point Road, its driver taking the curves carefully, the beams of the headlights lent solidity by the vapor, so that it would not have been so surprising had they shattered upon encountering some obstacle in their path. Two figures in the car, were anyone present to observe: a man and woman, the latter driving, the former snoring. They were both middle-aged and long married, for better or—periodically (whisper it)—worse. Music was playing, and the car was cooler than was comfortable; the woman was afraid of joining the man in sleep, and the nip kept her alert. They were almost home, though, and she drove by instinct, as though the car were not powered by an engine but pulled by horses familiar with the route, the scent of the stable in their nostrils.

"Jesus!"

The woman slammed hard on the brakes. Had her companion not been wearing his seat belt, he might already have been bleeding.

"What is it?"

Now he was wide awake, and about time too, in her opinion. He'd slept since Kittery, aided by three beers, a pizza, and exposure to the conversation of friends who'd interested her more than him.

"A child," she said, "a little girl. She ran across the road in front of me."

The woman opened the car door and stepped into the night.

"What are you doing?" her husband asked. "It's freezing out there."

"I'm telling you, I saw a child."

Reluctantly, he exited the car and watched as his wife crossed the road and peered into the gloom.

"Hello?" she called. "Honey, are you okay?"

But there was no reply and no movement.

"I don't want to say you imagined it—" her husband began.

"Then don't."

He closed his mouth, keeping any swearing to himself. Black Point Road was empty, with no other cars visible. Houses stood some way ahead and behind, but here it was marsh on both sides. He joined her as she moved onto the grass and was alert enough to spot the depression she failed to notice, so fixed was her gaze on the landscape beyond, or what little of it could be discerned in the fog.

"Careful!"

He grabbed her by the arm just as she began to slip, and the two of them nearly ended up on the ground. She stepped back onto the road. Behind them, the car beeped a warning about the open door on the driver's side. If another vehicle did come along, it might well take off the door as it passed, and he'd be the one nominated to explain the damage to the insurance company. He recrossed and pushed the door mostly closed, but didn't let it click. He'd once managed to lock a rental car with the motor running and the keys still inside—don't ask—and his wife had never let him forget it, just as she'd never let him forget the time he went swimming with the keys of another rental car tied to the string on his swim shorts, which hadn't ended well either. Add to that the occasion on which he'd lost the key of their own car while walking the dog, and you had an explanation for why the key was now kept on a lanyard, which he was under orders to wear around his neck if it wasn't actually in the ignition.

When he looked back, she was using the flashlight on her cell phone to search the marsh, but she might as well have struck a match for all the good it was doing in the fog.

"Hello?" she said again, but he could hear from her tone that she was beginning to doubt herself. He was sure, or pretty sure, that she'd briefly nodded off—one of those microsleeps drivers were constantly being warned about—and the child was part of a dream. He went for *pretty* sure because, well, there were stories, incidents, call them what you will, about the area between Route 1 and Prouts Neck, many of them involving a child, or a child and her mother: glimpses, flashes, but no more. He generally ascribed them to Mainers wanting to put the frighteners on flatlanders like him and his wife. They and their three kids had been living in Scarborough for nine years, ever since the bank had offered her a promotion if she moved to Maine from Boston. They'd done their best to involve themselves in the life of the community, but rarely did a week go by without some old fart reminding them of their roots elsewhere or asking them how they were "settling in," when their eldest daughter had already made it through middle and high school and was now studying at Bowdoin. Those coots could take a running jump with their stories as far as he was concerned, but there were others, men whom he trusted not to bullshit him, who'd mentioned catching sight of figures on Ferry Beach or Western Beach when the night was clear. A woman and a child, seen and then gone.

His wife stared at him, and he knew from experience born of twenty-two years of marriage that she was thinking the same thing.

"Let her go," he said softly.

She killed the flashlight on her phone and put it away. Her husband thought she might be close to tears, so he hugged her.

"I wonder who she is," she said. "I wonder why she stays here."

"I guess she must have her reasons."

"I guess she must."

They got back in the car and went on with their journey. Neither glanced at the driveway they passed on the left or the silhouette of the house barely visible at its end, a single lamp burning in one of its windows, and only when they were safely departed did the ghost of a child continue walking in the direction of the light.

CHAPTER III

In Santa Ana Tlachiahualpa, far from snow and marshes, Antonio Elizalde's life, like all lives, moved inexorably toward its close. Had a clock been ticking off the seconds of his existence, he might have noticed the sudden acceleration of its cadence; without such a clock, he was conscious only of a sense of danger. He hadn't let the gun drop, keeping it at waist height and directed at Seeley. Now he raised it higher, and the little man put up his hands in mock surrender.

"Don't shoot," said Seeley, his smile never wavering, broadening even, as though Elizalde's threat was a welcome move in the game, an indication of his willingness to play. "Me good Indian."

Seeley wiggled his fingers, then raised his elbows to let his hands drop down, like a marionette operated by secret strings, and shook his sleeves.

"I'm not armed, beyond what's in here"—Seeley tapped a forefinger to his left temple—"so don't go testing out your popgun on me, not until you hear all I have to say. You don't want to shoot an unarmed man. That brings with it all kinds of legal complications."

"An unarmed *intruder*," Elizalde corrected. "That brings fewer complications, especially down here."

Seeley conceded the point with a dip of his chin and resumed his former posture, his hands once more clasped in his lap.

"I hear you're ailing," he said. "Lung cancer, right? That's a bad card to turn, but you can't say you weren't warned. I mean, I've seen the pictures on your Mexican cigarette packs, all those diseased lungs and women with one titty. I even saw a pack of Luckies with a dead baby lying on a bed of butts. That would surely make me think again—though you're a Marlboro man, right? Bob Norris, that was the name of the guy who played the cowboy in those TV commercials. You know, he never smoked a cigarette in his life? Didn't let his kids smoke either. Most of the rest of them Marlboro cowboys, they picked up cancers, or emphysema, but not old Bob. He just cashed the checks and tried not to think about Philip Morris's name at the bottom. You got health insurance?"

"Yes, I have insurance," said Elizalde.

"You're a wise man. You never know what's going to come around the corner and hit you right in the kisser—or in your case, in the lower left lung. Typical carcinoid tumor is what they tell me, which means it's slow, and slow is good. Once they catch it early enough, a man might live to fight another day. Expensive business, though, getting rid of it. You got your wedge resection—that's what's on your slate for the week to come, according to the surgical notes—and then chemo or radiation, maybe both. If you don't have good insurance, it all adds up, unless you're lucky enough to win the public care lottery, and who wants to play those odds, right?

"Except your insurance isn't so good, Mr. Elizalde. Your insurance will barely get you in the hospital door. Fortunately, you also have a nest egg, thanks to all those treasures you've sourced for your customers down the years. They ask and you provide, given enough notice, so you're not just relying on the local boys to strike it lucky on an illegal dig. In a way, you're like one of those spiders there, building a web and sitting at its heart, but instead of hunting for delicacies you tap a thread and someone brings the spoils right to you: from a museum, a private collection, an official site. You know all the people that matter, and they know you.

"And because you're very quiet and listen hard, you have an awareness of plunder that few others possess, information to be filed away for when the right client comes calling with the correct sum in mind. But you're cautious into the bargain. You wouldn't have survived so long, in life as in trade, if you weren't. Only you stopped being careful because of the cancer. You gambled, because you had nothing to lose but a disease-riddled mess of days. In this matter, sir, you could say that I represent the house, and I'm here to give you the bad news: your gamble didn't pay off, and now it's a matter of how you choose to settle the debt."

Elizalde didn't bother with bluff or denial. The fact that Seeley was here made both redundant.

"I could kill you," said Elizalde, "and worry about settling debts later. I have enough money to leave the country and seek treatment elsewhere."

"You could, you could," agreed Seeley. "Of course, apart from the unlikelihood of your being *able* to kill me—shooting a man is a lot harder than it looks in the movies—it also assumes that I came here alone. Which, being prudent, I didn't."

"I see no one else," said Elizalde, "only you."

"That's because you're not looking in the right places."

Seeley stood, or perhaps "uncoiled" might have been more accurate, because there was a serpentine ease to the movement. Elizalde could see that, upright, the interloper was slightly taller than he'd previously thought, with handsome, intelligent features. He looked like someone a stranger might be inclined to trust, an asset for a salesman, even if you weren't convinced you wanted what he was selling. Elizalde didn't wish to die, making him a reluctant mark unless Seeley had something better to offer than a death, easy or otherwise. But the man's patter was almost hypnotic. It demanded that one hear him out, one reasonable human being to another, and neither party could leave until he'd finished his pitch.

Seeley gestured to the statue of the Great Goddess of Teotihuacan.

"Do you think the gods talk to one another?" he asked. "Do they love, hate, fear, and mourn like we do? Me, I was raised Presbyterian, so one deity was enough, even if He had to be divided into three to spread Himself around better. The church doesn't see me much now, not even at Christmas. I was a doubter from youth, and that hardened into atheism in adulthood. I figured we were all alone on this rock, with nothing above but sky and only damp earth below.

"But since I was required to venture into your fine country, I must admit that Hamlet had a point and my philosophy may have been inadequate. At first, I thought it might be exposure to excessive sunlight, because I do like my shade and AC. Soon, though, I came to an understanding—a new philosophy, if you will. I've decided that gods may be just another kind of creature. I don't think they have a form, or none beyond the ones we give them, which we create from what's familiar to us, whether frightening or consoling. Some gods endure and some don't. A few don't even want to make themselves known to us, so we don't get a perception of them, not ever. Others, they drift in and out of belief and can slumber like spiders, waiting to be jerked into life by being remembered again. Your goddess here, she's pretty much *all* spider, which is why she's surrounded herself with them. She summoned them out of fear."

Elizalde glanced down at the totem of the Great Goddess. Now that Seeley had drawn his attention to it, he could see that the spiders had formed a mass around her, like a wall of bodies set against an approaching enemy.

"Fear," repeated Elizalde. "Of what? Of you?"

"Of the one I came here with. To be honest, Mr. Elizalde, I generally prefer to work alone, but the difficulty is that I'm not by nature a violent man. I don't like inflicting pain, never have, although I'll do it if I have to; if it's them or me, so to speak. Like I told you at the start, I'm primarily a fixer, a negotiator, with a Rolodex for a brain and a talent for squirreling out connections that others have missed. I like to leave behind as little mess as possible—blood, bodies, widows, orphans—because mess attracts attention."

Seeley sighed theatrically.

"But unfortunately," he resumed, "it seems to me that this job is going to involve a great deal of suffering and no small amount of killing. It's more than I can handle alone, reluctantly or otherwise. In fact, it's already begun, and you're next in line."

Something struck Elizalde on the back of the head. His vision blurred, and the office nook grew muddied around him. He crashed against his desk before dropping to his knees, the dimensions of his beloved store altering, its walls drifting away, its ceiling descending, so that he experienced simultaneous surges of agoraphobia and claustrophobia. It all happened in just a few seconds, from the striking of the blow to the pain of his knees hitting the floor, though Elizalde felt that he might have been falling for a long time—for all his life—and the landing, when it came, would be final. He kept his head down while he waited for the feeling of dislocation to pass. When he peered up, Seeley stood closer, and someone else was moving behind Elizalde.

"I'd stay down there if I were you," said Seeley, as the other finally came into view. "After all, that's how a man ought to greet a lady."

CHAPTER IV

With the smell of salt in the air and the road through the marshes empty once more, the ghost of the girl stood before the house. She was present yet unsubstantial; the mist surrounding her had more solidity than she. The lamp in the window flickered beneath her gaze. It always shone in the night, even when her father was away from the house, because he kept it on a dark-activated timer. It burned, she knew, for her, so that she might know she was not forgotten.

However, she was aware that perhaps he thought of her less often now than in the past, and not only because she had been dead so long; more than two decades, even as it felt like less to her, time passing differently in the place where she waited, if it really passed at all. Sometimes, it seemed as though only days had elapsed since she arrived at the lakeshore, there to sit on a promontory between worlds, watching as the dead immersed themselves in the water, wading deeper and deeper before being lost to the great sea. At first, she tried to keep count of them, but they were too many and too similar; different, yet all the same. Some noticed her, but only momentarily, curiosity being for the living, the dead having no use for it.

She had learned not to wander beyond the environs of the water. Hills bordered it, and forests, but these were not uninhabited. They were largely the abode of the irretrievably lost: the angry, the insane, or those who, because of their pain, were unable or unwilling to surrender themselves to what lay beyond. A few, she thought, were somewhat like her—watching, waiting—but unlike her, they did not move between worlds. She believed they might be content to let her do it for them, so she became their agent, their intelligencer. Now and again, she caught some of them regarding her from the shadows, even if they did not approach. Those ones were always children. She felt they were frightened of her, even as they also desired what she desired: revenge.

And she would think to herself: *You have no reason to fear me. That's for another.*

SHE ENTERED THE HOUSE, occupying its spaces, her fingers passing over chairs, books, scattered possessions, without disturbing even a single speck of dust. She paused by a photograph of herself with her father and mother, when all three of them were unruined. Mother and child had died together, leaving the father behind. The girl no longer knew where her mother was. She had hidden herself away: a disunited being, unpredictable, so that even her daughter was wary of her. But she had been beautiful once, as the picture showed. The girl could remember being held by her, read to, loved. No more. All gone.

On a shelf nearby stood another series of photographs, these of her father with his other daughter: Sam, the dead girl's half sister. In only one were they joined by Sam's mother, Rachel. There were, the girl noted with something like amusement, more pictures of the dog, Walter, who had left this house with Rachel and Sam to go and live with Rachel's parents in Vermont. Walter was now gone from the world. Sam had been aware that he was dying, but she was unable to prepare herself because she had not yet been exposed to mortality on an intimate, personal level. She still had her parents and grandparents and had not lost any friends to death. She had been fortunate, but that luck lasted for no one. The blow, when it came, would hit hard. That was the first lesson death taught. The second was that so many of the losses to follow would hit even harder.

The dog had been with Sam since early childhood, and she was a teenager now, if not for much longer. When the dog was finally put to sleep, her childhood was laid to rest alongside him, and the bond between the girl and Sam had frayed still further. They had been close when they were younger, the dead girl shadowing the living, whispering to her, sharing some (though not all) of what she knew. But as Sam entered adolescence, the girl could not connect with her as before. The girl was both trapped in childhood and strangely ageless, but Sam was neither. Part of their growing estrangement, the girl understood, was a consequence of that awareness of difference, but she felt it more acutely than Sam because the latter was progressing toward an adulthood that had been denied the former. Sometimes, the girl struggled to contain her envy at the experiences Sam had already enjoyed and those yet to come, and her rage at the unfairness of it all.

She had watched from the dark as Sam received her first kiss from a boy; had stood amid daffodils as Sam's grandfather taught her how to fish for bass; and had crouched by the bathtub as Sam realized she was having her first period, its coming already prepared for by her practical mother but its arrival nonetheless greeted with a combination of embarrassment, discomfort, and pride. After every such event, the dead girl had retreated to her sentinel post by the water, where she briefly contemplated joining the ranks of the dead and embracing unknowing. It had taken all her resolve to wait for the urge to pass, aided by the glimpses of herself that she caught in mirrors and glass when she traveled to the other side: a bloody, ravaged creature, eyeless but not blind. The damage reminded her of her purpose and made her patient once more.

From above came the sound of bedsprings protesting and the coughing of a woman: Sharon Macy, who was sharing her father's bed that night, as she did once or twice each week. The girl had seen them becoming ever closer, ever more intimate. They shared secrets, whispering them to each other when the world was quiet; softly, body to body, though the girl could hear, when she chose to listen. Her father even spoke of her to the woman, which concerned her. It was unwise. But as with Sam and her progress toward womanhood, the girl was conscious of other emotions beyond fear of the harm that might result from her father's sharing of confidences with his lover: jealousy, a sense of betrayal—and sadness.

He no longer thinks of me as often. His pain is less intense.

The girl had never felt more alone.

CHAPTER V

The last of the spiders had returned to their webs, the insects to the gloom, and the statue of the Great Goddess lay in pieces on the floor of Antonio Elizalde's store. Elizalde, too, was no more. His pain was over, his spirit departed. He had suffered at the end, but not as much, Seeley reflected, as he would have had cancer and the medical profession enjoyed their way with him. There was less blood than Seeley had anticipated, though he had decided to step away at the climax. By then, Elizalde had given up all he knew. What came after was pure punishment.

Seeley's eye was drawn to the pack of Marlboros. He hadn't smoked in years, but if he was ever going to start again, this would be the time. To avoid temptation, he crushed the pack in his gloved hand and disposed of it in the trash. It was time to leave, but first, Seeley went through the shelves of rare books and manuscripts in Elizalde's office in case they contained anything worth rescuing. To his pleasure, if not entirely his surprise—Elizalde's taste, unlike his judgment, had never been in doubt—Seeley discovered a volume of posthumously published poems by the seventeenth-century Mexican poet and nun Sor Juana Inés de la Cruz, part of an edition of her complete works printed in Madrid in 1700, just five years after her death from plague. The original vellum binding was in desperately poor condition and the leather ties were missing, but Seeley could work with what remained. He even had a buyer in mind. Elizalde might have approved, had he still been in a position to do so. Seeley swaddled the volume in paper, followed by a couple of layers of bubble wrap. He then found a suitable box, laid the book inside, and sealed the folds with tape.

Seeley made a final check of his surroundings to determine that nothing obviously incriminating had been left behind. There was little he could do about stray skin and hair, but he wished the Mexican authorities luck with their investigation—should there ever be one, which he very much doubted. Seeley had already made a call about Elizalde's body, and his employer would ensure that it was gone within the hour. As for the police, their attention would be drawn to the fact that Elizalde was a sick man, facing an agonizing struggle with illness. It may have been that his courage failed him, and he had taken himself off to die. In the unlikely event that they persisted with their inquiries, pressure would be applied. Seeley's employer would not want anything to impede progress and had a way of encouraging obedience. But should Seeley encounter further resistance, other measures were available.

Briefly, Seeley regarded what was left of Elizalde, and the fragments of the Great Goddess, her subordinate position in the pantheon of deities now confirmed. Seeley reflected on the money he was being paid and decided it wasn't enough to compensate a man for having his beliefs about life and the universe upended so spectacularly. Regrettably, it was too late to back out now, not unless he wanted to end up like Antonio Elizalde. Still, he was forced to admit to a particular curiosity about what was to come.

"*Vámonos.*"

Seeley couldn't help but shiver. If dust could have spoken, it would have sounded thus. He hoped the current situation might be resolved quickly, leading his employer's agent to return to wherever she'd come from. He also hoped he'd come out of it with his life, because he really didn't want to die. Before he had taken this job, he had feared only the pain of death; now he was concerned about what might come after. He conceded the possibility that his employer might be so in name only, and he was in fact working for another, *this* other.

Which, Seeley decided, would be very unfortunate indeed.

CHAPTER VI

To the north, in Scarborough, the bedroom door was ajar. The girl stood on the threshold and regarded the sleeping figures: the woman on her right side, her back to the girl's father; and he, also on his right side, his left arm outside the comforter, his hand resting on the woman's exposed shoulder.

You have forgotten who you are, the girl thought. *It cannot last.*

Her father's eyes opened. He sat up and looked toward the door. Delicately, so as not to wake the woman, he pushed aside the comforter and stepped from the bed. He was naked from the waist up, and despite the dimness, the girl could make out the healed wounds, the physical evidence of torments that ran older and deeper than even he could recall.

"Jennifer?"

He whispered her name, and there was such tenderness to it, such longing, that she wanted to run to him. He would hold her against him, and she would feel safe.

Feel safe: Another illusion, because feeling and being were not the same. The girl and her mother had learned that to their cost. He had not been able to protect them, and they had died for it. She did not blame him. The forces ranged against him, against all three of them, were more powerful than they could have imagined. Had he been with them that night, he too would have been killed.

Again.

Why don't you remember? All those lives, all the torment. All the punishment.

Her father walked toward the door, only to pause on his side of the gap.

You have made recompense over and over, but still it's not enough, and it never will be. That's why it has to come to an end. We will bring it to an end, together.

"JENNIFER."

I spoke the name again to the dark, but now there was only absence.

She was gone.

2

And her being dead was filling her like fullness.
For like a fruit all of sweetness and dark,
she too was full of her immense death.

Rainer Maria Rilke, "Orpheus. Eurydice. Hermes."

CHAPTER VII

For more than two decades, the first Friday of each month had been Art Walk night in Portland. During the summer, craft stalls sprang up along Congress Street, galleries opened late, and local artists took advantage of the occasion to launch new collections. In winter and spring, when the days were too short and the nights too long, the Art Walk added liveliness to the city and gave people an excuse to move around instead of hunkering down in one place while waiting for the sun to return. You didn't necessarily have to love art to enjoy the Art Walk; you just had to like it better than nothing at all.

The Triton Gallery was the latest addition to the Maine art scene. Situated in an old warehouse off Forest Avenue, within striking distance of the upmarket Batson River Brewing & Distilling, the gallery's considerable square footage had already proven popular with artists who favored large-scale installations. Of course, those artists first had to impress the owner, Mark Triton, but Zetta Nadeau must have managed it because her latest pieces were now filling its spaces. Zetta worked in metal, creating abstract and figurative sculptures, and was gaining a national reputation. A former state governor had even asked her to design and construct a pair of ornamental gates for his property, a lucrative commission at a time when Zetta needed the money. She'd told him to take a hike on the grounds that he was a jackass, and while she couldn't prevent jackasses from buying her art, she wasn't about to start producing it at their behest.

No former governors were present at the Triton Gallery on this particular evening, but enough of the local great-and-goods had shown up to add color to the society page of the *Maine Sunday Telegram*. Triton himself was absent, but he wasn't a Maine native and had business interests that extended beyond the Northeast. Instead, the gallery's curator, Grace Holmes, took care of the introductions, praising Zetta as one of the state's most striking and innovative young artists and lauding the works on display as evidence of a new phase in her development. I thought Holmes went on too long, and there was an edge to her voice that hinted at desperation, as though she was trying hard to argue a case about which she remained unconvinced. It explained a mood that felt restrained—so much so, in fact, that I'd heard someone ask when we might be permitted to view the body. This was Zetta's first exhibition since a disastrous opening in New York three years earlier, the subject of a legendary takedown in *The New York Times*, the kind that acquaintances discussed with sympathy tinged by secret relish and rivals shared with outright joy, if tempered in the wiser by a sense of "There but for the grace of God . . ." Where the *Times* led, others followed, resulting in a pile-on that had almost destroyed Zetta's confidence, not to mention her career.

Now here she was, presenting her first show since the *Times* mauling, albeit on a local stage. She specialized in oversized compositions in bronze and steel that, on closer examination, revealed their resemblance to tortured beings, in the manner of that old Warren Zevon lyric about trees like crucified thieves. For the Triton Gallery, Zetta had reined herself in somewhat, and alongside a central sextet of compositions ranging from six to twelve feet in height were smaller works that did not exceed two feet, with a few no more than half that size. In truth, they looked lost in the vast zone, like afterthoughts to a conversation that had since moved on.

Sharon Macy peered at the price tag on the figurine nearest us, which resembled a twisted angel.

"It's eight thousand dollars," she said. "Can it be worth that much? I once paid five hundred dollars for a painting and didn't sleep right for a month. If I spent eight thousand, I might expire from insomnia."

"Ask Louis," I told her. "He knows more about art than I do."

Behind her, Louis sipped his wine—and it really was his. He'd brought his own bottle, slipping ten dollars to the kid at the drinks table to ensure it was kept for private consumption. Louis had been at Portland exhibition openings before and wasn't about to have his taste buds violated if it could be avoided. He wore a light brown tweed jacket over a near-matching vest and rust-colored trousers, finished off by a box-fresh white shirt and brown brogues. He looked like he ought to be hunting foxes or whipping a footman.

"I like the piece," he said. "Not eight thousand dollars' worth, maybe, but I do like it. The rest, not so much."

Beside him, his own Angel said: "You don't even like me eight thousand dollars' worth."

"True," said Louis, "but at least the art will age better."

Angel had dressed up for the occasion, which meant a strict no-sneakers policy and passing acquaintance with an iron. He, too, was drinking Louis's wine. We all were. Out of solidarity with the masses, I'd tried what was on offer, but it was too sweet for my liking. It would have been too sweet for a kiddie alcoholic.

Macy squinted at Louis. Small and dark, she had long since recognized that the advantages of being underestimated because of her appearance and gender far outweighed the disadvantages—not that anyone in Maine police circles had any illusions about her abilities. Macy acted as liaison, official and otherwise, between the Portland PD and external agencies, including the AG's office, the state police, and the FBI, but was far from being a suit. As a rookie, she'd been blooded in a gun battle out on Sanctuary Island that left a lot of people dead or missing. Some of the bodies were never found, but then Sanctuary was an odd place and always had been. Macy rarely spoke of what had happened there, not even to me. I knew enough about Sanctuary to be grateful for her discretion.

"What?" asked Louis, as she continued to give him the stink eye.

"You're mean," said Macy.

"Is that my wine you're drinking?"

"Maybe."

"How is it?"

"Perfectly palatable."

"Do you want to keep drinking it, or would you prefer to take your chances with the stuff in the box?"

Macy turned to Angel.

"You're on your own," she said.

Only in recent months had Macy begun to socialize with Angel and Louis. In fact, only lately had Macy and I let it be known around Portland that we were an item. I wasn't well-loved in the law enforcement community, local or national, and Macy's involvement with me, a serving detective in the Portland PD, brought complications. As for Louis and Angel, they preferred to keep their distance from police in any shape or form but had, for my sake, made an exception for Macy. In turn, she appeared to have bonded particularly with Louis, who rarely bonded with anyone. Each seemed to have discovered something of theirself in the other, which I regarded as worrying.

I watched Zetta Nadeau circulate. I'd known her since she was a kid and wished her well, which was why we were here. She was shepherded by an older man who kept her supplied with sparkling water. From the way they touched, I thought they might be intimate. I hadn't seen him around before.

"Who's the guy?" Macy asked.

"I'm guessing a new boyfriend," I said. "He's got some city miles on him."

"Huh," said Macy.

She and Louis exchanged a glance.

"You too?" said Louis.

"Yeah, me too," said Macy.

"What am I missing?" I asked.

"The new boyfriend, if that's what he is—" said Macy.

"Is on edge," finished Louis.

"He's been watching the guests enter and leave," said Macy, "checking faces, sizing people up, only showing his back to the ones he doesn't regard as a threat."

"He gets close to anyone he's worried about," said Louis, "so he can brush against them."

"Looking for weapons," said Macy. "He's pretty good, knows what he's doing."

"It could explain why he's wearing that jacket despite the heat in here," said Louis. "He may be carrying."

"Perhaps his girlfriend's worried about hostile critics," said Angel.

"They tend to come armed with pens, not swords," I told him.

But Macy and Louis were right about Zetta's new guy, and had spotted it before I did. I hid my irritation—at myself, not them. Well, possibly at them as well.

"Has anyone threatened Zetta Nadeau?" Macy asked me.

"Not to my knowledge."

"Would you have heard?"

"Probably."

"Then it could be it's not her safety he's concerned about," said Louis.

"If not hers," offered Macy, "then whose?"

I saw the boyfriend making his way toward Zetta again.

"How about we wish her well before we leave," I said, offering Macy my arm, "and take a closer look at the newbie while we're at it."

We cut a path to where Zetta was accepting compliments, sincere and otherwise, her arms folded defensively across her chest, her smile too fixed. She wore a cream silk dress that concealed some of her tattoos and the absence of extraneous flesh on her bones. Her hair was naturally very red and cut short. Combined with the dress it lent her a resemblance—as Angel remarked—to a decorated matchstick.

I introduced Zetta to Macy, and she freed one arm for long enough to shake hands.

"It was good of you to come," said Zetta, and the analogy of a wake arose again.

"This is quite the turnout," I told her.

"I guess."

"Is everything okay?" I asked. Clearly, everything wasn't. Seen up close, her smile was not merely fixed but brittle, and she seemed near tears.

"First-night nerves," she said.

Before either of us could respond, the new boyfriend appeared, placing a hand protectively at the small of her back. Zetta introduced him as Wyatt Riggins and presented us to him in turn, but got no further than naming names because Grace Holmes came along, men with money trailing behind, and Zetta was forced to turn aside to speak to them.

Wyatt Riggins was about a decade older than Zetta, and thin the way 304 stainless-steel wire is thin, so they made a good couple. His hair was blond, veering toward gray in places, and he wore it shaggy, though not studiedly so. His skin was tan and bore traces of sun damage around the eyes. As Louis had noted, he kept his jacket on, but if he was packing, it was probably something compact: the jacket was baggy, but not so as to be able to conceal a cannon. The way he carried himself suggested ex-military. His expression wasn't unfriendly, but it was definitely guarded.

Behind Riggins, Angel ghosted by, barely touching him. Riggins picked up on it nonetheless, but by then Angel was gone. If Riggins hadn't spotted that we were sizing him up earlier, he knew it now, and was aware he was being assessed by experts—or, given my earlier failure, some experts and me. I watched a veil descend over his eyes, like electrified gel activating on airplane glass as a shield against the light. He didn't offer to shake hands, and I didn't force the issue. He smelled faintly of pot, but that wasn't remarkable. A good share of the city's population smelled of it. You could attend a cremation in Portland and get high when the body began burning.

"Where are you from, Wyatt?" I asked. "You don't sound local."

"The South, originally."

"There's a lot of South."

"Just the way we like it. We fought a war for it."

"Well, that and slavery," said Macy. She smiled at him so sweetly that only an idiot could have mistaken it as anything but false, and Wyatt Riggins didn't scream "idiot."

"For the most part, I'm not in favor," Riggins replied. "Though I make an exception for the Chinese prisoners who sew my sneakers."

He returned Macy's smile. It emphasized his wrinkles, and I thought he might have had even more miles on the clock than I'd originally guessed. Still, I could understand why Zetta was attracted to him. He exuded a strength and shrewdness—and toughness, too. I'd have deliberated hard before crossing him.

"Where did you serve?" I asked.

"What makes you think I did?"

"Just a hunch."

He drawled the answer, all "aw, shucks" modesty.

"I moved around, but I was just a Remington raider. I liked my desk, where the biggest risk of injury was picking up a paper cut."

"Your desk must have been by a window. You got some sun."

"It was hard to avoid."

"Out there in Around."

"Yeah. It's big, like the South. And what do you do, Mr. Parker?"

"I'm a private investigator."

"That explains the questions." He turned to Macy. "And you, ma'am, I didn't catch your occupation."

"Police."

Riggins's expression didn't falter, but that gel dimmed another tone.

"Sounds like you two were meant to be together," he said. "It's nice when things work out that way."

He placed a hand on Zetta's arm—"You need anything, just let me know. I'll keep an eye on you"—before wishing Macy and me a pleasant evening and fading into the crowd.

The moneymen, if that's what they were, had moved on, Grace Holmes with them. Macy discreetly disengaged herself from me so I could speak with Zetta alone. More guests were closing in on her, one or two watching Riggins, wanting to be sure he was gone. They might not have known any more about him than I did, but they sensed he didn't belong, and his presence made them uneasy. Over to my right, Holmes put a red sticker on one of the smaller pieces. Someone applauded. Zetta acknowledged them by raising her glass before looking away.

"This is more than first-night nerves, Zetta," I said. "Is there anything I can do?"

"Not unless you can rewind time," she replied. "I don't have to read the reviews to know I'm dead in the water. I've been found wanting again, but I figured as much as soon as we began assembling the show. It doesn't work."

"Is it the venue?"

"It's the artist. It's me. Something's gone wrong, and I can't figure out what it is. See that red sticker? It's a pity sale. I'll bet you a bright new nickel that Mark Triton left instructions for Holmes to buy a minor piece or two if the mood warranted. If it doesn't start a rush, it'll save some of my blushes."

She was only moments away from throwing her glass at the floor and vanishing into the night. Hers was a very particular and public humiliation, all the more intense for being so subtle.

"Any other kind of trouble?" I asked.

"Just with my career. Wait, was that what Wyatt's grilling was about? I overheard you interrogating him."

"He strikes me as being a little on the tense side. I wondered if it was solely on your behalf. How long have you two been a couple?"

"Just a few months, but I like him. As for tension, this is unfamiliar territory for him. He's not comfortable in the art world, or what's passing for it tonight. Also, I think he had a harder time in the service than he admits." She paused. "He cries out in the night."

I let it go. Riggins was solicitous of Zetta, and she was a grown woman. If she was making a mistake with him, she'd earned that privilege. I kissed her cheek.

"Good luck with the show," I said. "I hope you're wrong about it."

"Yeah, me too."

She prepared to accept the embrace of a man wearing overlarge red spectacles and the kind of check suit last favored by vaudeville comics.

"Hey?" she added.

I looked back at her.

"Thanks for caring enough to ask. About Wyatt, I mean. But you don't have to worry. He's okay."

Which was probably what Charles Forbes said about John Wilkes Booth before admitting him to Lincoln's theater box. Still, it was none of my business, and I had no shortage of other people's troubles to occupy me. If that ever ceased to be the case, I'd be out of a job, but it wasn't likely in the short term.

"So?" asked Macy.

"Zetta says she's okay. She says Riggins is okay, too."

"That's reassuring," said Louis. "Be a pity if she became the first woman to make that mistake."

"No gun," said Angel, "and his pants are too narrow to take an ankle holster, but he's carrying a knife: something short with a fixed blade, worn horizontally, not vertically, the handle within easy reach when he hitches the jacket."

"Maybe he whittles," said Louis.

"A gun would be better," I said.

"Not for whittling," said Louis, "but unless he tries to whittle one of us, he's someone else's problem. Let's go eat."

So we prepared to leave. I paused by the door and saw Zetta Nadeau's head bobbing at the center of a crowd while Grace Holmes hovered at the periphery, all strained smiles. Wyatt Riggins's attention was elsewhere. He was leaning against a wall, playing with an old flip phone, like a man waiting—or wishing—to be summoned away.

"Riggins?" guessed Macy.

"Just curious."

"What's he doing?"

"Nothing," I replied. "But a lot of it."

CHAPTER VIII

We had reserved a table at Batson River, so we didn't have far to walk. What used to be a somnolent zone between Congress and I-295, mainstays like the Bayside Bowl excepted, was now much livelier, with Batson River as one of the anchors. At the start, I feared the bar might be too flashy for Portland. With its deer antlers and moose head on the wall, and its stone fireplace, it might have been designed for Telluride or Park City and somehow been misdelivered. But what did I know? Rooms at the more upscale hotels in town cost $800 a night on summer weekends, with breakfast extra, so an $18 pizza at Batson River counted as a bargain.

While we waited for our food to arrive, I spotted Moxie Castin at a private reception in the back room. I did some work for Moxie, who was also my lawyer. He liked to assure me that when he could no longer keep me out of jail, he'd come visit once a month and do his best to ensure I had a cell with a view. I caught his eye, and he stepped away to join us. He kissed Macy and scowled at Angel and Louis, already anticipating a hard time from one or both of them.

"Nice suit," said Louis, fingering Moxie's lapel. "I like the shine. It's hard to get the blend right so the natural fibers don't overwhelm the nylon."

"It's silk, you barbarian." Moxie batted Louis's hand away. "I got it made special. The stitching's invisible."

"If it rains, you'll be in trouble. The soap holding it together will turn to bubbles."

Moxie decided to ignore him. I admired Moxie's optimism.

"It doesn't look like a gathering of lawyers in there," I said. "No accident victim is being circled."

"My secretary's daughter got married," said Moxie. "I wanted to wish her better luck than I've had." Moxie had been married so often that inviting him to a wedding was like bringing a burn victim to a bonfire. "What's your excuse?"

"The opening of Zetta Nadeau's new show."

"She's a good kid, but flighty. I took care of some contract stuff for her, back before that last show in New York, the one nobody liked. You suppose they're going to appreciate this one more?"

"Zetta doesn't think so."

"She ought to have gone into law. She still wouldn't have been liked, but the money's better."

"She has a new boyfriend."

"So? Zetta always has a new boyfriend. It must be a creative thing. From your tone, I gather you don't approve of this one."

Now that Wyatt Riggins had come to my attention, I found him difficult to dislodge.

"He gives the impression of trailing aggravation."

"Well, if it's any help, Zetta will have another guy soon enough. Remember, it's not your issue unless someone pays you to make it yours. Call it the Cynic's Maxim. The corollary is that the issue stops being yours once the money runs out. You'd avoid a lot of heartache if you kept that in mind."

It was an interesting philosophy. In his bleaker moments, Moxie might even have been convinced of its veracity, if only briefly. He glanced at his watch and pulled a piece of paper from his inside pocket.

"I have to get back inside. I promised to say a few words before dessert."

"Be sure to bill for the full hour," said Angel.

"Fuck you, the full hour. I've known the kid since she came out of the womb." Moxie adjusted his tie. "She gets a discount."

CHAPTER

IX

Macy didn't come home with me that night. She had an early start the following day, but she also liked her space as much as I enjoyed mine. It came with getting older and growing comfortable in your own skin and with your own company. Once you got used to negotiating the territory you'd carved out for yourself, sharing it could be complicated. Macy and I were still trying to find a way to make that work.

Sitting at my desk, I was tempted to perform a cursory internet search on Wyatt Riggins, but I had other matters to occupy me, some of which would even help pay my bills. This was becoming an increasingly pressing concern because my daughter, Sam, would soon be starting college. Her mom's parents had offered to help with the fees, but Rachel and I were determined to cover the cost ourselves. To be fair, the impetus came more from me than Rachel, but she understood and accepted it. Since our separation, Rachel had raised Sam in a house adjacent to her parents' place in Vermont. The grandparents had been an integral, positive part of Sam's development, and Rachel's father and I had even reached our own form of détente after years of discord, but they would have been happier had I excised myself entirely from the lives of their only daughter and grandchild. Rightly or wrongly, I believed that accepting college money from them would give them a further claim on Sam, aside from any question of personal pride.

I turned off the office light, leaving just the lamp burning, and stared out at the blackness of the marsh, with its slivers of fragmented moonlight. I thought of the dream I'd had and how I'd woken to the certainty that Jennifer was in the house with me. She still felt close now. She was out there, somewhere. I used to fear that she was lost, wandering, until I came to accept that it was I who was lost.

Grief and loss are not the same. Loss has a fixed point: a date, a place, a moment. I know when and where my wife and daughter were killed, and that is the locus of my loss. As the days passed in the aftermath, some of them now recalled with more clarity than others, I found myself seeking the cessation of time. I did not want to depart from that locus. In doing so, I would leave them further behind—or rather, I would be loosed from the instant before they ceased to be, when they were still in the world.

But the current of time is too strong. Whatever contrary speculations scientists may offer on the intermingling of past, present, and future, by our perception the clock moves inexorably forward and will, without fail, carry us away from those we love. As much as the dead withdraw from us, so also do we withdraw from the dead.

Grief—real grief, the kind that never heals—is an expanding orbit. Each circuit, which lasts a year, brings us to within sight of that original nucleus of bereavement, but at a greater remove. The distance, ever increasing, lessens the pain, even as we never lose sight of that hub, however tiny it may appear, flickering like the light from an ancient star. Ultimately, that light may even bring a trace element of comfort. It is never utterly cold, unless we make it so by forgetting.

"Good night," I said to the dark, to my daughter. "Good night."

CHAPTER

Jennifer Parker watched the light go on in her father's bedroom before she entered the marshes, following trails familiar to her from years of similar vigils. Before her lay the ocean, but she knew that she would never reach it. As she approached the water, the landscape would morph, and she would once again be by the lakeside, watching the dead lose whatever of themselves remained while she waited and waited . . .

Jennifer paused. Ahead of her, standing on the surface of a marsh pond, her feet not disrupting the surface tension, was a woman wearing a summer dress. Unlike Jennifer's, her face was not a mask of ruination, only a blur. Dark ovals marked her eyes, and her mouth was the barest suggestion of a line. It had been a long time since she had shown herself.

mother, said Jennifer, although she was uncertain if this remained the case. Part-mother, perhaps. Echo. Revenant. But "mother" would suffice.

The line of her mother's mouth widened, lips moving as they attempted to form a reply. Jennifer wondered when last she had spoken aloud. The effort it cost her was visible, her neck straining like that of Julie Krakowski, a girl in Jennifer's first-grade class who used to struggle with a stammer. The two syllables that finally emerged were between a whisper and a cough.

daughter

is that all you have to say to me, mother, after so long?

Another effort at speaking, this one less stressful. Her mother had found her tongue now.

why do you continue to visit him?

for the same reason that i wait, Jennifer replied.

Her mother shimmered as a surge of unfamiliar emotions coursed through her. Jennifer picked up on all of them: hate, jealousy, grief, betrayal—and love. She thought it might be the last that caused her mother's remnant the most confusion.

perhaps, Jennifer added, *a reason we share*

Her mother shook her head, but the word, when it came, lacked conviction.

no

Jennifer elected not to pursue the matter. It would serve no purpose beyond enraging. Then her mother might leave, and Jennifer was curious to discover why she had come. Jennifer was aware that her mother also sometimes circled her father. In the beginning, Jennifer feared she might have been trying to find a way to harm him, though this turned out not to be the case. Her mother blamed him for what had happened to them in a way Jennifer did not, but then her mother's history with him was longer and more complex than Jennifer's, with other hurts and failings to compound the final one. Eventually, Susan Parker, or this vestige of her, had grown tired of haunting the edges of her husband's existence. Now she had returned, and must have had some cause. Jennifer would not let her go without revealing it. But it was also true that, whatever the incomplete nature of this manifestation, she remained, in part, Jennifer's mother, and the child in Jennifer still loved her.

mother, why have you come?

because you grow careless

here?

here, and elsewhere ~ *you are drawing attention* ~ *did you think you could pass unnoticed forever?*

not forever, said Jennifer, *just long enough*

i fear you were wrong

is it too late?

that remains to be seen

thank you for the warning, said Jennifer.

you don't listen

i'm listening to you now ~ *i'll be more careful, i promise*

listen better

i dont understand. i—

listen now

And then Jennifer heard it. In her defense, there was so much background noise in this world, so much distraction, that she had learned to tune it out in order to focus on her father. As a result, she sometimes missed things.

Like this.

it's a child, said Jennifer.

try again ~ *i told you: you have to listen better*

Jennifer did. She closed her eyes, concentrating only on one sense.

children, she said at last. *i can't tell how many, but one is closer than the rest*

good, very good

i can't make out what they're saying ~ *i don't know the language*

you don't have to know it to understand its meaning

Now that she had isolated the sound, Jennifer picked up on the emotion behind it.

they're crying out, calling to someone

and someone, said her mother, *has heard*

but what has it to do with me?

Jennifer's mother looked beyond her to where the house stood concealed amid trees.

nothing this is for him alone, though he may regret his involvement what is coming for the children is very . . . pure

can i help him?

no, because something older and far more dangerous is coming for you

what must i do?

Suddenly, her mother was close, so close that the blurring could no longer conceal what the Traveling Man had done to her. When she spoke again, she sounded almost human.

hide

CLASSIFIED

UNITED STATES DEPARTMENT OF JUSTICE
FEDERAL BUREAU OF INVESTIGATION

File Number: REDACTED

Requesting Official(s): REDACTED

Task Numbers and Date Completed: 1000210, Work Request Number 1000210, 3/11/24

Source File Information/Name of Audio File: 031124_0638_pm BERN_Phone_Call.wav

VERBATIM TRANSCRIPTION

Participants: Aldo Bern B
Devin Vaughn V

Abbreviations: Unintelligible UI

031124_0638_pm BERN_Phone_Call.wav

BERN: The Mexican didn't make his medical appointment.

VAUGHN: Maybe he had second thoughts about the treatment.

B: For lung cancer?

V: He had a hard road ahead.

B: And went to a lot of trouble to be able to afford to walk it.

V: If I were him, I'd want to take a few days to enjoy myself before they started poisoning me. Once they got going, I might not have the chance again for a long time, or not ever.

B: I never met him, but from what I hear, he wasn't that kind of guy.

V: I never met him either, but you hear the clock ticking and you become that guy. Have you tried calling him?

B: It goes straight to the machine. He doesn't own a cell phone. He's old.

V: The fuck does that have to do with it? Your mother's old, and she has a phone.

B: He's real old, like his stock.

V: If something happened to him, how would we know?

B: Maybe it would make the papers, and maybe it wouldn't. Depends.

V: On what?

B: On what happened.

V: We have someone we can ask?

B: You mean to knock on his door? No, we keep our distance. Right now, nothing links him to you, but if I go asking people to ask other people, that changes.

V: Is this where you tell me again that I ought not to have done it?

B: No, this is where I tell you again that you should have come to me before, not after.

V: You're jumping at shadows.

B: If a shadow exists, I want to know what cast it.

V: [UI]

B: Okay, but someone will have been sent to recover them. He'll want them back.

V: They're not his. They never were.

B: I suspect you and he may differ on that.

end of 031124_0638_pm BERN_Phone_Call.wav

CHAPTER XI

Howie's Pub stood almost in the shadow of Tukey's Bridge, a structure connecting Portland's East End—which, confusingly for people from away, seemed at least as much north as east—with the south part of East Deering via Back Cove. Tukey's Bridge was named after an eighteenth-century Portland toll collector and tavern owner named Lemuel Tukey, who'd continued to levy tolls even after they'd officially been abolished, an act unlikely to have endeared him to many of his fellow citizens. His name endured, though, which said much about Mainers' capacity either to forget a grudge or to nurture one.

Howie's wasn't fancy. It was a dive bar, and proud of it, but served better pizza than a stranger had any right to expect and fresh whoopie pies for those who, having settled on a steady diet of pizza and beer, felt that abstemiousness in any further form was pretty much pointless. But Zetta Nadeau was not of that stripe. She might have enjoyed the ambience of Howie's, but if she'd ever ingested any of its food, or much food at all, she'd done so only thanks to the particulate nature of smells. Without flowing fabric to conceal her angularity, she was so thin that, had I gripped her waist in my hands, my fingers would have come close to touching. Mind you, I would have been lying on my back by then, wondering what had hit me. Zetta might not have had much meat on her, but what was strapped to her bones was all muscle. A lot of it was currently on display thanks to a seasonally unwise black crop top and a pair of denim shorts that, if discarded and found later, might have been mistaken for an adolescent's. Except for her neck and face, her visible skin was covered in tattoos. Given her paucity of flesh, I could only guess how much getting them done had hurt.

Because Zetta was so thin, and had endured the upbringing of nightmares, she looked older than thirty. After being transferred from foster home to foster home for much of her early childhood, and enduring occasional disastrous reunions with her birth parents, she had finally come under the care of a late-middle-aged couple named the Scovells, who were capable of offering her the patience and kindness she required. Zetta remained with them until she was almost nineteen, by which point she had won a full tuition scholarship to the Maine College of Art & Design. The Scovells, who had no children of their own and had never fostered before, were as pleased and proud as if they had tended Zetta since she was an egg in the womb. Then, in a freakish piece of bad fortune, the Scovells' little Honda Fit was annihilated by a swerving semi on I-495 just a few days before Zetta was due to start college. That was as close as Zetta came to breaking—finally, fatally. But she didn't. Two days after the funeral, she showed up at MECA&D. Whatever her pain, she hid it well.

Meanwhile, her nominal parents continued to consume valuable oxygen, which, as with the accident that killed the Scovells, was enough to make one wonder if God was paying as much attention to human affairs as He should have been. Ammon, Zetta's birth father, and her mother, Jerusha, had both served time on various charges relating to the mistreatment of their only daughter early in life, from endangering the welfare of a child to domestic violence. Ammon and Jerusha had been together since their early teens and looked set to remain that way until death finally parted them, courts, imprisonment, and estrangement from their daughter having served only to bring them closer. They currently lived on the outskirts of Anson, Maine, a small city with lousy employment rates, where nearly a third of the population subsisted below the poverty line and many of the rest were walking it. Ammon and Jerusha were failed people but kept themselves to themselves and rarely troubled Zetta, except when their landlord threatened to evict them for nonpayment of rent, which happened about once every year or so. Then Ammon would come crawling to Zetta, cash would change hands, and a life absent of any more meaningful interaction would resume.

From what Zetta had told me, her mother regarded her as a traitor to the family, a child whose whining had brought the police down on her progenitors, causing them to be incarcerated for no crime worse than imposing necessary discipline on an unruly child. But then Jerusha had always been hard on Zetta, claiming that the girl had stolen her beauty and ruined her insides. Whether Jerusha had ever actually been beautiful, I couldn't say; if so, it was long before I knew her and was true no more. As for Ammon, he had always struck me as a craven entity, a crooked, stunted tree eclipsed by his wife, their poisons transferring back and forth between them and their union thriving on the resulting infusions.

But we have to be wary of the judgments we pass on others. Much of my knowledge of Zetta's parents was gleaned from what she had shared with me in passing over the years, combined with the mentions of Ammon and Jerusha in local arrest reports and whatever gossip filtered through from my dealings with law enforcement. What I learned might have colored my view of them. I wouldn't have been human otherwise.

Yet on the night of the launch of Zetta's first solo exhibition in Portland, at the now vanished June Fitzpatrick Gallery, I was driving along Congress shortly before midnight when I noticed a figure peering into the well-lit space. It was Ammon Nadeau, trying to glimpse as much of his daughter's work as he could. I can remember pulling over on the opposite side to watch him. I thought he might be tempted to hurl a brick through the glass, but no, his curiosity about Zetta's art—and, I believe, his pride in it—was genuine. He remained there for a while before drifting into the shadows, head low, lost in reflection.

In theory, Ammon could have visited the exhibition during the day and nobody would have commented on his presence, unless Zetta had posted pictures of her parents with an exhortation to have them escorted from the premises should they show their faces. In practice, I doubted Ammon had ever set foot in an art gallery and probably feared being ejected based on his demeanor alone. But I suspect he also feared meeting his daughter on her territory, and the awkwardness and hostility that might result from the encounter. It was interesting, too, that he had gone to the gallery alone. Of his wife there was no sign. I sometimes considered sharing with Zetta what I had seen that night, but always decided against it in the end. If her father had wanted her to know, he'd have told her, and the breach between them would not be healed by my account of a troubled man mired in regret.

Now here was Zetta, perched like a stork on her barstool, a gin and tonic by her right hand, a bandage on her left, the latter the result of a disagreement with a steel edge in her studio, or so she claimed. I didn't question the story. For the moment, I was here to listen, because just ten days after the opening of Zetta's show at the Triton Gallery, Wyatt Riggins had dropped off the map.

"You hadn't been seeing him for long, if I remember right," I said.

"Two months, give or take," she replied, "but I was as happy as I'd ever been in a relationship. I thought Wyatt felt the same way. It was good, or so I believed. I still believe it, or I wouldn't be talking to you now."

Before our meeting, she had sent me a series of pictures of her and Riggins together, selfies for the most part. As at the gallery, I thought they complemented each other, in appearance if nothing else.

"I checked him out, obviously," said Zetta, "before we got too serious."

"You mean you googled him?"

"Yeah. I didn't hire someone to investigate him. I'm wary, but I'm not paranoid."

"And what did you find?"

"Not a lot."

"Meaning?"

"Less than I might have expected. Wyatt didn't leave many footprints."

"That didn't worry you?"

"I asked him about it. He said it was to do with his time in the military."

"And you accepted his explanation?"

I didn't manage to keep the skepticism from my voice and immediately apologized.

"I think," said Zetta, "that his service might have involved more than riding a desk."

"Did he elaborate?"

"No, and I didn't press him. I had no reason to."

"But now you *are* trying to hire someone to investigate him."

"If you'll accept the job. I just want to know that he's okay."

"Have you reason to fear he might not be?"

She sipped her drink, buying herself time to consider how she might respond. I was nursing an alcohol-free beer for appearances' sake. I preferred to keep a clear head when meeting clients. If someone insisted I order something stronger, I would, but I'd allow it to remain untouched before declining whatever job was being proposed. People who insist that you drink with them are best avoided.

"Is it usual for a person to abandon a place he shares with a woman without retrieving his possessions?" she asked.

I thought of Jack Nicholson in *Five Easy Pieces*, leaving Karen Black to get coffee as he goes to a gas station restroom, only for him to hitch a ride alone on the first truck heading out. Occasionally, people didn't want to put themselves through a painful conversation, or not one that wasn't about to alter the finale. It was a coward's way to end a relationship, but it happened.

"When you say he left his possessions, what are we talking about?"

"Clothes, books, some money," said Zetta.

"How much money?"

"Seventy-three dollars, ninety-two cents."

"That's not a lot."

"There was a time when I'd have fought a bum for a tenth as much."

"But not now."

"No, not now."

"What about Riggins? Is he the kind of man who'd feel the loss?"

"He refers to C-notes as 'Texas pennies,' so I guess not."

I watched as a man named Gibson Ouelette stepped into Howie's, walked to the bar, and ordered the cheapest beer on offer, which he'd do his best to make last. Gibson acknowledged me, and I nodded back. He'd just emerged from Bolduc Correctional Facility, to which he'd been transferred from Maine State Prison for the final three years of a nine-year stretch. Bolduc was a minimum-security facility that resembled a farm, but only from a distance or if one wasn't looking hard enough. Gibson, who'd seen the inside of enough cells to count as an expert, once told me something interesting. He said that the worst part of getting busted, worse even than being caught in the first place, was the period between capture and conviction. He told me that it was like being trapped in limbo, but as soon as the judge passed sentence, he felt a sense of relief, because a decision had been made and he could now set about figuring out how to accommodate himself to it. There was nothing worse than not knowing, he said, which might have explained why Zetta Nadeau was willing to spend money establishing the whereabouts of a man who could simply have run out on her because it was easier than discussing why he no longer wanted to be with her.

But I used the word *might* advisedly, because I'd spent enough time listening to people tell me stories to be able to spot gaps in a narrative. I knew Zetta was holding back, and in whatever was being concealed lay the pitfalls: for her, for her boyfriend, and for me, if I agreed to help her—which I wouldn't unless she came clean. That was another lesson hard learned: the risk lay in what was hidden. With risk came hurt, and I'd had enough of that. I ached more than any man in his fifties ought to, not unless he'd been through a war. I was in pain from the time I woke to the time I went to sleep, and I slept less than I would have liked because of it, which exacerbated the situation. I'd been prescribed medication for the toughest nights, but I didn't like using it because it left me foggy for too much of the following day. It also caused me to sleep *too* soundly, which meant that I was less likely to wake if something happened. I suppose one could call it caution on my part, but that wouldn't have been entirely accurate, so call it what it was. Call it fear.

"What did he do for a living while he was here?" I asked.

"Wyatt worked at BrightBlown, but mainly for the discount."

BrightBlown was one of the many dispensaries that had proliferated since Maine legalized the recreational use and sale of cannabis. They weren't all going to survive, but for now, Portland resembled the Wild West in cannabis terms—or the Laid-back West, if you preferred. The down-and-outs who would previously have argued over bottles of Flash Point or Fireball were now to be seen negotiating the use of medical marijuana cards, while storefronts that might once have housed the kind of businesses that lent variety to a city had been taken over by weed distributors. Rents were being pushed up, restaurants and bars were struggling to retain staff because selling weed paid better, and, as was inevitable, the money to be made had attracted criminals of various stripes, from thieves targeting cannabis-growing operations to organized crime gangs engaging in illegal cultivation and mass distribution.

But apart from that, my experience of pot smokers was that some of them were the dullest people you could meet, because what they were most interested in was weed—where they were going to get it, when they were going to smoke it, and how they were going to feel when they did it—which made them poor company for anyone with all their synapses firing.

Zetta smirked.

"You're wearing the same look of disapproval I saw on Ammon's face the first time he caught me smoking a joint," she said.

"Lord, I hope not," I said. I didn't want to think that my features might resemble Ammon Nadeau's. Otherwise, I'd have to start covering up the mirrors in my house and walking the streets only after dark. "But weed isn't my bag."

"Wyatt only smokes on weekends. He's an organized guy."

An organized guy who worked at a weed store and was content to abandon all his possessions, including cash and a girlfriend, seemingly on a whim.

"Could he have been involved in anything illegal?" I asked.

"At BrightBlown?" Zetta snorted. "Jesus, they're about to open a yoga studio."

But Zetta kept her face turned away from me as she spoke.

"What about involvement in anything outside of BrightBlown?"

She didn't answer.

"Zetta, you asked me to meet you because you're anxious about Wyatt. If you were sufficiently upset, you'd have gone to the police. Instead, you're here at Howie's, where the only cops are off-duty and minding their own business."

"This is new territory for me," she said. "I've never had cause to deal with a private investigator before, or not professionally."

"At least you admit that you might have cause," I replied. "Look at you, making progress on talking about your feelings."

"You have an interesting line in sarcasm. Does anyone ever hire you twice?"

"You're in trouble if you have to hire me once. Hiring me twice means you may have a taste for it, which would make me disinclined to become involved again."

Zetta fished around in her tote bag and seemed to locate what she was looking for, but didn't immediately display it.

"Is everything I tell you confidential?"

"Largely, unless you tell me that you're planning to kill someone, in which case I might feel obligated to inform the authorities. Are you planning on killing someone?"

"Not yet, but the night is young."

"Then you're probably in the clear. But there's a difference between my legal and moral obligations. The latter I take more seriously than the former."

"That's what I was told."

She removed her hand from the bag. She was holding a red flip phone in a Ziploc, either an old Nokia or a new one designed to look old. She placed it on the bar.

"This is Wyatt's phone," she said, "or one of them."

"How many does he have?"

"Just two. This one and an Android. The Android is for daily use."

"Where is it now?"

"With Wyatt, I suppose, but it goes straight to voicemail when I call the number. If he's picking up his messages, he's not replying."

"And the Nokia?"

I held the bag up to the light. The phone, I thought, was probably the same one I'd watched Riggins opening and closing at Zetta's show.

"It was found at Tandem Coffee Roasters on Congress five days ago.

One of the staff recognized it as Wyatt's. She recalled him using it before he left and was holding on to it until he returned, because Wyatt likes Tandem a lot. When he didn't show, she gave it to me."

"Are you a regular at Tandem too?"

"With Wyatt, though I don't really drink coffee. I stopped by after he went missing, in case someone had noticed anything odd last time he was in."

"And had they?"

"Just his lost phone."

So her boyfriend had dropped one phone, wasn't answering another, and had fallen from sight, leaving behind what appeared to be all his worldly goods. But once again, it was me to whom Zetta was speaking and not the police.

"I'm waiting," I said.

"For what?"

"For the punch line. I know it's coming."

She played with her drink again, giving her something else to do with her hands while she debated what to reveal and what to conceal.

"I noted the passcodes for both his phones."

Wow. I was no analyst, but I thought Zetta might have trust issues.

"And why did you do that?"

"Because I've been stung before by guys who cheated on me or lied about who they were, where they went, what they were doing when they got there, and with whom."

"It sounds like you need to be more selective about your boyfriends."

"I blame my upbringing. I'd hoped Wyatt might be different, so I took his word about the military thing. The passcodes were just a precaution."

"And was he different?"

"I could only read opened messages and emails, but he seemed to be. All I found on the Android was stuff relating to BrightBlown."

"Anything on the Nokia?"

"A short series of contacts in the address book, but only as letters, not names, and no calls were listed as either made or received. Those contacts had been deleted when the phone was found. One text message was left in the inbox, which Wyatt hadn't deleted."

She took the Nokia from the bag, entered the code, and showed me the message. It consisted of a single word: RUN.

CHAPTER XII

Roland Bilas figured he was screwed the moment he disembarked the afternoon flight from Mexico City to LAX. Actually, he suspected he might already have been screwed before boarding, but Bilas always worried when he was working. A man could become convinced that everyone in uniform was looking at him, so either he began looking in turn at everyone in a uniform or he tried not to pay attention to anyone in a uniform while simultaneously being aware of their presence. The trouble was that studied avoidance seemed to draw their attention more rapidly than a direct gaze, as though acting innocent released some kind of pheromone that trained customs officers could scent, causing the pack to descend.

Most of the time, there was no reason to be nervous, other than the fact that smuggling was an illegal act and illegality brought nervousness as a matter of course. Bilas didn't know anyone in his business who was nerveless. No, correct that: he didn't know anyone nerveless who was *still* in business. He could name a couple who were in jail and a few who were dead, but a certain degree of tension, like a moderate amount of stress, was healthy in the criminal world, both being conducive to long-term survival.

Not that Bilas liked to think of himself as a criminal. His view was that criminals represented a category of individuals who harmed others, and Bilas did his best to restrict the harm he did in every aspect of his life. After all, he wasn't moving narcotics or weapons, or offering to transport desperate folk across the border only to abandon them in the desert. In fact, he didn't even use drugs, didn't own a gun, and felt that anyone from Latin America who wanted to work in the good old U.S. of A. should be facilitated, not least because Bilas didn't care to clean his own hotel bathroom, bus his own table, or deliver his own Chinese food. While he could probably have listed on the fingers of one hand those on whom he wished real misfortune, none were poorer or less powerful than he.

Thus, Roland Bilas considered himself to be, by most standards, a relatively good guy. The likelihood that some in police circles would have disagreed with him was neither here nor there. It was simply a matter of perspective. Bilas, while waiting for his flight, had found his gaze drawn to the television screen in the departure lounge, only to quickly avert it when faced with apartment blocks being demolished by Russian missiles or, because this was Mexico, dismembered human remains being disinterred from under buildings or discovered in garbage bags by the side of the road. Back in 2022, Bilas had spent a week in an upscale hotel on Playa Condesa in Acapulco. On the afternoon of his departure, the outgoing tide had revealed a body roped to a cement anchor, the kind of event that inevitably cast a shadow over an otherwise happy vacation, even if vacationing contentedly in Mexico required the exercise of a certain willful blindness to a hundred homicides a day.

Bilas loved Mexico and its people, but when it came to human butchery, he took the view that the country was seriously fucked. He used to argue with Antonio Elizalde about this, once their transactions were concluded and Elizalde had opened a bottle of something old and curious to celebrate. Elizalde would respond to criticism of his nation by pointing to the number of gun fatalities in the United States, or the high rates of maternal mortality among Black women in what was supposed to be a first-world country. Bilas would retort that nobody in the United

States was making a busload of forty-three trainee teachers vanish, or murdering women at the rate of ten a day, and so a free-spoken evening would pass for both men.

But Bilas hadn't met Elizalde on this latest trip. Elizalde had thought it best for them to remain out of contact, even allowing for his imminent medical treatment. Bilas had sent him a good-luck card, signed only *R* and without a return address. He wished the older man well; if Bilas *was* a criminal, then he, like Elizalde, was one from a more civilized time.

Flying from Mexico to the United States invited a degree of attention from the authorities, but Bilas had never yet set off any alarm bells. Primarily, the uniforms were looking for narcotics, as well as targeting those individuals with no right to enter the country, and Bilas didn't check either of those boxes. He was a second-generation American, a little overweight but not trying to hide it. He dressed smart-casual for flights, always carried a book in one hand as he proceeded through customs, and wore his glasses on a nylon cord around his neck. He was polite with the authorities, but not excessively so, and any search of his bags would have revealed only a fondness for the kind of souvenirs set to reside on a shelf before being broken during a spot of careless dusting. His reading material evinced an amateur's fascination with the history of Central and South America, and entry tickets to various temples and archaeological sites of interest served as bookmarks throughout.

The best kind of smuggling does not resemble smuggling at all, in that there is no apparent attempt at concealment. Bilas's business was the smuggling of antiquities, many acquired to order for collectors untroubled by the legalities of acquisition. His particular area of expertise was Peru, particularly pre-Hispanic cultural artifacts. Unauthorized excavation of Peruvian archaeological digs and the exportation of pre-Hispanic treasures had been prohibited by legislation since 1822, and successive Peruvian administrations had added to that body of law, even as government officials were assisting with export documents and shipping arrangements, often due less to corruption than a lack of awareness of the unique nature of what was being sent abroad. With so many sites still to be explored, and with too many artifacts already unearthed to ever be able to display more than a fraction, permitting duplicates or near-duplicates to be exported had, for many years, seemed no great sin.

So it was that Hiram Bingham III—who, in 1911, made public the existence of Machu Picchu, even as one of his workers was tasked with erasing from its stones the names of Peruvians who had visited the site before him—was permitted to transport thousands of human bones, pottery, and other items to Yale University, along with a quantity of gold concealed in a trunk, in return for vague promises that the hoard would be repatriated should the Peruvian authorities ever submit such a request. The Peruvians quickly realized, to their cost, that taking Americans at their word was a bad idea, and control, once ceded, was hard to regain. When they asked for the Machu Picchu cache to be restored to them, they received forty-seven cases of human remains, none of them from Machu Picchu, and so began almost a century of stalemate.

The Peruvians might have lived to regret their earlier decision to facilitate Bingham, but they did learn from it. Repatriation proceedings were expensive, difficult, and time-consuming, so it was better not to have to repatriate antiquities at all. In 1981, a memorandum of understanding was signed between Peru and the United States, allowing the Peruvians to be informed of any seizures by U.S. Customs, followed by the immediate return of those items, with U.S. officials aided by a list featuring general descriptions of Peruvian treasures in seven categories. Admittedly, the agreement essentially ignored items that had been smuggled into the United States before the signing of the agreement, but the perfect was the enemy of the possible. Those battling the smugglers had bigger fish to fry, not least the sheer quantity of sites, many of them in remote areas, that were easy prey for *huaqueros*, looters who left their spoor in the form of scattered bones, ransacked altars, and a marked absence of textiles, ceramics, and gold.

Which was where Roland Bilas came in, because a considerable expanse of territory, much of it occupied by voracious middlemen, lay between *huaqueros* and prospective buyers. Bilas knew by name many of the leading *huaqueros* and their bosses—because everyone except God worked for somebody—and maintained a spreadsheet of collectors in Europe, North America, and Asia, as well as their preferences and wish lists, so he was ideally positioned to put the appropriate item into the appropriate hands for the appropriate price. Because Bilas had a reputation as a fair dealer, he had managed to prosper without leaving too much wreckage behind. This was as much a conscious decision on his part as a consequence of any better aspect of his nature. The existence of genial souls like Antonio Elizalde notwithstanding, the acquisition and sale of antiquities was by no means always a civilized trade. The easiest way to make it one was to pay properly and promptly, and charge no more than the market could bear—even a little less, which might encourage return business. Greed, in Bilas's experience, was the great undoer, and much misfortune could be laid at its door. Roland Bilas was that rare breed: a man who understood the meaning of enough, or had until recently.

Partly, Bilas blamed his internist. The previous year, Bilas had been diagnosed with atrial fibrillation, which caused the internist, Dr. Minhas, to inquire whether Bilas was dealing with high levels of anxiety. Bilas was tempted to reply that, as a smuggler, anxiety was part of the job description, but decided that Dr. Minhas might have filed that under TMI: too much information. Still, Bilas admitted that, yes, his line of work—"I'm in imports and exports"—did have its associated pressures, though he believed he'd been handling them well, all things considered. Dr. Minhas begged to differ and indicated that Roland Bilas was well on his way to a stroke unless he instituted some profound life changes. Dr. Minhas's recommendations included regular exercise, a better diet, and practicing mindfulness, none of which appealed to his patient.

But Dr. Minhas also advised that, at fifty-seven, Bilas might like to consider working less if he could afford it. The difficulty was that Bilas *couldn't* afford it. True, he made a decent living, but laundering the proceeds to hide them from the IRS meant taking a hit of twenty-five to thirty percent, and he had overheads in the form of travel expenses, bribes, and losses due to breakage, theft, and seizure. If Bilas wanted to relax, never mind retire, he needed to begin properly feathering his nest, and fast, before a blood vessel burst in his brain. In this regard, as in others, he and Antonio Elizalde had much in common.

So Roland Bilas, like Elizalde, had involved himself in the sourcing—well, theft, to be scrupulously honest about a dishonest act—and transportation of an unusual hoard, for which he'd been generously recompensed. Bilas subsequently reinvested a generous percentage of those funds in a selection of fine erotic Moche pottery dating from AD 100 to 700, with accompanying paperwork and invoices describing them as replicas, nothing to see here, Officer, etc. To further obscure their origin, Bilas acquired two additional pieces that *were* replicas, with similar paperwork, from one of which he'd permitted the tape to come away, making it more accessible in the event of a search. One of those replica pieces was in his carry-on bag along with a genuine ceramic, and the other was with the three remaining originals in his checked baggage. An expert with time to compare and contrast would be able to spot the difference between the real and the fake, but fingers crossed, it wouldn't come to that. Customs and Border Protection had more important matters with which to occupy their time, given that some five thousand pounds of drugs were seized at U.S. ports every day, with ten times as much getting through undetected. A little perspective here, fellas.

But the ceramics were the support act, not the main show. That honor fell to a pair of immaculately preserved mantas from the pre-

Incan Nazca culture, for which Bilas had paid $35,000 apiece, with the expectation of earning five or six times as much from the right buyer. Bilas had wrapped the textiles in polycaprolactone/polystyrene sheaths infused with extract of chamomile oil to guard against contamination by microorganisms before fixing the resulting packs between the interior hard shell of his suitcase and a layer of padding, ostensibly to protect his "replica" ceramics from damage. Finally, he had arranged for the goods to be transported from Peru to Mexico because Mexican customs officials were less watchful than the Peruvians.

It was set to be among the more lucrative runs of Bilas's career. He'd taken a chance by returning south of the border so soon, but the mantas were special. If he didn't move on them immediately, the seller would try to offload them elsewhere, which wouldn't be difficult. And it wasn't as though Bilas could just wire the money and ask for the mantas to be FedExed to him because a) the seller had no interest in leaving a trail at his end and b) Bilas might as well have sent a personal invitation to the FBI's Art Crime Team to come visit him and make themselves at home.

So Bilas had gone to Mexico City, but stayed only two nights. He'd also made an appointment with a private dental clinic in Polanco for a consultation about possible implants and crowns to provide a plausible reason for such a short trip, should anyone elect to question him upon his return. As for the officials at Mexico City International Airport, they'd displayed no interest in the Moche ceramics as the items passed through the scanner in his carry-on bag. Similarly, the checked baggage had been placed in the hold without a hitch, although Bilas didn't start to relax even a little until the wheels left the ground.

Then he landed at LAX, and from the moment he entered the terminal, he felt eyes on him. He couldn't pinpoint the source and therefore couldn't be sure he wasn't overreacting because of the value of the cargo. But that cargo, and the money tied up with it, meant he couldn't just walk away. Even if he did, they'd take him before he left the terminal, whether he picked up his bag or not. Bilas knew that random searches by customs officials rarely uncovered high-value goods; targets were usually identified before they even took their carry-on bag from the overhead lockers on the plane. If they were onto him, there was nothing he could do about it. He could only hope that the false paperwork would cut the mustard, and the mantas' sheathing, which had been constructed as a perfect fit for the case, would remain unrevealed. But with each step he took, more hope fell away, so that by the time he reached the baggage carousel, he was resigned to his fate. When they came for him, just as he began walking toward the exit, he was almost relieved.

CHAPTER XIII

In Howie's, I looked again at the single-word text message on Wyatt Riggins's phone. The sender's number was listed.

"Did you try calling the number it came from?"

"I got an out-of-service response," said Zetta. "It was probably sent using an anonymizer app. One of my exes stayed in touch with his other girlfriends that way."

I didn't know how to respond so I said nothing, which seemed safest.

"And a boyfriend," Zetta added. "Though I'm not judging."

I waited for further relationship revelations. Thankfully, none were forthcoming.

"It may not have been an app," I said. "The only reason for carrying around one of those old phones is to limit the possibility of being monitored. It's not a perfect solution, but it's better than using a smartphone, unless the smartphone is heavily secured. A Nokia is a simpler, cheaper option. The fact that Wyatt kept it close and reacted decisively to the only communication he received suggests that it was a warning device, with the sender using a similar phone. It would make sense to be consistent and not risk compromising the system in any way by introducing apps. You're sure you have no idea why Wyatt would be part of an arrangement like this?"

"None. I'd tell you if I did. I'm genuinely worried about him, and lying to you won't help."

"No," I told her, "it won't. Did you, by any chance, make a list of those earlier contact numbers?"

"I didn't. I would have, had I thought something like this was going to happen."

"Don't let it bother you. I couldn't have done much with the contacts anyway, not without going to a lot of time and expense. I doubt anyone would have answered had I called, or cooperated if they did."

"Because whatever Wyatt's involved in is presumably illegal, right?"

"Which doesn't necessarily make Wyatt a criminal. He and at least one other individual—whoever sent the message—might have crossed paths with the kind of people who are better avoided. That can happen through bad luck alone, though it's rare."

Zetta touched the index finger of her right hand to an area of uninked skin on her left arm.

"I'd been thinking about getting his name tattooed here," she said, "if things worked out between us."

"Lucky you didn't rush into it."

"Actually, I might have stuck to initials. They're easier to alter later. Will you look for him?"

I informed Zetta of my hourly rate and the weekly minimum. She didn't blink hard or start laughing, which was always a good sign. She even offered payment in advance without being asked, putting her in the running for Client of the Year.

"I'll need a list of friends, acquaintances, anyone with whom Wyatt had even passing discourse," I said. "Did he use social media?"

"Never. He claimed only chumps put their lives online."

I wasn't about to disagree, but it removed what might have been productive lines of inquiry.

"I'll also want to go through whatever he left in the apartment," I said. "If you could put together any paperwork—bank statements, employment records, anything official or, better still, unofficial—that would be useful, along with a list of his email addresses, his regular cell phone number, his hat size—"

"He didn't wear hats," said Zetta, then frowned. "Oh. That was a joke, right?"

"Investigative humor. It kills at conventions."

"I'll bet. A lot of that stuff I already brought with me"—she patted her tote—"but call by the house whenever suits. We can even go there now if you like."

She had a gleam in her eye. It signaled that if I were to make a move on her, she wouldn't object. Zetta might have been worried about her boyfriend, but not *that* worried, even if I was old enough to be her father. She was one of those artistic free spirits. Trouble, in other words.

"Tomorrow morning will be fine," I said. "How about after ten? I'm not an early riser."

That sounded like an unfortunate double entendre under the circumstances, but Zetta managed to hide any disappointment she felt and no tears of regret stained the bar as she wrote down her address for me.

"After ten it is," she said. "If I'm working, I may not hear the bell, so call my phone. I'll see it light up."

She ordered another gin and tonic. I left her to it. Outside, the evening wind was baring its teeth enough to nip but not bite. Across the street, an intoxicated man argued loudly with a marginally less inebriated woman, who walked away from him with her head high. Having no one else to argue with in her absence, he continued arguing with himself before heading after her. I shadowed him from the other side as he caught up, but he displayed no signs of violence toward her, nor she to him. I saw only some conciliatory gesture from the former and what might have been grudging acceptance from the latter. They walked on, together but apart, which was about as well as it could have ended.

I thought about calling Macy to see if she wanted to meet, but if I did, the evening would drift—not unpleasantly, it should be said—and perhaps the night as well, and I had things to do. I speculated on what it might say about me that I should opt for paperwork over the company of a woman who cared. Whatever it was, it wasn't good.

I heard footsteps behind me, and Gibson Ouelette appeared. He hadn't spent long in Howie's. Gibson didn't spend long anywhere except prison cells. I'd always gotten along okay with Gibson. He wasn't a bad guy, just an unlucky one, and many worse men had never spent even an hour behind bars.

"How you doing, Gibson?"

"You know, getting by."

He stared at the sky, which was cloudless and filled with stars.

"Beautiful night," I said.

"Someone once told me all those stars were dead," said Gibson, "but he was an asshole. It's just old light, from thousands and thousands of years ago, that's only reaching us now. We're looking back in time, staring at fragments of the past scattered above our heads."

Gibson was like that, a philosopher trapped in the body of a petty criminal. He could conduct a searching moral inventory while emptying a cash register. As I watched, he made a shape with his hands, creating a narrow rectangle.

"That was as much as I could see of it through the window of my last cell," he told me. "Just that. But it was enough. All this"—he gestured at sky, land, river—"is too much."

Gibson wished me good night and walked on. I guessed he'd be back in jail before the year was out—not because he wanted to be, but because after years spent in a room eight feet by six, the outside world was often too big, and the past too close. Departed, but still haunting the living.

CHAPTER XIV

Roland Bilas had never seen the interior of an interview room at LAX before and had hoped to without being able to say he'd had the pleasure. The room smelled of sweat and old coffee but was otherwise clean and tidy, even if the decor extended no further than various official notices in English and Spanish that told him little he didn't already know.

Bilas didn't panic. He was too experienced for that and had blustered, threatened, and lied his way out of tougher situations, some involving men who carried machetes as a matter of course and not because they were passionate about agriculture. When the customs officials ordered Bilas to go along with them, he hadn't made any more fuss than might have been expected from an innocent man who believed an unfortunate error had been made, to be cleared up as soon as someone took the time to listen to what he had to say.

Bilas elected not to mention the Moche ceramics before determining the lay of the land. If they were the reason for the search, he would protest that he had the requisite invoices, and the paperwork was, so far as he was aware, completely legitimate. For the present, he made sure that when he spoke, he gave away nothing that might incriminate himself. He could have—perhaps even should have—immediately requested access to a lawyer, but again, he preferred to see what might unfold before committing. More to the point, he was aware that he wasn't legally entitled to representation during primary or secondary inspection by Customs and Border Protection, so if he kicked up, they could tell him to go fuck himself. If they found something and elected to charge him, *then* they'd have to let him call a lawyer, and the contest would begin in earnest. So Bilas asked only for a glass of water, which was provided, and for the novel he was reading to be returned to him, which it was not. After that, he was left alone with his thoughts.

The room didn't have a clock, but Bilas still had his watch. An hour went by before two female CBP officers entered the room, accompanied by a young guy in shirtsleeves who was prematurely balding and appeared too somber for his years, as though playing at being a grown-up. One of the officers placed Bilas's laptop and both of his cell phones, an iPhone and a red Nokia 2660 flip, on the table between them.

"What were you doing in Mexico, Mr. Bilas?" asked the younger of the two CBP officers. Her name tag identified her as Flores. The older one, who looked like she chewed barbed wire for fun and profit, was tagged as Schroeder. Mr. Somber wore no badge at all. He was also sweating through his green shirt, indicating a recent, even hurried, arrival. Bilas instantly had him pegged for non-CBP, a specialist of some kind. Bilas's worry meter crept up a notch.

"I had a consultation about dental work," he replied. "I'm considering getting implants and don't want to have to refinance my mortgage to pay for them on this side of the border. I have the appointment letter in my bag, along with the estimate for the procedure."

"What about the contents of your baggage?"

Bilas decided to play a card, see what unfolded.

"You mean the pottery? What about it? They make those things by the thousands to sell to tourists. I mean, okay, mine might be a little risqué, but I'm a single man living alone and my mother is dead, so I don't see who could be offended by them."

"And you bought them all from the same store?"

"The same dealer, yes. I don't think I'd describe his premises as a store. A stall, maybe, but not a store. If you've seen the ceramics, you've seen the invoice as well, because I made sure to pack it alongside them. You know, just in case."

"Just in case of what?" asked Schroeder.

"Just in case I was asked to prove they weren't originals."

"And why would that be a problem?"

"Look, I travel a lot in Latin America. I love the people, the landscape, the food, but most of all, I love the history. I know it's illegal to export pre-Hispanic artifacts without a license, though been offered the opportunity to acquire items under the counter more than once. I don't know a regular visitor who hasn't."

"And you've never accepted?"

Bilas decided he'd said enough.

"Please," he said, "just tell me what this is about."

Schroeder and Flores surrendered the floor to Mr. Somber.

"My name is Morgensen," he said. "I'm attached to the Cotsen Institute of Archaeology at UCLA, specifically the UCLA/Getty Interdepartmental Program in the Conservation of Cultural Heritage. Mr. Bilas, it's my opinion that only two of those Moche ceramics are replicas. The rest are originals."

"That can't be right," said Bilas.

"I'm afraid it is."

"But you said it was just your opinion. You could be mistaken."

"I don't believe so."

Bilas shook his head in bewilderment.

"Huh," he said. "Well, what do you know."

"Actually," said Flores, "we're more interested in what *you* know, specifically about a pair of Nazca mantas concealed behind the padding of your suitcase."

Which was when Roland Bilas went from suspecting he might be screwed to knowing for sure that he was.

"I'd like to speak to a lawyer," he said. "Right now."

CHAPTER XV

Howie's proximity to the highway meant that I was back in Scarborough in the time it took the radio to play only a couple of songs, none memorable enough to hum along with or offensive enough to turn off. Once home, I made a mug of instant coffee, took it to my office, and read through the material that Zetta Nadeau had provided about her missing boyfriend. It didn't amount to much. Riggins had an account with a bank in Portland, but it contained only a few hundred dollars. I could try to have the account monitored, which would reveal when and where any withdrawals were made, but gaining access would be expensive and illegal, and I preferred not to go down that road unless absolutely necessary. The rest of the paperwork related to his employment at BrightBlown and not much else. I searched in vain for a photocopy of his driver's license, and none of the paperwork, not even the BrightBlown material, included Riggins's social security number. Either he'd stored the critical material—military discharge papers, birth certificate, photos, his dad's old wristwatch, a lock of his mother's hair—back at Zetta's place and she'd missed it, or he was keeping it elsewhere. I was leaning toward the second option. Like Zetta said, Wyatt Riggins was a man who didn't like to leave a trail.

Zetta had declined to give the Nokia to me, which was fine. Not much could be gleaned from it anyway, and maybe she was hoping Riggins might call, if only in an effort to establish whether anyone had found it. But I doubted the phone would ever ring again. The Nokia had served its function. It had alerted Riggins to an approaching threat, which raised two issues: first, the nature of that threat, and second, whether it was still heading in this direction.

Because if someone was hunting for Wyatt Riggins, Portland was the last place in which he'd been seen.

IN THE MARSHES, in the moonlight, Jennifer Parker listened. The children were calling out again, the same words repeated like an incantation or a summoning, howling like animals desperate to be found.

no, not that alone, she thought.

Desperate to be reunited.

CHAPTER XVI

In a suburb of St. Louis, Missouri, two men had just finished dinner, consuming between them a massive cowboy rib eye with pepper sauce and sides. They were now making a pair of brandies last while waiting for their arteries to recover. They had also drunk two glasses of red wine—less than they might have preferred because they had business to conduct the following day, business that involved some driving, thinking, and negotiating, all activities better undertaken with a clear head.

Aldo Bern was, at best, ambivalent about St. Louis and tried to give it as wide a berth as possible, which was easy when a man put his mind to it. On the other hand, he did like Olive + Oak out in Webster Groves, which meant the city and its environs had at least one redeeming feature. If his sixty-plus years on earth had given Bern any insights worth sharing—and the older he got, the more he had his doubts—among them was that it was a whole lot harder to maintain a halfway decent restaurant than people seemed to think, and really hard to operate a great one. After centuries of trying, a man was still more likely to be served an average meal than a good one. Bern didn't know whether Olive + Oak qualified as a great restaurant in the minds of those who measured the distance between the silverware to make sure it lined up and dined with a notebook to hand, but by his standards, it was damn fine.

As for his companion, Bern figured that he'd probably enjoyed the experience as well, though with Devin it could be difficult to tell. Devin Vaughn went through life like someone had severed his smile muscles, and he kept compliments to a minimum, but it was widely accepted that he was more highbrow than the criminal norm. Devin counted as cultured not only in the circles in which he and Bern moved—where reading more than the sports pages and the funnies qualified you as an intellectual—but also in wider society. Devin had a library that was more than a shelf long, collected art that didn't involve dogs playing poker, and always dressed as though he was either going to or coming from somewhere more formal. He kept his shoes shined, his clothes pressed, and had never been known to wear denim, or not since he'd passed thirty. In the past, those habits had led some less-enlightened associates to question his sexuality, but nobody did that anymore. The ones who used to had learned their lesson fast, and at Devin's hands.

A young woman passed their table, tightly packaged and barely old enough to drink legally. Bern's eyes flicked toward her: he was only human, even if he could have passed for her grandfather. Mercifully, Devin's eyes didn't stray from the table. Since the breakup of his marriage, he'd begun sleeping with girls who'd been born only this century, an indulgence Bern hoped he'd tire of before too long, since the next step was marrying one of them. In the eighties, Bern had spent a few years on the West Coast working under Devin's father, God rest his soul, when they were both younger men on the make, and a ready supply of coke could gain a man entry to all the best parties. The experience had taught Bern never to be a user, only a seller, and that while sleeping with much younger women was nice work if you could get it, marrying them was no course of action for a sensible man, not unless he aspired to bleed himself dry with future alimony payments.

On a practical note, Bern had also learned that the first lesson in being a successful drug dealer was not to look, dress, or act like one. It was a lesson he had later drummed into Devin because, in his final years, Devin's father, paralyzed and rendered mute by a stroke, wasn't able to drum much of anything into his only son. Bern felt that Devin might have taken the lesson to extremes, given the cost of some of his suits, but he was forced to admit that the boy always looked classy. If you passed him on the street, you'd have taken him for an investment banker or a corporate lawyer, not the head of a criminal organization.

That was the other thing about Devin: He specialized. He ran coke, MDMA, heroin, fentanyl, and pot, the latter in both legal and illegal forms, and the quality always guaranteed, but that was it. No gambling, no whores, no protection rackets, and no construction scams. The money was laundered at a hefty premium, coming back so clean it gleamed, before being invested in legitimate businesses managed by individuals who, in most cases, had no idea that the parent firm—protected by subsidiaries, shelf companies, and enough layers of bankers, lawyers, and offshore addresses to confound God Himself—was founded on pot, pills, and powder, and their paychecks ultimately cleared thanks to the custom of addicts. It was Devin who had expanded the empire, and rarely did he put a foot wrong—until recently.

A series of calamitous occurrences, over only some of which Devin could have claimed control, had led to the present difficulties. It began with the seizure of a $10 million cocaine shipment from Mexico at a time when cash flow was already sluggish, followed by a disagreement between supplier and buyer over who was responsible for the failure of the shipment to reach its ultimate destination. It might just have been bad luck that customs agents had searched the container, but Devin was of the opinion that luck, bad or otherwise, had nothing to do with it, and someone on the Mexican side had tipped off the U.S. authorities. If it came from the cartel, then it had been authorized by Blas Urrea himself, though Bern had reserved judgment on that score until more information became available.

Then, while Bern's investigation into the seizure was still ongoing, some new cryptocurrency had collapsed, and it turned out that Devin had bet, if not the entire house, then at least the first couple of floors on a different outcome. Bern didn't know from cryptocurrency, but he could have told Devin that trusting millions to kids who did business in shorts and T-shirts, and who didn't own a proper pair of shoes among them, was never going to end well. The people who advised Devin to invest, most of whom didn't wear proper shoes either, had assured him that his investments would bounce back, but weren't able to say when. Might be a year, could be two. Unfortunately, Devin didn't have two years, or even one. Combined with the loss of the shipment—and the lingering aftereffects of COVID, which had royally fucked with both the legitimate and criminal sides of their operation—Devin probably had three to six months of wiggle room before the cracks began to show. Once that happened, the vultures wouldn't just be circling, they'd be plucking eyes from heads. The situation wasn't beyond retrieval, but it remained an existential threat. It was important that everybody stayed calm and didn't do anything rash—which was when Devin, unbeknownst to Bern, had decided that rash was the way to go, and moved against Blas Urrea behind Bern's back. Now they were in St. Louis, trying to cut a deal on fentanyl, because they needed an alternative source, and quickly.

"Maybe we should call for the check," said Bern, raising a hand to their server as he spoke. "Devin, you hearing me?"

Devin's eyes were glassy. If Bern didn't know better, he'd have suspected Devin was dipping a wet finger in his own supply, or what was left of it.

Devin came back from wherever he'd been.

"What did you say?"

"That we should call it a night."

"Uh-huh."

"You feeling all right?"

Devin rubbed at the corners of his eyes.

"I haven't been sleeping so well."

"You have a lot on your mind."

"Yeah," said Devin. "That too."

"Too? Is there something else I should know?"

"Just bad dreams."

Bern wasn't surprised. Bad fucking dreams? It was a wonder Devin was sleeping at all after what he'd done to Urrea, and with what he was keeping at home.

"Take a pill," said Bern.

"I take any more pills, I'm going to rattle when I walk. They don't stop me dreaming."

Bern didn't know what else to say. Well, he did, but Devin wouldn't want to hear it, not again. What was done was done, and all they could hope was that Urrea didn't find out Devin was responsible. If he did, Urrea would declare war, and that was a fight they'd lose, weakened as they were.

Bern placed his right hand on Devin's arm.

"You're like a son to me," he said. "You understand that, right? I told your father I'd look out for you, always, and I've kept the promise as best I could."

"I know that. No one could say different."

"But I'm getting tired, Devin. It comes with age. I have pains in my joints and my guts hurt."

"You didn't tell me that before. They hurt, how? Did you see a doctor?"

Bern instantly regretted opening his mouth. He took his hand away, used it to wave for the check. Anything for the distraction.

"It's stress, is all. I take Pepto-Bismol, it helps. What I'm saying is, I don't have energy like before. Once we were in the black again, I was planning on easing out. I was just trying to find the right time to tell you. I'd still be around to offer counsel, but on a day-to-day basis, I'd be done. Now, with this Urrea thing, and you not being able to sleep without having nightmares—"

Despite himself, Bern was singing the same song again.

"Bad dreams," Devin corrected him. "And they'll pass."

"Give back what you took. I'm asking you for the last time. You and the others, you leave them somewhere safe, we make a call. Urrea doesn't ever have to know it was us."

"I've told you before: They stay."

Bern sat back. He was about to say "Then I can't" when his cell phone rang. Bern checked the caller ID and felt life lining him up for another punch to the gut. The last time a call had come through from this number, it was to inform him that their shipment of cocaine was now in the hands of the U.S. government.

Bern put the phone to his ear and began thumbing bills from his money clip as the check arrived.

"Yeah," he said to the caller. "I know who this is."

Bern listened. He turned the check to its blank side and scribbled some notes.

"Okay. You tell her she needs to get him out, whatever it takes. Make sure she appreciates there will be consequences otherwise. Anything changes, you call me."

He hung up. Devin was watching him.

"How bad?" Devin asked.

"Roland Bilas got picked up by customs at LAX. He was flying in from Mexico City with a handful of obscene statues and some old blankets in his suitcase."

Devin closed his eyes. Bilas had been told—no, *ordered*—not to head back across the border for a while. He'd also been paid well for his part in the Urrea operation to ensure he had no cause for complaint. Devin wasn't about to dismiss Bilas as greedy or stupid—the man had never struck him as either—but that wouldn't stop him from having Bilas's hands stomped to paste once he was out of custody.

"Has he lawyered up?" Devin asked.

"As soon as he was charged. I have the lawyer's name."

"Anyone we know?"

"Not that I remember, but someone will get in touch with her, tell her we have an interest."

Bern didn't think Bilas would hold up well under pressure. Bilas had never been arrested and would be scared even before hard-faced officials began talking about jail time, time that might go away if he was prepared to name names.

"He'll know better than to give them anything," said Devin.

"You think? Jesus, Devin, my granddaughter would have a better chance of holding up under questioning, and she's six years old. We need to make sure Bilas isn't kept anywhere worse than a holding room at the airport. God forbid they use the weekend to put him in lockup with a copy of the Prison Rape Elimination Act as a fiction option."

It was all unraveling. This was the beginning of the next stage. Bern could feel it.

"Make sure the lawyer is aware that if Bilas talks, we'll be the least of his problems," said Devin. "No matter what protection he's promised in return for testimony, Urrea's people will find him. Silence is his best chance of staying alive."

"It's in hand."

"I want *you* to call her, not anyone else. Fix it, Aldo."

Bern headed for the door to make the call outside. Devin Vaughn remained seated. He still had a little brandy left in his glass, but Bern had barely touched his. Devin reached across and added Bern's portion to his own because alcohol helped more than pills. The fucking child kept crying, that was the worst of it. The nightmares he could handle, but not the crying. Still, Devin wasn't sorry for what he'd done.

Because the child was beautiful.

CHAPTER XVII

Many miles to the east, in a Virginia town unloved even by those who lived there, or perhaps by them most of all, Harriet Swisher woke to find her husband, Hul, absent from their bed, the sound of the wind replacing his soft snoring. She immediately began to worry. The Swishers were both in their seventies, but Hul was in poorer health than his wife, and Harriet spent more time fretting about him than he did about her, even if she suspected he might well outlive her, ornery cuss that he was.

But what would he do without her? She buttered his toast every morning and laid out his jammies on the comforter last thing at night, had done since the day after their wedding. He rarely made a decision without first consulting her, and while he didn't always agree with her point of view, he'd take time to consider what she'd said, which was more than most men she knew did when presented with a woman's opinion—and probably most men she didn't know, too.

Sometimes, Harriet feared Hul might manage better in her absence than she and everyone else believed, because husbands could be frustrating that way, strategically incompetent until they could afford to be no longer. After she was dead, Hul might well discover previously untapped abilities to butter his toast, lay out his jammies, and make sensible decisions without her input. But should he suddenly begin dating some local jade a month after the funeral, she'd come back from the grave to haunt him, she swore she would. He and his tramp wouldn't know a moment's peace.

Harriet called out to him.

"Hul? Where are you?"

Nobody addressed him by Hurrel, his given name, not since his mother had gone to her reward back when Reagan was president. His middle name was John, but for reasons lost to history he didn't care to be known by that either, so most everyone knew him as Jack. Except to Harriet he didn't look like a Jack Swisher, which for her evoked connotations of rakery, even homosexuality. At the very least, it brought to mind someone who wore two-tone shoes and smelled of scents stored behind drugstore counters, which was not her man. He was tall and robust, with a handsome, weathered face, and smelled of nothing more exotic than Aqua Velva. Over the years, she had contracted Hurrel to Hul, which meant his gravestone, when the day came, would be crowded with letters: Hurrel "Hul" John "Jack" Swisher. Jesus, people would think three or four people were buried down there. If he did predecease her, she'd try to cut a deal with the stonemason for a discount. But she didn't want to outlive him. What would she do without him?

Harriet listened for the hum of the exhaust fan in the bathroom, which came on with the light, but no noise was heard.

Christ, she thought, *what if he's fallen?*

She got out of bed, eased her feet into her slippers, and put on her robe. The room was icy because the cost of heating oil had soared. Harriet blamed the Russians, while Hul blamed the Democrats, if only because he voted Republican and didn't know any Russians. Whoever was at fault, the Swishers now dressed in layers and slept under extra bedding, and the recent welcome influx of funds hadn't altered those habits. They might be glad of the money down the line, and frittering it away on heating when they had sweaters and blankets to spare didn't make much sense now that spring was coming. It helped that, the vagaries of old age apart, they were both of pioneer stock. Harriet could live with her twinges, and as for Hul, well, a battle with neck cancer a few years previously, and the radiation treatment required to tackle it, had damaged his thyroid, so he was more likely to complain about being too hot than the opposite.

Harriet stepped into the hallway and let out a yelp of surprise. Hul was standing before the oxeye window immediately to her left, with his back to her and his right hand raised.

"You about scared the life from me," she said.

"Hush."

"Don't you hush me! What are you doing, standing out here in the dead of night?"

He turned to her, and she saw the look of puzzlement on his face.

"Can't you hear it?" he asked.

"Hear what?"

"Just listen."

Harriet did.

"I don't hear anything," she said, after five seconds or so had gone by. "What am I supposed to be listening for?"

He lowered his hand, and she took it. Rarely did they remain in proximity for long before one of them reached for the other. It was why their marriage had endured without offspring to bond them.

"A child. A girl."

"A child? Where?"

"I didn't see her, only heard her."

"What was she doing?"

"Speaking, but it wasn't any language I recognized."

Harriet held her breath for fear that whatever sound had drawn him out here was so faint that she might have missed it the first time around.

"No," she said at last. "There's nothing."

She hoped he wasn't succumbing to Alzheimer's. He'd been growing more forgetful over the past year or so, certainly since the cancer, but then he'd always been absentminded. Even when he was in his prime, one of her daily tasks was to ensure he wore matching shoes and his fly was zipped before he left the house.

"Let's go back to bed."

She tried to lead him away but he didn't follow. He raised his left hand as high as his ear and tilted his head.

"There!" he said. "Do you hear it?"

"I told you, I don't hear anything."

It was a lie, but a white one. There might have been something, if she chose to listen, but she elected not to.

"At first, I thought I was imagining it," said Hul, "but it's her."

"Don't talk foolishness."

"We ought not to have consented to it," said Hul, which was just like him. He had many good points, but some lesser ones too, among them the habit of being wise after the fact. But then he qualified what he'd said: "Splitting the children up like that."

"It's too late for regrets," said Harriet. "What's done is done, and half the money's already spent. You weren't so contrite when the roof was being fixed."

She was still clinging to his hand, even while they bickered. *Such a pair we are.*

Against her better judgment, Harriet decided to yield some ground, or else she might never get him back to bed. If this was madness, she could only hope it was the passing kind.

"If it is her, she'll get tired soon enough. All children do. And she has company."

"The boy's different," said Hul. "I think he might be retarded."

"There's nothing we can do about it now." Harriet squeezed her husband's hand. "Come on, we can't stay out here all night. We'll catch our deaths."

She tugged, and he followed. They were on the threshold of their bedroom when Hul paused for the final time.

"I think they're names," he said. "She's calling out names."

"What names?"

"The names of gods."

CHAPTER XVIII

Roland Bilas spent a long, uncomfortable night in a holding cell at LAX before being arraigned the following morning in federal court on felony smuggling charges. No objection was made to bail, which was set at an eye-watering $60,000, though Bilas was required to surrender his passport. Dates were also set for a felony dispositional conference and, depending on the outcome, a preliminary hearing the following month, while a search warrant was granted for Bilas's home and storage unit. Bilas kept his mouth shut throughout, as his lawyer had instructed, but it was a close-run thing because Bilas had once again felt a childlike urge to admit to everything just so people wouldn't be angry with him anymore.

His attorney was a woman named Erica Kressler. She had looked after his affairs for years without any acknowledgment of his involvement in the illegal movement of antiquities, even as she suspected him of engaging in some form of criminality. Following the arraignment, and the signing of the paperwork with the bail bondsman, Kressler drove Bilas to her office, requested a pot of coffee, sat back in her chair, and said: "Tell me straight: What are they going to find?"

"Less than they expect," Bilas replied, "and nothing as valuable as what was in the suitcase."

"Do you have any storage facilities you didn't mention during questioning?"

"None."

"You're sure? Because if you're lying and the feds find out, any hope we have of cutting a deal at the dispositional conference will be gone. You could be looking at serious time, along with fines that will leave you destitute until the grave."

"I told them everything," said Roland, and hoped his face gave nothing more away.

The coffee arrived. Kressler poured a cup for each of them.

"Do you want something to eat?" she asked. "We have croissants and doughnuts."

Bilas declined both. All he really wanted was to shower and change his clothes, but before he did, he needed to get to a laptop and start insulating himself financially. The seizure of the mantas was going to seriously undermine his retirement planning, as would the premium Kressler was charging for her services in this instance. The bail bondsman's ten percent he could swallow. That was the least of his worries, since the alternative was a jail cell.

"How bad will it be?" Bilas asked.

"If you've been straight with them, and the federal warrant doesn't uncover the treasures of Montezuma, you're looking at probation and a fine."

"That doesn't sound so bad."

"You haven't heard about the small print," said Kressler. "A happy outcome will require cooperation on your part, a guilty plea, a prosecutor who doesn't want to put you on the rack, and a judge who's had a good lunch and doesn't suffer from indigestion. Look, Roland, you were caught with antiquities worth a mid-six-figure sum concealed in your suitcase, and from what you've just told me, a search of your home and storage unit will reveal additional items that shouldn't be in your possession. If you picked them up from another party in the United States,

I guarantee the feds will want all the details as a condition of the plea bargain. If you declare that you acquired the antiquities during your travels, then you can't claim the mantas were a one-off, which is likely to make a judge less sympathetic."

She watched Bilas add four sugars to his coffee. Her previous dealings with him had been mundane for the most part: assisting with his late mother's estate, drafting a will, ironing out contracts. But she'd had her suspicions about Bilas for a few years, thanks to escrow arrangements on his behalf with the kind of Latino lawyers who raised red flags among even the halfway sentient.

"I got a call," she said, "not long after you contacted me, from a man who didn't leave a name. He told me to make sure you knew your friends had your back and advised that what you could do in return was—and I quote—'keep your fucking mouth shut.' Now what would that have been about, Roland? Did you have partners in the acquisition of the mantas? Because I have to tell you, this man didn't sound like someone big into textiles, not unless they could be used as shrouds."

Bilas swallowed half the coffee. It was bitter and lukewarm. For a country that seemed to run on coffee, it was hard to get a cup worth the money. Bilas blamed Starbucks for transforming the taste buds of a generation. It was another reason why he preferred Latin America, though now he was dearly wishing that, on this last occasion, he'd stayed at home.

"The mantas and ceramics are mine alone," he said. "I set up the deal and used the bulk of my ready cash to buy them. Their seizure has left me drowning."

"You're breaking my heart," said Kressler, "not to mention making me concerned about my bill."

"You're covered. I said I used up a lot of my ready cash, not pawned everything I owned. And I have other accounts."

"That's a relief. You still haven't answered my question."

Roland finished the rest of his coffee. Whatever the taste and temperature, the sugar had done the trick.

"I maybe helped some people with a thing," he said.

"Well, thanks for clearing that up, and so succinctly, too. What people, and what thing?"

So, figuring he had nothing more to lose, Bilas told her.

CHAPTER

A last-minute hitch with one of Moxie's clients, who was due to appear before a judge that morning but instead decided that flight might be right, meant I didn't get to Zetta Nadeau's place until late in the afternoon, but I'd advised her of the delay. Her home and studio lay on the southeast of Cousins Island, not far from the Chebeague Island ferry dock. Cousins Island, part of Yarmouth Township, was connected to the mainland by what was colloquially known as the Cousins Island Bridge. The Cousins Island Bridge was officially the Ellis C. Snodgrass Memorial Bridge, but hardly anyone called it that, with the possible exception of the descendants of Ellis C. Snodgrass himself.

The house was a small A-frame situated on the grounds of a larger property that, had it been advertised for sale, would have promised little change from $2 million. The A-frame might originally have been staff quarters for the main dwelling, but Zetta had cut a deal with the owner to keep an eye on everything during winter and spring. She had also designed and constructed—at a knockdown price, and because the client wasn't a governor she didn't like—the gates that guarded the driveway. This was how artists survived. It might also have helped Zetta secure her show at the Triton Gallery, since the cottage's owner happened to be Mark Triton.

As instructed, I called Zetta on arrival. I didn't have much choice, as locked security gates at either side of the house denied access to the yard unless I was prepared to scale a boundary fence. I made three attempts to reach Zetta before the call was answered, but they weren't a consequence of being ignored. I could hear what sounded like an angle grinder at work and pictured Zetta in coveralls and a welding mask, with ear protectors in place—which was essentially the vision of her that presented itself to me a couple of minutes after she finally picked up, except with the mask raised and the protectors hanging around her neck. The coveralls looked too big for her, but then Home Depot probably hadn't yet grasped the potential of the waif market.

"Sorry," she said. "Were you waiting long?"

"My clothes were still in fashion when I got here."

"Unlikely. Still, I bet you'll be the dandy of your retirement community."

I followed her behind the house, where the smell of scorched metal was acrid enough to make my eyes water. Zetta's workspace resembled an auto shop's cut-up area as much as a studio. Through the open door, I could see what looked like steel fingers or flames linked at the base, each at least as tall as I was.

"What are you working on?"

"I'm not sure yet. It may come to nothing." She stared at whatever it was. "I'm exploring new possibilities."

"Why?"

"Did you see the review of my show in the *Maine Sunday Telegram*?"

"I read it, but I can't claim to have understood all the big words. Still, everyone likes 'Local Woman Makes Good' stories."

"Is that how you read it?"

"Like I said, some of it went over my head."

"My pieces were described as 'impressive but chilly.' It was suggested that they lacked a human dimension, which is more or less what *The New York Times* said in its hatchet job last time out. Even if I felt the new work wasn't quite what it might have been, I still believed I'd developed in the interim, but maybe I haven't. I think I need to go in a more radical direction."

I wasn't about to get into a discussion about the shortcomings or otherwise of conceptual art. Other than the gates she'd made for her patron, I couldn't say that what Zetta did appealed to me, but I wasn't the target market. Zetta was watching me, waiting for a response. I might have said that "chilly" came with her territory, but that would have been a good way to alienate a client.

"I'm not sure you should let them get under your skin," I said. "In every critic lies a frustrated artist who couldn't make the grade."

"Yeah, that's what we tell ourselves. I don't know if it's true."

She wiped her face on her sleeve. At first, I thought she was removing sweat, but then I realized she was crying—not sobbing, just silently weeping.

"I'd always dreamed of being reviewed in *The New York Times*," she said, and she suddenly sounded very young. "That's when I'd know I'd arrived. I wanted them to love what I did. Instead, I felt like I'd been nailed to a tree. The trouble is, maybe they were right, and now I've started second-guessing myself. It wasn't the words themselves that wounded so much as the fact they made me doubt the validity of what I was doing. My confidence took a hit."

She recovered, finding it in herself to smile.

"And those folks under the Russian jackboot think they have problems, right?"

"Yours is a calling," I replied. "The rules are different."

"I suppose we have that much in common. Come on, I'll show you the house, then leave you to nose around. I don't want to hang over you while you do whatever it is you do: dust for fingerprints, or listen for dogs that aren't barking."

"I don't do fingerprinting since we unionized," I said. "And there's always a dog that isn't barking, or else I'd have to find another racket."

She led me to the back door, which opened into a small kitchen, which in turn opened into a living room that wasn't much bigger. To the left was the hallway and the front door, and beyond the hallway was another narrow room with a dining table and too many chairs. The whole place felt dark and claustrophobic. I couldn't imagine one person living here happily, or not for long, let alone two.

"I know what you're thinking," she said, "but I don't spend much time down here. Upstairs is prettier, with better light. You'll see."

"How did you and Wyatt divide up the space?"

"What there is of it, you mean? He kept some of his stuff in the dining room. It's all still there. I started going through it after he left, then stopped, the paperwork I gave you excepted. It didn't feel right. I have less of a problem with you poking around because that won't be personal. We shared the bedroom and had our own closet spaces. Wyatt wasn't messy or anything, not like some guys I've known—though, to be honest, the women I've lived with were worse than any boyfriends I've had. But Wyatt didn't have many possessions. It's hard to make a mess if it's just you, two bags, and a few books."

She showed me upstairs. She was right about the layout. It was nearly all bedroom, freshly painted in creams and whites, with paintings and prints on the walls, an Indian rug on the pine floor, and a comfortable armchair by one of its two windows to catch the afternoon sun. The closets were built in and might have been oppressive but for the rattan inlay on the panels. To the right of the bed was a closed door, which presumably led to the bathroom. Through the windows, I could see blue water.

"Toiletries apart, Wyatt's things are in the closet on the left. The rest, as I said, are in the dining room. If you want to go through my belongings, feel free, unless you blush easily."

I told her that probably wouldn't be necessary, and she tapped her welding mask.

"Back to the great effort," she said. "If you need coffee, there's a Nespresso machine by the sink and milk in the refrigerator. Soda, too—or beer, if you're the type that likes to start early. Anything stronger, you'll have to buy yourself."

"Coffee when I'm done. We can talk again then."

"Okay." She looked sad and young again. "I really did like Wyatt, you know."

"I know."

"But when you find him," she said, "I'm going to bill him for your time."

CHAPTER

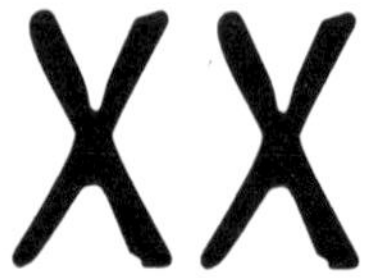

Roland Bilas had been raised Catholic, even if it was years since he'd darkened a church door. Nevertheless, Catholicism was a hard habit to break, and after sharing with Erica Kressler what he'd done, he at last experienced something of the release that came from a shriving. He wasn't even required to do penance, or not beyond enduring Kressler's look of mixed incredulity and disgust; he had no intention of sinning again in a similar fashion, because he didn't think it would actually be possible, some offenses being unique.

When he was done, Kressler let him stew before she spoke.

"I wish you hadn't told me," she said.

"You asked," Bilas pointed out, not unreasonably.

Kressler capped her pen, seemingly fearful that if she did not, she might be tempted to use it, thereby committing to paper that which was better left unrecorded.

"Clients of mine have been threatened in the past," she said. "Deciding how to handle it is where idealism meets reality. Ideally, we'd ignore threats; in reality, that's not always an option. My instinct is that you'll have to throw the feds a bone, one with marrow in it. When the Mexicans are notified of what you were carrying in your suitcase, they'll want to know how you came by them, which will require you to cooperate. The feds will encourage you to do that because it'll keep the Mexicans happy and maintain good relations. If you don't cooperate, they may decide to make an example of you. Worse, the Mexicans could seek your extradition, given the value and rarity of the items. We can fight the request, but it'll cost you, and there's still a good chance you'll lose. Have you ever seen the inside of a Mexican prison, Roland?"

Roland admitted that he'd never seen the inside of any prison.

"The only Mexican prison I've seen was in a Netflix documentary," said Kressler. "It didn't appeal, even at one remove, and I doubt you'll like it any better in person."

"Technically, the mantas and pottery are Peruvian," said Bilas. "I just acquired them in Mexico."

"Really? How interesting. And do you think a Peruvian prison will be significantly more luxurious than a Mexican one?"

"Probably not."

"Then shut up. How much crossover exists between your personal activities—meaning the textiles and the pottery—and what you did for this man, Devin Vaughn?"

"None, or very little."

"They're not the same thing. Which is it, Roland?"

"A middleman in common, that's all. He looked after the logistics for the Vaughn business, including transportation to the border, but had no idea of the cargo."

"Not back then, but are you sure he hasn't worked it out by now?"

Bilas was sure he had, because the middleman wasn't dumb and had made it clear that the sale of the mantas and pottery represented the last dealings he and Bilas were likely to have until Christ returned to claim his kingdom.

"If he has, he didn't say anything about it, or not explicitly," said Bilas.

"Because he had the good sense not to raise it with you. He's trying to pretend it never happened. If we offer sacrifices to the feds, can he be excluded without the whole narrative collapsing?"

"Of course."

"Don't speak to me like I'm an idiot for even suggesting it. You really are testing my patience, Roland. Whatever you tell the feds needs to hang together, which means it has to be tied by truths. They're not amateurs. If you lie, they'll spot it. Omissions, though, we can find a way to gloss over."

"So what do you want me to do?"

"I want you to sit in the lobby and put together a timeline and a list of names, with the middleman left out. You're going to go through it over and over, and when you're satisfied, you'll come back in here and I'll try to pick it apart. If it holds, we have something to offer the FBI. After that, I'll burn the paper you wrote it on."

She slid him a yellow legal pad and a pen.

"Now get to work. And Roland?"

"Yes?"

"When we're done, you should find a new lawyer."

CHAPTER

XXI

I wasted three-quarters of an hour going through Wyatt Riggins's possessions. I could have done it in half the time, but I didn't want Zetta Nadeau to think I wasn't trying. As she'd indicated, Riggins traveled light: any lighter, and he'd have been capable of levitating to wherever he needed to get to next. None of his clothes were new, though they weren't so worn as to indicate he was struggling financially. He'd left behind one pair of good boots, one pair of dress shoes with leather uppers and rubber soles, and one pair of black Chuck Taylors. His wardrobe didn't include a tie and leaned toward casual jackets, shirts, and jeans—a man after my own heart. I searched every pocket, checked the lining of his jackets, and shook out his footwear but found nothing, not even a spare nickel or crumpled store receipt. The two bags he'd arrived with were made of brown leather and had seen heavy use. They were empty too.

I tried the bathroom. A hanging toiletry bag from L.L.Bean had been folded and placed on the medicine cabinet. It held the usual male products, none fancy, a pack of generic ibuprofen, and a Tricare prescription box of Tofranil, indicating that it had been supplied two months previously by the Naval Branch Health Clinic in Kittery, Maine. I looked up Tofranil on my phone. It was a brand name for imipramine, an antidepressant that worked by altering naturally occurring chemicals in the brain to lift the mood, prescribed for those who, for whatever reason, couldn't or didn't want to take regular inhibitors like Zoloft or Prozac. Side effects could include anxiety and nightmares—and an increased sensitivity to sunlight, so it was unlikely that Riggins had been taking the pills while serving abroad. I pocketed the medication. My memories of attempting to get information out of the U.S. military were not happy, but that wouldn't stop me from trying again. If we don't have hope, we have nothing at all.

Downstairs, I found books—classic fiction, bought used, and a small collection of paperback volumes of military history, none dealing with any conflict more recent than Vietnam—and a white envelope containing $73.92. I went through all the books, flipping the pages, but nothing revealing fell to the floor: no mysterious maps, no matchbooks from private members' clubs, no photographs of Riggins with a mystery woman or kids he'd neglected to mention to Zetta Nadeau.

Back upstairs, I stood at the window and watched sparks fly from the studio. Zetta had given me permission to search the room, and I was beyond embarrassment by this stage of my life, so I went through her closets, wearing disposable gloves out of politeness. Only a vibrator that could have been used to coldcock a burglar, excuse the pun, gave me any real pause.

But as I went, I tapped every surface and tested every piece of cabinetry, including the baseboards. I then returned to Riggins's closet and did the same. Finally, I went to the bathroom and methodically worked my way over each surface. I found what I was looking for behind the toilet and beside the outflow. It made sense. Nobody went poking around there unless they had to or were being paid for it. Using the blade of my penknife, I eased away a section of baseboard.

Behind it, in a Ziploc bag, was a pistol.

CHAPTER XXII

Roland Bilas had always fancied himself a writer, so being asked to construct a plausible story about his recent buying trip to Mexico presented a welcome challenge. He had lots of ideas for novels, many of which featured a taller, funnier, more attractive version of himself performing impressive feats, some involving beautiful women in a state of undress, yet whenever he tried to write them down, the air went out of both him and his story. The ideas themselves had to be worth something, though. He had vague notions of hiring a hack to put words to them, said hack being so grateful to good old Roland for having done all the hard work of coming up with a plot that he'd consent to a thirty percent share for his efforts, or twenty-five if the idea was strong enough.

Unfortunately, in the absence of a hack writer hanging around Erica Kressler's office with nothing better to do, Bilas was forced to wrestle his story into shape unassisted. But after some crumpling and many crossings-out, he had assembled a version of the truth he could stand behind. Kressler found thirty minutes in her busy schedule—which would be billed to Bilas as an hour because she didn't do fractions—and she and Bilas went through it a couple of times, with Kressler testing for flaws and expecting Bilas to address them. He managed without great difficulty, as it was easy to leave out the middleman and establish a direct line of contact between Bilas and the seller. Bilas experienced minor guilt at the prospect of giving up associates, and a degree of shame since nobody liked a snitch. But no greater self-love had any man than that he lay down a few passing acquaintances to save his skin, as the Bible didn't say—though it ought to, because a dime would get you a dollar that self-love was more widespread than self-sacrifice.

"Okay," said Kressler, when they were done. "We now have something to offer the feds should they decide to play hardball. Meanwhile, I want you to think again about anything in your collection that you might have forgotten to mention earlier. And don't bullshit me: If the aim is staying out of jail—Mexican, Peruvian, or American—then it's going to cost you, and if you don't feel the pain, it's not costing you enough."

Bilas nodded miserably. Even with the funds he had squirreled away, this whole mess threatened to bleed him badly. The only way he knew to make some of that money back was the very thing that would land him in prison if he was caught—and he would be caught, because his name would now be on every watch list from here to hell itself.

"I guess you can tell my mystery caller that Devin Vaughn has nothing to worry about," said Kressler. "You can also share your new bedtime story with him, to set his mind at rest. While you're at it, I'd appreciate your asking him never to pull a stunt like that with me again. You've had your shot, Roland, and I won't be the messenger a second time. If it comes down to choosing between my license and your life, you don't need me to tell you which way I'll go."

Bilas didn't need her to tell him. He'd be sorry to lose Kressler as a lawyer once this was over but it couldn't be helped. If she kept him out of jail, he'd send her flowers as a farewell.

He got up to leave. The authorities had seized his laptop, which was inconvenient, and his iPhone, which was more bothersome still. But beyond inconvenience, and straying into the potentially life-threatening, was the fact that they had also confiscated the red Nokia flip phone.

When asked about it, Bilas told them he'd picked it up for its nostalgia value but also to use as a cheap backup device, because sometimes simplest was best. They hadn't believed him, suspecting—rightly, as it happened—that the phone was a burner.

Because Bilas was wily, he didn't use fingerprint or facial identification to open his laptop or smartphone. He might not have been a dangerous criminal, but he was still a habitual lawbreaker. He'd read up on his rights, including the prerogative, even under arrest, to decline to surrender passcodes or passwords to one's devices. A suspect's biometrics might not have been protected by the Constitution, but their mental processes were. If the authorities wanted to access Roland's contacts and data, they'd have to obtain another warrant, which Kressler assured him she'd fight, even if she doubted she'd win. She could delay, not postpone indefinitely.

That was when Bilas had come closest to panicking. He had erred in returning to Mexico, and erred further by being apprehended on his return to the United States, but he had blundered on a cataclysmic level by allowing the Nokia to find its way into the hands of the law. Once opened, the Nokia would be found to contain a handful of numbers in its contacts list, each identified only by a letter. Bilas didn't know all the names hidden behind those letters, but he was sure of a couple and could guess at more. He was also aware that each of those people possessed a Nokia similar to his, a phone that was never to be used to make or receive calls, only to send or receive short messages, with any follow-up call to be made on another device. Bilas, by his actions, had put that warning system at risk. It was still potentially rescuable, though. The process might already have begun, given that one of Devin Vaughn's people had been in touch with Kressler, which meant Vaughn must have figured out that Bilas's Nokia was either compromised or about to be. It would be a matter of ditching the old SIM cards, acquiring fresh ones, and circulating the new numbers. Bilas wouldn't be Vaughn's flavor of the month afterward, and would pay a price for his carelessness, as well as for failing to heed the injunction to remain north of the border. Bilas didn't think Vaughn would have him killed, but he would certainly have him hurt.

"You mind if I use your phone before I go?" he asked Kressler.

"Yes, I do mind."

"Seriously?"

"Roland, your parents are both dead, you're an only child, and you have no friends, so whoever it is you intend to call, it's almost certainly someone you shouldn't, or not from my office. If you need a flight or hotel room booked, my secretary will handle it. Otherwise, go find a public phone or buy another burner."

"Jeez," said Roland.

Still, he had his wallet, including cash and credit cards. He felt miserable and alone, but he also needed to sleep and was in no state to drive all the way home to Palm Desert. The thought of a bed, even a cheap one, was irresistible, so on the way out he asked Kressler's secretary to recommend the nearest place with clean sheets and a strong lock on the door, and was directed to a motel a few blocks away. The secretary even called ahead to ensure it had a room available and put together a care package of snacks, including chips, fruit, soda, and a protein bar. It was such a kind gesture that Roland came close to hugging her.

He decided to wait until he got to his motel room before settling on a means of getting in touch with Vaughn's people. Because he no longer had his phones, he didn't have any contact numbers—nobody remembered phone numbers anymore; Bilas could barely recall his own—so reaching out would entail leaving a message at one of Vaughn's businesses and waiting for someone to get back to him. The motel was an upscale place with a tiki bar and a pool in back, and the rack rate was enough to make Bilas's eyes water, but the room was comfortable and quiet, and more important, it had a phone. Bilas knew that Vaughn's cannabis stores were all owned by a single corporate entity, DeVinarex Growth Services, and the motel's receptionist looked up its head office number for him. The woman who answered claimed to have no knowledge of any Devin Vaughn, but Bilas told her to cut the shit and get a message to Vaughn or Aldo Bern. He left the name and number of the motel and hung up. Then he lay down and instantly fell asleep.

BILAS WAS WOKEN BY the phone. It rang three times before stopping, so he kept his eyes closed and drifted off again. Seconds later, the phone resumed ringing. This time, it got only as far as two rings before the noise ceased. Bilas heard a rattle as the phone was returned to its cradle. Someone was in the room with him.

He opened his eyes. To his left, on the other twin bed, sat a small man in a lightweight sky-blue suit. His longish gray-blond hair was brilliantined in place, and Bilas picked up the distinctive scent of chrysanthemum and jasmine, familiar from his father. Alongside it was another smell that reminded Bilas of the desert. The man didn't appear to be armed, which was good. Perhaps Vaughn had sent him. If so, the messenger might have had the decency to knock instead of intruding on a stranger's rest. Next time, Bilas thought, he'd make sure to put the safety lock in place and—

He realized he was babbling in his own head.

"Who are you?" he asked.

"My name is Seeley. I was waiting for you to wake, Mr. Bilas. I didn't want to disturb you. You've had a trying time."

Bilas ran through his limited options. He could shout for help, make ineffectual threats, or try to overpower the intruder. Before he attempted any of those things, though, it would be best to pose the obvious question.

"Who sent you?"

Bilas didn't ask him straight out if it was Vaughn. *No names.* He might have been scared, but he wasn't scared stupid.

"Who do you think?" Seeley replied.

"I'll need more than that."

Seeley tapped his fingers on his thighs and nodded to himself.

"Of course you will."

He reached into his jacket, produced a small reinforced brown envelope, and handed it to Bilas.

"Open it."

Bilas did. Inside were photographs of Antonio Elizalde. He looked dead. He was certainly blind: his eyeballs had been punctured.

"We're going to talk, Mr. Bilas," said Seeley. "And if we don't like what you have to say, you'll end up like your Mexican friend."

Bilas threw the only thing close to hand, which was a pillow. It distracted Seeley momentarily, enough for Bilas to leap out of bed and sprint for the door. Only then did he spot the third person in the room, one who had been standing in the shadows throughout.

If we *don't like what you have to say . . .*

Bilas managed to shout one word before Seeley leaped on his back and put a hand over his mouth. That word was *please.*

CHAPTER XXIII

I made two cups of coffee, put a carton of milk under my arm, added a can of soda to my jacket pocket, and went outside to speak with Zetta. She had stopped grinding metal for a while and was examining a pile of what resembled spearheads cast in bronze.

"I brought coffee," I said, "or a soda if you're hot. If you need sugar for your coffee, you can add the soda."

"I'll take the coffee," she said. "The soda will keep."

She set the soda on a shelf, added milk to the coffee, and sat on a folding chair by the door, her legs outstretched.

"So, Sherlock, have you found the solution yet?"

I leaned against the wall and took out my notebook. Macy had gifted me a slim Kaweco fountain pen in brass, and the notebook had a hollow spine into which the pen fit neatly. I'd started liking the arrangement despite myself, even if I felt I should be writing my notes in sonnet form.

"You mentioned that Wyatt was reluctant to talk about his military service," I said. "But he must have revealed some details to you."

"Not many. He told me he'd done two tours in Afghanistan, but didn't mention anywhere else. He spoke of boredom punctuated by moments of fear, but he may just have read that somewhere and was using it to deflect questions. I didn't want to pursue the subject, not if he wasn't comfortable talking about it. I hoped that might change with time."

"Did you notice tattoos, military insignia, anything that offered a clue to his unit?"

"No, nothing like that. Wyatt has no tattoos. But then, I have enough tattoos for both of us."

"He has no tattoos at all?"

"Nope. I checked out every inch of him for myself."

She flicked a pierced tongue at me. Had I been twenty years younger, I'd still have run a mile from Zetta Nadeau, though not without regrets. If she wasn't the girl my mother warned me about, it was only because my mother couldn't have conceived of anyone like her.

Wyatt Riggins's avoidance of tattoos wasn't necessarily shocking, but it was unusual. I'd known my share of men and women who'd been in the military, and some Millennials who were currently serving. The latter were so enamored of body modification that the army had been forced to adapt its policy on tattoos to permit them on the hand, ear, and neck. But even decades earlier, tattoos were more common than not. It was a conviction passed down by soldiers from generation to generation: warriors marked themselves as such.

"You told me he had trouble sleeping?"

"Sometimes. Pot helped."

"And prescription medication?"

"So you found his pills. I was going to tell you about them, but I decided you might prefer to discover them for yourself. If you hadn't, I'd have mentioned them, probably just before I dispensed with your services for missing them in the first place."

I took out the bottle I'd discovered in the bathroom.

"According to Dr. Google, these are sometimes prescribed by military doctors for ex-servicemen suffering from PTSD, though that doesn't necessarily mean Wyatt was traumatized, not the way tranquilizers are handed out these days. Kids on playgrounds may be taking Tofranil with sips from their juice boxes. But Wyatt was anxious enough to seek help, which is interesting. Next: Do you own a gun?"

"No," said Zetta. "I don't like guns."

"Was Wyatt aware of that?"

"I told him I wouldn't allow a gun in the house. He said he was okay with it and that he didn't need one."

I removed the pistol, still in its Ziploc bag, from my jacket pocket. It was a Sig Sauer P226, chambered in .40 S&W. The gun had seen service, but was clean and well-oiled.

"This was hidden behind the baseboard in the bathroom," I said. "Unless it was left by a previous tenant, Wyatt may not have been telling the whole truth about a weapon. It still has its serial number, which means it can be traced from manufacturer to dealer to buyer—or the original buyer, anyway. If it was stolen or sold on, that line of inquiry peters out."

I studied Zetta carefully, but she appeared genuinely shocked at the sight of the Sig.

"Assuming it's Wyatt's, why did he hide it in the bathroom?" she asked, which wasn't a bad question.

"I imagine he'd have preferred to keep it closer but couldn't risk your finding it. Also, you have a house alarm, right?"

"It was already installed when I moved in. It's linked to the main property, and the studio is connected to the same system. My tools and equipment cost me a lot over the years. I don't want some asshole addict stealing them to sell for chump change."

"So Wyatt wagered that if someone came at him while he was in the house, he'd have time to get to the gun, day or night."

"What about when he was working?" asked Zetta. "If he was worried enough to have a gun here, wouldn't he want to be armed the rest of the time?"

"Either Wyatt brought this one with him when he left each day and returned it to its hiding place when he got home, or he had another gun stashed somewhere. I'd go with the second option, because there was a chance you'd notice if he was carrying, however briefly."

For the next twenty minutes, I peppered Zetta with questions, only a handful of which she could answer. Wyatt Riggins's parents were dead. He had one sibling, a stepbrother in Utah or Idaho who was a pastor in some Holy Roller church, but they weren't close, or so Wyatt had informed her. The stepbrother's name was Regis, but whether he shared Wyatt's surname Zetta couldn't say, and she had made no effort to trace him. Wyatt owned a vehicle, a blue Toyota Camry worn around the edges but sharp inside. She knew its license plate number. She'd written it down on the chalkboard in the kitchen because—well, just because.

What did it all mean? That's what Zetta wanted to know. On the one hand, the gun shouldn't have come as a surprise: a man who leaves everything behind on receipt of a cell phone message advising him to run isn't living his best life, and fear might be occupying some of his bandwidth. Given Riggins's military background, the acquisition of one or more guns would be a natural response to a threat. On the other hand, he was working at a cannabis store and attending gallery openings, so he wasn't exactly hiding in a cave. Yet as soon as the RUN message came through, Riggins walked, and in a manner beyond all but the most disciplined of men. He hadn't said a last goodbye to his girlfriend, hadn't collected his modest belongings, and hadn't even tried to retrieve his gun. That suggested he might have had cause to vanish before.

There are two ways to lie low, one more permanent and extreme than the other. The permanent way is akin to witness protection, a new name and a new existence, far from friends and family. You stay away from places you know and people who might know you. It's what you do when you think your life is in danger and is set to remain so until you no longer have any life left to lose. The second is less extreme but more hazardous, as it's based on unknowns. It may be that someone wants to find you, someone from whom it might be better to stay out of reach, but you can't be sure and you don't want to cast all to the wind on the off chance. So what do you do? You temporarily divest yourself of as many encumbrances as possible—job, romance, whatever dump you're renting—and find somewhere quiet and safe. And because you don't yet have cause to reinvent yourself, which is a time-consuming and costly process, you keep your name, and maybe the place you choose isn't entirely devoid of friends, the type you can trust to help you if the hammer falls or keep their mouths shut when that special person comes asking after you.

My instinct was that Wyatt Riggins fell into some version of the second camp. He might have had feelings for Zetta Nadeau, but if he did, they weren't deep enough for him to write a note letting her know he was okay, no hard feelings, ships passing in the night, you know how it is. But he had left the text message on the Nokia, despite taking the time to delete the contacts list. Then, rather than dump the phone, he had dropped it somewhere it might be found, and by someone who knew it was his. It seemed that he wanted to let Zetta know he'd been forced to skip town and wasn't just ditching her after a good time. He'd struck lucky with her because her home—secure and out of the way—was the perfect spot for a man who might be on edge, but he hadn't known Zetta before he got to Maine. So, why choose the state as a base while he waited to see how things panned out? A plausible answer was that he had contacts in the Portland metropolitan area, folks who could act as a support structure, help him find work, and brush away his tracks if he had to scoot again. He might have stayed with them for a night or two when he first arrived, but they wouldn't have wanted him so close for too long, not if he was marked.

"What about friends?" I asked Zetta.

"His or mine?"

"Both, if relevant."

"Wyatt didn't socialize much with my friends. I didn't mind. If he and I stayed together, that would come with time. As for his, he didn't really have any, except for this one guy, Jason, who also works at BrightBlown. They'd known each other back when they were kids in the South. But Wyatt didn't see a lot of Jason, even at work. In fact, I think he was surprised to find out that Jason was up here."

"Does Jason have a last name?"

"If Wyatt told me, I've forgotten. BrightBlown will know who I'm talking about. He's been working for them since they opened."

I threw a few more curveballs at Zetta, but she'd told me all she could. I assured her I'd stay in touch and urged her not to worry too much. Wyatt Riggins struck me as a man with a well-developed sense of self-preservation. If I failed to find him, Zetta might choose to take that as a good sign: If I couldn't find Wyatt, there was a chance that the people he was running from wouldn't be able to find him either, in which case I told her I'd consider refunding any overpayment of my fee, but rounded up to a full day. In return, Zetta gave me the finger and returned to her art.

I considered visiting BrightBlown on my way back to Scarborough, but it had been a long day and I didn't feel any great sense of urgency about Wyatt Riggins, who currently didn't want to be found. If that meant Zetta Nadeau struggled to get to sleep for worrying about him, she could take a pill. I no longer had the energy to fight every battle on other people's terms. As Riggins might have confirmed, had he been around to offer an opinion, that was a sure way to lose a war.

CHAPTER

XXIV

The National Museum of the American Indian in New York is situated in the Battery and occupies part of the Alexander Hamilton U.S. Custom House, a stunning Beaux-Arts building with a footprint covering three city blocks. While the white-marbled rotunda, with its oval skylight and muraled walls, was the most spectacular of the museum's rooms, the most atmospheric and intimate, at least in Madeline Rainbird's view, was the Collector's Office, all Tiffany oak panels, subdued lighting, and depictions of seaports.

Rainbird had been with the museum for ten years, starting out as an intern in Collections Care before becoming a member of the conservation team, specializing in pesticides and pest management. This meant ensuring that the museum's relics remained safe from insects or rodents and applying chemical analysis to establish what pesticides might have been utilized in the past. Until 1972 and the passage of the Federal Environmental Pesticide Control Act, the use of pesticides was unregulated, which meant that even culturally and historically valuable items were often exposed to potentially harmful agents. The fact that Madeline had recourse to the words *insecticide*, *fungicide*, and indeed *rodenticide* in her daily life went some way, she felt, toward explaining why she continued to struggle on the dating front.

Some pesticides were active for only a short time, but others—

organophosphates and organochlorides, for example—could retain their toxicity for years. This presented a particular problem when it came to the repatriation of holdings to tribal communities, because it would obviously be unwise to hand back funerary objects or human remains laden with mercury or arsenic. But the museum couldn't conduct tests without permission from tribal stakeholders, some of whom took a dim view of any further perceived assaults on the dignity of their ancestral dead. One of Madeline's roles was to explain why such tests might be in everyone's best interest and reassure tribal elders that the examinations would be conducted with the maximum respect and the minimum of intrusion, since Madeline herself would be responsible for them. Madeline was a member of the Passamaquoddy tribe, and had been born just outside the Sipayik reservation in Washington County, Maine, which meant that those with whom she was dealing could be sure she wasn't paying lip service to their concerns. To further gild her credentials, she had accrued additional expertise in the care and preservation of human remains—another reason, perhaps, why she could sleep on either side of her bed most nights—which meant she was unlikely to be short of work in her lifetime, not when at least one North American university still held the bodies of up to seven thousand Native Americans in its collection. Making certain such relics were restored to their communities was high on the agenda of many at the museum, Rainbird included.

But all the museum's efforts came with a cost attached, so it was constantly in search of funds to support its activities. It wasn't as though it could rely on the resources of the Native American community, which had the highest poverty rate of any minority group in the country. More Native Americans might have been completing high school and going on to college than ever before, but many were also struggling to find jobs, since the kind of employment opportunities on which they used to rely—construction and manufacturing—continued to contract. As for casinos, if Madeline had a dollar for every time someone had suggested opening a gambling den as a way out of poverty for Native Americans, she could have bought herself better shoes and used them to kick the person in question hard in the ass.

So when a donor came along, especially one offering money without too many onerous conditions, it was cause for celebration, which was why Madeline, along with about a dozen of her co-workers, was currently standing in the Collector's Office, a glass of sparkling wine in one hand and a napkin in the other, while trying to eat a particularly awkward canapé. The donor being acknowledged was a widow named Elle Louise Douglas, whose late and by all accounts unlamented spouse, an investment banker named Darryl Douglas IV, was a direct descendant of one of the Eel River Rangers. The Rangers were a group of settlers and gunmen led by Walter Jarboe who, over six months between 1859 and 1860, killed almost three hundred Yuki braves, and perhaps at least as many Yuki women and children, in an attempt to annihilate the native population of Round Valley in Mendocino, California, thus facilitating further white settlement. The killers had then billed the state for their services.

Darryl Douglas IV—in common, presumably, with Darryls I, II, and III—was proud of his heritage and regarded the Rangers as fearless protectors of the men and women who had built this great nation. The Yuki, according to Douglas family lore, were cattle thieves and murderers who had provoked the settlers into acting against them. As for the fatalities, the warriors had died in battle, which was how they would have wanted to go, while the Rangers sustained only a handful of casualties in the engagements, suggesting that "massacre" could more aptly have been superseded for "battle." Per the Douglas version of history, the numbers of women and children killed in the conflict had been greatly exaggerated for political ends, besmirching the courage of their forefather and his fellow fine Americans. Quietly, Madeline Rainbird hoped that the spirits of Darryl Douglas IV and his predecessors were wandering the afterlife eyeless, eternally lost and afraid.

It was small consolation that Darryl Douglas IV felt the same way about Blacks, Jews, Latinos, and Asians as he did about Native Americans, being a hardened proselytizer for the merits and accomplishments of the white race. He was also, as it emerged after his sudden death on a golf course at the age of sixty-eight, a cocksman of the highest order, incapable of passing a crack in a wall, or possibly even a hole on a golfing green, without wishing to stick his dick in it. Admittedly, his much younger wife had suspected him of a certain level of infidelity, accepting it as part of their marital arrangement, but the scale of it revealed after his death, including payoffs for three abortions, appalled even her. There was also the humiliation of learning that mutual friends had been aware of Darryl IV's behavior, so she felt as though intimates had been laughing and whispering behind her back for two decades.

Consequently, the widow Douglas set out to use some of her husband's estate in ways calculated to kill him were he not already dead, including a substantial donation to the National Museum of the American Indian, her only stipulation being that the donor plaque should acknowledge payment being made in recompense for the actions of the Douglas family against the Yuki. This was why she and her three children were now being honored with a small reception in the Collector's Office. They had brought with them a man named Mark Triton, a dealer in Native art and antiquities, both North and South American, whom the Douglas woman had met at a charity event and who had suggested to her that a contribution to the museum might be an appropriate form of atonement for the Douglas family's historical failings.

While he had an interest in contemporary art, Triton principally sold Native American ceremonial pipes, weapons, totems, carvings, beadwork, parfleches, clothing, and pottery, generally higher-end material from the late nineteenth and early twentieth centuries. He maintained lines of contact with the museum, and was outwardly scrupulous about ensuring that antiquities of unusual importance or sensitivity found their way back to their rightful tribal owners, sometimes taking a financial hit along the way. But despite Triton's reputation for probity, Madeline still had reservations (and how many times had she heard that particular pun thrown back at her?) about his dealings because fetishes, totems, and similar objects had particular spiritual and hereditary associations for their tribal claimants that he could not possibly share, no matter how many Native Americans he had working for him or how many good causes he supported.

Triton had also clashed with museum curators and tribal representatives over issues of provenance, because it wasn't always possible to establish how a seller might have come by an item, especially if someone claimed to have discovered it in Grandpa's attic after the old coot bought the farm. Triton might have been prepared to roll over in exceptional circumstances, but he remained a businessman who reserved the right to buy and sell as he saw fit and wasn't about to run every acquisition past a committee. Neither was Madeline so naive as to believe that Triton didn't discreetly pick up and dispose of certain collectibles without ever letting it be known they'd passed through his hands, cutting lucrative deals with connoisseurs who preferred not to have their collections come to the attention of tribal representatives or the authorities. Thanks to his network, Triton also acted as an agent and intermediary, bringing buyers and sellers together and taking a cut for his efforts, which made it even less probable that he would always raise moral objections to an exchange. Finally, he was reputed to have a sideline in pre-Hispanic antiquities, and more than once the Mexican and Peruvian authorities had failed to halt auctions in the United States and Europe in which Triton had an interest, silent or otherwise. Mark Triton might have been honest by the standards of many in art and antiques, but that was a low bar.

In recent years, Triton had commenced stepping back from his business concerns, not only to write a long-mooted book on Native American tribal art but also to enjoy his own collection, which was reputed to be modest in size but very carefully curated and undoubtedly valuable. This reception represented Madeline's first opportunity in years to question him personally about his plans for Triton Rarities, as she had last been in his company before the COVID pandemic. He hadn't changed much in the interim, aided by having gone bald in his early thirties and keeping his head shaved for the three decades plus change that followed—like a man, someone once quietly joked, who feared being scalped and had decided to make the effort as worthless as possible. Triton was very bronzed, very slim, and eschewed the Western dress styles favored by some in his trade, preferring casual suits and white shirts worn without a tie. The shirts matched the brilliance of his dentition, so that shirt and teeth might have been composed of a common material.

Madeline finished the canapé without leaving too many crumbs on her clothes and placed the napkin and glass on one of the tall tables scattered around the room. A series of brief speeches commenced, although the widow Douglas was not among the speakers, which was for the best as she had already consumed most of a bottle of Schramsberg Blanc de Blancs and wasn't letting any food spoil her appetite. Offered the floor, she might have felt compelled, not for the first time, to unburden herself publicly about her late husband, and nobody liked a messy widow.

The plaque honoring the donation was displayed on a small wooden stand, alongside a gift from the museum to the donor: an early twentieth-century beaver totem, beautifully painted. Beaver totems were associated with avenging wrongs, so it was a suitable offering. The widow volubly expressed her approval of the totem as it was presented, helped by a chorus of quietly impressed noises from Triton, but she greeted the sight of the plaque only with a grimace of satisfaction. Her children—

two boys and a girl, all in their mid- to late teens—looked variously bored and bewildered. Madeline wondered if they were ignorant of the resentments underpinning the endowment. Probably not, she decided. Even allowing for the general self-absorption of teenagers, they couldn't have been unmindful of the imperfections in their parents' marriage. Madeline hoped the widow Douglas had set aside some of her bequest for family therapy.

Madeline disengaged herself from a quartet of her colleagues and headed in Triton's direction. He saw her approaching and excused himself from the widow's company. He and Madeline might have had their differences over the years, but he respected her expertise and regularly sought her advice and assistance. She never refused him, and any help she gave was always reciprocated with a donation to the museum from Triton Rarities. It was also a means of keeping open communication channels and facilitating dialogue over problematic sales or acquisitions.

"It's been too long," said Triton. He opened his arms but did not immediately move to embrace her. "Are we doing this again? I'm never sure. If it helps, I've had all my shots."

They hugged. Madeline had to admit that he remained a striking man; not exactly handsome, but singular in looks and with charm to burn. Thankfully, she was immune to his more carnal aspects, which he wasn't above exploiting. Three failed marriages and a string of conquests to his name indicated that Mark Triton had more in common with Darryl Douglas IV than his widow might have cared to hear. Triton's current squeeze, Tanya Hook, a buyer for his company, was a quarter century his junior but could have pleaded another five years in the right light. Madeline watched her discreetly dissuade one of the waitstaff from refilling the widow Douglas's glass while the widow's older son took less discreet glances at Tanya's breasts.

"I tried contacting you a month or so ago," said Madeline to Triton, "but your secretary said you were on a buying trip. Anywhere interesting?"

The barest flicker, but enough of a tell for her to note it.

"You know how it is," Triton replied. "Always looking and rarely finding. I don't recall seeing a message."

"I didn't leave one. It was a curiosity call more than anything else. I hear that your plans for divesting yourself of Triton Rarities have accelerated. I was wondering what replacement management structures you might be considering."

"It's not just Triton Rarities of which I'll be divesting myself, though I might hold on to one or two galleries. Will you miss me that much?"

"Better the devil you know."

Triton sipped his soda water. Madeline had never seen him consume alcohol.

"Are you familiar with *King Lear*?"

"I scanned the CliffsNotes in high school," said Madeline, "so let's go with yes."

"When I was taught the play in college, we were told that Lear's error lay in challenging his three daughters to say which of them loved him more—an old man's vanity, in other words. But I learned later that a contemporary audience would have blamed him for dividing his kingdom, as a kingdom divided cannot abide. I want to reward the most loyal and long-serving of my staff with a portion of Triton Rarities. I also want to guarantee its continuance—and cosset myself with a comfortable old age—by selling a significant percentage to an outside investor."

"Have you had expressions of interest?"

"Any number of them. Despite your periodic interventions, I've managed to build a solid business, and therefore a saleable one, as long as I agree to remain in an advisory capacity for a year after purchase. The issue going forward is how to continue to combine moral and financial obligations in a way that doesn't threaten to fracture the company."

He swirled his soda. Madeline waited. She could see that he had more to say.

"You and I get along, don't we?" he asked.

"We've had our ups and downs, and I feel you've occasionally behaved badly. But for the most part, yes, we've maintained a civil, even friendly, relationship."

"Beneficial?"

"I suppose," said Madeline, "if more for you than for us."

"I won't insult you by asking you to keep it between ourselves, but perhaps, down the line, I might run some names by you—from both inside and outside Triton Rarities."

"To what end?"

"To minimize the risk of friction between this museum and the company that will continue to bear my name—and, by extension, to be sure that the Native American community has the least possible cause for unhappiness with us. I don't want my legacy, however modest, to be tarnished by acrimony or bad publicity. In fact, I even considered trying to poach you from the museum by offering you the position of CEO."

Madeline was surprised. She had heard no whispers of this.

"Why didn't you?"

"Because I knew you'd decline."

Yet there was to his words an undercurrent that implied otherwise.

"A girl likes to be asked. It's flattering."

"The chance hasn't entirely passed. Any new owner would be delighted to have you on board. Would you be open to joining?"

Madeline gave it a couple of heartbeats before replying.

"No, but thank you for the opportunity to refuse."

"What if I could assure you that you'd be of greater value Triton Rarities?"

"I told you: I don't want to be a CEO."

"What about being a well-paid private conservator?"

"Of?"

"The priceless."

"I'm too much of a realist to accept that term," said Madeline. "Everything has a price."

"Even you?"

"Even me."

Intentionally or not, Madeline had stepped into a negotiation. What surprised her was that she did not immediately retreat from it; Triton spotted it also. A decade was a long time to spend in one institution, the prospects for advancement were few, and Madeline was still young. She had, on occasion, struggled to disguise her impatience with bureaucracy, parsimony—enforced or elective—and the tenacity with which the old clung to their positions. Triton was known to pay well and trust his employees.

But more than that, Rainbird's home county of Washington suffered from the highest poverty rate in the state of Maine, and a declining population. Its towns were dying. Worse, the four Wabanaki nations of Maine—Maliseet, Mi'kmaq, Penobscot, and Rainbird's own Passamaquoddy people—suffered a disadvantage that tribes in the other Lower 48 states did not: they lacked genuine tribal self-government. Under the Maine Indian Claims Settlement Act of 1980, or MICSA, the state of Maine was empowered to block nearly all federal Native American self-determination policy unless Congress authorized a federal override, and that had occurred only once. Even the simple act of digging a well on Passamaquoddy land required permission from the state. Millions of dollars in federal funds had been denied the Wabanaki, causing tribal development in Maine to stagnate. If Triton could be persuaded to invest in Washington County, and select Machias or Calais as the site of a permanent museum home for his collection, it might be the harbinger of real, fundamental change, especially if Rainbird had access to businessmen, lawmakers, funding . . .

"I understand that you've been approached about a pair of mantas seized at LAX a couple of days ago," he said.

"You're well-informed."

"They don't sell mantas at Target. Interested parties comprise a select constituency."

"We've been asked to consult with the Cotsen on their preservation," said Madeline. "The smuggler claimed not to know the source of the mantas or how they might have been stored before he bought them. They'll need to be checked for pests, damage, decay—"

"And then they'll be returned, I presume?"

"You know they will. The Peruvians will have the main claim, and the Mexicans won't object because they'll be offered the Moche pieces sharing baggage space with the mantas. It's a good deal all around, except for the smuggler and the ultimate buyer. Our guess is that the mantas were acquired to order. Someone will be out of pocket."

"But justice will have been served," said Triton.

"You don't sound convinced."

"Those mantas may never see daylight again. The Moche pottery will gather dust in a Mexican cellar. If sold, at least a buyer might have derived a degree of pleasure from them."

"We take a very different view of these matters, you and I," said Madeline.

"Yes, on occasion. At other times, we think alike." Triton tapped his water glass, making it chime. "We should talk again. I have a further proposition for you, and it may be—no, it is—a matter of some urgency."

"Involving?"

"Saving the invaluable," Triton replied. "Preserving the unique. It would be a private contract, but I promise you'd have no regrets about accepting it."

"You seem very confident of that."

"I am. Without your help, something ancient and precious might vanish forever."

Over his shoulder, Madeline saw the widow Douglas's eyes flit over various faces and backs before alighting, somewhat unsteadily, on

Triton. One of her children received a tap on the shoulder and a whispered instruction that sent him toward them.

"I think you're about to be summoned back to the widow's side," said Madeline, but she no longer had Triton's attention. She thought she'd heard the beep of an incoming SMS in the form of the old Nokia Morse code alert, but Triton's Samsung Galaxy smartphone was on the table beside him, and its screen remained dark.

"Is that your—?" she began, but Triton was already walking away from her, heading for the door, his Samsung now in one hand, the other reaching for something in the inside pocket of his jacket.

"Excuse me," he said. "I'll just be a moment."

But he wasn't only a moment. Minutes elapsed: five, then ten, and still without any sign of his return. Madeline was about to check that he was okay when Tanya Hook appeared by her side.

"What's up?" Madeline asked.

"I don't know," she said. "Mark asked me to make his apologies and take care of Mrs. Douglas and her kids. He said he'd be in touch later."

"Is he feeling ill?"

"A business problem. I know he respects you a lot. You're friends, right?"

"We're friendly, which isn't quite the same thing."

"It'll do for now," said Hook. "Mark and I were supposed to be having lunch with the Douglases at Boucherie," she said. "I'm not sure I can deal with them alone. One of her sons keeps undressing me with his eyes. I swear, he's halfway to being a sex criminal."

"If you want support, I can join you. I'm used to flying the museum's flag at social events."

"You'd do that?"

"We've just received a generous donation, in part through the efforts of Triton Rarities. It seems like a small favor to do in return. Plus, I hear Boucherie is great."

And, Madeline thought, *who knows what I might learn?*

"Then consider it done," said Tanya, obviously relieved not to be left to handle the vagaries of the Douglas clan alone. "We'll be leaving shortly. Our reservation is at two-thirty."

"I just need to get some stuff from my desk. I'll meet you outside."

Hook returned to her post by the widow Douglas's side as Madeline slipped away. Had Madeline's back not been turned, she might have seen Tanya Hook smile.

CLASSIFIED

UNITED STATES DEPARTMENT OF JUSTICE
FEDERAL BUREAU OF INVESTIGATION

File Number: REDACTED

Requesting Official(s): REDACTED

Task Numbers and Date Completed: 1000210, Work Request Number 1000210, 3/13/24

Source File Information/Name of Audio File: 031324_0138_pm BERN_Phone_Call.wav

VERBATIM TRANSCRIPTION

Participants: Aldo Bern B
Unidentified Participant UP

Abbreviations: Unintelligible UI

031324_0138_pm BERN_Phone_Call.wav

BERN: I'm calling on behalf of your business partner, so no names.

UP: Has something happened to him?

B: Why would you say that?

UP: Because you're the one calling, not him.

B: He's okay, but he's in mourning. He just lost a friend, and it might not be the first.

UP: Which friend?

B: The one from Palm Desert. He had an accident in his motel room, a messy one.

UP: And the other?

B: The dealer down south. Missing, presumed not having a good time. He was the first, our desert friend the second. Someone is working their way up the line.

UP: What about the rest?

B: The ex-soldiers have melted away, but we're attributing that to caution on their part. We've no reason to believe they've been found. That's not how the connection goes.

UP: Which way does it run?

B: [UI]

UP: I didn't catch that.

B: Uh, southeast.

UP: I'm not sure that's what you said the first time, but never mind. Listen, I paid a lot of money to remain insulated.

B: And you are. This is a courtesy call. Nobody has your name.

UP: You have it.

B: I'm tactful, and steps are being taken to identify and isolate the threat.

UP: Obviously, the threat is coming from Mexico.

B: The origin isn't necessarily the same as the instrument. In the meantime, a new SIM card is on the way to you, and we're reviewing security procedures.

UP: That would seem wise. Anything else?

B: Get yourself a gun.

UP: I have a gun.

B: Then get yourself another.

end of 031324_0138_pm BERN_Phone_Call.wav

CHAPTER

I had arranged to meet Moxie Castin for lunch at David's in Monument Square. I could probably have worked full-time for Moxie had I wished because there was never a shortage of people doing dumb things on which the law frowned, or alternatively, cases of the law threatening to do things to people on which natural justice frowned. I called Moxie to let him know I was on my way and found a parking spot on Free Street, not far from the restaurant, which I took as a good omen.

Moxie was seated in the far corner of the restaurant, with a plate of Moroccan salmon in front of him and some vegetable potstickers waiting for me.

"That looks nearly healthy," I said. "You didn't get a final warning from your internist, did you?"

"What internist? And I ordered fries on the side. I'm not an animal."

The fries arrived, accompanied by a smile from the server for Moxie that could have lit up a cellar at midnight. Moxie—bald, overweight, and wearing a tie that looked like it had been cut from a Nudie suit—had that effect on certain women. It came down either to charm on his part or desperation on theirs, coupled perhaps with being temporarily blinded by his ties.

Moxie smothered his fries in ketchup to prove how evolved beyond the animalistic he actually was. He then watched in silence as I removed the arugula from my potstickers.

"What did arugula ever do to you?" Moxie asked. "You eat like someone with a disorder."

"We all have our quirks."

"You more than most. That's why I always ask for a corner table where you can feed yourself unobserved."

We talked about nothing much for a while before proceeding to a few jobs Moxie wanted me to take on, all but one of which I turned down because they were dull, laborious, or both, and I didn't need the money that badly. I told him about Zetta Nadeau, Wyatt Riggins, and BrightBlown. Moxie scowled when I mentioned the latter.

"Anything I should know?" I asked.

"It's a slick concern."

"Too slick?"

He ate his last fry. They'd survived barely long enough to start cooling.

"BrightBlown is gearing up for the long haul," he said. "A lot of these cannabis places will fall by the wayside over the next few years—it's already happening to the underresourced and overambitious—but BrightBlown won't. The Portland outlet has a wellness center attached, and they've acquired the building next door to be a health food store, with further plans to expand the brand. It's cannabis as part of a lifestyle choice for body and mind. Jerry Garcia must be turning in his grave."

"That's a significant outlay. Where's the money coming from?"

"A client of mine was looking at the building, the one tapped for health food. He got gazumped and didn't take it well, so he did some digging and came back with a name, even if he had to go through about a hundred layers of obfuscation to find it: Devin Vaughn."

"Who's Devin Vaughn?"

"Devin Vaughn is the son of the late Landon Vaughn, previously unknown to me but familiar to multiple branches of law enforcement. I have a copy of the client's research because it's a good idea to know who's trying to tip the scales in your town. Landon was a mid-tier mobster of the old dispensation, which meant he was disciplined and didn't get high on his own supply. No whores, no extortion, minimal violence. His territory was mainly the mid-Atlantic: DC, the Virginias, parts of Pennsylvania. When he died, his son did two things, one smart and the other not-so-smart. Smart was seeking to go legit as much as possible while using those legitimate businesses to launder proceeds from narcotics, which in turn supported the purchase of more businesses and more narcotics. For that, he needed cash-intensive entities, so we're talking convenience stores, parking garages, cigarette distributors, laundromats, vending machines, and private ATMs, followed by the acquisition of small restaurants, cheap motels—"

"And cannabis stores, right?"

"And some people claim you aren't bright," said Moxie, "although only out of earshot. If the business end is handled correctly, legalized cannabis is a license to print money—and launder it, too."

That much I already knew, just as I knew the main facilitator of the money laundering was the federal government. Because cannabis remained illegal at the federal level, and the federal government regulated banks and credit unions, financial institutions were reluctant to do business with the cannabis industry. Therefore, the industry had to be open to accepting cash, which meant that paying sizable bills became a problem, leaving cannabis sellers to rely on cashier's checks. But the upside, if you were crooked, was that you had a whole lot of cash washing around and no record of it beyond what you chose to include in your books. So you could elect to screw the IRS by underdeclaring and pocketing the difference or, if you had dirty money from other sources that you needed to launder, you could overdeclare, accept a hit on the tax, and—presto—you had clean money. In fact, considering the premium charged by criminal launderers, it was cheaper to let Uncle Sam do the job for you.

"According to my client's report," Moxie continued, "Devin Vaughn has some shrewd advisors, financial and otherwise, including his father's former right-hand man, Aldo Bern. Vaughn usually listens to what they say; if he was ever arrogant, he's reputed to have grown out of it, and he shares his old man's views on violence. It's not his style, or not habitually, anyway. He has a finance degree, invests in art and antiquities, and keeps his name out of newspapers and criminal courts. He's in the process of getting divorced, but not because he fooled around, or not that anyone can tell. Overall, Vaughn is a model of modern wrongdoing."

"So what's the not-so-smart aspect of his character?"

"He expanded too fast. To go straight, he needed more money, and to get more money, he had to be more crooked. He's overextended. Finding out how overextended, and what Vaughn might be doing to address it, was beyond the remit of the client report. But BrightBlown will survive. Either Vaughn will find a way out of this mess or he'll be forced to dispose of BrightBlown, which will be acquired by another vendor because its business model appears sound. But Vaughn will try to hold on to what he has; otherwise, it will be like a run on a bank. His more colorful debtors will come looking for their money, and they won't be resorting to bankruptcy proceedings."

The server returned to remove our plates and bestow another smile on Moxie. I was only surprised that she didn't write her number in lip liner on his hand.

"Which brings us back to your client, Zetta Nadeau, and her missing boyfriend," said Moxie, once we'd declined coffee, "because if Wyatt

Riggins was working for BrightBlown, he was working for Devin Vaughn."

"Then Riggins ups and runs," I said. "Is it too much of a coincidence that a man who may be under threat happens to be paid by a mid-level criminal?"

"I'd have said so. And unless Riggins was skimming from his employer, which would be ingratitude on a woeful scale, not to mention potentially fatally stupid, it can't be Vaughn who made him run. The mystery is for you to solve. I expect you to pick up the lunch check in return for all the spadework I've just saved you."

"Can you email me a copy of the client's report?"

"Sure, but I didn't leave out anything of note. I'm a lawyer. I know how to summarize. I also know how to give advice, which at this moment would be for you to tell Zetta Nadeau to forget about her boyfriend and find someone else to waste her feelings on, because this money will be hard-earned. Riggins is tied to Vaughn, and Vaughn is a dog being stung by hornets, with a whole other swarm of them on the way. You wade in, and you're liable to get stung as well."

I thanked him and paid the check. Moxie's counsel was valid, but picking up the odd sting was an occupational hazard. If you started getting scared of the pain, it was time to consider retirement. Otherwise, as day followed night, you were guaranteed to get stung more often.

It was sufficiently cool outside for Moxie to pull on his gloves and cover his baldness with a beanie.

"What have you got on your dance card for the rest of the afternoon?" Moxie asked.

"I'm going to visit BrightBlown and see what they might know about Wyatt Riggins."

"Despite my advice? Why is Zetta Nadeau so important to you?"

"Because I've watched her grow as a person, despite all she's been through," I said. "If she isn't important, who is?"

"You remember that stuff I said about Devin Vaughn and his sparing use of violence?"

"Yes?"

"I wouldn't take that as applying to you," said Moxie. "After all, why should he be the exception?"

CHAPTER XXVI

Eugene Seeley was in his workshop. The cover of the poetry book was in worse condition than he'd hoped and he could only speculate how long it had been languishing on the shelves of the late Antonio Elizalde. But then, the cover wasn't his priority. Seeley had some expertise as a restorer but preferred repurposing old volumes, making something new from what was in a parlous, even seemingly unrecoverable, state. He enjoyed rebinding, and adding new capitalization and alternative illustrations while retaining the spirit of the primary text. The clients to whom he sold his books were not interested in acquiring first editions as close to their original state as possible, although some were happy when Seeley was able to oblige. Instead, they admired how he could take a battered, ill-used book, like this collection of Sor Juana Inés de la Cruz, and from it forge a hybrid of the antique and the modern. Purists would object, of course, but Seeley wasn't selling to purists and labored for his own satisfaction. Books didn't keep him in bread and wine, but they were a useful disguise for what did. Working on them was also a source of calm and helped him think.

Now, as he picked at the spine of the de la Cruz, he was considering what had been learned from Roland Bilas, who was given up before his death by Antonio Elizalde, just as Elizalde had been named by a man named Manuel Chacon Pocheco, who had, a year earlier, performed electrical repairs at a property in Zirandaro, Mexico, owned by one Blas Urrea, currently Seeley's nominal employer. Bilas was the most important link yet established in the chain. Pocheco knew only of Elizalde, and Elizalde knew only of Bilas and some former soldiers, but Bilas knew many names and had surrendered all of them before he died.

Seeley had elected to leave Bilas's body in the motel room; there was little point in moving it, and not only because of the risk of attracting attention. Bilas's blood had soaked through the sheets and into the mattress, so disguising the fact of his death would have been difficult. Nobody who had bled that much was likely to survive, but the corpse would also serve as a warning to Bilas's accomplices, a harbinger of what awaited them as punishment for their transgression. Seeley was not worried about the pigeons scattering. It would have happened sooner or later, even without what was left of Bilas to focus their minds.

Most usefully, thanks to Bilas, Seeley now knew the identities of the culprits, and he possessed an instinct for the hunt. Bilas's murder might even encourage them to consider handing over the children, although Seeley doubted it. They were not stupid people—foolhardy, yes, but not unintelligent—and must have realized that relinquishing the children wouldn't save them. Seeley might have been of a forgiving nature, but Blas Urrea was not.

As for the other party, currently seated in a corner out of reach of daylight, staring vacantly at a silent television, Seeley wasn't sure of her nature, wasn't sure of it at all.

CHAPTER XXVII

The BrightBlown Dispensary and Life Store was on Forest Avenue, close to the Morrills Corner intersection. It was far enough from the center of town to avoid competition from the plethora of cannabis outlets around Congress Street and the Old Port, but not so distant as to make potential customers think twice about making the trip. The premises had previously housed a discount furniture outlet, but the functional nature of the building had been softened by the addition of a new brick facade and the installation of arched windows. Inside, it resembled an upmarket tanning salon, with mood lighting, inoffensive music, potted plants, and stripped pine furnishing. It even had its own line of clothing, which showed just how far we'd all come. I was old enough to remember when wearing a T-shirt promoting cannabis was an invitation for a cavity search. Then again, the last time anyone had offered to sell me pot, the dealer in question looked like he'd been dragged backward through a hedge and smelled strongly of skunk, both vegetal and animal. The young man behind the counter at BrightBlown wore a branded black T-shirt and clean black jeans, and smiled like a relieved cultist who'd drunk the Flavor Aid and hadn't died. His hair was bunched in an intricate topknot that would force him to censor his photos in later life so his children didn't laugh in his face, and he wore a sparse beard that appeared to be growing back after he'd accidentally set its predecessor alight.

Lord, I thought, *I'm getting cranky in my middle age.*

"Help you?" He eased a basket of gummies toward me and invited me to try one. "They're gluten-free and vegan."

"Sorry," I said, "I'm on a diet."

"It's okay," he replied, taking back the basket. "I don't like them much anyway."

I showed him my identification and asked if his boss was around. He told me she was in her office and went to find her, leaving me alone to make the place look untidy. He returned with a woman in her late thirties, also wearing a BrightBlown T-shirt, but with hair that wouldn't be a source of regret to her in years to come.

"I'm Donna Lawrence," she said. "I'm the manager."

She lifted the hatch on the counter and invited me to follow her. BrightBlown was messier behind the scenes, but that wouldn't have been hard. We passed a handful of employees, none older than thirty, variously engaged in tending, weighing, and bagging, who barely glanced at me as I passed. Mellow classical music came from a Bluetooth speaker by a window.

"Is that good for the plants?" I asked Lawrence.

"It's good for my sanity," she replied. "If I give the employees their head, they play stuff that sounds like we're being burgled."

She led me to a large, glass-sided office with a desk, a couch, and a pine meeting table with four matching chairs. On the desk was a photograph of Lawrence with a woman who could have been her darker-haired twin and two young children, a boy and a girl. The only decorations on the walls, pinboards and work rosters apart, came from children's paintings. They gave the place the air of the principal's office at a kindergarten.

"Family?" I asked, indicating the photograph.

"Wife and kids. There's also a dog, but she doesn't sit for pictures."

Lawrence suggested we talk at the table. She offered me coffee, water, or soda. I opted for soda. She handed me a can from a mini fridge, retrieved a maté gourd with a silver bombilla from among the papers on her desk, and sat across from me.

"So," she said, "I hear you turned down a gummy."

"Was that some kind of test?"

"It helps put new customers at their ease and promotes sales. Do you indulge?"

"Not me. I'm high on life."

"Then you mustn't be paying sufficiently close attention to it."

Ah, so we had ourselves a cynic. That made me happy. One could negotiate with a cynic, but not an idealist.

"Not paying close attention certainly helps," I said. "But pot was never to my taste, maybe because I never smoked cigarettes either. I'm dull that way."

Lawrence drank her maté.

"I'm old enough to still enjoy reading newspapers," she said. "I'm familiar with your background, and you're not dull at all. In my experience, only dull people claim to be interesting. The intriguing ones don't need to advertise." She regarded me appraisingly. "You know, this is the first time I've ever met a private investigator."

"If it helps," I said, "this is the first time I've ever met a big-time cannabis dealer who wasn't facing charges."

She laughed.

"I've never thought of myself that way, though I suppose you're right. And I may be out of line, but I sense you don't entirely approve of what we're selling."

I shrugged. "Like cell phone stores and Starbucks a few years ago, it's not the presence or the product I object to so much as the ubiquity. I feel the same way about vape shops: they don't add a lot to the life of a street. When it comes to cannabis stores, we don't so much have an industry here as an outbreak."

"I agree, which is why we're on Forest and not downtown. Soon, the city may have to start restricting new openings around Congress and the Old Port, like it did with fast-food outlets back in the day. We felt it was better not to get caught up in that debate. But I doubt you came here to lodge a formal protest."

"No, but you did invite an opinion."

"Guilty as charged. So why are you here, Mr. Parker?"

"I've been hired to find one of your employees, Wyatt Riggins. He skipped town and there are concerns about his safety."

"Is he in trouble?"

"Probably, but not with me."

"Can I ask who hired you?"

"You can ask."

I had decided that it would be better to leave Zetta Nadeau's name out of the investigation for the present, even if her relationship with Riggins might be common knowledge in some circles. Whoever Riggins was running from might track him to the Northeast, and I didn't want them knocking on Zetta's door to find out what she knew, not because of something I might have disclosed to the wrong person.

"I can probably guess. Unless it was family, and Wyatt didn't speak much about them, I'd say his girlfriend stumped up the cash. There must be money in bad art."

Ouch. I wondered whether Zetta had crossed Donna Lawrence. Unless Lawrence was bisexual and unfaithful, it couldn't have been over Riggins, yet he was the point of contact between them. Perhaps Lawrence simply wasn't a fan of conceptual sculpture.

"Everyone's a critic," I said, but it seemed sensible to cut short any further discussion of Zetta. "Where did the taste for maté come from? That's not something one sees often in the cold Northeast."

"It's a recent development. I was getting jittery on coffee, and we discourage staff from using our products during working hours, so I was trying to set a good example. It took me a while, but I've grown to appreciate maté."

"Have you traveled much in Latin America?"

"Not me. I'm a homebird."

"So the gourd was a gift?"

"You can pick them up north of the border now," she said. "We live in a globalized world."

Which was, I noticed, not answering the question.

"I should tell you," Lawrence continued, "that I don't know a great deal about Wyatt, and he hasn't been in touch since he started missing shifts."

"Were you worried when he didn't show?"

"I was annoyed. We're struggling to retain staff as it is. There's a lot of competition in the industry for anyone with experience, and don't get me started on wage inflation. When Wyatt didn't materialize, I had to cover for him on what was supposed to be my day off. If he did come back, I'd be tempted to fire him if we didn't need people so badly."

"So he had experience in the industry?"

"He'd been arrested a few times during the late nineties and early two thousands, twice in New York State and once down south. I don't remember where offhand. Misdemeanor and felony marijuana possession, but the most he ever spent behind bars was ninety days, so he was lucky. We have a guy working on our farm who did three years in Arkansas for possession: four point one ounces, and that point one was the difference between a rap on the knuckles and what amounted to ten percent of his life in prison. Wyatt had both used and sold, which wasn't—and isn't—unusual, and he knew a bit about cultivation, so he was just what we were looking for. Convictions for cannabis-related offenses aren't an obstacle to working for us. They'll bump you right up the list so long as no violence was involved."

"Do you perform criminal record checks?"

"Of course," said Lawrence. "There are still conservative elements in this state who aren't convinced that legalization was the way to go. We don't want to give them any excuse to come after us."

I was taking notes as she spoke. I always took notes. It made me look like I knew what I was doing when mostly I was just stumbling around in the dark. But if you stumbled around long enough, you typically found the light switch.

"And Wyatt Riggins just showed up here one day, looking for a job?"

Lawrence didn't immediately reply, which raised the question of who or what she might not be keen to discuss.

"Listen," I said, "I don't want to make anyone's life more complicated. My client just wants to know that Riggins is safe. If he overstepped a line, I'm not interested in what he might have done or who might have helped him to do it unless someone got hurt."

"But if you find out he's done something illegal, don't you have to tell the police?"

Which was also what Zetta Nadeau had asked me before speaking in more detail about her missing boyfriend. Perhaps Wyatt Riggins was simply cursed with one of those faces. Perhaps I was too.

"Only if asked about it directly in the course of a criminal investigation, or if the crime involves a child. The rest I tackle on a case-by-case basis, but I incline toward discretion. It's better for business."

Lawrence toyed with her silver straw. Like the gourd and BrightBlown itself, it was shiny and new but would weather with time. Weathering was good, tarnishing not so good, and Lawrence had BrightBlown's reputation to consider.

"Wyatt was recommended to us by one of our budtenders, Jason Rybek," she resumed. "Jason's been here longer than I have. He should really be a dispensary manager, but he doesn't embrace responsibility." She hacked up a humorless laugh. "That's another thing about the industry: it attracts individuals who've been smoking pot for so long that they may lack motivation. Some of them are surprised by how hard the work is, but those ones often fall by the wayside. Jason is just laid-back enough."

Maybe I'd been right to take that parking space as a good omen. Lawrence had given me Jason Rybek without my having to reveal my interest in him. If I'd been a gambling man, I'd have bought a Megabucks ticket on the way home.

"Is Jason around?"

"He's off today, but he'll be at the farm tomorrow. He likes to spend a few days a week working directly with the plants. Says it gives him a better sense of them. He knows his stuff, so who am I to argue?"

"Would you have his address, or a phone number?"

But that was as far as Lawrence was willing to go where Jason Rybek was concerned.

"Why don't you speak to him face-to-face tomorrow, Mr. Parker? I prefer not to give out the personal contact details of employees. It's a trust issue, not to mention a legal one."

It might also give her time to contact Rybek and advise him that a private investigator would soon be asking him questions about Wyatt Riggins.

"Did Riggins appear frightened lately, or overly watchful around strangers?" I asked.

"Wyatt was always edgy. I think it was his disposition, or had become part of it. He served in the military, but I'm sure you know that. He told me he was taking medication for PTSD and was careful about what he bought here with his staff discount. He wanted to be sure it balanced with his meds."

Lawrence checked her watch. "I have to go, Mr. Parker. I have a Zoom meeting at four that I need to prepare for."

I put away the notebook. We were done, more or less. Lawrence escorted me back to the dispensary.

"By the way," I said, "does the name Devin Vaughn mean anything to you?"

"I don't think so." But she didn't look at me as she answered.

"You have a boss, right?"

"Yes."

"And he has a boss?"

"I would assume so."

"Well, my understanding is that somewhere between that boss and God is Devin Vaughn."

We were at the counter now. Lawrence unlocked the hatch so I could leave.

"Why are you telling me this, Mr. Parker?"

"Because sooner or later, Devin Vaughn will discover that I'm trying to find Wyatt Riggins. When he does, be sure to spell my name right."

CHAPTER XXVIII

Seeley sat at the bar of the Springwater Supper Club & Lounge in West Nashville. Despite being the oldest continuously operating bar in the state of Tennessee, or so it was said, the Springwater was not among his usual haunts. He didn't drink beer, which was the only alcohol served there. Neither did he like playing pool, darts, or listening to live music. In fact, Seeley didn't like very much at all, books excepted, and was close to just one person, though the physical aspect of their relationship had ceased years before. The woman in question knew him as well as anyone alive, even if that knowledge didn't extend to his real name. She was aware it wasn't Eugene Seeley, but since that was the only name she'd ever called him, she was content to delve no deeper. More to the point, she was familiar with his activities, and facilitated them. Without her, Seeley would have struggled. If love and need were the same, he supposed he loved her.

It was 2:30 p.m., and happy hour at the Springwater began at 3:00, so Seeley had half an hour before the afternoon drinkers drifted in. His soda stood untouched. He'd ordered it only to have a reason to stay. At 2:45, a man in his mid-twenties entered, ordered a Tiny Bomb, and laid his *Tennessean* on the barstool before heading to the restroom. Only someone looking closely might have spotted that there were, in fact, two copies of *The Tennessean*, though when Seeley departed moments later, just one remained.

Seeley was a man who understood the danger of electronic footprints; while the internet was undoubtedly useful, he preferred to let others utilize it at his behest. In his car, he removed the envelope concealed between pages six and seven. In addition to assorted documents unrelated to the immediate issue but still potentially informative, it contained photographs of a number of Maine properties captured by drone cameras by both day and night, a review of a new art exhibition in Portland, catalog images of the same, and a picture and biography of the artist, a young woman with what Seeley regarded as too many tattoos—that is, any at all. Seeley examined the catalog images before reading the review and deciding that the latter was unduly harsh.

He looked again at the picture of the artist. She had fierce, sad eyes. Seeley felt sorry for her. He wondered how much Riggins might have shared with her. However much it was, he hoped that should the time come, she wouldn't require too much convincing to reveal it. He didn't want to be forced to watch her die.

CHAPTER

XXIX

Back home, I set about locating Wyatt Riggins's stepbrother, the preacher. An internet search revealed no trace of a Regis Riggins serving as a pastor in either Utah or Idaho—which assumed Zetta Nadeau wasn't misremembering either his name or location to begin with—and even broadening the search to anyone named Regis who showed religious inclinations didn't produce promising results. I made a list of church and religious organizations in both states, from the Utah Valley Interfaith Association and Mission Northwest to the Rocky Mountain Ministry Network and the Idaho Episcopal Foundation, then set about calling each one, or emailing those that didn't answer the phone.

After a couple of hours, I started to feel a pang of sympathy for the courtiers who'd been dispatched to scour the kingdom for a virgin wife-cum-nurse to tend to the aging King David. One of them eventually returned with Abishag the Shunammite, who was, one assumes, prettier than her name. As luck would have it, David was by then too decrepit to sleep with her anyway, so she was called upon only to keep him warm with her body, which, though probably not always pleasant, was at least better than being required to service him in other ways. The Playboy bunnies should have been so lucky toward the end of Hugh Hefner's days.

Eventually, I got a call from a woman at the Utah Division of Multicultural Affairs who told me that, while she couldn't be sure, she thought the pastor of Christ the Risen King Community Church up in Logan might be the man I was looking for. He signed his name "Edward R. Collins," and the official forms he'd filled out for the division indicated that the *R* stood for "Regis." An hour later, I was on a Zoom call with Pastor Edward R. Collins himself, who admitted that he'd googled me before responding to my message. He confirmed that he had a stepbrother named Wyatt, and while they weren't exactly estranged, they were not in regular contact. Wyatt's father had died in a mining accident before Wyatt reached his teens, and the widow remarried a year later to a widower, one Kobe Collins, a woodworker and part-time preacher. Kobe passed on both vocations to his older son, Edward, the only child from his first marriage, Wyatt being uninterested either in woodworking or the ways of the Lord, mysterious or otherwise.

"Wyatt and I don't perceive the world similarly—this one or the next," said Collins. He was a small, round man with heavy-lensed glasses and a haircut last seen on J. Jonah Jameson in the Spider-Man comic books. However, he'd rejected the matching Hitler mustache, which was always a wise decision. His magnified eyes were watchful and gentle and his mouth settled naturally into a soft smile. He didn't strike me as a fire-and-brimstone type, more as someone who had studied the New Testament and the Old and decided that, on balance, the New offered the better guide to living.

"Wyatt isn't a Christian man, then?"

"I think Wyatt has seen too much of war," said Collins. "That makes some men look to God and others cease to believe. But Wyatt was always inclined to stray from the path—or follow his own, to be more charitable."

"Did you get along?"

"We weren't alike, but we didn't fight, or not often. My father found

Wyatt frustrating, but he wasn't a man easily roused to physical discipline, especially with children. He preferred reason and understanding, which worked with Wyatt, if only to a degree. Wyatt and I began to drift apart during our late teens. I grew closer to Christ and he grew closer to—well, everything that wasn't Christ, I suppose. Once that began to happen, what little we had in common fell away. Wyatt left home, my stepmother—his mother—succumbed to breast cancer, and my father joined her in the next life not long after. Takotsubo cardiomyopathy: he died of a broken heart, a surge of hormones following the stress of her loss. The last time I saw Wyatt was at my father's funeral, which was seven years ago now. Why did you say you were trying to contact him?"

"I've been hired by his girlfriend," I said. "Wyatt left her without saying goodbye."

"That sounds like him. On the morning we buried my father, Wyatt said he'd see me back at the house but never showed. Some people don't like farewells."

"There may be more to it than that," I said.

Collins tugged at a small wooden cross around his neck. "I thought as much."

"Why?"

"Because if every woman whose boyfriend skipped out on her started hiring private detectives, I might be tempted to set up an agency and reap the benefits. And—"

I waited.

"You're not the first person to come asking after Wyatt," he finished.

"Who was the other?"

"A man, an odd one. Shorter than the average and smarter, too. He didn't bother with a Zoom call but cut straight to the chase by coming to see me in person a few days ago."

"Did he give you a name?"

"Seeley. I'm figuring it's spelled with three *e*'s, though I have no reason other than it's how I pictured it in my head. No card or anything like that, just a name and a handshake. Knew his Bible, but only in the manner of the devil quoting scripture. He asked about Wyatt, and I told him what I've just told you, if without the additional family history. He thanked me for my time and proceeded on his way."

"What about contact details?"

"None. Seeley accepted that I was telling the truth, or so I assumed. But later, after he was gone, I spotted that the lock on my storage shed had been broken, and I saw footprints in the mud at the back of the house: small ones, like an undersized man might have left. If he chose to believe me, it was only because he'd taken the trouble to search my property. He may even have been in the house while my wife and I were out, because she picked up a male scent, like an old-fashioned cologne or aftershave. I couldn't detect anything, but if she says the house smelled strange, it did. Her senses are keener than mine."

"Did this Seeley explain why he wanted to find Wyatt?"

"He told me he was a friend from back home who had lost touch—we were raised in Maryland, Wyatt and I—but Logan, Utah, is a long way for a friend to travel, and Mr. Seeley, for all his cordiality, didn't strike me as a man of friendly mien. Furthermore, I didn't recall him from my youth, and while his accent was close, it wasn't Maryland close. He had the dates and places right, even named some names that meant something to me, but he could have found those on the internet or in the obituary columns. All told, he didn't hold water, and I was glad when he went away."

"Did he arrive by car?"

"On foot, but I live in town. He might have parked nearby, but I watched him from the window as he left. He must have walked two blocks before he turned."

"He didn't want you to see the vehicle or the license plate," I said.

"That was my reckoning." Collins tugged at his cross again. "Strange, isn't it?"

"What?"

"That I didn't trust Seeley," he said, "yet I've told you all I know. Why do you suppose that might be?"

"I like to think I radiate goodness."

"I'll grant you efficiency, and I take you for someone who prefers not to lie."

"Lies don't serve anyone well in my profession," I said. "They have a habit of coming back to bite."

"With poison in those fangs, I'd venture. If there's nothing else, I ought to be about my business. I have a layer of varnish to apply to a table and a similar gloss to add to a sermon."

"If you do hear from Wyatt—"

"I'll let you know, if only so you can inform the woman that he's safe. Oh, and Mr. Parker?"

"Yes?"

"If you persist in your search, there's a good chance it will bring you into contact with Mr. Seeley. I don't know whether he can be avoided, but my feeling is that if he can, he ought to be, if you take my meaning. 'Be sober-minded; be watchful. Your adversary the devil prowls around like a roaring lion, seeking someone to devour.' That's from St. Peter, who ended up crucified for his troubles."

"Upside down."

"Apocryphal. But even if true, I doubt he found it an improvement."

"Thank you for the warning."

"If it's any consolation," said Collins, "I'd probably have warned Mr. Seeley too, had I known about you before his visit. May God watch over you, Mr. Parker. In fact, may God watch over both of you."

SO I NOW HAD a name for another party interested in Wyatt Riggins and—if the preacher was correct about that party's intentions—not out of concern for his well-being. I called Zetta Nadeau to ask if Riggins had ever mentioned someone called Seeley, but she told me the name didn't ring a bell. I suppose I could have tried mentioning him to Donna Lawrence at BrightBlown, though only so often did a man care to be lied to by the same person.

By then, Moxie had emailed me a PDF of the intelligence on Devin Vaughn. A lot of the property details were of no interest, but the rest confirmed that Vaughn was a) a criminal; b) a dealer in narcotics stronger than cannabis, including heroin and fentanyl; and c) hurting for money, given how many of his business interests and properties he'd been forced to sell over the last eighteen months or so, some of them for significantly less than the original purchase price.

I showered before calling Macy to tell her about my lunch with Moxie and my conversations with both Wyatt Riggins's stepbrother and Donna Lawrence at BrightBlown.

"Are you asking me if the Portland PD is aware of Devin Vaughn's involvement in BrightBlown?"

"No," I said. "If I want to know something, I'll ask you straight."

And I meant it.

"For what it's worth," said Macy, "we are, but we already have enough outright criminality to occupy our time, and BrightBlown appears legit, with clear space between it and Vaughn. Given that Vaughn's companies operate in multiple states, we're hoping the feds will do the hard spadework for us."

She didn't have to elaborate; pointedly, she avoided doing so. She'd told me enough: the feds had Devin Vaughn in their sights.

"I'd let this one drop if I were you," said Macy. "I'm not sure Wyatt Riggins is worth venturing into Vaughn's territory to find."

"I took Zetta's money," I said. "I accepted the case."

"You like her, don't you?"

"She's interesting, and she's elevated herself against the odds. If someone like that isn't deserving of my time, no one is."

"If one of your ancestors wasn't a martyr," said Macy, "I'll be shocked."

She wished me good night and added a murmur as she ended the call. I might have been mistaken, but I thought she said she loved me.

CHAPTER

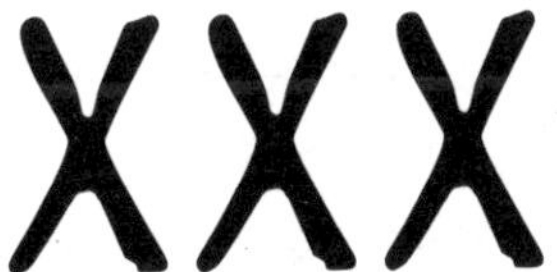

That night, I joined Angel and Louis at Isa on Portland Street, where they'd nabbed a prime window table. Across from us, the fairy lights were illuminated at Bubba's Sulky Lounge. To its right, what had once been the more downmarket Rockin Rickey's Tavern was an empty shell, mourned only by the terminally alcoholic. Soon, there wouldn't be anywhere left in the city where a man could get blindly, malevolently drunk and not have do-gooders attempt to kill his buzz.

Meanwhile, condos were rising all across Portland, and property prices with them, but few locals would be able to afford to buy. The new units would go to out-of-towners looking to rent them to the highest bidder, or with enough spare cash lying around that spending more than $2 million on a summer-use unit overlooking Becky's Diner struck them as a good deal. Down on Commercial Street, more and more stores didn't even bother putting prices on their window displays for fear that some passing Mainer with a delicate heart might collapse from shock, which would be bad for the city's image. But along Congress, a person could still while away a happy hour buying used vinyl records in any number of outlets; Strange Maine endured, home to eight-track cartridges and used board games, with a sign in the window announcing NO PROUD BOYS SERVED; and Longfellow Books and the Green Hand both sold new as well as used books. There remained reasons to be cheerful, even if they were increasingly compressed into a few city blocks.

Louis ordered a calvados cocktail for himself and a bottle of Portuguese wine for the table. Angel stuck with beer. He'd cut his alcohol consumption to weekends and nights out and looked better for it. He also continued to receive the all-clear from his doctors, with no recurrence of the cancer that at one point had threatened to take him from Louis. The latter was cropping his hair closer and closer to his scalp—mainly to hide the gray, even if he'd never have admitted it. His face, I suspected, was clean-shaven for the same reason, but like Angel's bloom, the look suited him. Anyway, I didn't like to be reminded of these men growing old and of what must inevitably follow. I'd miss them too much.

As though picking up on my mood, Angel spoke.

"Loney died," he said, "out of Ditmars. We just heard this morning. He had a stroke."

"Wow, that's terrible," I said. "Who's Loney? Wait, was he the guy with the huge head?"

"That was his cousin," said Angel, "Moonface Loney. If he went out at night, the tides changed. This is Lineup Loney."

Now I remembered. Lionel Loney, better known as Lineup, was a reasonably honest guy with an unfeasibly dishonest face, his features combining to create an ur-criminal aspect that meant he couldn't walk down the street without being stopped and searched by police. Loney spent so much of his life explaining himself to cops that he was forced to keep a diary so he could accurately respond when asked where he'd been on any particular date and at any specific time. If he visited a shopping mall or department store, he attracted the attention of security the way a magnet attracts iron filings. So untrustworthy were his features that the cops in the 114th Precinct in Queens took to asking him to participate in lineups at ten bucks a pop to add a degree of verisimilitude to the usual collection of passing detectives, police clerks, and the unemployed. Loney became so popular in lineups that the 108th, the 110th, and the 115th also began to call on his services, and it wasn't long before he was adding all the lineups to his diary as well while earning decent walking-around money along the way.

The difficulty was that due to his blighted countenance, some element of Loney's face—his eyes, the shape of his nose, the curve of his mouth—seemingly inevitably corresponded to a suspect's, which meant that witnesses who were on the fence defaulted to Loney on the basis that, if he looked like a criminal, he probably was. Various cops then began to wonder if maybe Loney might not be guilty of something after all, given the number of eyewitnesses who were prepared to finger him for anything from bag-snatching to criminal battery. Eventually, Loney twigged why detectives in four precincts were peering at him more closely than usual and he knocked his career in lineups on the head. He returned to keeping his regular diary, complete with movie stubs, bus tickets, and lunch receipts, but the nickname stuck. Forever after, he would be Lineup Loney. Now he was gone, another splash of color vanished from a world that could ill afford the loss.

Our food arrived, and over it I told Angel and Louis about Wyatt Riggins, his preacher stepbrother, BrightBlown, and Devin Vaughn. Louis, who had an encyclopedic knowledge of malfeasance, vaguely recalled Vaughn Senior but not the son. He was on surer ground with Devin Vaughn's right-hand man, Aldo Bern.

"He's solid," said Louis.

"And that's good, right?"

"As long as you don't collide with him, which you may be about to."

"Bern and his employer can use BrightBlown for whatever they like," I said. "Zetta Nadeau just wants to know that Wyatt Riggins is okay."

"If he was okay," said Angel, "he wouldn't have any reason to be running."

Which was true.

"Does the Lawrence woman know who she's working for?" asked Louis.

"Yes, despite her denials. I doubt much gets past her."

"Then as soon as you left, she would have called Bern or someone close to him. If Riggins's disappearance has anything to do with Devin Vaughn's operation, there's a chance you may be hearing from Vaughn's people. But that was what you intended, right?"

"I'm hoping they're reasonable men. They don't want me nosing around in their affairs any more than I want to get that nose cut off. If Riggins was frightened of Vaughn, he wouldn't have been working at BrightBlown. It may be that they're as eager as Zetta to find out where he might have gone, or it could be they don't care. Clarity would be welcome either way."

"I'd suggest pursuing further diligence on Vaughn, now that you're rattling his cage," said Louis, "though it might have been wiser to do it before you started. I can make some calls."

Louis maintained murky sources in shady places, and the more umbrous the spaces, the better those sources. Admittedly, his contacts had diminished in number as the years went by, sudden and violent mortality being an occupational hazard in the volatile circles through which Louis had once moved—and still moved, when the necessity arose, though he had grown selective in the autumn of his days. Death would welcome him in time, but Louis saw no reason to rush to greet it.

"Actually, Misstra Know-It-All, I have done some research," I told him, "or at least I've read someone else's."

I shared with them the contents of the dossier put together by Moxie's client while Louis tried to determine if throwing a Stevie Wonder reference at him counted as tacit racism.

"That's great," said Louis, when I was done. "Now, if Vaughn ever decides to float on the stock market, you won't get screwed on the share price."

I had to admit the report was light on insights into criminal behavior, and it would be wise to learn more about who Devin Vaughn's friends and enemies might be. Basically, you couldn't know too much about people who ran around with guns, especially if some of those guns might end up pointing in your direction.

"Fine," I told Louis, "make your stupid calls. And while you're at it, ask if anyone has heard of a guy named Seeley."

CHAPTER

XXXI

From the marshes, Jennifer Parker watched her father return home. With him were Angel and Louis, these men he loved and who loved him in turn. She was glad he was in their company. Sometimes, when they joined him on nights like this, they would sit around the kitchen table reminiscing, or discussing a case. Jennifer would listen by the window, less to the substance of the conversation than to the sound of their voices. The visitors would drink wine or beer from a store her father retained for their use, while he usually stuck to coffee. Often, Angel and Louis would stay the night, and when they did Jennifer would experience a sense of peace. With them, her father was safer. With them, he was no longer so alone.

Jennifer moved away—from the house, from that world. The children were calling again, demanding to be rescued and reunited. Whoever took them had decided to separate them, and they didn't like it; they were frightened and angry. Jennifer also felt that one of the children—a girl, from her voice—might be drawing nearer. She was being brought to the Northeast, into the orbit of Jennifer's father.

After crossing back between realms, Jennifer made her way to the lake. She was distracted by her concerns about Sharon Macy. Jennifer was convinced that her father had been unwise to share with Macy his belief that his dead daughter watched over him and communicated with his living child. Jennifer trusted Angel and Louis to keep quiet about what they knew, but she could not say the same of Macy. To whom would Macy talk? If her father and Macy were to end their relationship, might she speak of his strangeness to others? Should she decide to do so, the story would spread, and others were listening, always listening.

By now, Jennifer was once again within sight of the water and the endless torrent of the dead. So attuned was she to this environment that she sensed the change in it moments before she discovered the reason. She also noticed that the dead, who rarely paid attention to the shore, were now focused on it, even as they immersed themselves in the waters and were carried away.

Two figures were standing by the mossy rock that was Jennifer's preferred vantage point, close to the edge of the forest. They were facing away from her, one dressed in a dark suit, the other in a plain cream dress that fell below her knees. Both had bare feet. They shimmered, like presences viewed through a heat haze, and Jennifer knew them for what they were.

Angels.

CHAPTER XXXII

Jennifer had long ago realized that what she saw was not a real lake or was it more properly an unreal *lagoon*? She could never be sure—just as the dead were not being carried out to an actual sea. Instead, it was like a film projected on a layer of smoke over a chasm, a falsehood concealing the terrifying vastness beneath: call it, perhaps, eternity. Whatever name it was given, the reality would be sufficient to unnerve even the dead were they to be confronted by it. Better to disguise it, to present it as something welcoming: a warm, still body of water that lulled whatever passed for their remaining faculties, gently tranquilizing them so the transition would not be so disturbing and they would accept an easeful drowning.

The stone thrown by Jennifer broke the surface but left no ripples as it sank. Slowly, and without obvious surprise, the figures by the lakeside turned to see who had thrown it. In their faces, Jennifer glimpsed versions of all those she had loved or who had cared about her in life—friends, a kindergarten teacher, her favorite crossing guard, her mother's family, her mother—the angels presenting themselves as amalgams of joy and consolation, drawn from whatever they picked up from her, because Jennifer could feel them sifting through her memories, seeking what they might use to calm her. They were considerate intruders, but intruders nonetheless.

But they had underestimated her. Time moved differently here, if it could really be said to move at all, but whatever the manner of its progress, Jennifer had spent too much of it in that place to be so easily fooled. Just as she had come to grasp the reality of the lake and sea, so also did she perceive what lay behind the angels' facade: the awfulness of their beauty, the violence of their passions, the blindness of their loyalty. Under the skin of each—spotless, unwrinkled—cyclonic spirits roiled.

She had been preparing for their coming, even before her mother's warning. Now, as they tried to comb her history, drifting through the version of her former home in which she stored all she once had been and something of what she now was, they came upon doors locked against them, toyboxes that would not open, photographs that disintegrated at a glance, books that could not be read. Jennifer felt their puzzlement shade into annoyance. She was a child and a child should not be able to do this. But surely a child had nothing to hide, or nothing worth hiding, so they had no reason to be worried.

"Hello, Jennifer," said the female, and in her voice, as in her appearance, Jennifer detected dissonance. The form the angels had assumed bore no relation to their actuality; they had appeared as a man and a woman because that would be less threatening to a child.

"Hello," said Jennifer.

The female took a step forward and Jennifer retreated a step in turn. The female looked to the male, as if uncertain how to proceed in the face of such wariness.

"We don't mean you harm," he said. "We saw you by the water's edge and were concerned for you. We'd like to know why you stay here, why you don't join the others."

Jennifer had to try not to lie; the angels would pick up on a lie of commission. But a lie of omission? That, she thought, was different. It was why she had spent so long training herself to visualize locked doors and keyholes without keys.

"I'm waiting for someone," she replied.

"For whom?"

"My father."

"If he's not here, it's because it's not yet his time. He will be with you soon, I promise. In the end, all pass this way. But it's not right that you should be so isolated. Those who wander are often unable to find their way back, or they're taken by the ones in the woods. It would be safer for you to come with us. We will walk with you into the sea, and when you surface, it will be into a new life."

"I'm afraid that I'll forget him," said Jennifer. "I'm afraid that he'll be lost to me and I to him."

She spotted a crack in the male's veneer. Redness flared, and she knew she had hit upon a truth.

"It is a different way of being," he responded, but only after a pause.

Ah, so you have to be wary of lying too.

"Nevertheless," said the female, "we think you should let us take you away."

Jennifer regarded the angels. To them, she was a misguided, mildly recalcitrant child who required only to be steered gently in the right direction. They did not know who she was, which meant they were also unaware of who her father was. Either they had not been given that intelligence before being dispatched or—

Or he had been forgotten. Was that even possible? If so, the cycles of pain he endured were the actions of a system set automatically to repeat, like a torture device activated before being left unattended, or an eternal oubliette. Jennifer, her face as much a mask as those of the angels, endured a cascade of emotions. First, rage at such a punishment for its own sake; then, despair that it should continue without the possibility of an ending, whether through mercy or redemption; and finally, a chilly sense of conviction.

We will stop it, he and I.

"I choose to remain," said Jennifer.

The female looked sad, the male angry. Jennifer prepared to run, though she doubted she'd get very far. If they were determined to force her to leave, there would be nothing she could do to stop them.

Suddenly, Jennifer became aware of footsteps approaching from behind. She reacted to the new threat, expecting to be confronted by another angel, only to see a burly, bearded man wearing a clerical collar with a worn black shirt, his hands buried deep in the pockets of ill-fitting trousers. Through the straps of his sandals, gray socks showed, his big toe poking from a hole in the left.

"Why don't you two just fuck off back where you came from," he said, "and not be bothering young girls."

Understandably, the angels looked dumbfounded. Even Jennifer was taken aback by the newcomer's temerity. After all, what kind of priest swore at angels?

In the end, it was the female who spoke first.

"You are lost," she said to the man, not without pity. "You want company in the purgatory you've created for yourself. But the path has never been closed to you and never will be. It was you who elected to turn away from it. Like this child, you can choose to come with us. There is a place for you, Martin, as there is for all. But if you're not yet ready to accept it, don't lead her astray out of malice. You were a shepherd once, when that collar still meant something to you."

The man addressed as Martin tilted his head, like one listening to a melody formerly familiar but now bygone.

"It's been a while since I've heard that name spoken aloud," he said. "I'd almost forgotten it was mine. And you're not far off quoting Matthew 7:7 to me, which I regard as a cliché that should be beneath you. Next, you'll tell me that Matthew himself is somewhere over the rainbow, ready to give me a personal performance backed by an orchestra of harpists and a choir of cherubim."

The male angel extended a hand.

"Let it end, Martin. Show the child that she has nothing to fear. All you have to do is reach out."

But Martin kept his hands fixed in his pockets.

"You heard what she said. She doesn't want to go with you. She's waiting for her father. If you're worried about her being alone, which is a credit to your tenderness, let your minds be at rest. I'll keep an eye on her, because I don't want to go with you either."

The male let his hand drop. Nothing more was said by him or the female, and then they were gone.

Jennifer looked to Martin.

"Will they be back?" she asked.

"That depends. They can't compel you to go with them, but they'll try to wear you down, so eventually you might be tempted to give in just to shut them up. Those two are bureaucrats, divine box-checkers. The Vatican was full of fuckers like them. Your presence here is an irritant. You're a child who refuses to line up with the other kids at school and risks setting a bad example. They'll stew over the problem and try to devise a different approach. They may even decide it's in their best interests to say nothing more about it and pretend they never noticed you. But if that doesn't work—"

His expression became apprehensive.

"Well," he continued, "others might be summoned, and it would be best for you to avoid some of them."

"Why?"

"Because they could pick up on what the first two missed: that you're different, and if that's true, the one you're waiting for may also be different, which is when the real probing will commence. You'll have to watch your step from now on. Like the poet said, the woods are lovely, dark, and deep. I'd consider keeping to them, if I were you. Out of sight, out of mind."

Jennifer stared into the trees.

"I don't like the woods," she said. "They scare me."

Martin laughed. It was a great, booming sound, and Jennifer saw the drowning dead react with confusion to this alien outburst of joy.

"Let me tell you this," he said. "Anything in there is more scared of you than you could ever be of them. You move between worlds, with agency in each, which makes you very special and very dangerous. Even the ones who don't actively fear you will keep their distance. They certainly won't try to hurt you. It's not in their interests. They've decided that whatever you're up to, it can't make their position any worse."

"And what about you?" Jennifer asked. "Are you frightened of me?"

The laughter had left behind a smile. Jennifer watched it die.

"Oh yes," Martin replied, "very much so, because I have an inkling of what you plan to do when your father finally arrives. You see, I knew him many years ago, when your half sister was just an infant. We were looking for a statue, a statue of an angel. He found it. I died. I thought he was an unusual man then, but I was wrong: he's so much more than that. Now he's the only thing that frightens me more than you do."

"Will you try to stop us?"

"Stop you? I doubt that I could, even if I wanted to—which I don't. Like you, I've had an opportunity to reflect. Pain will do that to a man. I can remember my death, the agony of it. I'm just glad I no longer have cause to sleep, or else I imagine I'd be revisiting that moment in my nightmares, which would be like dying all over again. Things are bad enough as they are."

He pointed to the dead.

"How many of them remember their passing, do you think? How many went easy? Fewer than went hard, I'd wager. So you and I, we'll wait together: for your father and for the reckoning to come. If you need me, call my name. You know it now. I'll never be far away."

He made as if to leave, but she called out to him.

"Stay." She realized her tone made it sound like an order, and she recalled what Martin had said about being scared of her. "If you'd like to," she added.

She saw from his face that he might be about to weep for gratitude. His loneliness was like a fog that surrounded him.

"I would like that a lot," he said.

He found a patch of grass to sit on and a tree against which to rest his back.

"Tell me about my father," said Jennifer. "Tell me how you came to know him . . ."

CLASSIFIED

UNITED STATES DEPARTMENT OF JUSTICE
FEDERAL BUREAU OF INVESTIGATION

File Number: REDACTED

Requesting Official(s): REDACTED

Task Numbers and Date Completed: 1000210,
Work Request Number 1000210, 3/15/24

Source File Information/Name of Audio File:
0231524_1113_pm BERN_Phone_Call.wav

VERBATIM TRANSCRIPTION

Participants: Aldo Bern B
Devin Vaughn V

031524_1113_pm BERN_Phone_Call.wav

BERN: The bud lady got in touch. Someone is asking questions about Wyatt.

VAUGHN: [laughter] Well, if they get any answers, maybe they'd like to share them with us.

B: They warned us, him and Emmett both. At the first sign of blowback, they'd walk away.

V: So, no word from Emmett either?

B: None.

V: You think he and Wyatt are somewhere together—you know, safety in numbers?

B: I doubt it. Hard to hit two targets distant from each other with one shot. Not impossible, but hard. Safer to remain apart.

V: Let them. We have our own people. We're not like the old Mexican or that fucking Bilas.

B: We still don't know who's coming, but I may have a lead. It will cost us, but the source rings true.

V: [Pause] Go back to the someone asking questions up north.

B: [UI] — investigator.

V: Say again?

B: The one who's asking questions about Wyatt, he's a private investigator.

V: Could be worse. Could be police.

B: Not in this case. His name is Parker. He has a reputation.

V: What kind of reputation?

B: The kind that's deserved.

V: What's his interest in Wyatt?

B: The bud lady says Wyatt's girlfriend may have hired Parker to find out where he's gone. It would be better not to have this man sniffing around, not right now, not ever.

V: Can he be dissuaded?

B: Others have tried and failed. He may regard dissuasion as a form of provocation.

V: Family?

B: A daughter.

V: We could remind him of his paternal responsibilities.

B: And thereby escalate potential provocation to an outright declaration of war.

V: Even weakened, we can deal with one man.

B: Parker's not alone. He has the last of the Reapers to call on.

V: An aging hired killer?

B: Worse, one who is no longer on the market. The only thing more dangerous than a hired killer, aging or otherwise, is a principled one.

V: Then let him investigate. If he gets too close to the truth, Urrea's people may do us a favor.

B: We can but hope.

V: And the girlfriend?

B: We can try scaring her some. That might work, or it could make matters worse. The best solution would be to reach out to Wyatt and have him talk to her, get her to call off her PI dog.

V: Which brings us back to not knowing where Wyatt is.

B: I'll work harder on it. But you can bet that his antennae are twitching, and his buddy Emmett's, too. I'll pass on a message, the same way we found them to begin with. If Wyatt cares about the woman, he'll make the call.

V: He didn't care enough about her to stick around.

B: Or he cared enough not to.

V: This contact, when will you hear back?

B: As soon as the first installment is paid. That'll establish bona fides on both sides. She wants confirmation that we're not going to screw her over.

V: How much are we talking?

B: More than you'd prefer to pay, but if she comes up with the goods like she's promising, it might save your life. All our lives.

V: Let me think about it.

B: Devin—

V: You heard me, Aldo. Don't push this.

B: There's a clock ticking.

V: I hear that, too.

end of 031524_1115_pm BERN_Phone_Call.wav

CHAPTER

XXXIII

Jason Rybek, friend to BrightBlown's buds and bud of his own to the missing Wyatt Riggins, had just finished putting the second of his bags in the trunk of his car when I called his name.

I'd been waiting outside Rybek's condo in North Deering since before dawn. Zetta Nadeau had located the house for me. I'd called her the evening before to ask if she had any idea where he might be living. Zetta told me that she and Wyatt Riggins had been out to Rybek's condo only once, and she hadn't been in a hurry to return. The place was bordering on filthy, and something in the mangy carpet had bitten her on the ankle. She'd also experienced a contact high from the pot Rybek and Riggins had shared, which left her with a headache and required her to launder everything she'd been wearing to get the smell out. Worst of all, they'd insisted on playing the Red Hot Chili Peppers while smoking indica-dominant Strawberry Glue, and except for maybe two or three songs, Zetta really hated the Red Hot Chili Peppers.

Zetta didn't recall the number or the street, only the general area. Still, she told me she'd recognize the condo if she saw it because of what she described as its "higgledy-piggledy" construction. So, bless her heart, she'd headed to North Deering that night and driven around until she located Rybek's building. She spotted his Daewoo Lanos, which he'd bought because Danny McBride's character owned a similar model in *Pineapple Express*, even if Rybek's was lime green, not yellow. It was into the same Daewoo Lanos that Rybek was currently piling his belongings as a prelude to exploring pastures new, or so I presumed.

Donna Lawrence had given me Rybek's name, but only because she calculated that it was better to appear cooperative than the opposite. I imagine calls had subsequently been made and a decision reached that, all things considered, it might be better if Jason Rybek found somewhere else to listen to the Red Hot Chili Peppers for a while, possibly on BrightBlown's dime. When Rybek failed to show up at the farm the following day, Lawrence could shrug her shoulders and remark on the general unreliability of potheads these days.

I could have tackled Rybek immediately after Zetta called back with his address, but knocking on strangers' doors late at night, even strangers of the mellower kind, was best left to the police or people who enjoyed being shot at. Anyway, if what Zetta said about Rybek's evening routine was correct, he was more likely to head for the hills come morning, especially if he'd been informed that I'd be looking for him elsewhere later in the day, which would give him a head start.

Rybek was in his late thirties or early forties, with dark curly hair heading for a mullet unless someone staged a crucial intervention, and the calves of a runner or rock climber. He was wearing cargo shorts despite the morning cold, a puffer vest over a long-sleeved T-shirt, and tan boots. His eyes were clear when he turned to face me. As Donna Lawrence had intimated, Rybek might have lacked ambition but not discipline—especially if it meant avoiding a potentially unwelcome conversation with a private investigator, a prospect that might encourage a person to get up early and get gone.

"Shit," he said. "You're him, right?"

"Depends on who you were or weren't expecting," I replied. "I may need more details."

He rubbed his nose. It was chilly enough to cause it to run. He could have done with another layer of clothing, or pants that reached his ankles.

"The PI," he said, "the one who visited BrightBlown."

"That's me."

I kept my distance, but more out of good manners than anything else. Rybek didn't strike me as a threat. He didn't even look worried, just resigned, as though this happened to him all the time and he was forever on the verge of making a clean getaway before being pulled up short by Fate.

"On your way to work?" I asked. "I was told you wouldn't be expected until ten, but meeting a self-starter is always heartening."

He leaned against the car and regarded his boots silently.

"I have to advise you," I said, "that I'm not a morning person, so I was already in a bad mood before I arrived to find you only moments away from making this a wasted trip. If I'd hit that snooze button, you'd have been in the wind, forcing me to hunt you down for needlessly depriving me of my rest. That might have made me fractious."

Over by the garbage containers, a one-eyed cat was picking at a fallen chicken carcass, its claws scratching against the plastic. Rybek gave the impression that he'd have been happy to change places with the cat, one-eyed or otherwise, because he knew how the carcass felt.

"I'm not supposed to talk to you," he said.

"Yet here we are, standing in the cold, talking."

He nodded miserably.

"Your boss at BrightBlown informed me that you're good at your job," I said.

"If they find out we've spoken, I won't have a job."

"There are others. Given your skill set, I doubt you'll be unemployed for long. Or—"

Rybek looked up.

"We talk," I continued, "you drive away, and the bosses at Bright-Blown are none the wiser. My only interest lies in establishing that

Wyatt Riggins is safe. That's what I was hired to do, so unless you buried him in your yard, I have no reason to make your life difficult. Not yet."

I let the last two words hang in the air so they could do their work. For Rybek, it was a question of balancing minor inconvenience now against major inconvenience later. Unfortunately, it was my experience that many people opted to kick the can down the road because they were dumb. Jason Rybek, I hoped, was not dumb.

"He's not buried in the yard," said Rybek, in case I was tempted to take hesitation as confession and look for a spade.

"That's reassuring to hear. Do you think Wyatt is buried someplace else?"

"He's trying his best not to be." Rybek kicked at the gravel of the driveway. "I wish he'd never shown his face here. I like this town. I had a good thing going."

"You still do. I make my living from prudence."

"And shooting people, according to Donna Lawrence."

He looked directly at me as he spoke. Despite myself, I was beginning to like him, even if he had almost cost me a few hours' sleep with nothing to show for it but a headache.

"That stings," I said. "If it helps, I pinkie swear not to shoot you. But if I don't get a cup of coffee soon, I may pistol-whip you to release some of the tension."

"I'll just have to take your word on that prudence, won't I?"

"Embrace optimism. Begin the day with a smile."

"Shit," said Rybek. "Okay, so Wyatt may have screwed up . . ."

CHAPTER

XXXIV

Rybek suggested we go elsewhere to talk. Some of his neighbors would already be up and about, and we might be seen together. If we continued our conversation outside—or worse, if I was seen entering his apartment—he'd have no latitude should someone from BrightBlown come asking what he did or did not reveal to me. I gave him five minutes to lock up and warned him that if he tried to abscond, I'd imbue the rest of his existence with enough misery to cause even the spirits of tormented Christian martyrs to wince in sympathy. Just to be sure, I found a parking spot that offered a view of both the rear of his building and the jutting trunk of the Daewoo. I just hoped Rybek wouldn't try to make an escape on foot, giving me no choice but to run him over.

In the end, he backed out of his drive with thirty seconds to spare. I followed him north to the Dunkin' in West Falmouth Crossing, which opened at 4:30 a.m. to cater to those for whom the morning just didn't sit right unless it started with a gallon of coffee and a sausage, egg, and cheese sandwich. I ordered the smallest coffee they could offer, while Rybek went for chai tea and a bagel with cream cheese. I asked whether he minded if I took some notes, and he replied that he didn't so long as his name didn't appear. I labeled him "Mr. B," *B* for Bud, which he told me he might adopt as his superhero identity.

"I was surprised when Wyatt showed up in Portland," Rybek began. "I knew him back home, though I hadn't seen him in a few years, not since he finished with the army. We didn't have a falling-out. Life just sent us our separate ways."

"But he was aware that you were living in the city?"

"He told me he heard from a mutual friend. I didn't expect him to start at BrightBlown, though."

"You mean you didn't get him the job?"

"No, it was pure coincidence that we ended up working there together. I was out at the farm, and the day supervisor asked if I'd mind training the FNG—you know, the Fucking New Guy. That was Wyatt. When Donna Lawrence found out we were acquainted, I sensed she wasn't overjoyed. Nothing was said, but Wyatt and I were rarely scheduled together. That had to be deliberate on Donna's part."

"But they couldn't stop you from socializing."

"No, though we didn't meet up often. Wyatt kept to himself more than he used to, and later he had his girlfriend, Zetta, so he was spending time with her. He didn't like it this far north, though. Wyatt's a Southern boy through and through. He didn't feel like he belonged in Maine, especially in winter."

I couldn't blame him. Outside Dunkin', a customer misjudged the depth of an icy puddle in the parking lot and sank to his left ankle. At times like that even I, a committed Maine psychrophilic, might have been tempted to gaze longingly in the direction of sunnier climes. The guy with the wet leg shook it, cursed whatever god he believed in, and went on his way.

"At least his day can only get better," Rybek remarked. "Unless it's a sign that he ought to go home and lock his doors."

"Do you believe in signs?"

"I'm starting to—bad omens, anyway. No offense meant."

I had a natural suspicion of people who opened up to me too quickly: it frequently meant they were either being deceitful or had an agenda.

Rybek, I believed, might be innocent of both. He came across as someone for whom dissimulation was too much effort.

"What?" he asked.

"I was just trying to decide how trustworthy you are."

"And I haven't even arrived at anything worth lying about yet."

"You have the benefit of the doubt so far," I said, "but I'm happy to withdraw it at any time."

"It must be hard to have cynicism as a default mode."

"Sentimentality wasn't working, so I learned to live with the burden."

"You need to smoke some weed, take up yoga, anything that could help. You're a very wound-up person. I mean, that pistol-whipping threat, was it kind? Was it necessary?"

He spoke so sincerely that, for an instant, I really did want to hit him.

"You were speaking about Wyatt's sense of dislocation," I said.

"Yeah, he was unsettled," Rybek resumed, "but he was also more nervous than I remembered. The old Wyatt had a calmness to him, while the new one—well, if I said he was always looking over his shoulder, it wouldn't be far from the truth. I put it down to his time in the military. I've seen the army do that to people, especially if they served hard, like Wyatt."

I paused in my note-taking.

"Wyatt claimed to have been a desk jockey—that he didn't see any real combat, or only from a distance."

"He told strangers that just to head them off. He wasn't one of those blowhards who likes boasting about their time in uniform or showing off their tats to chicks in bars. But I'd heard stories about Wyatt down the years."

"What kind of stories?"

"I'm betraying confidences here," said Rybek.

"If it helps, think of me as a priest."

"I'm not religious."

"Then think of me as a selective amnesiac, but one with a short fuse before noon."

Rybek gave me a sad look. "I bet you have no friends," he said.

"Not at this hour."

Rybek gave up.

"Wyatt might have started out in the National Guard," he said, "but that's not where he ended up. He worked in Army Special Operations. They call it Civil Affairs, which was how come Wyatt was able to make it sound like he was a desk jockey if someone tried to pin him down. But Civil Affairs was a whole lot more than shuffling paperwork."

"How do you know this?"

"Because we discussed it, not long before he melted away. I told you, we've known each other a long time, Wyatt and me. A few weeks ago we had one of those nights where you hit the town and properly renew old acquaintances. We got real drunk, then real high, and exchanged war stories, except in Wyatt's case, they literally were war stories."

He stopped talking.

"You sure you don't mean him harm?"

"If he's in a jam, I can help. I'm not in the habit of making people's lives harder than they already are, not unless they deserve it."

"And who decides that, you?"

"Let's say I have faith in my own judgment."

"Then I suppose I'll just have to rely on it too," said Rybek. "From what Wyatt told me, and what I dug up later on the internet, Civil Affairs personnel operate in four-man teams. They go into places where the natives are hostile or where U.S. forces can't admit to operating, and deal with threats to and from the civilian side. Wyatt was a civil recon sergeant, a technical reconnaissance expert. He was one of the operatives who assess critical infrastructure and civilian networks and figure out the crossovers with a view to disruption or protection. Frankly, my stomach tenses up just thinking about it."

That would explain the absence of tattoos. A member of the U.S. military operating undercover in hostile territory couldn't have permanent markings that might give him away.

"How long did he serve?" I asked.

"Four years before he moved to Civil Affairs, and another five or so after, mostly in GWOT—the Global War on Terror."

"So when did he leave?"

"In 2017, maybe early 2018."

"Donna Lawrence said he had a record for possession. That didn't impede his progress in the military?"

"I doubt they gave a rat's ass. If the army turned down everyone who'd messed up early in life, the system would collapse."

"And what did Wyatt do after he was discharged?"

"Drifted. Spent some of his lump sum, then more of it, until soon there wasn't much left. He started taking short-term contracts in the private sector: guarding executives, risk analysis, that kind of thing. A few of the jobs were in Latin America, places like Mexico, Colombia, parts of Peru. He'd spent time down there before, possibly early on with Civil Affairs, though he wouldn't confirm that part. He spoke good Spanish, as far as I could tell—better than high school, which is all I have. Whatever he earned from a contract would keep him in clover for six months, after which he went looking for another payday. It suited him, living that way, or did for a while. But once forty was looming, and his bones started to hurt more, he decided it might be time to go out on a lucrative high and invest whatever he made in a bar or a store, something that would produce an income without requiring him to wear a gun. So he took a job he wouldn't otherwise have accepted."

Rybek licked his lips.

"I'd usually have a smoke right about now," he said. "It's like you and your morning coffee, but without the urge to pistol-whip someone if it's withheld."

"I only have a few more questions. Look upon it as delayed gratification."

I didn't want to push Rybek harder, but neither did I want to give him the opportunity to reconsider. Standing outside, smoking something of which Dunkin's head office would almost certainly have disapproved, he might decide to clam up. I'd then have to work on levering him open again. I could do it, but it would be tiresome for both of us.

"Fine," said Rybek. "Wouldn't want you thinking I'm an addict. You have kids?"

"A daughter."

"Bet you've warned her about the dangers of dope."

"She's a teenager, so I've warned her about the dangers of everything, but I couldn't swear to how much she took in. And you?"

"A son. I was married until I wasn't. My boy lives with his mom up in Houlton."

"Have you warned him about the dangers of dope?"

"He's four, so yeah." Rybek had relaxed again. "I told him only to accept a hit from a friend."

"Go back to the job Wyatt accepted," I said.

"Right. As I said, Wyatt was coiled, like a spring, so I suggested that a night on the town might not be a bad idea. We ended up in Ruski's, heads down. We weren't too drunk, but I still wouldn't have wanted either of us behind the wheel. Later, back at my place, we got more drunk and I broke out the good stuff. At Ruski's, we just had a buzz on.

"It turned out that Wyatt hadn't been sleeping so good, and the VA had given him pills for anxiety. They'd also offered him psych sessions, but he told them he wasn't ready for therapy yet. Wyatt let them assume it was PTSD, or whatever you want to call it, but with me, he claimed it wasn't. What he'd seen and done overseas hadn't affected him, he said, or not in a way that couldn't be dealt with by a couple of days spent fishing or hiking. No, this came from something more recent: his last detail down in Mexico. He'd spent a month there, October into November last year, working on the advance logistics. The main thing, for him, was that nobody would get badly hurt—on either side. He was very insistent on that: no losses, especially CIVCAS, or civilian casualties. He was tired of seeing bodies."

"What sides were these?"

"Wyatt didn't say, exactly. I only know he was part of a group, each member with a specialization, though only Wyatt and this other fella, Emmett Lucas, had military experience. Wyatt and Emmett grew up together in Weverton, Maryland. I come from Lovettsville, just over the Potomac in Virginia, which is how we got to know one another. We all used to smoke pot, drink beer, and chase girls down by the river on weekends."

"Who else was in the Mexican detail?"

"Again, Wyatt wouldn't say, but they weren't all operating in the same location. It was like a chain or relay, with the goods being handed along, one to the other, until they were safely out of the country. *Goods*. That was the word he used, but, you know, fuck that."

For the first time, Rybek looked disturbed.

"Are we talking narcotics?"

"No," said Rybek, "we're talking children."

CHAPTER

I haven't learned a lot during my years on this earth, or not much worth sharing. Getting shot hurts, but you probably worked that out already, while getting shot more than once constitutes carelessness, a death wish, or a message from God to seriously reconsider your lifestyle choices. The great mass of people are fundamentally decent, but the worst make the most noise and do harm out of all proportion to their numbers. Fear is more prevalent than hatred, but the first morphs easily into the second, which is why moral courage is essential. Never trust strangers who call you pal, buddy, or friend, because they mean you no good.

And here's something else: most people want to talk. They want to share their thoughts. They want to be heard, to be recognized. The ones who don't are either without insecurity or insane—which, when examined closely, is the same thing. If you give them the opportunity, and are patient, men and women will tell you a great deal more than they might originally have intended, especially in the case of those who have been asked, perhaps out of friendship or weakness, to conceal knowledge of an act they believe to be wrong.

The noise of Dunkin', the comings and goings, faded away, leaving only Rybek, me, and the last word Rybek had spoken: *children*. I broke the silence.

"Wyatt Riggins was involved in a kidnapping?"

Rybek appeared miserable but relieved. The wound had been lanced. The poison was flowing out.

"What he admitted was that they took children out of Mexico in December, and it was a real bad idea. Which, you know, maybe goes without saying."

"Who were these children?"

"He didn't say. He wasn't crying when he came clean, not exactly, but he was close. I could hear his voice catching. I could also see that he was worried, even scared."

"And how did you respond?"

"I probably wore the same expression you're wearing now," said Rybek. "Taking someone's kids is about as low as a man can sink, next to taking their lives. This wasn't the Wyatt I'd grown up with, and I told him so, but he said he hadn't known."

"Wait, he was engaged in an operation that required at least a month of preparation and he wasn't aware of its purpose? That doesn't sound plausible."

"He claimed he'd been employed to steal artifacts, except the word used was *transfer*. He'd been informed that those items properly belonged in a museum, except the museums down there had nowhere to display the stuff they already had, so they'd hardly be missed. They'd also been looted, which meant they were stolen property. Once they were in the United States, they'd be sold to private collectors. It was a victimless crime, unless you counted the original thieves as victims, which no one was in a hurry to do."

We were in no danger of being overheard, but still we kept our voices low, as though even to speak of this was somehow shameful.

"Then he gets to the location that's been targeted, and instead of looted treasure, he finds children waiting to be transported across the border?"

"Four of them," said Rybek. "That's the story, more or less. It began in Ruski's and unraveled further at my place, so Wyatt was pretty messed up toward the end. We both were, and I might have missed some of the particulars. Plus, Wyatt was rubbing his face and mouth, and mumbling some, so I couldn't always make out what he was saying. By the end, he didn't even seem to be speaking to me. I think he was trying to apologize to those kids."

"Were they to be ransomed?"

"I asked him if they'd wanted to leave Mexico," said Rybek. "Like, whether it could have been a custody thing, with the kids taken south of the border against their will and one of the parents paying to have them snatched back to the United States."

"How did Wyatt reply?"

"He told me the children didn't say anything at all. Then he laughed, but not because he'd found something funny. He laughed because it was better than the other option."

Rybek flicked his fingers, like a man casting seeds to the wind.

"Which was when Wyatt said he needed to stop drinking, stop smoking, and particularly, stop talking. We were done. He called an Uber to take him back to Zetta's place. Like flipping a dime, he was sobering up. He warned me to keep my mouth shut before we parted, as if I needed telling. Not because of anything he might do—he wasn't threatening me—but in case someone else might hear."

"Did he give any indication of who that person might be?"

"I'm no detective, but whoever they stole those kids from would be my first guess."

Rybek let that hang, along with the implication.

"The second," I said, "being whoever employed Wyatt and the others to take them out of Mexico."

I closed my notebook, less to signal we were done than that whatever was said next would not be recorded.

"Do you think Donna Lawrence was instructed to find a position for Wyatt at BrightBlown?" I asked.

"Wyatt knew about selling pot to college kids," said Rybek, "and he could roll a joint better than I can, which is no faint praise, but he wasn't about to make employee of the month at BrightBlown. Unless he fell from the sky and was fortunate enough to land next to Donna on a day she was feeling uncommonly tolerant, which seems a stretch, I'd say that, yes, she was under orders to put him on the payroll."

"Do you know who owns BrightBlown?"

"I know the name of the holding company listed on my pay stub, if that's what you mean."

"It's not."

"I didn't think so. Yes, I know who owns BrightBlown ultimately: Devin Vaughn. I was one of the first hires and I did my homework before I signed the contract."

"Were you uneasy?"

"That a criminal was the beneficial owner of a cannabis concern? Until recently, everyone involved in the industry was technically a criminal. I was a criminal, with a record that said so. There's being particular and then there's being hypocritical. I'll concede that I had some questions, but I made sure to ask them quietly."

"Of whom?"

"Donna Lawrence. She told me shortly after I joined that Vaughn was only one of a number of investors in the business, even if he was the major stakeholder. BrightBlown, like his motels and stores, was legit and she was determined to keep it that way."

"Did you believe her?"

"I chose to. I don't count the cash at the end of the day, and I don't balance the books. Officially, I'm deaf, dumb, and blind, beyond checking on the plants and directing customers to their best high. Unofficially, I'd admit to suspecting that if BrightBlown has investors other than Vaughn, they're all linked to him and do his bidding. Also, even with my math skills, I can tell there might be some discrepancy between the amounts of cash taken in and those declared, if not so much recently."

"A large discrepancy?"

"I told you, I don't balance the books."

"Which isn't to say you don't glance at them."

"You know," said Rybek, "I really am sorry I agreed to talk to you."

"You'd have been sorrier if you hadn't. I'd have stuck to you like gum on your shoe."

"Huh. Is that where *gumshoe* comes from? I'd never thought of it that way."

"I believe it refers to rubber-soled shoes, which make less noise. So we just missed out on being called *galoshes*."

"Small mercies," said Rybek. "As for the accounts, I've seen inflated bills from some of our contractors, large and small. I only raised them once with Donna, in a jokey way, and that was during my probation period. She accidentally included an invoice from one of our courier companies, misfiled with plans for a reorganization of the customer displays. I found it, handed it back to her, and said I'd get a couple of kids on bikes to make deliveries for a quarter of the price. She thanked me for my input but advised me to mind my own business. I didn't bother to point out that she'd made it my business by misplacing the paperwork to begin with. I didn't think it would go down well.

"And on the cash side, even when we had quiet weeks, we didn't really, or not on paper. That's what surprised me, if only for, like, thirty seconds. I could understand a business underdeclaring to hide money from the IRS but not overdeclaring, until I remembered Devin Vaughn. If the feds arrest me for involvement in money laundering, I suppose I can always claim brain impairment and behavioral disinhibition due to my working environment."

I wouldn't have wanted to spend an evening at Rybek's condo listening to his choice of music, but if drollness ever became an Olympic sport, he was a shoo-in.

"But there's less of that now?" I asked.

"Yeah, now we're not overdeclaring, but the opposite. For us, cash is king and it goes out as soon as it comes in. BrightBlown is doing better than okay, but that doesn't mean some other part of the Vaughn empire isn't. Cannabis is making up the shortfall."

He gazed at me sadly.

"You know how they say confession eases the soul?" he asked. "I'd like to interrogate that view. I may just have implicated a friend in a kidnapping and my employer in criminal activity, and I don't feel happy about either."

"I'm still not going to talk to the police," I said. "What I have is a rumor that Wyatt Riggins may have been involved in the removal of four children from Mexico, and the possibility of poor accounting practices at a largely cash-only business. The second is none of my concern. As for the first, I'm being paid to establish Riggins's whereabouts, and one task may feed into the other. Have you been completely straight with me?"

"About Wyatt and BrightBlown? Absolutely."

"Then I'll keep your name out of it, whatever happens. But if you hear anything else, especially if Riggins gets back in touch, I'd appreciate you letting me know."

I passed him a business card.

"Try not to use that for a roll-up," I said.

He fingered the card dubiously.

"I prefer higher-quality material. Did you run these cards off yourself? Because I swear, we have a better grade of paper in the employee restrooms. What now?"

"You spend a few days out of town, just as Donna Lawrence instructed—or more than a few, if she's willing to cover the tab. Getting rid of you was a way to buy time, but would only ever be a temporary fix. I'm not even sure why she brought up your name. I think she might have panicked; that, or she was worried Zetta might already have mentioned your friendship with Riggins."

"It's a mess, isn't it?" said Rybek. "Even before Wyatt reappeared, I'd been considering working somewhere else. There's a startup outside Bangor that looks promising. It's honest, as far as I can tell. Then again, compared to where I am right now, Enron was aboveboard."

"I didn't know anything about Devin Vaughn's ownership of Bright-Blown until this week, when my lawyer informed me of it," I said. "He got the story from a client, who also heard rumors that Vaughn is overextended financially, which may be forcing him to blur the lines between his legitimate and criminal interests. If those rumors are in the air, you can be sure law enforcement won't be far behind. BrightBlown may soon come under intense federal scrutiny."

"Shit," said Rybek.

"In addition, Donna Lawrence's actions indicate that it may have been Vaughn who sent Wyatt Riggins to Mexico as part of a snatch team to abduct or retrieve those children. If that's why Wyatt disappeared, the operation has started to go bad. It can only mean someone has come looking for the children and, by extension, whoever took them."

"Double shit," said Rybek.

And if those people came hunting for Wyatt Riggins but failed to find him, they might instead apply pressure to those who knew him, which would put Zetta Nadeau in their sights, not to mention the man seated opposite me. The look of worry on Rybek's face implied he had reached the same conclusion.

"Being advised to skip town to avoid private investigators is not conducive to a contented life," he said, "but skipping town to avoid disgruntled Mexicans might be. I feel an extended vacation coming on, one that could shade into permanency. I may have been wise to talk to you after all."

"Wisdom comes with age," I told him. "Like arthritis. One last question: Did Wyatt own a gun?"

"I asked him the same thing," said Rybek. "He said he kept one at home and one taped under the driver's seat of his car, but I wasn't to say anything to Zetta—not that I would have, even if she and I had gotten on better."

"What was the problem?"

"A lack of common interests, Wyatt apart. She doesn't smoke and doesn't like the Chili Peppers." He shook his head in sorrow. "I can understand the first, but the second?"

We left Dunkin' and walked to our cars. Rybek paused beside his Daewoo. I urged him to get rid of it in favor of a less conspicuous ride. He might also want to avoid using his credit card for a week or so.

"I have enough cash to keep my girlfriend and me going for months," he said. "BrightBlown isn't alone in knowing how to work the system. What about my cell phone?"

"If you're serious about not returning to BrightBlown," I said, "get a new number, but be sure to share it with me. Look, we may be overreacting. Wyatt could have been talking through his hat after a long night, and his upping sticks may have nothing to do with Devin Vaughn or Mexico. There may be no children, in which case there's no threat.

"On the other hand, if what he revealed to you was true, he's left a spoor that leads here, and questions may be asked of anyone who's been in contact with him. Questioning comes in two forms. You've just been on the end of the first kind, and you don't want to experience the second. But even if Wyatt Riggins is a fantasist, my information on BrightBlown is solid. Devin Vaughn's house of straw is shaking. You don't want to be under it when it collapses and a torch is applied to the wreckage."

"If Vaughn was involved with the abduction," asked Rybek, "and he knows Wyatt has run, won't he be worried?"

"Probably, but Vaughn has men and guns. Also, if he tries to hide, especially with his other difficulties, he puts the larger operation at risk. His allies will sense fear, and his rivals will taste blood in the water. Whatever part Vaughn played in that Mexican grab, he has no choice but to let the consequences work themselves out and hope whatever gamble he's made pays off."

"One last thing," said Rybek. "If you're looking for Wyatt, and these people, whoever they may be, are also looking for him, doesn't it mean your interests and theirs may—"

"Coincide?" I finished for him.

"I was thinking 'conflict.' "

"Either way, the answer is yes."

"I hope you got paid in advance."

"Perhaps I'll name you in my will in return for your cooperation, so you feel invested in the outcome."

"You know," said Rybek, with feeling, "everything being equal, I'd prefer if you didn't name me at all."

CHAPTER XXXVI

Devin Vaughn and Aldo Bern sat in a storage room at the back of a produce warehouse on Baltimore's Frankford Avenue, their table illuminated only by early morning light. The business was currently another of Vaughn's legitimate operations, although it hadn't started out that way. In the beginning, fruit importation was a convenient means of smuggling narcotics. Perishables were usually fast-tracked through customs, even allowing for insufficient manpower to begin investigating random heavy crates of bananas and pineapples in the hope of uncovering contraband. In addition, Blas Urrea's contacts, who included corrupt officials at the points of departure and arrival, ensured that searches were the exception, not the rule, which meant Vaughn's losses were minimal, verging on nonexistent.

But all that was in the past. The animosity between Urrea and Vaughn had caused the collapse of all such arrangements, leaving Vaughn with a warehouse costing him more to maintain than he earned from selling its contents. Vaughn felt a fire coming on, followed by an insurance settlement. He'd have to be subtle about it, since the word was out that he might be having cash-flow issues. He didn't want arson investigators sifting through the rubble because close behind them would follow the DOJ whispering of criminal charges coming down the tracks. It was all about increasing the pressure on his operation, intensifying it until someone or something cracked.

To relieve some of that pressure, he and Bern had been seeking alternative sources for the supply and importation of more lucrative products than mangoes and grapes. Meanwhile, unbeknownst to Bern, Vaughn had planned, funded, and carried out his little Mexican expedition in December. Bern had to give Vaughn some credit for keeping the whole affair secret until it was concluded, but it didn't do much to make him happier. In Bern's view, it was a risk that should never have been taken. It might result in war being openly declared on them, pitting Vaughn's crew not only against Blas Urrea but also against his associates, some of whom made Urrea look like a declawed pussycat.

Yet the initial aim of the mission to Mexico had been achieved. The operatives had returned to the United States with their prizes, and no one on either side had been killed. Admittedly, the Mexicans had suffered nonfatal casualties, and one of Vaughn's people received a minor stab wound. Still, considering the other possible outcomes, this counted as a triumph.

Blas Urrea had then proceeded to do just what Bern himself would have done under similar circumstances. He began walking back the cat, testing the chain to establish who might have moved against him. Vaughn would have been on his list of suspects from the start, but probably not high. Urrea would first have looked to enemies closer to home because such a level of incursion required local knowledge. Since Vaughn had indeed been obliged to call on certain natives, even if they weren't aware of whom they were working for, the identity of those individuals was always at risk of being discovered by Urrea's men. So it came to pass, and once Urrea had the first link in the chain, he could proceed to the next.

Except Vaughn, to his credit, had been careful to distance himself and the other major shareholders in the venture. Until recently, the children had been held together in a secure location, and only a handful of people were intimate with every facet of the operation. Unfortunately, one of those people was Roland Bilas, who had been stupid and greedy enough to go back to Mexico while Urrea was on the warpath before managing to get himself picked up by U.S. Customs with contraband in his suitcase. By the time Bern had sent two of his Los Angeles contacts to the motel, Bilas was already dead, having most assuredly given up all he knew: that was not in question. Bilas was discovered naked on the motel bed, and Bern's people had stopped counting the wounds on his body once they reached double figures. Under similar duress, Bern would have capitulated, and he was a lot harder than Roland Bilas—but then, Jell-O was harder than Roland Bilas.

So Blas Urrea now knew that Devin Vaughn was responsible for the abduction of the children from Mexico, but no message or ultimatum had been received from Urrea, and Bern doubted any would be forthcoming. Even were the children to be returned, Urrea would not be minded to forgive. He would want blood, particularly that of Vaughn and anyone close to him, including family members.

Vaughn was nearing the end of divorce proceedings. It would be better if the full extent of his troubles remained concealed from his estranged wife, Karin, and her legal representatives, but she and their two children also needed to be protected. Bern's first task, then, as agreed with Vaughn, had been to persuade Karin and the children to go into hiding. That wasn't easy, for obvious reasons, not least work, school, and Karin's understandable anger at her unloved spouse for putting his family in a position of danger, even if its exact nature was not a subject for discussion. Bern had personally advised Karin of the need to safeguard herself and her children, but he also intimated that Devin Vaughn might be forced to reassess his uncombative approach to both funds and custody should Karin not cooperate, which helped focus her mind.

Karin had found employment with a start-up that was piggybacking on that Marie Kondo decluttering shit—wealthy people emptying their closets of once-worn clothes just so they could fill them with new stuff—and was reluctant to give up a position that paid well, especially when the commission she received from designer resellers was taken into account. Bern reminded her that there would be other start-ups, while she and her kids had only one life. Also, if she'd wanted a Regular Joanne existence, she shouldn't have hooked up with a man like Devin Vaughn to begin with, though Bern didn't have to say that aloud, Karin being able to join those dots for herself. As for the kids, it wasn't like they were studying for their SATs; they were four and six, for Christ's sake. As long as they had Mommy with them, they'd be fine. The result was that, as of the day before, the family had been packed off to Nowheresville, in Nothing County, Wisconsin, there to watch Netflix and eat cheese curds until—

Well, there was the rub, as someone much wiser than Bern once wrote. Karin had asked Bern how long they'd be expected to lie low. He guessed it would be no more than a month or so, but he'd hesitated before replying, which was when Karin put herself right in his face.

"Two weeks," she said. "Get this shit sorted by then or—"

She let it hang. Bern didn't push her with an "or what?" because that didn't sound clever even in movies. He knew she was just letting off steam. There was no "or" worth countenancing. Once she and the kids were safely housed, bodyguards would be with them everywhere they went, so trying to escape was off the cards. And what would be the point in running if Devin Vaughn's enemies were prepared to hurt them to get at him? Of course, Karin could turn to the feds if she was desperate, but their protection would come with a price, requiring her to share all she knew about her husband and his dealings. Nevertheless, if the crisis dragged on, or Urrea's people made their presence felt, she might regard it as a price worth paying. Bern would then be forced to shorten Karin's leash in case her desire to preserve herself and her children made her forget her obligations—to tighten it so hard she choked.

However, that was for another day. Today's challenge was Devin

Vaughn himself. In an ideal world he, like his family, would have holed up somewhere safe, but with his syndicate on the verge of collapse, the option of concealment was denied him. It was all about maintaining a front, keeping Vaughn simultaneously visible yet protected. Extra manpower had been drafted, and security overhauled. Bern was confident the main house in Manassas remained safe, so that would be their base for the time being. Any movement beyond its walls, such as that day's warehouse excursion, would be limited: planned well in advance, but revealed only at short notice.

And all the while, Bern was spending money they couldn't afford—and calling in favors he would have preferred to save—to gain some insight into Blas Urrea's plans. Until the previous day, he'd had no luck at all. South of the border, the news had spread that something valuable had been taken from Urrea, and the culprits, along with their families, their pets, and the bones of their ancestors, were now marked, as was anyone who assisted them or failed to share knowledge of their whereabouts.

But then a call had come through to Bern from a woman named Elena Díaz, who needed to get out of Mexico. If she didn't, a band of killers from Coahuila, Urrea's seat of power, were going to rape her, remove her arms, legs, and head, and hang her dismembered torso from the aqueduct in Saltillo, all because she had declined the advances of the wrong man. Díaz, therefore, urgently required money, and her immediate fear of torture and death had overcome her longer-term fear of Blas Urrea, especially because the man whose attentions she'd spurned was one of Urrea's senior lieutenants.

Díaz worked for a private Mexican bank, one that had long maintained a mutually beneficial relationship with the cartel boss. The funds it held for Urrea were both clean and officially unconnected to him, which meant that transfers did not attract undue attention, either domestic or international, and cursory government inspections found nothing to be alarmed about. The core banking team, of which Díaz was a member, was aware of the identity of some but not all of the clients through regular exposure to transfer and investment patterns, helped by hearsay and the occasional conversational nugget dropped by Las Tres Jefas, as they were known—because, unusually, the highest positions in the bank were occupied by women.

Regrettably, none of those women, all of whom were aware of Díaz's predicament, had proven willing to intervene with Urrea on her behalf. They might have been anxious not to endanger themselves or alienate an important client, but Díaz also suspected that Blas Urrea was more than a customer and might well be among the bank's owners, if not the principal. Díaz couldn't prove this, and even if she could, she knew there would be no smoking gun to entice the authorities, so scrupulously did Las Jefas adhere to the banking laws—or within reason, because any bank that appeared too honest was, quite rightly, automatically assumed to be hiding something, a situation not unique to Mexico but common to global finance.

So Díaz had been looking for a way out, and the raid on one of Blas Urrea's isolated compounds had unexpectedly provided her with a potential route. The details of what had occurred—and, more precisely, what had been taken—were unclear, but the result was that, a month after the first whispers about the raid reached the bank, Las Jefas had reactivated two accounts that Díaz knew to be dormant Urrea holdings. Díaz had processed the transfers as instructed, the funds moving from Mexico to Nashville, Tennessee, one of the cities frequently cited as a Buckle of the Bible Belt. The money landed in the No. 1 and No. 2 accounts of a company dealing in repurposed Bibles, both English and Spanish, from the cheap to the costly. An off-the-shelf website indicated that the Nashville Codex Corporation was additionally devoted to creating "unique books of worship from existing volumes," thus ensuring the "propagation of the Word" in a manner that was both "environmentally sustainable and historically appropriate," enabling buyers to become part of a "Christian continuum," possessors of beautiful books once owned by other worshippers, which could be passed on to the next generation.

The purpose of the payments, acknowledged in a formal, beautifully phrased, and unsigned letter of receipt, was for the production and delivery of eight impeccably restored eighteenth-century Bibles—four English and four Spanish—each with new artwork and capitalization, as well as fresh leather binding, gilding, and jeweled cases, within a time frame of not less than five years, a schedule somewhat at odds with the urgency of the transfers. The Nashville Codex Corporation also committed to sourcing up to five thousand used Spanish-language Bibles within the same period, which would be given new covers and marked as *un donativo penitencial de un pecador reformado*—a penitential offering from a reformed sinner. The total of the two transfers came to $500,000—which represented, Díaz thought, a hell of an investment in the hope of salvation, if that wasn't a contradiction in terms.

Against all protocols, Díaz installed stealth monitoring software to log all transactions to and from the Nashville Codex Corporation and illegally harvest historical financial records going back a decade. It was this information, starting with the name and location of the company, that she was now offering to sell to Aldo Bern. Devin Vaughn's name had recently been mentioned in unflattering terms in the bank's halls, and by the same Urrea lieutenant who had given Díaz to understand that, at a time of his choosing—whether days, weeks, or months in the future—she would be dispatched to the next world, but not before her body had been violated and sundered. It hadn't taken Díaz long to identify Vaughn's relationship to Blas Urrea, and then Aldo Bern's to Vaughn.

Díaz had named a non-negotiable price for her trove and given Bern the details of an account set up solely to receive those funds. As soon as the first tranche was safely deposited, Díaz would commence sharing all she knew. But Bern needed Vaughn to okay the transfer. This, in the environs of a soon-to-be-immolated produce warehouse, he was proving reluctant to do.

"How can we be sure she's straight?" Vaughn asked.

Vaughn was consuming a clementine, segmented and laid out on its peel. He ate methodically, chewing each piece for what seemed to Bern like precisely the same number of seconds, but with no obvious relish. Vaughn had contracted COVID in the early days of the pandemic, and his taste buds still hadn't fully recovered. Bern knew it had made Vaughn depressed, which might have affected his judgment and contributed to the current havoc.

"She knew your name," said Bern. "Urrea's associates are talking about you. She wouldn't have approached us otherwise."

"Or she figures we're desperate and can be played."

"She's at least as desperate as we are," said Bern. "We've both dealt with el Amante. If she doesn't get out of there, she's a dead woman."

El Amante was the nickname given to Urrea's lieutenant and Díaz's nemesis. It was what passed for humor in the Mexican underworld, referring to a compulsive rapist as "the Lover." Maybe, Bern reflected, el Violador was taken. There certainly wasn't any shortage of candidates for the title.

"But a hundred thousand dollars?" Vaughn continued.

He finished the clementine, tossed the peel in a garbage can, and wiped his hands on the pleats of his tan trousers. Bern spotted what he thought might be a urine stain beside the fly. Vaughn was letting himself go, though it wasn't for Bern to point this out. It might have been easier if Vaughn still had a wife to attend to his domestic needs.

"A quarter up front," said Bern, "and the rest in escrow, to be released once we're satisfied with the material."

"It's still twenty-five thousand in advance."

Bern was growing impatient. Only a couple of years earlier, Vaughn would have dropped $25K on updating his summer wardrobe, and regarded a conversation like this as quibbling over nickels and dimes.

"We need to know exactly where the threat is coming from," said Bern. "Right now we're in the dark, waiting to be hit."

"If Díaz screws us over, do we have anything to use against her?"

"She has a mother and a younger sister, but they'll vanish with her. She can't leave them for el Amante. If Díaz is as bright as she seems, she'll have tried to hide her snooping at the bank, but if she's that bright, she'll also know how hard it will be to eliminate all traces. When she drops out of sight, her employers may initially put it down to the threat of el Amante, but you can be sure they'll also review her recent activities. Whatever dangling ends she's left, they'll find, and Urrea will be informed."

Vaughn scowled.

"So she and her family are dead, no matter what she does," he said. "Another reason not to give her our money."

Bern wanted to grab Vaughn by the hair and beat his head against the table.

You fucking infant. You child. All this is because of your recklessness, your covetousness—

Bern took a deep breath.

"We need what she's offering," he said, "and she has a vested interest in ensuring we're satisfied. If Urrea goes down, so does el Amante. She wants us to succeed. It's the best hope she has for staying alive."

Vaughn was silent for a while longer before nodding.

"Then do it," he said, finally. "Give the bitch her money."

CHAPTER

XXXVII

Bern made the transfers, the first directly to Díaz's nominated account and the second to escrow. He could have arranged to cheat her on the remaining $75,000—it wouldn't have been hard—but they had enough difficulties without alienating someone with knowledge of Urrea's financial operations. As long as the intel she provided was solid, Bern was content to see the rest of the money released.

Yet when the material began to come through, he wondered whether Díaz was attempting to stiff them after all. A fucking Bible company in Nashville, Tennessee: What could that possibly have to do with anything? But further emails showed that Díaz's instincts were correct. Shortly after the arrival of the funds from Mexico, the Nashville Codex Corporation had acquired portable freeze dryers, ultraviolet- and infrared-filtered light sources, and equipment for atmospheric monitoring and modification, including a pair of portable nitrogen and oxygen generators. For reasons beyond all human understanding, Blas Urrea had, it seemed, commissioned the Nashville Codex Corporation to recover the lost children.

The flow of information from Díaz paused. Bern waited for the next anonymized email message. It arrived within seconds.

WANT MORE? RELEASE THE NEXT $50K.

By the time their business was concluded, Devin Vaughn was $100,000 poorer and Elena Díaz was $100,000 richer. Bern didn't begrudge the woman a single cent, even if Vaughn might. Díaz had saved them a huge amount of effort and thrown in additional financial details that would have cost Bern a small fortune in bribes to banking and business contacts had he been forced to source them for himself.

The owner and president of the Nashville Codex Corporation was a former Methodist preacher named Varick Pantycelyn Strawbridge Howlett, his first three names being those of early leaders of the church and the last his patronymic. Díaz's investigations revealed that the Reverend Howlett was ninety-three years old and currently residing in an assisted-living facility for those suffering from dementia, which meant he was unlikely to be accepting blood bounties from Mexican crime lords.

Tennessee was one of the less expensive states when it came to dementia care, which didn't mean it came cheap: Howlett's accommodation at Shining Stone Senior Living in Murfreesboro cost $7,000 a month. Howlett's account was safely in the black, and the $7K arrived regularly—religiously, even—in Shining Stone's account on the third of every month. The nominal payee was the company's retired accountant, himself in his late seventies and a resident of Palm Springs.

As for the Nashville Codex Corporation, it was, despite its name, a limited liability company rather than an actual corporation, which meant it had a simpler legal structure and less formalized accounting and tax-filing processes while remaining a separate entity from its owner. In other words, as long as someone fulfilled the minimum legal requirements, Howlett could eat soft food and believe he was the reincarnation of John Wesley for all the interest Tennessee's Department of Revenue might have taken in the NCC's activities.

Díaz had traced the Shining Stone money trail back through a series of companies and roadside churches—all of the former existing only on paper, and most of the latter rejoicing only in rodents and insects for their congregation—and come up with one recurring name: Eugene Seeley. It was Seeley who had, via the NCC and certain shell entities, rented or purchased the equipment itemized in the first section of Díaz's email. The receipts specified, presumably at Seeley's instigation, that it was required to preserve and treat "fragile manuscripts and bindings."

Díaz's paperwork showed that Urrea's wasn't the first such large payment received by the Nashville Codex Corporation, though it was the only one used to source specialized storage and transportation equipment. According to the records, sizable payments to the NCC were biennial, or annual at most. A number were derived from Latin American financial institutions less scrupulous than her own, and Díaz had helpfully added, in brackets, the cartels or criminal organizations with which they were most closely associated, many of them connected to the PCC, the Brazil-based Primeiro Comando da Capital, Latin America's dominant organized crime and narcotics syndicate, with which Blas Urrea's cartel was aligned. Eugene Seeley, it transpired, was the go-to guy in the southern United States for Latino reprobates, but to what end?

Bern printed off the most relevant documents and marked salient names and figures with a red pen. He then drove to Manassas, only to be told by one of the foot soldiers, Marek, that Devin Vaughn was in his basement and had left orders not to be disturbed. Bern had long ago decided that any such orders did not apply to him and brushed past Marek, who knew better than to try and stop him.

Bern descended noisily so that Vaughn would know he was on his way. The stairs spiraled, and the basement's interior was not visible until Bern reached the final steps. He had not been down there since the arrival of the child. Vaughn had invited him to visit her, but Bern was still too incensed to accept. Vaughn had taken the refusal personally and the invitation was not renewed. In fact, Vaughn ordered that nobody was to enter the basement without his permission, a permission that had not been offered or requested since.

Bern paused on the last step. Vaughn was kneeling before the child, leaning in so close that his face was just inches from hers. Only the glass prevented them from touching, skin to skin. Vaughn turned to look at him, and Bern understood, truly and for the first time, what it meant for a man to be haunted. Behind Vaughn's empty gaze, ghosts walked.

"What is it?" Vaughn asked.

"We know who's coming."

CHAPTER XXXVIII

Angel and Louis weren't noticeably keener on early mornings than I was, so I gave them some time to come to terms with the reality of another day before I got in touch. Instead, I headed home, eased myself of the burden of a bladder's worth of Dunkin' coffee, and caught up on some paperwork. Shortly after eleven, and to protect Jason Rybek, I drove out to BrightBlown's farm and asked after him, only to be told by the woman at the front office that Rybek had been in touch to say he was ill and would be taking a few days off. I'd been practicing my expressions on the way and had perfected "annoyed but not necessarily shocked." I gave it to her now, and received an apologetic shrug in return. I was about to leave, all bases covered, when Donna Lawrence arrived.

"I was going to call you," she said. "Jason is taking time off, but I have his permission to share his cell phone number with you, should you wish to reach out."

I took down the number for form's sake. Lawrence removed two bottles of water from a refrigerator and handed one to me. The bottles were made from recycled plastic and the water probably flowed from Eden itself, pure as the driven snow, pure as Donna Lawrence's soul.

"I feel that we've gotten off on the wrong foot," she said, "though I'm not sure how. Why don't I show you around? Who knows, we might even convince you to loosen up and try some of our products."

Now that she believed Jason Rybek was safely out of the way and any efforts to trace him were destined to end in frustration, she was happy to play the gracious host. But I was also sure that Lawrence had been in contact with Devin Vaughn or one of his intermediaries since last we'd met. In Vaughn's position, I'd have encouraged her to find out what the investigator might already know about Wyatt Riggins and his activities. I didn't see any downside to playing along.

The most straightforward means of approaching Vaughn would have been to knock on his door down in Virginia, specify that I liked my coffee with milk, no sugar, and invite him to fill in the blanks. That would also have been a fast way to incur broken ribs and a concussion, or potentially something more terminal, depending on what Vaughn might be trying to hide. If every conversation was also a transaction, there was no point in arriving empty-handed. Should I decide to approach Vaughn directly, I'd need leverage. Taking a look at his operation in Maine, and hearing what someone who was effectively an underboss might have to say about it, was a step in the right direction.

The farm was alive with noise as we walked. A construction crew was clearing an area to the north, destined to be the site of a new production facility twice the size of the existing buildings combined. Lawrence showed me inside one of them, a long windowless barn divided into separate rooms in which cannabis plants were growing in elevated trays under LED lighting. I could no longer hear the sounds of the backhoes and excavators, only the quiet hum of the units that controlled the temperature. Lawrence explained that these plants were either at or near the end of their growth cycle. Next to the growing area was a curing room, where the plants would be dried before the flowers were trimmed, separated from the leaves, and the two products bagged for distribution to the main store in Portland, a smaller store in Bangor, or to independent outlets supplied by BrightBlown.

"That seems like a lot of weed," I said, as Lawrence closed the door behind us.

"It is, but not as much profit. We were running at a loss for the first eighteen months, though we're now in the black. Capital costs are high, and finance is hard to come by because lenders don't want to be associated with cannabis or are prevented by statute from lending to our industry. Then there are taxes to be paid, but we're excluded from claiming certain credits and deductions; we're unable to trade across state lines; and, as you intimated when we first met, we have a glut of competition, both legal and illegal. We're expanding because we're optimistic that we've weathered the worst of the bad times, but we've been wrong before. We thought that when the Democrats returned to power, it would mean a loosening of federal restrictions, and that didn't happen."

I nodded along politely, but everything she told me had to be viewed in the context of a cash business—one, what's more, that was allegedly being used by Devin Vaughn to launder money. It wasn't that Lawrence was lying, just that she wasn't presenting the complete picture. We stopped on a rise to take in a view of the whole farm. To the east stood a shuttered coffee truck surrounded by picnic tables.

"We're going to add a pizza van for the summer months," said Lawrence. "We want BrightBlown Farm to become a destination for tourists and locals alike."

"It's all very idyllic," I said. "I hope Devin Vaughn will come up here to cut the ribbon personally."

"I asked around," said Lawrence. "That name wasn't familiar to anyone I spoke with."

"What about to the people they spoke with?"

She drank some of her water but didn't look at me.

"You don't give up, do you?"

"I've been told it's one of my better qualities," I said, "or one of my qualities, anyway."

Her tone changed, and the pretense of ignorance was dropped.

"Nothing has happened to Wyatt Riggins, or if it has, it's nothing to do with BrightBlown. Devin has never even set foot here. That's deliberate. We don't want anything to tarnish the company's reputation or draw heat. We have twenty employees, both full- and part-time, and we're hoping to double that number when the new facility is up and running. Like me, they love what they do and want to keep doing it. They're working with their hands, digging in the soil, growing plants.

"We have customers who come to us with epilepsy, cancer, MS, chronic pain. Before legalization, they might have been hooking up with some street dealer or trying to cultivate cannabis in their yard or greenhouse, always looking over their shoulder for a cop. Do I think there are too many outlets in the city? Of course, but I would say that, right? Whatever you may feel personally about what we do, it's not all bad, and we're here to stay. If Wyatt Riggins is in trouble, I hope he stays away from here, and if he tries to come back, he won't find a welcome or his old job. Have I made myself plain?"

"Very," I said.

"The man I spoke to asked me to pass on a message. He said that efforts were being made to trace Wyatt and make him calm his girlfriend down, which means persuading her to dispense with your services. He was hopeful of getting a message passed along to Wyatt. Once Wyatt's spoken to Zetta Nadeau and confirmed he's safe and well, we can all go our separate ways."

I finished my water.

"I'm never going to speak to Jason Rybek, am I?" I asked.

"I told him to leave town. Even if you find him, it won't change anything. BrightBlown is a dead end as far as Wyatt Riggins is concerned."

And I believed her. Thanks to Rybek, I knew more than she did about what Riggins might have been doing for Devin Vaughn. Unfortunately, it made me less inclined to drop the investigation.

"Thanks for the tour," I said. "I doubt I'll be bothering you again, but I can't say the same for Vaughn. When you next speak to your contact, you might share that with him."

"There must be easier ways to earn a living than getting in Devin's face." She shook her head. "And you'll receive no help from anyone here, because if he goes down, so do we."

"An enterprise like this?" I said. "No, someone will keep it running just as it is. They might change the name, but they'll have no reason to mess with the structure. I mean, you're getting a pizza van. You'll be okay."

I tossed my empty bottle in one of the many recycling barrels scattered around the property. BrightBlown was very eco-friendly, which proved that even miscreants like Devin Vaughn weren't all bad.

"Does that mean I can come to you for a reference should it all go south?" asked Lawrence.

"No need," I replied. "If someone's looking to employ an apologist for a criminal, I'll send them straight to you."

To her credit, she didn't take it badly.

"Maybe I can get a job working for Congress, or Big Oil."

"Reach for the stars," I said.

CHAPTER

XXXIX

With Aldo Bern gone, Devin Vaughn squatted before the child. He ran an index finger over the glass that separated them, following the curve of her cheek down to her mouth, which hung open in repose.

"I'm sorry, honey," whispered Vaughn, "but we're going to burn your twisted brother. I wish it didn't have to be this way, but it looks like the bad men will keep on keeping on, and we can't have that. So we'll set the boy alight and film the results. Maybe it'll convince old Blas to call off his dogs, because if he loves you enough, he'll want you to remain unharmed. It'll pain me, and I know it'll pain you, too." This Vaughn was curious about, though he did not say so aloud. He wondered whether the girl would react when the boy was incinerated. Would she know? Would Vaughn hear her scream? "All I can promise is that you'll be safe. You can count on it. You're mine now."

Vaughn listened to her reply. The girl's eyes remained closed, and if she spoke, it was in a voice only he could hear.

"Hush, now," he said. "Please, hush. It's okay."

But she would not be calmed, repeating a name, one that bounced around inside Vaughn's head like the slug from a .22, slowly tearing his mind apart.

CHAPTER XL

When I was certain that Louis and Angel would be showered and dressed, if not decent, I called to suggest we meet for lunch at Hot Suppa on Congress, since by that stage I'd been up and about for so long I was beginning to hallucinate.

I parked in the Walgreens lot, Walgreens now standing at one apex of a triangle dominated by two boutique hotels, Congress being the new location of choice for upscale, tony places to stay, leaving Commercial for the chains. The latest addition, the Longfellow, hosted a spa. I couldn't recall ever having visited a spa. I was pretty sure Louis had, though, which he confirmed when I joined him and Angel at the restaurant.

"See this skin?" he said. "You don't get skin like this at my age unless you care for it, 'Black don't crack' or not. You use retinol?"

I told him that I didn't think so.

"You got to use retinol, except it may be too late for you. Your face already looks like the sole of an old shoe."

"Do you use retinol?" I asked Angel.

"He barely uses soap," said Louis. "Hand him a bottle of retinol and he'd try to drink it."

Angel, calmness personified, let the wave break over him and recede. He was too occupied by the menu. Hot Suppa formerly opened for breakfast, lunch, and dinner, but not necessarily all three on any particular day, so it could be hard to remember which days it opened for which ones, or at all. Now it was strictly breakfast and lunch, with Southern food to rival even the Bayou Kitchen—though I wouldn't have suggested this to Louis, who regarded the Bayou Kitchen as a sacred space. Louis ordered the shrimp and grits, Angel the chicken and waffles, and I the Hollis: two eggs, toast, bacon, with hash browns instead of grits. This caused Louis to wince, but I'd never understood grits and never would. They reminded me of something out of Dickens, gruel and grits not being unrelated.

"You see this?" asked Louis, sliding a newspaper across the table. The lead article concerned the Italianate Victoria Mansion, one of the loveliest buildings in the city, constructed as a summer home by a Mainer–turned–New Orleans hotelier named Ruggles Morse in the mid-1800s. It was common knowledge that Morse had been an ardent supporter of the Confederacy and permitted slave auctions in his hotels, in addition to owning slaves of his own. Before the Civil War, Louisiana was a slave economy. If you did business there, it was slave business, and some of that money had made it north to Portland, leaving its legacy in the form of the Victoria Mansion. Had it not been so beautiful, it wouldn't have been so problematic.

"Do you have a solution to this thorny Portland quandary?" I asked Louis.

"Time-shares," he replied. "We run an annual lottery for Black folk and the winners get to stay at the Victoria Mansion for a week, meals included."

"A ticketed lottery?"

"Dollar a shot. We're not greedy."

"It's certainly an unconventional approach," I said. "I can have Moxie draw up some paperwork so it looks fully thought through when you present it to the board."

"Sounds good," said Louis. "I ought to give him a call, have him set up a meeting."

"No, I think you should turn up cold. Make it a surprise."

"So as not to give him time to get away, you mean?"

"That too. Then again, Moxie might agree just to see the looks on the faces of the board. He has a strange sense of humor."

Our food arrived. While we ate, I updated Louis and Angel on what I'd learned from Jason Rybek, and for what it was worth, Donna Lawrence. In turn, Louis had made those promised calls regarding Devin Vaughn.

"Yeah, Vaughn is in trouble," said Louis. "He's overstretched financially because he didn't have the resources to properly weather the pandemic, but he may also have made some bad calls on cryptocurrency."

"That hardly makes him unique," I said. "Smarter people than him have fallen into the same traps, and dumber people have survived them."

"But how many of those people," countered Louis, "also had a quarrel with a cartel boss?"

On his phone, Louis pulled up a mugshot of a man in his fifties who looked like he'd swallowed a swarm of wasps, but not before they'd done their best to sting him to death. Even his mother must have squeezed her eyes shut and hoped for the best before kissing him.

"Meet Blas Urrea," said Louis, "contender for the title of Guerrero's ugliest man. Oddly, it's said that he's restrained by cartel standards, but that's a low bar. It probably just means that he kills quickly unless he's bored.

"So: Devin Vaughn ultimately wanted to go straight, but to do that required significant investment to grow his legitimate activities, which meant he had to expand his criminal dealings, and that expansion inevitably resulted in disagreements—because for someone to gain, someone else has to lose. When it came to cannabis, even heroin and cocaine, he could reach an accommodation by agreeing to pay a percentage of the action to the locals, but other disputes proved harder to resolve, particularly once he expanded into illicit fentanyl, which is where the real money is right now.

"If you're dealing in fentanyl, you're buying from the PCC, a loose affiliation of drug lords based out of São Paulo in Brazil, of which Urrea is—or was, of which more in a moment—a member in good standing. Urrea started out strictly as a supplier, but he, like Vaughn, is also a fan of trade-based money laundering. Urrea similarly aspires to legitimacy, if not actual respectability, with clean investments to form the basis of his bequest to his family. He'd prefer to build that bequest in the United States. In Mexico, he'll be bled dry, and there's no guarantee that his kids will be able to hold on to whatever he's built after he's gone."

I watched pigeons fighting over a discarded sandwich on the street outside. Just because a metaphor is handed to you on a plate doesn't mean you should ignore it.

"Initially," Louis continued, "Vaughn bought cocaine from Urrea, and later fentanyl produced in China and exported to Mexico, all packaged and ready to be shipped north. Vaughn was a good customer, so in return, Urrea introduced him to his contacts in the Colombian illegal mining sector, allowing Vaughn to purchase gold at forty to fifty percent of its standard value, with Urrea taking a commission for brokering the deal. Vaughn then used tame aggregators—more commission for Urrea—to blend the illegal gold with legally sourced stock, and they in turn passed it on to refiners, also friends of Urrea's, who melted it together and re-formed it, so now there was no way to trace the origin of each bar. A portion of the gold, though, Vaughn arranged to be shipped directly to the U.S., concealed in batches of scrap aluminum because it seems it's now easier to smuggle gold than hard currency."

"Let me guess," I said. "Blas Urrea is also in the scrap metal business."

"If something can be bought or sold at a profit, Urrea is interested, especially if illegality becomes virtually indistinguishable from legality. He really does want his family to be clean within a generation."

"Urrea and Vaughn would appear to be brothers from other mothers," I said. "So what went wrong?"

"Guided by Aldo Bern, Vaughn used to invest in traditional financial instruments: bonds, funds, and equities bought and held through platforms in the Caymans, the Virgin Islands, and Labuan, an offshore territory run by the Malaysians," said Louis. "But Urrea encouraged Vaughn to approach Los Brokers, a money-laundering network out of Bogotá, Colombia. Los Brokers used front companies and fake export contracts to move funds for their clients, with a lot of Vaughn's money passing through Mexico and Costa Rica before ending up in U.S. accounts—or, more commonly, being converted into cryptocurrency. And before you ask, Urrea received a kickback from clients he referred to Los Brokers and entrusted them with some of his cash. But Urrea may have a bank of his own in Mexico, so he didn't need Los Brokers the way Vaughn did. Urrea also regarded Los Brokers as having too many moving parts, leaving the network vulnerable. In return for referrals, they gave him a favorable rate, which he took advantage of when it suited him.

"Then, in 2021, the Colombian government moved against Los Brokers. All their channels were frozen, and Vaughn lost heavily—could have been as much as twenty million dollars. Urrea, though, was untouched. He made the last of his transfers twelve hours before the Colombian authorities pounced, and later claimed it was pure coincidence. Maybe it was, but Vaughn chose to believe otherwise, just like he doesn't believe in Santa Claus or the Tooth Fairy. But Vaughn was a clown for taking Los Brokers at their word about crypto, because Urrea surely didn't. Whether he shared his reservations with Vaughn remains to be seen, but my guess is he kept quiet.

"That seems to be the origin of the dispute between Vaughn and Urrea, exacerbated by Vaughn trying to expand into markets ostensibly controlled by other clients of the PCC, who went crying to their contacts, who in turn advised Urrea to bring Vaughn under control or cut him loose. As a result, Urrea may have decided to seriously damage Vaughn using Los Brokers and let his rivals or the U.S. government do the rest."

Louis took a moment to order a refill of coffee but also to reconsider some aspect of what he'd just shared. I thought I might be able to follow the direction of his thoughts.

"Could Urrea have been trying to ruin Vaughn from the start?" I asked.

"If not from the start, then shortly after. Why work to build your own empire in the United States when you can take over someone else's? That prospect must have been at the back of Urrea's mind, but he might have waited until Vaughn became overextended before pulling the trigger."

"And if we've come to that conclusion—"

"Vaughn will have reached it as well," said Louis. "So his luck goes from good to bad, then bad to worse, and it doesn't look set to recover anytime soon, all of which he blames, rightly or wrongly, on Blas Urrea. Now Vaughn is reduced to shedding assets at fire-sale prices, and he can't lay hands on fentanyl because the PCC has cut him off. Vaughn is desperate and wants to hurt Urrea, because if he can make Urrea look weak, he may be able to work his way back into the PCC's good graces."

"You mentioned that Urrea was trying to secure his family's future," I said. "Which means he must have children, even grandchildren."

"No grandchildren yet, but four kids—two girls, two boys—and nieces and nephews in the extended clan."

"And they're all safe?" I asked.

"The source I spoke to didn't say otherwise, but I can check."

"Can I ask who this source might be?"

"You can ask."

"I may be better off not knowing."

"If you're worried about it getting back to Urrea that we're asking questions, it won't. My source has no love for him."

The loneliness of a drug lord. No wonder singers wrote *narcocorridos* about them.

"Assuming Wyatt Riggins wasn't lying to Rybek," I said, "and Devin Vaughn paid a team to target children in Mexico, it would make sense that those children were somehow linked to Urrea. Vaughn would have no reason to avenge himself on anyone else down there."

"If that was Vaughn's intention," said Louis, "he must have been very sure that whatever he did would leave Urrea with no room to maneuver. Urrea's not a man to turn the other cheek, and not just because one is as ugly as the other."

"But I still don't understand what advantage Vaughn thought might be gained by kidnapping children," I said. "What's he going to do, hold them for ransom until Urrea admits that he set out to ruin him and makes up the losses?"

"People have engaged in kidnapping for less," Angel pointed out.

This was undoubtedly true, but it still sat awkwardly with me. Nevertheless, if Vaughn's financial situation was as wretched as it appeared, he might not have been thinking straight when he moved against Blas Urrea; that, or he figured his predicament couldn't get any worse. On that front, at least, Vaughn was mistaken, since Urrea might be tempted to set aside his reputation for comparative restraint and skin him alive.

"What about Seeley, the one who bothered Riggins's stepbrother?"

"I got silence when I dropped the name," said Louis.

"What kind of silence?"

"The kind that doesn't speak volumes. There was no echo. But if I was Blas Urrea, I'd have someone on this side of the border, someone I could trust—not Latino either, but white and superficially respectable."

"Define 'trust,'" I said.

"Agreeing to a price for a service and keeping to the deal. Not playing off one side against the other."

"A lawyer?"

"Too limited. Also, lawyers aren't above introducing themselves as lawyers—they have no shame—and Seeley gave the preacher nothing. The American contact wouldn't be a hired gun either, or not exclusively. More of a fixer."

"But not above handling the rough stuff?"

"Not above it, but prefers not to. Clean hands."

"So who gets blood on theirs?"

"Whoever Urrea has sent north to assist."

"That's quite the insight you have into the souls of men."

"Women, too. I'm an equal-opportunity misanthrope."

I'd finished eating, leaving half my food untouched. I'd overestimated my appetite, but I'd also lost some of what I originally had. I realized that, in a moment of weakness, I'd wanted Urrea's hunters to catch Wyatt Riggins because Zetta Nadeau would be safe once they did.

"How much of this will you share with Zetta?" Louis asked.

"I may tell her that, like Jason Rybek, she should take a short vacation where nobody knows her and Spanish isn't even spoken in a Mexican restaurant. After that, I'll see if anyone in the U.S. military will talk to me about Riggins or provide a lead on his buddy and co-conspirator, Emmett Lucas. If I can get to Lucas, I'll be a step closer to Riggins."

"Or," said Angel, "you could just advise Zetta to find another boyfriend, especially if Vaughn's people can assure her he hasn't been dumped in a barrel of acid by Urrea's hunters. That would allow you to walk away."

"I could do that," I said, "but where would be the fun in it?"

CHAPTER XLI

Seeley was driving east, the light fading behind him and darkness ahead. Seeley drove nearly everywhere. He used airplanes only when they could not be avoided and rarely traveled beyond the United States. His recent trip to Mexico had been clandestine, and no record of his passage existed at any border crossing. Blas Urrea's people had been paid well to transport him safely over the border and back again, though Seeley had not returned to the United States alone.

Urrea was becoming impatient at the lack of progress, but Seeley had convinced him of the importance of not acting precipitously. If they did, it might put the children at risk or break one of the links in the chain that Seeley was so diligently exposing. Elizalde: found and dealt with. Bilas: found and dealt with. Now, after days of searching, of reaching out, twisting arms, making promises, paying bribes, Seeley had a probable location for Emmett Lucas, one of the two ex-military operatives hired by Vaughn and his associates to move against Blas Urrea. Wyatt Riggins was concealing himself well, but Lucas had not been so circumspect.

From Bilas, Seeley had learned that just as one, even two, of the conspirators had elected to keep Wyatt Riggins close, so had another drawn Lucas to his cause, or Lucas had offered his services to him for a price. Bilas had not been confident of the precise arrangement, but then he was dying as he tried to explain it, so some confusion on his part was forgivable. Regardless, Seeley now had the names of the three ringleaders, and those of Lucas and Riggins, the mercenaries employed to operate on their behalf. Of the principals, two, including Devin Vaughn, were dangerous men. The third, as far as Seeley could establish, was not, but had fallen into bad company out of avarice or zeal.

Seeley's contacts were among the best in the underworld, a network of intertwined threads that could be traced back to him only with difficulty. One of those threads had recently been tugged in Portland, Maine, by a private investigator asking questions about Wyatt Riggins. Seeley did not want anyone else looking for Riggins. He most particularly did not want this particular private investigator nosing around because Parker had a reputation for immunity to intimidation, damage, and, so far, death. Seeley saw no reason to make an enemy of him, and thus he was better avoided. But Blas Urrea had made it plain that Seeley was to assist in the punishment of all involved, as well as the removal of their hearts. At first, Seeley had regarded this latter condition as an unnecessary piece of theater—if Urrea wanted proof of death, a photo would suffice, or even a finger—but that was before he had been introduced to Urrea's agent.

If Seeley failed to fulfill the contract in full, it would harm both his reputation and his finances. More worryingly, the agent, seated beside him in the car, might take it amiss, and that would be unpleasant for Seeley in ways he did not care to imagine. Seeley had witnessed what was visited upon Elizalde and Bilas at the end. He had never seen a man's heart exposed before, not while it was still beating. Oh, Seeley had known it was possible to uncover the heart of a living man, if not for very long, but he would carry to his grave the image of long, skeletal fingers closing around that same heart, like the pale legs of a cave spider seizing its prey. He did not wish the last thing he saw before he died to be his own heart similarly gripped before being torn from his chest.

All this done by a woman. Seeley did not have a name for her, and she had not offered one, so he now thought of her only as "la Señora."

"You want some music?" he asked.

"No," said la Señora.

And so they continued on their way in silence.

TO THE NORTH, Devin Vaughn gave a series of instructions. Aldo Bern was to proceed against Eugene Seeley. The private detective Parker was to be watched, and actively discouraged from pursuing his investigation if he persisted. Finally, without Bern's knowledge, Vaughn ordered the immolation of one of the children.

3

But the day of the absolute is over,
and we're in for the strange gods once more.

D. H. Lawrence, *Kangaroo*

CHAPTER

XLII

It would not have been true to claim that I had good relations with the Veterans Administration. I knew one person in the VA who probably never wished to hear from or see me again, and she was the best contact I had. However, if I'd let such feelings stand in my way, I'd never have left the house. People not wanting to talk to me came with the territory.

Dr. Carrie Saunders was based at the Togus VA Medical Center in Augusta, where she specialized in PTSD. I'd met her some years earlier when a group of war veterans decided to get into the antiquities-smuggling business. It hadn't ended well, with the resulting fallout leaving me persona non grata in military circles. I could have tried pointing out that I wasn't the one who thought it might be a good idea to transport stolen artifacts halfway across the world, but it wouldn't have gotten me very far. Where the U.S. military was concerned, bad press was bad press.

I was waiting in the lobby of the mental health center when Saunders appeared. In fact, I'd been waiting for almost two hours, even though she knew I was there. It was my own fault. I hadn't told her I was coming, out of concern that she, like Jason Rybek, might feel a sudden hankering for someplace else. I'd shown up at reception, handed over a business card in a sealed envelope, told the receptionist I'd like the envelope passed to Dr. Saunders, and confirmed that I was happy to take a seat until she found a convenient gap in her schedule. I'd even brought a book to pass the time, along with a large coffee in my reusable Coffee By Design travel mug, which had nostalgia value since the original outlet on Congress Street, where I'd purchased the mug, no longer existed. Short of producing a pipe and slippers, I couldn't have looked more ready to make myself comfortable for the long haul.

Saunders stood over me as I closed my book. She was now in her forties, her blond hair still worn short, but she'd acquired a wedding ring since last we'd met, along with the altered physique that came with recent motherhood. She still looked like she could go three rounds with the champ, but would now try to put him down in the first to conserve her energy.

"I hope you're reading something improving," she said.

"*Little Dorrit*." I showed her the cover to prove I wasn't lying. "I aim to get through all of Dickens by next year, except after *Little Dorrit*, I only have the difficult novels left, the ones that make even hardened Dickensians suck their teeth in a concerned manner. I fear I may run out of steam."

"Or you may die. I'm surprised you've survived long enough to get as far as *Little Dorrit*."

"I hear that a lot—oddly, with the same tone of wistfulness you just adopted."

"It's important to live in hope. What do you want, Mr. Parker?"

"I'd like to buy you lunch."

"I'm married."

"We can sit at separate tables if it makes you happier."

"Nothing would make me happier about having lunch with you, except not having lunch with you."

She walked away. I fell into step beside her and held the door as we moved outside, because Mother raised a gentleman.

"I'm looking for a missing veteran," I said.

"Then I wish you luck, and better luck to him."

"He may have been involved in the abduction of children from Mexico."

Saunders stopped walking.

"You know," she said, "today was a good day until now."

"Sorry."

"Really?"

"Not so much," I replied. "But at least you won't have to pay for your lunch."

THERE WEREN'T MANY PLACES to eat by the VA Medical Center, so we drove in convoy about three miles northwest to the Countryside Diner, where I stopped for takeout sandwiches and sodas before continuing to the parking lot of the Viles Arboretum. I pulled in beside Saunders's Escalade, and we found a bench where we could sit and talk. I told her what I'd learned about Wyatt Riggins while Saunders ate an egg salad sandwich.

"They get themselves into such quandaries, these men," she said.

"Some more than others."

"And you've no idea who these children might be?"

"Only that if Jason Rybek is right, and Riggins wasn't fantasizing because of weed and booze, they're connected to Blas Urrea, who can hardly be faulted for coming after them. If Riggins is running, it's because he's afraid Urrea may have his name on a list."

"What do you intend to do about it?"

"Try to find Riggins—and the children too."

"Why not just go to the police with what you know?"

"Right now, all I have is a drunken hearsay conversation at Ruski's, and the person who told me about it could be at risk from his employer if it's discovered that he's been speaking out of turn—and by 'at risk,' I don't mean the loss of medical and dental, though he may need both once Devin Vaughn's people have finished with him. I'm not even sure I could get in touch with him again if the police asked me to. If I were Rybek, I wouldn't surface until winter comes around again. But I'm also worried that if I make this official, Vaughn may decide to cut his losses and dispose of the children, if he hasn't already. No kids, no evidence, no crime."

"Is Vaughn holding them for ransom?" Saunders asked.

"He's hurting for money, but kidnapping children possibly belonging to a Mexican crime lord doesn't seem like the most advisable way to improve his finances. Even if Vaughn succeeded in getting a ransom paid, Urrea isn't just going to walk away and swallow the pain. Vaughn would never be able to sleep with both eyes closed again."

"Revenge, then?"

"That may be part of it. If it's the only reason, the children are already dead, so I hope it's not the case."

But neither ransom nor revenge made complete sense to me, which left leverage. By holding the children, Vaughn was hoping to pressure Urrea, but that still left the certainty of Urrea seeking payback later. As Louis, Angel, and I had discussed, the only way I could see Vaughn coming out of this with some hope of reaching old age was by fatally weakening Urrea. Could Urrea have been responsible for protecting the children so that whoever had entrusted them to him would punish him for his failure?

Saunders folded the remaining half of her sandwich in paper and set it aside.

"The wreckage left by that Iraq incident still hasn't been fully cleaned up," she said, "and I doubt it ever will be. Your involvement hasn't been forgotten either."

Nothing makes a man feel anxious quite like being hated by an army.

"If I can track down Wyatt Riggins or Emmett Lucas, I may be able to handle this quietly," I said.

"Are you serious?"

For the first time since we'd met, Saunders grinned, though it might have had more appeal if she hadn't looked so skeptical.

"Okay, I'm being optimistic," I said. "With both Vaughn and Urrea involved, I'll be lucky not to end up dismembered or buried in a barrel."

"As I said earlier, your luck on that front is holding up surprisingly well. From what I've heard, you've been at Death's door so often, he's probably left a key under the mat for you."

She took in the park. A pair of dads, either stay-at-homes or guys goofing off with their kids for the day, were kicking a ball with three young boys while a white terrier did its best to complicate matters. I knew how the dog felt.

"I have two girls of my own now," said Saunders. "The youngest is less than a year old."

"Congratulations."

"If someone took them, I wouldn't rest until whoever did it was dead."

"That would be Urrea's line of thinking."

"So what do you want from me?"

"Whatever you can find out about Riggins: people he was close to in the service and people he remained close to afterward, including his childhood friend Emmett Lucas, as well as pertinent material from his medical records and anything else that might prove helpful. I'm in the dark here. It's down to his training, but Riggins is proving hard to locate."

"If your information is correct, and Riggins was attached to Civil Affairs, I may struggle for access. If I start digging too hard, alarm bells will sound. Do you have a name for the clinician who prescribed the medication found at the Nadeau house?"

I did: Noah Harrow.

"I've had some dealings with Noah," she said. "He's been working with the VA for a long time. He's a realist about the scrapes veterans can get themselves into. There may be some leeway with him."

I thanked her.

"Don't thank me yet. I could come up with a big fat zero."

She put the rest of her sandwich in her pocket and prepared to leave. I stayed where I was. I'd give her time to drive off before I returned to my car.

"If you decide to go to the police—" she began.

"Your name won't be mentioned."

"Likewise on my side, for obvious reasons. By the way, it was smart of you to seal your business card in an envelope."

"Sometimes I think I might even be able to make a career of this," I said.

Out on the grass, the terrier took a hard ball to the head and stopped running.

"Or maybe not."

CHAPTER XLIII

I decided to drop by and speak to Zetta Nadeau on the way back to Scarborough, since it wasn't much of a detour. I found her out front, using a dolly to move sheets of metal from the back of a pickup to her studio. She paused as I stepped from the car but didn't try to open the gate.

"Need any help?" I asked.

"No, I've got it."

And still the gate remained closed.

"Do we have an issue, Zetta?"

"I was going to call you when I was done. I've been thinking: I want you to stop looking for Wyatt."

"And why is that?"

"If he's so eager not to be found, let him stay that way. I don't see why I should waste any more of my time or money on him."

She folded her arms in anticipation of an argument. If so, she wasn't going to get one.

"That's fine," I said. "I'll bill you for the remaining hours, and our contract will be concluded."

Zetta looked relieved. Slowly, she unfolded her arms.

"I thought you'd be annoyed," she said, "or try to pressure me into continuing."

"You're the client. If you want to step back, that's your right."

I waited. Zetta wasn't dumb, so it didn't take her long to spot the catch.

"You're going to stop searching for him?"

"No."

"But I've asked you to, and I won't keep paying you."

"You're free to ask, but I'm not obliged to comply. As for the money, there's a certain liberation in working purely for pleasure."

Zetta approached the fence and gripped its links, like a prisoner begging for release.

"I want you to stop. I'm *telling* you to stop."

"When did he contact you, Zetta?"

She stared at me.

"I don't know what you're talking about." She spoke very slowly, as though wary of stumbling and leaving herself more exposed. "If Wyatt has gotten himself into trouble, I don't want it spreading to me—or you."

What she was saying might have some truth to it, but we both knew that she was using it in the service of a lie. Riggins had been in touch, and at the instigation of Devin Vaughn or one of his underlings.

"Where is he, Zetta?" I asked gently.

She closed her eyes and leaned her forehead against the wire.

"He didn't say."

"Zetta—"

"He promised me he was safe and well, and I told him I'd been so worried that I'd hired someone to find him. He wasn't angry, but he asked me to call you off, which is what I'm trying to do. If he's in no danger, you don't need to search for him. I want him left alone."

"Did he say why he'd run?"

"It doesn't matter."

"Actually, it does. I think your boyfriend was involved in the abduction of children from Mexico, and the man he seized them from has taken it amiss. That man is a cartel boss named Blas Urrea. He's filled deserts with unmarked graves, and now he's looking for Wyatt, which is why Wyatt left town without so much as a farewell kiss. Unfortunately for you, it's well known at BrightBlown that you and Wyatt were an item, and I think BrightBlown is owned by the same person who hired Wyatt to take those kids. There's a real danger that some unpleasant individuals are about to come knocking on doors up here, yours included, unless Wyatt does the right thing."

Even then, I doubted it would save him, but it might protect Zetta. Her face, though, remained impassive.

"I'd like you to leave now," she said. "I don't want you to bother me again."

"I can't promise that, Zetta, and it's not like you can call the police if I persist."

I moved closer to the fence, so close that I could smell her sweat. I saw in her face that nothing I'd shared had come as a shock.

"He told you about the children, didn't he? Was it before or after you hired me? Of course, it must have been after: you wouldn't have asked me to look for him otherwise. You'd have been afraid of what I might discover."

So Riggins had called her and admitted to some or all of what he'd done, but rather than cut him loose or persuade him to rectify matters, Zetta had doubled down. She was betting the house on Wyatt Riggins—and her life, too. I made one last push.

"Those children have to be returned, Zetta. Tell me who they are."

"They're none of your concern."

"I've elected to make them my concern."

"Then on your own head be it," she said.

And Zetta stalked off.

CLASSIFIED

UNITED STATES DEPARTMENT OF JUSTICE
FEDERAL BUREAU OF INVESTIGATION

File Number: REDACTED

Requesting Official(s): REDACTED

Task Numbers and Date Completed: 1000210, Work Request Number 1000210, 03/17/24

Source File Information/Name of Audio File: 031724_0405_pm BERN_Phone_Call.wav

VERBATIM TRANSCRIPTION

Participants: Aldo Bern B
Devin Vaughn V

031724_05_pm BERN_Phone_Call.wav

BERN: This Bible corporation, we're struggling to locate a warehouse or workshop.

VAUGHN: Maybe it exists only on paper.

B: No, it ships product. I had someone track down one of its books. Nicely made, if that's your thing. Our contact down there is doing his best, but I think I may have to deal with it myself. There's a lonely old man I'd like to visit.

V: This guy, See—

B: Christ, no last names.

V: I think we're beyond that now.

B: (Unintelligible)

V: You're sounding like a stuck record. Consider this a tap to move the needle. But have it your way. He can't be working alone. Nobody's that good.

B: Our banker friend says they sent someone north to assist. The bank funneled money to the couriers employed to get her over the border.

V: Her?

B: The couriers were told the package was female.

V: No one else, only a woman?

B: El jefe has gunmen on this side of the border, but from what we can establish, they haven't yet been mobilized. As of this moment, it's a two-person team.

V: Why would they send a woman?

B: I'll find out, I promise you.

end of 031724_0407_pm BERN_Phone_Call.wav

CHAPTER XLIV

It is not illegality that draws the attention of law enforcement but carelessness. Traditionally, Devin Vaughn's activities had been models of good practice, criminally speaking. Vaughn was ambitious but not greedy and didn't gamble unless the odds favored him. Like Blas Urrea, he aspired to respectability because respectable men had a better chance of avoiding prison time or a violent death. If Vaughn was successful enough, the origins of his fortune, like that of all the great robber barons of American history, might ultimately be forgotten. Small thieves, Vaughn's father used to say, get sentences, but big thieves get statues.

Devin Vaughn's financial difficulties, combined with his desire to hurt Urrea, had led him to take chances he would otherwise have avoided. The result was that he had become a person of interest to the U.S. Treasury's Financial Crimes Enforcement Network, the FBI's Financial Intelligence Center, and the Drug Enforcement Administration, with the FIC taking the lead. A federal court in Virginia had authorized electronic surveillance of Vaughn and five named accomplices, including Aldo Bern, which meant that federal investigators were now aware that Vaughn was under threat from a cartel boss, a consequence of a classic falling-out among thieves. It didn't take them long to identify the boss in question.

The FBI's contacts in Mexico's Policía Federal Ministerial and the Agencia de Investigación Criminal confirmed a recent flurry of unusual activity in Blas Urrea's camp. Something had been taken from Urrea, something valuable, and he was convinced Vaughn was the culprit. Pressure was put on the PFM's informants to provide more details, but most of them were at the periphery of Urrea's activities, not part of his inner circle. Nevertheless, whispers were overheard: Vaughn had taken "*los niños de Urrea.*" Except, as the PFM quickly established, Urrea's family was safe and well. If he had any illegitimate offspring, the PFM was not aware of them.

While efforts continued to establish the identity of the "children," a conference call between the FBI and DEA discussed the possibility of using Vaughn's difficulties to pressure him into becoming a federal witness in return for protection. Officially, it was decided that the two agencies would await further intelligence before engaging. Unofficially, and over Chinese food at Mama Chang's in Fairfax, the core members of the cross-agency team agreed that what they were waiting for was not more information but for Urrea to make a move against Vaughn. Federal agents would then have the opportunity to swoop in, and Vaughn would be advised that next time, they might not be able to save him. Metaphorically spilling his guts to law enforcement would be preferable to having them literally spilled by Urrea's torturers. It was a hazardous strategy, but with Vaughn under surveillance and the chance that Urrea would strike sooner rather than later, it was felt to offer the best prospect for a satisfactory outcome.

But should events go south, and the agents prove too slow to protect Vaughn from injury—or, saints preserve us, death—it wasn't as though the world would be significantly poorer. Vaughn remained a trafficker of narcotics and had, until recently, been the business associate of a Mexican whose preferred method of dispatching his enemies was to lay them facedown on a rock and split their skull with a sledgehammer.

In other words, and to use legal jargon, Devin Vaughn was screwed.

THE FBI HAD INSTITUTED three forms of surveillance on Vaughn. The first was termed *stationary-technical*: small cameras hidden in cars and vans parked near Vaughn's home in Manassas, the vehicles regularly alternated from a pool of twelve registered to phantom companies and individuals. Vaughn's home was also the subject of fixed surveillance from two points: an office block overlooking the rear of his property and an apartment for sale in a complex almost directly opposite, the locations employing thermal imaging and infrared cameras.

But the most important of the three, theoretically at least, was electronic monitoring, so his email and telephone communications, and those of his cohort, were now being shared with the bureau. But since Vaughn, for all his problems, hadn't fallen to earth with the last shower of rain, he did his best to avoid writing, transmitting, or saying anything that could be used against him in a court of law. As an added precaution, he had boxes of burner phones stored in his basement, and the numbers being used by the subjects changed on a near daily basis.

Unfortunately, even burners weren't protection against federal eavesdroppers. In Vaughn's case, the monitoring involved the use of StingRays and KingFish, or stationary and portable cellular phone surveillance devices. These mimicked wireless carrier cell towers, forcing devices within a set range to connect to them instead. With a grid established around Vaughn's home, it was a comparatively simple task for the agents to identify the new numbers upon activation and lock on to them accordingly, along with any other nearby phones.

So far, the eavesdropping on Aldo Bern's cell phone had provided the best material, which was unsurprising given Bern's responsibility for much of the day-to-day running of Devin Vaughn's operations. While

Bern had obviously instituted protocols against using proper names in calls, the agents were aware that he had identified at least one of those whom Urrea had sent against Vaughn, and some form of pre-emptive strike was about to be made. But where, or how, the agents were unable to establish.

CHAPTER XLV

Late the next morning, with Zetta Nadeau's duplicity still rankling, I drove down to Portsmouth, New Hampshire, to meet Sam, my other daughter, for lunch at Book & Bar. Sam was spending a couple of nights in the city with the Baylors, who were old friends of her mother's. The previous day, she had driven up to Portsmouth from Amherst, one of the colleges to which she had applied for a place in the fall, grades permitting. Rachel had offered to go with her, as had I, but Sam wanted to revisit the campus alone, and we respected that. She had her own way of doing things. Sam was an unusual child. I knew that better than anyone, and sometimes I believed her mother suspected it too, even if she had yet to discuss this openly with me—or, indeed, with Sam.

I hadn't seen Sam for six weeks, not in person. While we spoke regularly on the phone and via FaceTime, she'd been immersed in her studies and I'd been caught up with work. Now, as she stood to greet me, I marveled afresh at the young woman she'd become. She had much of her mother to her, particularly in the delicacy of her features, though a certain hardness to the set of her mouth, even in repose, signaled that anyone foolish enough to cross her would have cause for regret. She smiled easily but laughed less so. Her eyes were mine, and sometimes, in the right light, the specter of her dead half sister, gone before Sam was born, passed over her face, so that two souls stared back at me instead of one.

I caught a pair of men in their late twenties checking her out as we hugged and I speculated, not for the first time, on how much I might have to pay a judge and jury not to convict me for making an example of one festering sack of male hormones to discourage the rest. If I was busy, Louis would do it for free, and even take pictures I could store on my phone for moments like this.

"Hey, fellas, I saw you giving my teenage daughter the eye. Maybe you might like to take a look at the last guy who did that, or what's left of him . . ."

"Dad?"

"Sorry," I said. "My mind was elsewhere."

We ordered a pair of soup-and-sandwich combos, and Sam told me about this second trip to Amherst, which she thought was "fine," and made passing references to a few of the other options she'd visited earlier in the year, including Bard and Colgate.

"Were they 'fine,' too," I asked, "or is there something more to this lunch invitation from my daughter?"

Her mouth formed a horizontal S of amusement touched with mischief.

"I haven't discussed it with Mom, and I wanted to see Amherst one more time before raising the issue, but I've been considering heading in a different direction."

Generally, those were words a parent would rather not hear from a teenage daughter, right up there with "I'm dropping out of college," "Can you pay my bail?," and "I'm pregnant." I willed my brow not to darken.

"You haven't discussed it with me either," I said, "so that makes two of us. If you tell me you want to take a year off to find yourself, I can save you a lot of time and trouble by drawing you a map."

"Gee, thanks," said Sam. "Will it be very detailed?"

"It'll be an X on a blank sheet of paper, which I'll stick on your forehead to remind you that wherever you go, there you are. So tell me, what exactly constitutes a 'different direction'?"

She took a bite of her sandwich and, possessing good table manners, waited until she'd swallowed before answering. This also gave her time to think, even though I knew she must have planned this conversation long before arriving at Book & Bar. She was, after all, my daughter.

"Did you know," she began, "that I always keep some of your business cards with me?"

I hadn't known, and told her as much.

"I hold on to them in case I ever meet someone who's in difficulty, the kind of difficulty you might be able to help with," said Sam. "I'm careful about how I dispense them—so careful that, so far, I've only given away three, and one of those was just a few days ago. Each of the cards went to a woman."

She took another bite of her sandwich: chewed, swallowed, resumed.

"I've decided that I want to do what you do, or something like it. I want to help people who feel they have nowhere left to turn." She frowned. "This part is hard, but I'll say it anyway. I don't want to hurt anyone, not the way you have. If I can avoid owning a gun—or routinely carrying one—I will. I'm not sure you were ever like that."

"No," I said, "I don't believe I was."

"And I understand why. I think about your father taking his own life. I think about your wife. And I think a lot about Jennifer, her most of all. I know that what happened to them made you the way you are, or the way you *used* to be, because you've changed. Even Mom says so. You're not as angry anymore, and what you do is no longer an outlet for rage."

"You really do sound like your mother," I said.

"Would that be so bad?"

"Not at all. In some ways, Rachel always knew me better than I knew myself, and certainly better than I knew her."

"She still loves you, just as you still love her," said Sam. "I don't mean in a sexual way, because that would be, like, gross"—she was smirking—"but as two people who've been through a lot and care about each other. That makes me happy. It always has."

The grin dissolved.

"Can we talk about Jennifer?" she asked.

Some years earlier, Sam had opened up to me about her experiences of seeing and hearing her dead sister. We had touched upon the subject before, but Sam preferred to avoid it. That time was different. She said Jennifer had told her it was okay to speak to me, and that I would understand. It was a first step, and there had been further small steps since then.

"We can talk about whatever you like."

"She doesn't come to me so much anymore," said Sam. "That's the first thing. It started to change when I turned thirteen. She became like this annoying younger sibling, the little sister I didn't want bothering me while I tried to figure out how to be an adult. And just as I was impatient with her, I felt her annoyance with me—and her envy. Jennifer is older than she looks, but a part of her is still stuck at the age she was when she died, and she struggles with those two sides of herself. She realized why we were drifting apart, yet it didn't mean she wanted it to happen. At the same time, I was having all these experiences that were denied her, and she couldn't explore them through me because that was never the bond we had. So she stopped visiting. It's been months since I've sensed her near, and longer since I've heard her voice.

"But when I was younger, it was as if she was there all the time, or as good as. Even when she wasn't around, I was aware of her. I knew her name almost as soon as I knew my own, but I can't remember how. Now I think she was whispering to me from when I was little, so it became almost natural for me to see and hear her, except I grasped very early on that I wasn't supposed to speak of her to Mom, and sometimes not even to you."

"We've both kept our secrets," I said, "for good or bad. As you say, Jennifer doesn't like being spoken of, not without care."

"Because she's afraid of who might be listening, and not just here."

"By 'here,' I'm assuming you don't mean a bookstore-cum-bar."

"By 'here,' I mean this world. Why do you think that is?"

It was my turn to pause and reflect. Outside, people were going about their affairs on a day that finally felt like spring; inside, we were talking about a dead child who refused to be released, and it still felt like winter.

"She's frightened of being discovered," I said.

"Not for her sake alone, or perhaps not even at all. She's frightened for you."

"If that's true, I have no idea why."

"Really?"

"I wouldn't lie to you. Has Jennifer shared something else with you, something important?"

"No," said Sam. We were concealing nothing from each other now. "It's the secret Jennifer holds, the one she won't reveal: why it's so important that they, whoever 'they' are, don't find out about you."

"Much as I'd like to accept that the universe does, in fact, revolve around me," I said, "thereby proving any number of ex-partners wrong, your mother included, that makes no sense. After all that's happened, after all I've done, the worst of men—and worse than them—can't but be aware of me. I haven't hidden myself. I have the wounds to prove it."

"Unless you've hidden something from yourself, something crucial, and you've buried it so deep that it's been forgotten. Isn't that what happens if you stay undercover for too long? You start to become whoever you claim to be, and your real self gets buried so deep that you struggle to find it again."

"But the real self is never lost, not completely. It's in there, somewhere."

"Which begs two questions," said Sam. "Who are you, and what have you suppressed that's so dangerous?"

To that neither of us had the answers, and the one who might have was elsewhere.

"Can I ask you something in turn?"

"Of course," said Sam.

"What do you remember of the night Steiger died?"

The man named Steiger had died on the beach at Boreas, a resort town in Maine. A sand dune collapsed, suffocating him shortly after he had killed a woman and moments before he was about to shoot me. When the dune came down on him, Sam was standing nearby, watching. She had refused to speak of it ever since, even to a therapist friend of Rachel's, and I had let it go—until now.

"I remember being scared," she said. "I thought I'd be blamed for it. I blamed myself."

I waited.

"That man was going to kill you," she continued. "I was frightened, and didn't know what to do. Then—"

She closed her eyes, pictured, opened them again, resumed.

"It was like a series of images or outcomes came into my mind all at once: a gun materializing in your hand and firing, a wave sweeping him from the beach, the ground swallowing him up, all these things that couldn't occur, until finally, I saw an avalanche of sand. That was when Jennifer came. I felt her. She was in me and of me, and she *pushed*. She took what was in my head and made it a reality. I don't want you to think I'm trying to evade responsibility, because I'm not. I visualized Steiger's death. I wanted him to be buried under all that sand, conceived it as a solution, but I couldn't make it happen. Jennifer could, but she needed me to envisage it. So together, we killed him. Afterward, I was shocked, but I wasn't sorry. I'm still not sorry. He was a vile man."

"He was," I said.

Sam touched my hand.

"Can someone have no regrets about something yet still want to make up for doing it?" she asked.

"I think so."

"Then that's why I want to find a way to help others. And when I told you that Jennifer keeps her distance from me, I'm also keeping my distance from her. She came to me when I needed her—Steiger, the Dead King—and she'd come to me again if I called her, but it's better that I don't. I may not feel remorse for what happened to Steiger, but I didn't enjoy it. If he hadn't died, you'd have taken his place. It wasn't as though I needed time to consider the choice. But Jennifer *did* like it. Dad, she's angry, she's so angry: not at me or you, but at someone or something else. There's a nucleus to it, but Jennifer keeps it concealed. Like you, she hides her secrets. I wonder—"

She stopped talking, so I finished for her.

"If we're hiding the same thing," I said.

We ordered coffee and returned to Sam's plans for the immediate future.

"I didn't just visit Amherst on this trip, like I told you and Mom," she said. "I also went to Lowell. Again."

"Why Lowell?"

"They have a criminal justice program. I might have applied and forgotten to mention it."

"Ah."

"Yeah, 'ah.'"

"Have you mentioned pursuing a criminal justice degree to your mom, even in passing?"

"No," said Sam. "I could never find the right time."

"Because you feared there might never be one."

"Let's say I wasn't optimistic."

She was correct about that much. Rachel's brother had been a state patrolman, killed in the line of duty, and then there was also my history to consider. My father, an NYPD detective, had taken his own life after a shooting incident, and my experience with the same force had not been a happy one. My vocation as a private investigator had contributed to the end of my relationship with Rachel, put both her and Sam in danger, and left me with lifelong injuries, not to mention blood on my hands.

Any suggestion on Sam's part that she wished to pursue a similar line of employment might lead her mother to chain her to a D-ring on the basement floor until she came to her senses.

"Have you thought about becoming a police officer?" I asked.

"I'm not sure I'm cut out for it. Ultimately, like I said, I want to be a private investigator, but with a specialization. I'll run a female agency, taking on only women as clients."

I didn't doubt her. This wasn't a passing fancy.

"If you're serious, you'll need experience in the field after your formal education. It'll be a long haul, with little return for the maximum of effort."

"I could always come work with you. For you, I mean. At first. Like an apprentice."

"Or I could just start banging my head against a brick wall now, to get used to the pain. No, I think it would be better if you worked with a more—"

I searched for the right words.

"Conventional agency?" Sam offered.

"That about covers it," I agreed. "When it comes to the time, I can ask around. We'll find somewhere appropriate."

"I thought you'd say that, but I couldn't *not* raise the question of working alongside you. It would have been like I didn't want to, which isn't the case. I can't do what you do, or not the way you do it. I don't know—I haven't explained that part very well."

"You've been doing fine," I said, borrowing her own word. "If you'd said you wanted to follow directly in my footsteps, I'd have told you to stick to liberal arts. I'm very aware of how I ended up on this path. It was only through hurt, but it shouldn't have to be that way."

"And you won't try to talk me out of it?"

"Would it do any good?"

"It would only make me dig my heels deeper."

"What about your mom?"

"I was hoping you might be with me when I tell her."

I laughed.

"Even Louis would tag along for that conversation only if he was armed and wearing riot gear," I said. "As for me, I'd have to be dragged to Vermont, bound and sedated. No, that discussion is for you two alone. Seriously, if I'm with you, your mother will think we're ganging up on her, which won't help. Talk it through with her. Tell her your reasons. In fact, you can try telling me, because I still haven't heard them."

Sam sat up straighter in her chair, like a candidate at a job interview.

"I want to make a difference," she said. "Shit, that sounds so lame."

"A) There are other means of achieving that. B) Yes, it does sound lame. And C) Mind your language."

"Sorry, I must remember not to say 'shit' in front of my D-A-D."

"Funny, but you're not answering the question, or only with a platitude. That won't satisfy your mother. It doesn't satisfy me either."

She tried again, this time more hesitantly.

"The woman I gave your card to recently, she was crying in a Starbucks. I could have ignored her because that's what the other customers were doing. They all looked embarrassed, and some of them even seemed annoyed. She was making them feel bad when all they wanted was to stare at their screens on their lunch break, and I got that. They could even have justified their response to themselves by arguing that she wanted to be alone and by intruding they'd make her feel ashamed of a public show of grief, which might have some truth to it, if only a self-serving one.

"But if she'd wanted to be alone in her sadness, she wouldn't have been in a Starbucks. And if that was the case, what would it hurt to ask if there was anything I could do, even if it was only to listen? It turned out that her daughter had gone missing three years ago that day. She just vanished at the age of twenty-two. She—the daughter, I mean—had problems with depression and substance abuse, and was arrested a couple of times for soliciting. She got pregnant and had a son, who the mother helped look after. The daughter had gone AWOL a couple of times since the birth, for no more than a few days each time, after which she'd show up again, sadder and more bruised.

"But according to her mother, the girl had started to get her life back together in the months before she disappeared. She'd signed up for a beautician's course and was working nights in a bar to cover her fees. She loved being with her son and had met a guy who liked being with both of them. Then—poof!—she's gone. She doesn't come home one night from the bar, but because of her past, it may be that the police don't pull out all the stops at first—which is understandable, if not forgivable, though I accept it may just be the mother's impression of events.

"But many of the police she dealt with, from first to last, were men. And the mother, she's had her difficulties, too. She got married and divorced in the same year, before she and the groom could legally drink at the wedding, and has unwise tattoos, the sort that look like shit—sorry, my bad—when you're young and shittier—sorry again—as you get older."

"And she told you all this in one sitting?"

"I'm a good listener," said Sam.

"More than that, you must have asked the right questions."

"Are you saying I'm hired after all?"

"Not unless I took that bang to the head after all and didn't notice. Go on."

"So," Sam continued, "there's a particular law enforcement narrative from the start, and not one that favors mother and daughter. I'm not saying the police didn't do their job or don't care about the girl and what might have happened to her. What I am saying is that, from the beginning, mother and daughter were at a disadvantage. Now, after three years, her child's disappearance is officially a cold case. The police move on because they have to, and there's always a new kid to search for.

"Is this woman's daughter coming home? Probably not. Is she dead? I think so. If the mother calls you, can you do anything for her? Perhaps, even if it's only to help find a body for her to bury. But I want to be part of that 'perhaps.' In a world dominated by men who legislate, investigate, prosecute, and pass judgment, but who don't know what it's like to be a woman in that world, there's a place for a female enclave, a safe space, and I want to be part of that as well. Have I answered the question?"

I don't think I'd ever loved Sam more.

"Yes," I said, "you have. What's the girl's name?"

"Lynette Reynolds. Her mother is Julee Reynolds. And I didn't just give Julee your card, I also got her number."

She produced a notebook from her bag, tore a page, and passed it over.

"You can keep it," she said. "I've added her to the contacts on my phone."

"Look at you, all twenty-first century. I'm surprised you even own a pen and paper."

I folded the note and put it in my pocket.

"Thank you," said Sam.

"I haven't said that I'll talk to her."

"Not for that. I meant for not speaking about her daughter in the past tense."

"It's tied up with that same 'perhaps.' And what's *perhaps* but just another word for 'hope'?"

We prepared to leave. As I dropped some bills on the table to cover the tip, Sam asked: "Are you still seeing Sharon?"

Sam was one of the few people who referred to Macy by her first name. Macy had finally met Sam and me for dinner the last time Sam stayed over in Portland. They'd gotten along fine—not that I'd expected anything less of either. However, it was a relief.

"I am. And about what we've been discussing: she might be a good person to consult, either before or after you make your final decision. She might be a better role model, too."

"I'll bear that in mind," said Sam as we walked to the door. "Mom will come around, won't she?"

"It'll be hard for her, but there's a good chance she will, because she understands hope too."

I caught the two guys checking Sam out again.

"Eyes on the table, boys," I said, "unless you'd like them blackened."

They quit checking her out.

"Jeez, Dad," said Sam. "You know, you'll have to stop doing that at some point."

"I will," I replied. "As soon as you turn eighty, you're on your own."

CHAPTER

XLVI

A lull followed over the next thirty-six hours.

Zetta Nadeau declined to answer my calls, and I didn't see any point in scaling her fence just to argue with her some more, though I did leave a message on her phone. I reiterated that if she knew where Wyatt Riggins was hiding—and I believed she might—she ought to tell me, if only so I could attempt to reason with him. I thought again about the man named Seeley, who, if Louis's guess was correct, was working for Blas Urrea. I doubted Urrea employed cheap labor. Seeley had managed to connect Riggins and his stepbrother, and better yet, to find the latter, doorstep him, and search his property. Eventually, he'd locate Riggins too, even if he had to go through Zetta to get to him.

So we treaded water while the creatures we feared circled below.

I PASSED THE TIME by picking up some slack for Moxie before joining Sharon Macy for flatbread and wine at Novel Book Bar & Café, the new place on Congress. We spent the night together at her apartment, where I did my best to prove that age was not withering me. Over breakfast, I told her as much about the Riggins affair as I felt comfortable sharing, which meant excluding any mention of children and Mexico.

"I know you're leaving something out," she said.

"Only because I have no proof that it's true."

"Will it compromise me if you tell me? Will I be obliged to act on it?"

"It might, and you could."

She ate some grapefruit.

"This is difficult, isn't it? Balancing us and what we do, I mean."

"Too difficult?"

"Not for me, not yet. You?"

"No, but then I'm not police."

"You were, so at least you appreciate the predicament."

I stole a segment of grapefruit. Because I was on statins, I wasn't supposed to eat grapefruit. The joys of middle age.

"Sam wants to become a private investigator," I said.

"Are you surprised that she'd choose to follow in your footsteps?"

"A little."

"You're too hard on yourself. Are you going to work together, like in *Donato and Daughter*?"

"God, I hope not—and how do you even know about *Donato and Daughter*?"

"I saw the movie on cable. You don't resemble Charles Bronson, though. Then again, he did look like he'd been carved from ancient stone, so that may not be such a bad thing."

"It was a book before it was a movie."

"I hope the book was better."

"The book was good."

"How will Rachel feel about Sam wanting to be an investigator?"

"She may struggle with it."

"Is that an understatement?"

"Almost certainly," I said.

Macy finished her grapefruit.

"The Riggins tangle, the part you don't want to talk about, how bad could it get?"

"As bad as you can conceive."

"So what will you do?"

"I'll give it another day or two, but then I may hand it off to someone."

"Police?"

"Or the FBI," I said.

"When you're ready, call me. I may be able to smooth the way."

"Okay."

"Just try not to get me fired," said Macy.

"If you do get canned, we can go into business together."

"In that case, it would be Donato and Woman-Who-Looks-Young-Enough-to-Be-His-Daughter."

I patted her hand.

"That eye exam is long overdue."

Macy grimaced.

"It's on the list."

4

What lonely death am I to die / In this cold region?

John Keats, *Endymion*

CHAPTER

XLVII

Loudoun County was situated in the Commonwealth of Virginia, with a population of some 430,000 spread over more than five hundred square miles. Loudoun had always been prosperous, even before Dulles Airport opened near Sterling in 1962. After Dulles, the only way for Loudoun was up, with aviation, defense, and tech companies mushrooming along the border with Fairfax County, as well as, more recently, a slew of new data centers to serve Amazon's needs. The result had been a migration from the countryside to urban areas and the growth of planned communities to meet housing demand, making parts of Loudoun hardly more than commuter suburbs of Washington.

On the other hand, the farther west one went, the sparser the population, and out beyond the lower southern ridges of Catoctin Mountain, the natives regarded themselves as geographically distinct from the rest and looked askance at what they considered to be unrestricted development threatening their way of life. To that end, the region of Catoctin, with a heritage that was largely German and Quaker, had been rumbling about seceding from Loudoun since the end of the last century, the efforts of its citizens being stymied only by what they regarded as vested interests in Richmond, who had no desire to offend developers capable of facilitating jobs and enterprise and were not unknown to make generous campaign donations come election time.

All of which made the job of sheriff of Loudoun County, while undeniably a powerful position, a challenging exercise in diplomacy, though not one that was the recipient of universal acclaim. The sheriff's office had only recently avoided seeing the county switch from an elected system to a police department under an appointed chief. This would have made Loudoun one of the outliers among Virginia counties, traditionally the fiefdoms of sheriffs. The pushback against the move had been successful, not least because the transition would have cost more than $200 million at the most conservative estimate, tax dollars which many of the good folks of Loudoun preferred to see spent in other ways.

This would have been just so much background chatter were it not for the fact that, on this particular March evening, a pair of Loudoun County sheriff's deputies had arrived within minutes of each other at the entrance to a disused property off Chestnut Hill Lane. That property adjoined the homestead of the Dolfe clan, one of whose scions, Katie Dolfe, not only sat on the board of supervisors but was also among those most hostile to the current law enforcement dispensation. Katie, an attorney, no longer lived in the area, having long since decamped for fancier digs in Leesburg, but most of her kinfolk remained in the Dolfe heartland, and the extended family had no more affection for the sheriff and his department than their beloved Katie had.

The Dolfes' territory was off Route 9, bordered by Chestnut Hill Lane to the west, Berlin Turnpike to the east, and the Potomac to the north. The strip was long but narrow; the Dolfes had never tried to claim more territory than they could control. The landscape—all hollows, decaying trees, and falling rocks, spotted with trailers, junkyards, and private property signs—was a reminder of the persistence of an older, often poorer Virginia alongside the fancy wineries and farm shops, a relic of a time when people didn't advertise the presence of distilleries on their land. The Dolfes claimed descent from one of the First Families of Virginia, even though the connection was tenuous-verging-on-nonexistent, the general view being that, frankly, the Dolfes were clutching at fucking straws, genealogically speaking. Nobody with an ounce of sense cared to be caught up in that inbred FFV horseshit, the Commonwealth of Virginia having more than enough horseshit to be getting along with. On the other hand, there was no accounting for cussedness, delusion, and the deep-seated human desire to declare oneself better than one's neighbor. The Dolfes might have been hillbillies, but they were hillbillies with pretensions.

What the two Loudoun County deputies were trying to clarify, before they proceeded any further, was whether the Dolfes, blue-blooded or otherwise, had succeeded in purchasing the land on which the property stood. Given the nature of the 911 call received, the two deputies, who were both local, technically didn't require the Dolfes' permission to enter, but politics and common sense dictated that they step with care, even as representatives of the county. There was also the matter of a barrier erected across the road, consisting of a tree trunk on two X-shaped supports, attached to which was a sign reading PRIVATE ROAD—ARMED RESPONSE. If the Dolfes had posted it—and it was hard to conceive who else might be responsible—they weren't kidding about the armed-response part, and nobody wanted to get into an argument in the dark with a bunch of gun-toting Dolfes. Their ancestors had been partisans during the War of Northern Aggression, killing Union soldiers at will before melting back into the woods, and the years since had failed to dilute the Dolfes' fondness for a fight.

While they awaited the go-ahead, one of the deputies, Eric Wen, spoke with two young women standing by a red Dodge Challenger near the turnoff for the blocked road. In Wen's view, Dodge Challengers and Chargers were the chariots of choice for those who believed irony was an adjective, somewhere between coppery and steely. Loudoun County had a lot of Challengers and Chargers.

Wen was known locally as Chinese Eric, but didn't consider it worth making a fuss over. In his experience, incidents of racism—the whole "Chinese Eric" business apart, which might have counted—were encouragingly rare, helped by the fact that he was six feet tall, possessed a neck broader than his head, carried a big gun, and brooked no nonsense from anyone, regardless of race, color, or creed.

The two girls, Britney and Paris (*Heaven preserve us*, thought Wen), were both eighteen, and their breath smelled so strongly of mint that it made his eyes burn. Stashed somewhere nearby, no doubt, were some unopened cans of Coors or PBR, and possibly a half-drunk bottle of cheap vodka. He wasn't about to give them a hard time over it, not yet, and then only should they prove recalcitrant. He first wanted to hear what they had to say, and didn't want to frighten them more than was necessary in case it came back to haunt him in court.

"Tell me again what you saw," he said.

"A man, tied to a post in the middle of the barn," said Britney—or maybe Paris, because they both looked the same to Wen: white blondes with perfect teeth, puffed-up lips, and the kind of makeup applied by the pound. Britney—or Paris; anyway, the one doing most of the talking—struck him as the smarter of the two, though even a rock might have given her buddy a run for her money. The latter had dull eyes that weren't going to get any brighter as she grew older, just like her future. "He was naked, with blood all over him: his body, his mouth. And—"

"The flower," said the other one. "Tell him about the flower."

"Like, I was just going to. He had a flower stuck to his chest."

"A flower?"

"An orange one."

"Did you touch him?"

They both shook their heads, before the sharper one—Wen concluded it was definitely Britney—added: "We just went over to check. You know—"

"If he was, like, alive," said Paris.

"But he wasn't," said Britney.

"Nuh-uh," said Paris, shaking her head again. "He was dead for sure."

She started to cry again. She'd been crying when the deputies arrived but stopped soon after, distracted by all the activity. Britney had remained dry-eyed throughout, but she was paler than her friend, even under all the makeup. Wen guessed that Paris would make a drama out of it the next day. Britney would be more subdued, and what she had witnessed in the barn would stay with her for longer.

"Did you recognize him?" asked Wen.

"No," said Britney.

"He was all messed up," said Paris.

"Why were you in the barn to begin with?"

"We just wanted to hang out," said Paris, who had commenced a theatrical hiccuping hyperventilation.

"Somewhere that wasn't home," added Britney with feeling, and Wen made a mental note to check on Britney's domestic situation when he had the chance.

"You go up there alone?"

Hesitation gave them away. Wen let them see there was no point in lying.

"We were meeting someone," Britney admitted.

"A couple of someones," Paris added.

"Guys?"

They nodded.

"You want to give me their names."

They shook their heads.

"That wasn't a question," said Wen.

"Ah, hell," said Britney. "They didn't go inside the barn. They were slugging it, and by the time they got to us, we were already halfway to the car. We told them to make dust."

"Slugging it" was local parlance for dragging one's heels. Wen, being first-generation Virginian and raised by parents with aspirations—not to mention notions of superiority, if not quite on the FFV level—

preferred not to use colloquialisms. He was already enough of a disappointment to his mother and father, who had groomed him for entry into a profession they could be proud of. As a teenager, when he'd told his father over dinner one evening that he wanted to be an actor, his old man turned to the rest of the table and said, "It's spelled 'doctor.'" A life in the performing arts continued to remain out of Wen's reach for the present, but to get himself through the bad days, he liked to think of himself as an actor temporarily moonlighting as a sheriff's deputy.

"I'll still need their names," said Wen.

Britney exhaled hard enough to visibly deflate.

"Taylor Goff and Levi Hixon."

Bang goes your local pot source, thought Eric. Goff and Hixon, twenty-eight and twenty-nine respectively, were minor local trouble-makers inexorably mutating into something worse. Goff was reputed to like his girls young, and Hixon liked them even younger. Britney and Paris would have earned whatever they were due to consume in that barn—earned it, and then some.

"Did you see them walk away?" asked Wen.

"I wasn't looking back," said Britney. "I just wanted to put distance between us and that barn."

Whatever Britney might claim to the contrary, Eric doubted Goff and Hixon had exited without first taking a peek for themselves. He just hoped they hadn't screwed with the scene. Detectives would also need to ask them how often they convened their little social club up at that barn, in the faint hope that they might have noticed something odd in the preceding days. Wen didn't make Goff and Hixon for killers, though, or not like this. If they ever got around to doing the deed, they'd be smart enough not to abandon the body to be found by a pair of teenagers they were due to meet in a sex-for-joints arrangement.

"Are we in trouble?" asked Paris.

"We'll see," said Wen, keeping them dangling. He'd leave any further questions to the detectives, in case one or both of these girls knew more about the man in the barn than they were telling. "For now, I want you to get back in your car and stay warm."

"We'll need the keys to turn on the AC," said Britney. "The other cop took them from us."

"That's not going to happen," said Wen. He didn't want anyone panicking and deciding to lead law enforcement on a merry dance. If a call from Broadway or Hollywood didn't result from his work in local theater, Eric Wen hoped to make a career of policing by rising through the ranks, and nothing was better guaranteed to wreak havoc on those plans than having witnesses—or, worse, potential perpetrators, whatever his instincts to the contrary—flee the scene because a sheriff's deputy was foolish enough to leave them with keys in the ignition.

Wen headed over to his colleague, Inge Schuler. Her first name was actually Ingina, from High German, and Wen could only begin to imagine how much grief that had caused her during her school years. Some relief would have arrived with adolescence because Schuler was tall, blond, and striking, bordering on beautiful. Wen might have fallen a little in love with her were he not already in love with his Chinese-American fiancée, and were said fiancée not above burying him upside down in a hole in the woods if she suspected him of so much as contemplating relations with a rangy Germanic blonde, or even a short one.

"I don't like this," said Wen. "We ought to be up there already."

"Do you want to get shot by the Dolfes?" asked Schuler.

"I don't want to get shot by anyone."

"Neither do I, which is why we're still down here."

Schuler hadn't called the dispatcher but instead contacted the station commander at Western Loudoun directly, because some conversations were better off not conducted across open lines. He'd promised to get back to her in five minutes, but the best part of ten had elapsed by the time her cell phone rang again. Wen was beginning to fret about when the medics might get there, for fear the two witnesses were wrong about the guy being dead. Schuler put the call on speaker for Wen to hear, but kept the volume low so it didn't carry to the girls in the car.

"That's not Dolfe land, not yet," they were assured. "There's a holdup on the paperwork. The Realtor responsible for the sale says she doesn't know anything about any barrier or sign on the road, so you just take it down and get on up to that barn to secure the scene. Backup's on the way, with medics and detectives close behind."

Wen could already see the lights of the first of the approaching vehicles as the call was ongoing, which meant that someone would be available to watch Britney and Paris. The deputies might have to draw straws to pick who stayed behind and who got to enter territory that the Dolfes now regarded as theirs, with all the potential associated difficulties, but the more guns they had once they moved past the roadblock, the better. Perhaps they could handcuff the girls to the steering wheel and deal with the civil rights implications later.

"What if someone starts shooting?" Wen asked the station commander.

"You have my permission to shoot back, and possibly the sheriff's too, if he thinks you have any chance of hitting a Dolfe."

"Seriously."

"I am being serious. What it comes down to is, the Dolfes don't own that land and have no business pretending otherwise. Now do what you have to and find out whether there really is a body in that barn or someone is playing games with a scarecrow."

The station commander hung up. Wen stared at Schuler, and Schuler stared at Wen. They were then joined by a third deputy, Howard Negus, who had just arrived and commenced staring at both of them.

"What's the deal?" Negus asked. "You find out who the dead guy is yet?"

"Nope, but the Dolfes think they own the land that barn sits on," Schuler told him.

"The Dolfes think they run the whole county," said Negus, who was not Virginian by birth and walked with a heavy tread.

"You want to be the one to knock on their door and tell them they don't?" asked Wen.

"Fucking crackers," said Negus. "I have a shotgun in the car, if that helps."

"I think they prefer 'hillbillies,'" said Schuler. "Still, I'd get that shotgun if I were you."

"What about the kids?" asked Wen, indicating Britney and Paris. "Someone ought to stay with them."

"Pussy," said Schuler.

"It was worth a try. The question stands."

Schuler walked to the Dodge, where the two girls sat huddled in their coats, looking miserable. Schuler opened the passenger door and Paris whined: "You going to give us our keys back? It's cold."

Schuler held out a hand.

"No. Driver's licenses, both of you."

The girls surrendered their licenses, which Schuler photographed with her cell phone before returning them.

"You move from that car," said Schuler, "and I'll personally make you wish you'd died in the womb."

"What if whoever killed that guy is still around?" asked Britney, which Schuler had to admit wasn't an unreasonable question.

"All the more reason to stay in the car." Schuler pointed to the southeast, where more lights were scouring the night. "But they'll be with you in a matter of minutes."

"We could be dead in a matter of minutes," said Paris.

"Then you'll get fired," said Britney. "And sued."

"Jesus," said Schuler. "Fine, we'll stay until they get here."

They waited until a fourth car arrived, which disgorged a deputy named Eustace Ferris, known to his colleagues as Useless Ferris, even to his face. Useless Ferris's portrait could have been used to illustrate the word *timeserver* in a picture dictionary.

"You're the babysitter, Useless," Schuler told him, jerking a thumb at the Dodge.

"Better than being shot at by Dolfes," said Useless, but he was already speaking to Schuler's back. Wen followed after, leaving only Negus. He'd gone to his car to get the shotgun. In his experience, the sight of a big pump-action was useful for focusing attention and calming unrest.

"Don't you object to being called 'Useless'?" asked Negus.

"I've been hearing it since high school. I don't much notice anymore."

Negus turned away.

"I would," he said.

"That's because you're sensitive," said Useless, unwrapping a stick of gum. "If you get killed up there, I'll make sure it's mentioned in the eulogy."

CHAPTER

XLVIII

The three sheriff's deputies came within sight of the old horse barn, sheltered by a hill to the north. Although it hadn't received a coat of paint or preservative in many years, it remained structurally sound with an intact roof. A lot of these older barns were being renovated as houses, rental properties for tourists, wineries—and even wedding venues, Wen and his fiancée having visited a few. Unfortunately, it would be some time before anyone decided to exchange their vows in this one if the girls were telling the truth about what they'd discovered.

Beside Wen, Schuler gazed to the west, and the boundary with the Dolfe homestead.

"What is it?" asked Negus.

"Men's voices, but still a ways off."

"Might not be anything to do with us. It's not as if we sent up a flare."

"The Dolfes won't need an invitation. They've been in Loudoun so long they can probably hear the grass grow."

"Fuck them if they do come," said Negus. "We're law enforcement investigating a probable homicide."

"I'm with you on most of that," said Schuler, "but I'll let you be the one to tell them."

Wen raised a hand, urging silence. The barn had a pair of sliding doors on its southern side. These were closed, but a side door was partway open. While the girls had only seen what appeared to be a dead man, it didn't mean that whoever was responsible for making him that way was absent from the vicinity. The deputies padded slowly toward the door, Wen and Schuler from the west, Negus from the east, pausing only to allow Schuler to conduct a quick circuit of the building to check the rear. They kept their distance from the sides of the barn and tried to make the least noise possible. While the timbers looked solid, a shotgun or rifle could blow a hole right through them, along with anyone who happened to be standing on the other side at the time. Once they were in position, Wen identified himself as an armed sheriff's deputy and instructed anyone inside to make themselves known and lie down on the floor with their arms outstretched. All he received in return was silence.

Wen closed his eyes and took a deep breath. His palms were sweating and his heart was beating very fast. This was how men got themselves shot: by standing in a doorway, silhouetted against the stars. Eric Wen very much did not want to be killed that way. In fact, he didn't want to be killed at all.

Wen used the barrel of his gun to push the door open wider. He tensed for the sound of firing, but none came.

"Well, shit," he said.

Wen ignited the flashlight on the underside of the gun barrel and made his move.

CHAPTER

XLIX

Lyman Bouchard had inherited the Old Hatch bar in the southwest of Loudoun County from his father, who was also named Lyman. That Lyman had previously taken over the running of the Old Hatch from *his* father, another Lyman. In the ordinary course of events, they would, respectively, have been Lyman Bouchard III, Lyman Bouchard II, and just plain Lyman Bouchard, but the Bouchard family had always distrusted nominative numerals, even at the cost of confusion, so instead there had been Lyman, Lyman Jr.—also known as Young Lyman—and Little Lyman, the Old Hatch's current incumbent, who weighed enough to cause anyone forced to share an elevator with him to fret for the duration of the ride.

The Old Hatch, perhaps unsurprisingly, was referred to by regulars as the Nuthatch, or occasionally the Old Nuthatch. Like all local bars, it had its share of eccentrics and deadbeats, but fewer than its nickname might have signaled because Little Lyman didn't hold with eccentricity and had even less time for deadbeats. As far as he was concerned, only rich people could afford to be eccentric. Anyone else displaying signs of unusual behavior was just crazy. Deadbeats, meanwhile, were irritants who struggled to rustle up the price of a couple of bottles of Bud Light, neglected their children, and regularly felt compelled to raise the possibility of one on the house only to complain when they were rebuffed.

The Old Hatch was not unprepossessing. It was clean and well-run, and even during the worst times, when other bars and restaurants were raising their prices, Little Lyman found ways to make food and drink affordable for all, even deadbeats. Mostly, he achieved this by barely keeping his head above water, but thankfully, his needs were few. He was a single man and his own boss. He owned the premises and lived in a trailer behind the bar. The Old Hatch was his life and gave purpose to his existence. Without it, he would have been working on a production line, greeting shoppers at the door of the Walmart, or—and this he knew, even if he would never have admitted it aloud—occupying a regular seat in a bar much like the Old Hatch and asking for one on the house the day before his unemployment or disability check came due. Perhaps this was why Little Lyman was ambivalent about the Old Hatch's deadbeats: they were the ghosts at his feast, the shadows that haunted him.

Currently, the Old Hatch was nearly empty, apart from an older couple, the Swishers, finishing up a basket of chicken tenders and a game of Chutes and Ladders that had been part of the bar furniture for so long that the faces of the kids on the board were greasy blurs; a pair of young strays in a deuce by the window, who were either running from trouble or soon to run into it; and a small man in a midnight-blue tweed suit seated at the end of the bar, the suit having seen better days and its wearer possessed of a rueful demeanor signaling that he, too, had seen better, and was resigned to seeing worse. His legs were so short that the tips of his shoes barely touched the footrest, his arms were strangely spindly, and his torso was curiously overdeveloped so that he gave the impression of having been assembled from the discarded parts of others, like the last human in line on the sixth day when the Lord was letting the clock run down. Still, Little Lyman had to admit that the man was weirdly compelling, and his eyes flickered with the fires of an intelligence that would not easily be smothered.

Like many bartenders, Little Lyman was an observant human being and an astute judge of character—bad judges of character made poor businessmen and poorer bar owners—but for the life of him, he couldn't get a handle on the stranger. Yes, his suit was tired, its color faded in parts, but it was clean and would once have constituted an expensive purchase. His reddish-brown shoes were old, comfortable, and well-polished, with fresh rubber soles and heels. His white shirt was ironed and bore no stains, while the red-and-black tie was silk, anchored by a gold stud shaped like an eye, with a green jewel at its core that might have been an emerald.

The man was sipping top-shelf whiskey—the Old Hatch's sole bottle of Redbreast—and reading a copy of *The Washington Post* through a brass-handled magnifying glass. He had barely spoken except to order a drink and comment on the change in the weather, and his scent was Pinaud-Clubman, familiar to Little Lyman from the barber shops of his youth. He was clean-shaven, his skin very smooth apart from a vertical striation on each cheek, the marks so deep they might have been incised by a blade. When he'd taken his first sip of the whiskey, Little Lyman half expected to see some of the alcohol pour from those slashes and dribble down the stranger's collar. His hair was gray-blond, kept long, and combed back from his forehead to tickle the nape of his neck. His eyes were the same green as the jewel in his tie stud; when he turned his gaze on Little Lyman, the latter felt observed by three orbs instead of two. At regular intervals, the man took time out from his newspaper to monitor what was happening around him, and the corners of his downturned mouth would drop deeper, as though what he saw had conspired to further disappoint an already disenchanted soul.

The Swishers concluded their game, settled their bill, and took off into the night. The strays in the deuce tossed a coin to decide if they'd stay for one more. It came up tails and they departed, leaving only Little Lyman and the stranger. By now it was nearly 10 p.m., and while the Old Hatch was known to stay open as late as midnight, it might also close while there was still light in the sky if business was slow. On the other hand, Little Lyman didn't have a whole lot to do once he'd locked up, given the floor and tables a cursory clean, and counted the takings—not that the last was going to occupy much of his time, not tonight and not last night either, or the one before. The pandemic had loused up the Old Hatch, just as it loused up so many businesses, and custom had never returned to its former level. But change of habit alone wasn't enough to account for the falloff at the Old Hatch, because Little Lyman had counted the dead during the pandemic. He still couldn't look at some of the tables or stools without remembering the people who once occupied them, and who died straining for breath with their chests on fire and no family to keep them company at the last. One of these was a woman, Helena, with whom Little Lyman had occasionally shared a bed when they were both lonely enough, so he didn't hold with vaccine scares, Fauci-blaming, or any collective amnesia about the awfulness of what had occurred, and anyone who did could shut up or find someplace else to drink.

Tonight, Little Lyman wasn't in the mood for staring at the walls of his trailer, brooding on Helena and wondering if this was as good as life would get for him. He might as well leave the lights on here, the TV playing soundlessly in the corner, and permit the little man in the tweed suit to finish reading his paper. Who knew, he might even have another Redbreast for the road and tip commensurately.

Little Lyman strolled to the end of the bar, where a window looked out on the lot. He counted three passing cars in as many minutes. The rest of the time, Little Lyman stared only at his reflection. He was not an especially good-looking man, but he was also not an unkind one, and he was a business owner, which counted for something in his community. A few women, like Helena, had circled him over the years, but he'd never fallen hard enough for any of them to take the relationship to the next level. He might have been holding out for something better, because none of them was any more of a looker than he was, and a man had to be optimistic. Now Little Lyman had reached a stage in life where the choice was to keep lying to himself for the rest of his days, or stop lying and make the most of them. Love didn't seem set to find him anytime soon, or lust either, but contentment, or some semblance of it, still might. If it hadn't been for the virus, Helena might have become the source of it. Then again, maybe not. The dead were simpler to idealize than the living.

He heard a rustling from behind and turned to see Mr. Blue Tweed neatly folding his *Post* before draining the last of his whiskey. Little Lyman wandered back to stand before him.

"One more for the road?" he asked.

Blue Tweed checked his pocket watch. It was brass, not gold, and dangled from a chain threaded through a buttonhole in his vest.

"Where does the time go?" His voice held the same whispery rustle as the action of folding the newspaper. Had he not seen Blue Tweed's lips move, Little Lyman might have been convinced that *The Washington Post* had itself posed the question.

"Funny," said Little Lyman, "I was thinking the same."

Blue Tweed glanced around the bar, though the mirror before him would have confirmed that he was now the sole customer.

"I wouldn't want to inconvenience you."

"I got nothing else to do," said Little Lyman. "If you're happy, I'm happy."

"And I'm not happy until you're not happy."

Little Lyman frowned.

"The man who taught me my trade used to say that," continued Blue Tweed. "He called it the Bad Salesman's Mantra. You know, I think I will take a last glass."

"Same?"

"Unless you got better."

"Only worse."

"The same it is, then."

Little Lyman heard the sound of the Swishers' old F-150 starting up. It had taken them a while to leave the parking lot. Might be they'd been arguing about the game of Chutes and Ladders, for they took their amusements seriously. The F-150 dated from 1976 and counted as a classic. Its body and interior could have done with some work, but there was nothing wrong with the engine. Jack Swisher kept its workings in such fine order that the Ford looked bound to outlive its owners, who were good people but staring down the barrel of eighty. Little Lyman would miss them when they were gone. Like the F-150, they weren't making models like the Swishers anymore.

CHAPTER

L

The beam of Eric Wen's flashlight was fixed on a body tied to a stanchion with baling wire. Just as the girls had described, the man was naked, with orange flowers pinned to his chest like a corsage. The girls had been wrong about that much; it wasn't one bloom but three or four.

He was white, although the only way to tell the color of his skin was from the lower thighs down because the rest of him was dark with blood. If he wasn't dead, he would be wishing he was, but Wen reckoned him for long gone. However, Wen had to be sure, so he edged into the barn and went to the right, Schuler following and moving to the left, her pistol raised, the flashlight in a fist grip alongside it, her left arm acting as support for the gun, just as they'd been taught. Above them was a half loft lacking an access ladder, so it was doubtful anyone was up there lying in wait, not unless they could levitate. The barn appeared unoccupied, one probable decedent excepted, but neither of the deputies was taking any chances.

Wen approached the man but didn't lower his gun. It was easier to keep it where it was—possibly wiser too, because the appalling damage inflicted on the victim was becoming visible: broken fingers and toes; one ear, the left, half-severed, and the right eye gouged from its socket;

exposed flesh on the thighs and the abdomen, where skin had been excised; and the groin—

Wen shifted his gaze upward. He'd seen enough. Aided by Schuler's flashlight, he prepared to check for a pulse he knew he wouldn't find.

"Is he dead?"

The sound of Negus's voice breaking the silence caused Wen's feet to almost leave the ground from shock.

"Damn," he said, "you cost me a year of my life."

"Well, is he?"

For form's sake, Wen slipped a blue plastic glove onto his right hand and touched his fingers to the man's neck, but he might as well have asked him to turn a somersault for all the chance there was of a sign of life. Wen glanced at the tips of the glove and saw no trace of blood. Whatever was on the victim had dried, which meant he'd been dead awhile. His injuries made it hard to tell with any degree of accuracy, but Wen surmised that, from the swelling and the smell, it might be as much as forty-eight hours.

"I suppose he could be deader," said Wen, "but it's hard to see how. Best call it in, tell them what we've found."

Negus nodded and went back outside.

"He wasn't killed here," said Schuler, "that's for sure." She let her flashlight play over the dirt floor of the barn. "There's hardly any blood beyond what's on him."

Wen squinted at the spray of flowers on the man's chest.

"Bring that flashlight closer," he said. "Shine it here."

Schuler slowly played the beam on and around the blooms.

"What is that, bougainvillea?" she asked.

"Lord, I don't know." Wen peered behind the flower. "It looks like it's concealing a wound—a big one. Christ, he's been sliced down the middle."

"His cheeks are swollen," said Schuler. "He's got something in his mouth. At first I thought it was his tongue protruding, but that's no tongue."

Schuler directed the flashlight to the lump of flesh between his lips. Wen regarded it for a moment.

"No," he said, "I believe that came from lower down."

Which was when Negus reappeared at the barn door.

"We've got company," he said. "It's the Dolfes."

CHAPTER LI

Harriet Swisher waited until Little Lyman's place had receded from view before speaking.

"Hul, you think that was one of the people we was warned against," she asked, "the ones the Mexican sent?"

"Might be," Hul replied. "Whoever he is, he doesn't belong around here, that's for sure."

"Looked like he belonged nowhere but the circus."

"He did smell like a carny," said Hul, "all tricksy. A low man."

"Ought we to sound the alarm?"

"Let's not get carried away. We don't want to go raising a clamor for no good reason and come off as frightened old fools."

Hul Swisher reversed into a turnoff so the truck was facing the road before he killed the lights. The lot held only three vehicles when they'd emerged from the Old Hatch: the Swishers' truck, Little Lyman's Honda Accord, and a black Mercury Marauder so well-preserved that it must have spent most of its life under a tarp. The only clue to its owner was a box of Bibles on the rear seat. The Marauder had to belong to the little freak in the tweed suit. As for the Bibles, they just made the Swishers suspect him even more. It wasn't that they weren't religious—the Swishers were Christians of a loose kind, which meant they prayed only when they were in trouble—but anyone who possessed more than one Bible wasn't in the religion business, just the sales one.

Four cars came by from the direction of town over the next fifteen minutes, but none was the Marauder. Hul, at least, started to relax.

"No sign of him," said Hul. "He stayed where he was or left for elsewhere. Whatever he's here for, it's not us."

His wife scowled.

"You don't think that, if it was us he was after, he wouldn't take the time to find out where we lived or be smart enough not to come racing out on our heels?"

"If he knew where we lived, why would he be watching us at a bar?"

Which was a fair point, Harriet had to admit. Still, the man made her agitated. He resembled a figure that had stepped out of someone's bad dream.

"Let's go home," she said, "but keep an eye on what's behind."

Hul did, all the way, and detected no signs of pursuit or surveillance. To make sure, he didn't immediately pull up in front of the house but made a circuit of a mile. No unfamiliar cars were parked nearby, and certainly not the Marauder. Hul's phone, which was linked to the home alarm, displayed no alerts.

"I believe we're clear," he told his wife.

"For now. But they're out there, you can count on it. That Bern fella, he knows his beans."

"Just because they're seeking doesn't mean they'll find."

Harriet patted her husband's liver-spotted right hand.

"I hope so," she said. "If they do, it'll go hard on us."

Beside her, Hul's eyes closed briefly. It was, she thought, a wonder he'd managed to get them home without falling asleep at the wheel, given how much sedative she'd slipped into his last bourbon, but he always drove, and she didn't want to make him suspicious. With luck, he'd be safely asleep within the hour, leaving her to do what Devin Vaughn had instructed.

Harriet opened the car door and stepped into the cool of the night.

"Come on," she said. "Let's get you to bed."

CHAPTER LII

Deputies Wen, Schuler, and Negus were lined up in front of the barn. Facing them was a quartet of Dolfes, three men and one woman, with more almost certainly on the way because the Dolfes came in packs: one for all and all for one, like hillbilly musketeers. Unfortunately, right now this felt to Wen less like a scene from Dumas and more like the gunfight at the O.K. Corral. He didn't think the Dolfes would be foolish enough to use the weapons they carried, not without provocation—but with them, it didn't take much incitement.

Yet the Dolfes were not ignorant. Hard, yes, and intolerant of outsiders, but their children all finished high school, and some even progressed to college. Wen had only once been up to the big house, which was still home to the patriarch, Donald Ray, and was surprised to find one room fitted out as a library, complete with a ladder on rails. Elsewhere, he'd spotted statuary, antique vases, and a plethora of Native American artifacts, while the walls were adorned not only with a gallery of Dolfes, living and dead, but also with more general subjects, including a smattering by Virginia artists whom Wen recognized, among them a dog study by Thomas Verner Moore White and a pair of landscapes by Horace Day.

But balanced against this perhaps unanticipated display of artistic appreciation was that family history of violence, proven or suspected.

The three deputies were currently facing Donnie Ray's eldest son, Roland, his daughter Clementine, or Clemmie, and two of his nephews, Joe Dunn and Andy, the latter more commonly known as "Stomper" after a fondness for using the heel of his boot in fights. The three men were armed with pistols. Clemmie carried a Winchester rifle. For the moment, the pistols remained holstered, and Clemmie's rifle was slung on her shoulder. All four Dolfes were in their thirties, Roland and Clemmie being products of Donnie Ray's second marriage, his first having ended childless after that wife, Missy, died in a stable fire that had left Donnie Ray with lifelong scars, physical and psychological.

"You're trespassing, officers," said Clemmie. "Unless you have a warrant, in which case you ought to have served it before entering our property."

Although Clemmie was younger than Roland, the latter routinely deferred to her, as did the rest of the Dolfe family, Donnie Ray excepted, and even he paid attention when she spoke. Clemmie wasn't married and had so far shown no urge to alter that status. If she was wedded to anything, it was to the family and their land.

"This isn't your property," said Wen.

"As good as," said Roland.

"'Good as' cuts no ice with the law," said Negus.

Wen noticed that Negus had tucked his thumbs into his belt, his fingers forming a V around the bulge of his crotch. At least it would give Clemmie something to aim at.

"Stow it, Howie," said Clemmie. "What you know about the law could be shat out on a square of toilet paper. Even your fucking uniform doesn't fit right."

Negus opened his mouth to respond, but couldn't come up with anything better than "Fuck you too, Clemmie," before adding, "And it does so fit."

"This isn't getting us anywhere," said Wen. "Whatever claim you have on this land hasn't been signed off on, and now it's a crime scene."

"What kind of crime scene?" asked Stomper. His eyes were too big for his face, giving him the appearance of one constantly surprised by life, though Stomper would have been surprised by a word with more than two syllables. It was a miracle he hadn't yet killed anyone, even if Wen was aware of one victim who'd been left mildly brain-damaged after one of Stomper's assaults.

Schuler spoke for the first time.

"You know anything about what's in that barn, Clemmie?"

"Not unless you tell me, or let me see for myself."

Wen wasn't about to let Clemmie Dolfe or anyone else from her clan take a look at what was in there, not unless he fancied a career handing out parking tickets in purgatory. But as before, he doubted that anyone in the Dolfe brood—even down to some of the extended family who didn't function at the higher intellectual level of Clemmie or Donnie Ray—would be fool enough to kill a man in one place before taking him to another property next to their own, a property to which they were, additionally, laying claim. He decided to test the waters.

"Someone left a body in there," he said.

Stomper's eyes couldn't have grown any larger than they already were, but Clemmie's certainly did.

"Whose body?" she asked.

"We don't know yet," Wen replied, "but just a few moments ago you were laying claim to this acreage, which presumably includes the barn as well. I think you and your kin are going to be answering some questions when the detectives arrive, because let me tell you, Clemmie, that boy in there went out screaming."

Clemmie considered this.

"I have to make a call," she said.

It wasn't as though Wen could stop her, so he just shrugged.

Under similar circumstances, a lot of folk would have contacted their lawyer. Clemmie Dolfe called her father.

CHAPTER LIII

Donnie Ray Dolfe arrived at the barn at the same time as the deputy medical examiner from the Northern District office in Manassas. It turned out the DME had been staying over at a motel in Leesburg after a conference and so was barely a hop, skip, and a jump from the body. She nodded to Donnie Ray as they exited their vehicles together, the law in Virginia not being unacquainted with him, and he fell in step with her. Nobody tried to prevent Donnie Ray from approaching the barn. Frankly, some actions just weren't worth the effort, and his children and nephews, who were more likely to kick off, were congregated at a safe distance, with Schuler keeping an eye on them. If any more Dolfes appeared, Wen thought, it would resemble a clan reunion.

Two detectives had reached the scene before Donnie Ray and the DME, and they were currently in the barn. Wen knocked on the door, which was now nearly closed to discourage the lookie-loos among the Dolfes.

"Medical examiner's here," he said. "And Donnie Ray."

Hicks, the more senior of the two detectives, turned to the younger, Elkins.

"You stick with the medical examiner," she said. "I'll take a moment with Donnie Ray."

"I won't fight you for the pleasure," said Elkins.

They exited together, Elkins making a beeline for the deputy ME and Hicks moving to block Donnie Ray, indicating that Wen should join her. Since Wen had briefed the detectives on everything that had happened so far, he knew as much as anyone on the scene and would, therefore, be useful to have at hand.

Although he was nearing eighty, Donnie Ray Dolfe remained an imposing figure. Age might have diminished him, but there'd been a lot of Donnie Ray to start with, so he still had a couple of inches and more than a few pounds on Hicks. He had been handsome once, and the ghost of it still haunted his features, and only some disfigurement below his left ear hinted at the damage the fire had done to the rest of him.

Donnie Ray didn't look displeased to see Hicks. She might have been Black, female, and partly responsible for putting some of his people behind bars over the previous decade, but Donnie Ray wasn't a racist, respected women, and didn't take legal reverses personally. The Dolfes had their issues with the sheriff's office, but Donnie Ray regarded Hicks as someone who played the game fair and square. Hicks, in turn, respected Donnie Ray, but respecting wasn't the same as liking.

The Dolfes—or their agents, at any rate—were among those pressing legislators to establish a legal marijuana market in the state and were making progress. In the meantime, they continued to grow cannabis deep in their rural fastnesses, supplementing the crop with narcotics purchased from elsewhere, including cocaine and fentanyl. Their major supplier, according to the latest DEA briefings and local scuttlebutt, was Devin Vaughn, a local boy made good who was happy to help his own, for a price. The fentanyl-and-cocaine angle had caused Hicks to sour some on Donnie Ray, even if she suspected Clemmie had pushed her old man in that direction.

"Detective," said Donnie Ray, "my daughter tells me you found a body."

By now Clemmie had joined her father, but didn't interrupt.

"On land your daughter is claiming for the Dolfes," said Hicks. "If that's the case, it would complicate matters."

"My daughter may be mistaken," said Donnie Ray, "if only on an issue of detail. We're in the process of purchasing this land, but for the present, it isn't ours. We have no issue with how it was entered or why. It's none of our concern, not on that level, so it's nothing to get pressed about."

"Well," said Hicks, "ain't that a relief for all?"

She wasn't being entirely sarcastic, either. Donnie Ray was canny. No one had ever denied it. He was already distancing the family from his daughter's earlier claim while making it clear to Hicks that he was retaining an interest in whatever had occurred or might yet unfold as a consequence. In other words, he wouldn't make life difficult for the investigators so long as he was kept in the loop.

"You have a name for whoever's in there?" Donnie Ray asked.

"Not so far, but we will soon enough. It's hard for a body to remain anonymous in this day and age."

"You think I could take a look without stepping inside? Might be I'll recognize the face."

Hicks didn't immediately reply. Given that at least two kids had already seen the corpse and perhaps snapped a few images with their phones—she'd have to set Schuler on it to ensure they weren't circulated on social media—it wasn't as though the fact of its existence was a state secret. She couldn't have Donnie Ray traipsing around the barn, but she didn't see the harm in letting him view the body from a distance. It might even prove advantageous.

"How about you and Clemmie both ease up to the door?" said Hicks, finally. "We have some lights on the decedent, which should help. A note of warning: Whoever killed him took their time, and his features are distorted. If either of you are going to be sick, be sure to do it in the bushes. I don't want my people stepping in it."

Clemmie looked as though she might have preferred had the offer not been made, but she wouldn't show weakness in front of her father or Hicks. Donnie Ray's features, by contrast, were impassive.

Hicks led them to the barn and asked Wen to use his frame to block the gap when the door was opened wider, so only Donnie Ray and Clemmie would be able to see inside. The deputy medical examiner was shining a flashlight on the wound to the chest, and the area was further lit by a couple of additional flashlights set on their bases with the bulbs exposed, rendering the corpse visible and potentially identifiable, even from a distance. But Hicks wasn't looking at the corpse. She was watching Donnie Ray and Clemmie.

"My God," said Donnie Ray. Clemmie just put her hand to her mouth.

"Well?" asked Hicks.

Donnie Ray shook his head. A few seconds later, Clemmie followed suit. She then headed directly for a pile of stones dug from the earth years before and assembled into a cairn, but she didn't puke, or not that Hicks noticed.

"It was worth a try," said Hicks, "but we'll be knocking on doors over the next twenty-four hours. I know we can rely on the cooperation of you and your family. Right, Donnie Ray?"

"We'll answer any questions we can," he said. "Until then, we'd best let you get on with your job."

He gestured to the three Dolfe men, indicating that they should follow him off the land. Like Clemmie, all were now unarmed, Hicks, on arrival, having advised them to store their weapons. Clemmie, Hicks noted, was already walking ahead of the rest. She gave the impression of wanting to vacate the property as quickly as possible.

Elkins joined Hicks.

"We going to start selling tickets next?" he asked.

"Donnie Ray offered," said Hicks, "in case he could help with the identification."

"That kind of public spiritedness is out of character for him."

"We're all God's children."

"Even Donnie Ray?"

"Him, maybe not so much. He said he didn't recognize the victim."

"And Clemmie?"

"She didn't say anything. She didn't have to."

Elkins squinted at Hicks.

"You saying she knew who he was?"

"Oh yeah," said Hicks, as the Dolfes disappeared from view. "And if Clemmie knows, you can be sure Donnie Ray does too."

CHAPTER LIV

Blue Tweed had gone to the restroom, spending so long in there that Little Lyman began to worry he might have collapsed—that, or Little Lyman would have let in a lot of fresh air later, and possibly go to work on the bowl with a brush and some bleach.

"You okay?" Little Lyman asked when his sole customer eventually returned.

"Things don't move as easy as they once did," came the reply. "I could write a thesis on the texture of stall doors."

Little Lyman thought he might have to tackle the restroom after all. He opened the bottle of Redbreast and kept his hand heavy.

"You'll go broke pouring so freely."

"I got low overheads," said Little Lyman, "and lower expectations."

"Then life will struggle to disappoint you."

"I got to say, it's doing its damnedest anyway."

Blue Tweed inclined his glass toward the Redbreast.

"Care to have one on me?"

"It's kind of you, but I'll stick to coffee." Little Lyman refilled his mug from the last of the pot. "A lesson I learned from my father, who learned it from his: Never drink in your own bar, like that mantra you shared earlier."

"The Bad Salesman. But that was advice not to be followed."

"That your line, selling?"

"Isn't it everyone's, in some form?"

"I suppose so," said Little Lyman. "Unfortunate if nobody wants what you have to sell, though."

"A good salesman can make you buy what you don't need. A *very* good salesman will make you feel that you always needed it but never realized until he came along to point out the hole its absence had left in your life. But I don't want to sell folk stuff they don't need. There's too much of that already, and it leaves a sour taste in the mouth. I want everyone involved to walk away happy from the deal. Hence, the Bad Salesman's Mantra."

"And you're not one of the bad salesmen?"

"I aspire not to be." He took a sip of whiskey. "I notice you haven't asked me what it is that I sell."

Little Lyman hadn't asked him his name either. In his experience, men who wanted you to know their name shared it. Men who didn't want you to know wouldn't offer, and wouldn't thank you for inquiring either. Here, Little Lyman gathered, was a member of the second tribe.

"Because I don't want you to waste your time," said Little Lyman, "or mine. Whatever it is, I don't want it, and even if I did want it, I doubt I could afford it. And if I could afford it, I'd be someplace else right now."

"Really? You wouldn't be here?" Blue Tweed made the Old Hatch sound like a veritable nirvana, somewhere only a halfwit would abandon.

Little Lyman ruminated on the question. There was even a literal element to the act, because it was his habit to nibble at the inside of his right cheek when a subject required contemplation, lending him the aspect of a perturbed herbivore.

"I'd still own the bar," he declared at last, "or *a* bar, but I'd have someone else doing the heavy lifting. Spring and fall, I'd be planning a vacation, just some time to catch my breath. Odds-on, I'd already be gone by now, and you'd be talking to an underling instead of me."

"Florida?"

Little Lyman shook his head.

"I don't care for Florida. It's full of too many of the people I'd be going on vacation to avoid. No, I'd visit Europe. My grandfather, he fought in Italy during the war and liked it—the country, I mean, not the fighting. He always meant to go back and see how he felt about it when he didn't have to kill anyone."

"Lucky I'm not selling Boca timeshares, then," said the man.

"I guess it is," said Little Lyman. He polished some glasses that didn't require polishing. Blue Tweed studied his whiskey like one who had posed the fates a question and anticipated the response to be disclosed in amber.

"I sell Bibles," said the man, "among other items, generally of a religious nature"—though Little Lyman had studiously continued not to ask.

Little Lyman hadn't been aware that selling Bibles was even an occupation anymore. As far as he could tell, people were prepared to give away the word of God for nothing. Every second Saturday, a handful of evangelicals would gather in Leesburg, holding signs proclaiming the love of Jesus and handing out texts to anyone prepared to share their email details. If someone was of a mind to, they could give a fake email address and walk away with a shiny copy of the New Testament, though Little Lyman didn't imagine God would approve of someone lying and accepting the New Testament in the same breath, seeing as how it cut against the grain of the whole transaction. If they were happy to listen to the whole spiel, and drop ten dollars as a sign of goodwill, they could take home a full bells-and-whistles set containing the Old Testament alongside the New, with a cheap tin cross on a ribbon that doubled as a bookmark, the ribbon-bookmark treatment not extending to give-aways.

Failing that, assuming you weren't the sociable, giving, or lying type, you could wait for the opportunity to spend a night in a hotel and depart with a Gideon Bible, if only by ignoring the injunction to leave it where you'd found it and call the Gideons if you wanted a copy of your own. Little Lyman reflected that, in a curious sense, selling Bibles was a little like dealing in anything other than the most specialized of pornography in the internet age: no need to pay hard cash for something when it was available for free at the push of a button, even if the porn providers had finally cottoned on to this and now cut most of the movies before the money shot, or so Little Lyman had been reliably informed by a friend.

Despite himself, Little Lyman was intrigued by the man's vocation. Even as he spoke, he wondered if this was part of the pitch, and by being drawn in, he was destined to conclude the evening by parting with some of his hard-earned money in return for a doorstop with a fake leather cover and colored endpapers.

"That must be a tough way to earn a living," said Little Lyman, "what with the Gideons and their like undercutting you at every turn."

"The Gideons," Blue Tweed scoffed, as though Little Lyman had posited alien instead of human involvement in the distribution of Bibles. "Has anyone ever met a Gideon? I sure haven't, not in all my years. Me, I like to be able to see the man who's selling me something. I want to look him in the eye and question him about his product. I want to touch it, smell it, and while I do that, I'm watching him. It's a game, and if two aren't playing, one is being played. And you don't want to be played, not when lucre is involved. It sets a bad precedent for buyer and seller because the buyer will be unsatisfied and the salesman corrupted. Whatever happens, whether I make a sale or not, I leave with my principles intact."

He took another mouthful of whiskey, holding it for a while before swallowing.

"This nectar is making me garrulous," he said. "Next, I'll be giving you something for nothing, lessons in selling apart."

"The conversation's enough."

"Could be that you're a better salesman than I am. After all, I came in for a well bourbon and ended up drinking Irish whiskey from the top shelf. I stay here long enough and you'll run me out broke."

"You're forgetting the heavy pour," said Little Lyman.

"Ah, but it wasn't too heavy, just heavy enough. Too heavy, and I'd have no cause to order another should the mood strike. Too light, and I'd feel cheated. You hit it just on the nailhead."

"I don't believe I put that much thought into the matter."

"You didn't have to because it came naturally. If it didn't, someone else would be in possession of your premises, and you'd be an employee instead of the proprietor. We have that in common. We're both our own bosses."

"You don't work for a company?"

"I used to. I started out with Southwestern Com. You know them?"

The Southwestern Company had been in the door-to-door sales business since the nineteenth century, beginning with religious tracts before progressing to cookbooks, home medical reference volumes, and dictionaries.

"Sure I do," said Little Lyman. "My momma was from Nashville. She said you guys were the bane of her life, and her momma's too. 'Healthy, happy, terrific,' right?"

Blue Tweed chuckled. "The Southwestern slogan, or good as. Start at eight in the morning, work until nine or ten at night. Thirty house calls a day minimum and no more than twenty minutes with each customer. If they hadn't bitten by then, they weren't ever going to. I'd talk softly, so they had to lean in close to hear me. On hot days, I'd arrive looking fit to faint and ask for a glass of water. Most would invite me in for a minute to catch my breath, which was when I knew I was halfway home. I'd work six weeks during the summer, eight at a push, and make enough to cover me for the year, then spend the next ten months preparing for the following summer. It was my version of Bible study."

"But you don't work for the company any longer?"

"Selling books, even the Good Book, just got harder and harder.

People don't have as much regard for the written word these days. They don't see the reason for it, don't value it, not like previous generations. So I found other ways to make ends meet, but I couldn't quite give up on selling—or books, for that matter. I take pleasure in them, so I retain a range of Bibles and religious material in the car, and one or two on my person as well, just to keep my hand in. And you know what the funny thing is?"

Little Lyman replied that he did not.

"I'm not sure I even believe in God," said Blue Tweed, "or not the God of the Bible—which is not to say that the book doesn't contain truths, because it does, and a man could do a lot worse than live by the New Testament's edicts. But as for the rest, it means about as much to me as a fairy tale."

Little Lyman frowned.

"So why should anyone buy a Bible from you if you're selling something you don't much believe in?"

"But I *am* selling something I believe in, something that has value. I'm selling the artifact of the book."

As he answered, Blue Tweed reached into a pocket and produced a black copy of the New Testament, about the size of his hand. The page edges were gold, the spine ribbed. It was in good condition while betraying its age, a volume that had seen use but not abuse. The man laid it carefully on the counter beside his glass.

"This dates from 1854," he said. "The binder did a hell of a job on it, a hell of a one. His craftsmanship lasted a century before it began to wear, so I just had to help him out some. Touch it. Go on, sir, it won't bite."

Little Lyman did. The leather was smooth, and warm beneath his fingertips, almost certainly from its extended proximity to the salesman's torso—*almost*, because Little Lyman had the strange sense that the book might have been warm even had he stumbled across it on his doorstep one chilly morning. It felt to him like a living thing that was slumbering, a metaphor that might have appealed to religionists of a certain stripe but was inapplicable to Little Lyman, who had faith only in a distant God.

"What do you mean by helping the binder out?" inquired Little Lyman.

"I had to perform restoration work," said the man. "The gilt was worn away from some of the page edges, and the leather was split on the front cover. See if you can spot the join. I bet you a dollar you can't."

Admittedly, Little Lyman was no expert on bookbinding, but nothing was wrong with his eyesight. Try as he might, he could discover no trace of mending on the cover. Assuming the stranger was telling the truth about the damage in the first place, he surely had an aptitude.

"So you sell only restored books?" asked Little Lyman.

"Why would I sell new ones? You said as much yourself: People are giving them away, so why pay for what can be acquired free of charge? I have to offer something different, something unique. I'm selling a beautiful item, a piece of history, so the buyer can become part of a continuum. A book like this might lead a reflective individual, someone with a spark of self-awareness, to consider their place in the universe. It's a form of stewardship. You take care of it and pass it along when you're done, or it gets passed along once life is done with you."

Little Lyman opened the volume, but gingerly. Ordinarily, he'd have been tempted just to flip through the pages of a book, and if the cover was sufficiently soft, he might have bent it in the process, but he was sure Blue Tweed would frown on any mishandling. Little Lyman noticed that the capital letter at the start of each book was printed in gold, which glowed in the light of the bar.

"I did those," said Blue Tweed. "I enjoy gilding."

"It's pretty," said Little Lyman. "No, it's more than that. It's beautiful."

"Then it's yours."

"For nothing?"

Blue Tweed shrugged as if to say *Sure, if that's how it's got to be.*

"I can't take it," said Little Lyman, handing it back. "It wouldn't be right."

Blue Tweed wagged the index finger of his right hand approvingly, like a tutor noting a student's prowess.

"Because you understand that it has value, and we don't value what we receive without cost, not even love."

"I suppose that's true," said Little Lyman, who had never been in love, or not so that he'd been able to identify it as such.

"So what would a book like this be worth, do you think?" asked Blue Tweed.

"I couldn't say. I suppose it would depend on the buyer, wouldn't it?"

Blue Tweed raised his finger again, this time wagging it more forcefully, his whole frame practically vibrating with satisfaction.

"You see," he said, "you get it. There are factors outside the seller's control, and the more unusual the item, the more those factors come into play. There isn't another book like this, not anywhere. It's one of a kind. As the seller, I have to find a buyer capable of appreciating how special it is, and that buyer and I then have to agree on a price, because financial and intrinsic value are not the same. When we're done, we'll have settled on the correct sum if both of us emerge from the deal equally satisfied—or unsatisfied, the two not being unrelated.

"But beyond that, as not only the seller of this item but also its creator—because I've put time and effort into the restoration, and I've left my mark in the form of the gilding on the capitals—I want the book to find the *right* buyer, and that may not be the one with the most money. Would I want this book to end up in the hands of a collector of religious curios, to become just one more addition to their shelf, a bauble to be taken out for examination and display maybe once a year, if that, but otherwise touched only to be dusted off? No, I would not. I don't need money that badly. I want this volume to be appreciated, to be cherished, so that in fifty years, or a hundred, a man not unlike myself, a craftsman if not an artist, might take it in hand, fix its scars, retouch its gilding, and find another owner for it—but again, the right owner."

Blue Tweed stroked the book's cover. His gaze grew fixed. He was staring beyond Little Lyman, at a place or a period of which he alone was cognizant.

"The right owner," he repeated. "Wrongful ownership is not far removed from outright theft, because it's depriving another of what should properly be his. For those who care about such matters—and there are fewer of us than there ought to be—it's an error that cries out for correction, a necessary restoration of the natural order."

Movement returned to his eyes, and they flicked to Little Lyman. "Men," he concluded, "have died for less."

Little Lyman, who had never stolen from anyone, not unless holding back from the IRS counted, which it didn't, saw no reason to disagree.

"So I'll ask you again," said Blue Tweed. "What do you think a book like this might be worth?"

Little Lyman swallowed hard. He knew he'd be buying the book. Part of him didn't want to disappoint the little man by not purchasing it, but he also feared bad luck might follow if he failed to oblige, even if he could not have said why. He'd been played, but played well.

"Fifty dollars?"

Blue Tweed pantomimed offense, but there was genuine hurt behind it nonetheless.

"Fifty dollars? Why, that bottle of whiskey cost more and it's not even sui generis. This book, there isn't another like it and never will be."

"But I'm not sure I want it," said Little Lyman.

"We're negotiating, aren't we? That means you do want it, deep down. The only question is: How badly? Two hundred badly?"

"I own suits that cost less than two hundred dollars," said Little Lyman.

"So two hundred is too much?"

"Yes."

"Well, now we're in the ballpark. It's between two hundred dollars and fifty dollars. I'd be happy with a hundred, but I believe you'd consider that excessive."

"I would."

"But for me, seventy would be too little, though you might be content."

"Not very."

"Content enough, though, or significantly more than I would be. So what about eighty? I'd be desirous of a larger sum, but I could take the pain. You'd have wished to pay less, but you still might have paid more. Eighty it is."

He extended a hand. Little Lyman, despite himself, took it, and they shook on the deal.

CHAPTER

LV

Donnie Ray Dolfe and his daughter drove back to the main compound together, leaving Roland and the others to follow behind in their truck. After a time, Clemmie couldn't take the silence any longer.

"That's a message," she said.

"Really? You think so?"

Clemmie ignored the sarcasm.

"Why didn't they just come?" she asked. "Why leave Emmett Lucas displayed like that?"

"There are too many of us to strike at directly, and we're well armed. Urrea wants to avoid a confrontation because of the risk of harm to the children. But if we don't take precautions, next time it could be one of us tied to a pole with a hole in our chest and our balls in our mouth. Well, not you, obviously, but I'm sure they'd find an appropriate variation."

"So what are you going to do?"

"Devin has set Aldo Bern to work. If Bern can strike first, we'll have more time, and time is what we need. The longer this goes on, the harder it will be for Urrea to maintain his authority."

"Or you could just give them back your child and leave the others to make their own choice."

"I could, if I thought it would satisfy these people." Donnie Ray chewed a piece of skin from his lower lip. "It wouldn't, though. Further reparation would have to be made."

"Money?"

"I doubt money would cut it."

Clemmie stared out the window, watching their land roll by. This was their kingdom, and she had always felt secure here. She had never known what it was to be frightened before, not like this.

"You don't believe Vaughn will return his child, do you?" she asked.

Donnie Ray turned right, taking them onto the dirt road that led to the main house.

"No, I don't believe he will, just as I won't, nor our other major partner. Is this the point where you tell me again that I should never have become involved?"

"I didn't understand it then," said Clemmie, "and I still don't. We could have found another supplier and left Vaughn to drown."

"The beef with Blas Urrea was only some of the reason. Yes, by taking the girl and her siblings, Devin and I have weakened that Mexican, because what was done to Devin also damaged us. But I admit that I desired the child. She's an adornment to our family—or will be, once it's safe to bring her into the fold."

Clemmie shook her head.

"I don't want her in the house."

"That's not your decision to make."

"It's my home, too."

"It may be your home," said her father, "but it's my house, and you just live in it. But the girl stays where she is, especially after what happened to Lucas. I'll warn the Swishers to be on the lookout. I don't know how much Lucas revealed before he died. By rights, he shouldn't have known anything about the Swishers, but he always did conceal more than he revealed, him and Riggins both. It made them good at their jobs."

"Not good enough to avoid being killed—not Lucas, anyway."

"True, but nobody's perfect. And I'll tell you one more thing: Riggins will keep himself well-hidden until all this is over. He likes his balls just where they are."

"And when will it be over and done with?" Clemmie asked.

"When Blas Urrea is no more."

"I still don't see how taking the children will bring about his end."

"I told you: they're his good-luck charms. Without them, Urrea will be doubting himself, and that's the beginning of the end for a man. But he'll also be weakened in the eyes of his rivals once it's discovered that he let the children be spirited away from under his nose, with hardly a drop of blood spilled. The word is already spreading that Urrea could be there for the taking."

"The same word that says Devin Vaughn may also be? And by extension, us?"

Donnie Ray patted his daughter on the thigh.

"There's a line between realism and pessimism," he said. "Sometimes I fear you overstep it too often."

Ahead of them, the house loomed, but no longer as welcoming to Clemmie as before.

"I'm serious, Poppa," she said. "I really don't want to share a house with her."

"You'll get used to it," said Donnie Ray. "You always did say you wanted a little sister."

CHAPTER

LVI

In the basement of her home, Harriet Swisher took in the figures of the children through the glass of their respective cases. The girl had been swaddled tightly, so that only her face and feet were visible. She had died seated upright, the same position she currently occupied. Her features showed no signs of suffering or distress. She had passed away in her sleep, taken by the cold. There were, Harriet reflected, worse deaths.

The boy, by contrast, was less well-preserved. His features were distorted, barely recognizable as human, and his posture reminded Harriet of an insect that had died while trying to escape its chrysalis. The boy had been older than the others, and Hul was of the opinion that someone responsible for administering the sleeping draft might have misjudged the dose, causing him to wake before the cold took him. Unlike the girl, his death hadn't been so easeful.

THE SWISHERS' HOARD HAD spread throughout the main house and expanded into a number of outbuildings and a series of adjoining tunnels, as well as an old bomb shelter built by Hul's father during the Cuban Missile Crisis. The collection was displayed on collapsible tables, in lighted glass cases, and on tiered metal shelving, each item carefully labeled. While some of the pieces had been acquired from smugglers, or purchased from or swapped with other collectors, many had been found by the Swishers during decades of travel and digging. What they sold funded a modest lifestyle as well as further exploration and acquisition; for example, the sale of a pair of rare dwarf mammoth tusks, laced with vivianite, which they'd found in a wood in Alaska, had kept them solvent for a year and paid for a trip to Palenque, Mexico, to look for Mayan ruins. While it was known locally that the Swishers were collectors, and schoolkids were even occasionally invited to view arrowheads and fossils, the scale and value of the trove was the Swishers' secret. While they thought of themselves not as criminals but as conservators, or even repositories of knowledge, they were aware that the law might not view them in quite the same way.

The Swishers' basement functioned as a workshop, but it also contained minor artifacts deemed worthy of retention but not display, including a few partial animal and human skulls. These were kept in boxes on the shelves that lined the walls, with the central space being taken up until recently by a lightweight desk that Hul and Harriet used for cataloging, dusting, and repairing acquisitions. The desk had since been folded up and stored, to be replaced by the two children.

Had Harriet been a mother, or yearned for a child of her own, she might have felt more tenderness toward them, but she had no maternal instincts. She and Hul had never even owned a pet. Each had found in the other all the company they required, and they had passed their years together in a state of contentment colored by regular moments of passion. They still made love twice a week and had never lacked for conversation, or more important, felt the need for it when a shared silence would suffice. Meanwhile, their common fascination with the past—they had first met at a museum exhibition on the Incas—combined with a shared disregard for legal niceties when it came to adding to their collection, had bonded them more strongly. Their intimates had long regarded them as separable only by death, and Harriet could have numbered their major arguments on the fingers of one hand.

But something dreadful had come between them in recent weeks. Harriet had known couples whose initial years of bliss were spoiled by the birth of their firstborn, even to the extent of causing a fatal fracture in the marriage. How strange, then, that the arrival of dead children into the Swisher home when the couple were in their final years should have led to a similar sundering in their relationship. Hul was like a parent who had become besotted by an infant daughter, so much so that it had led him to neglect his spouse, his every waking moment absorbed by thoughts of the girl. It would have been unhealthy even under normal circumstances, but was doubly so when the child in question had been dead for centuries. Christ, he thought he could hear the girl calling to him—or to someone else, which might be even worse. Harriet couldn't decide which was the more appalling prospect: that Hul was finally succumbing to Alzheimer's, or that he might not be and was instead receptive to a voice to which she was, or chose to be, deaf.

Harriet was no committed skeptic about the supernatural. She had grown up around women—they were always women, it seemed—with gifts of insight and foresight beyond natural explanation. She had, therefore, always tried to keep an open mind. The problem in this instance was that her husband had never previously shown any indication of preternatural abilities, being almost absurdly average. She had even occasionally wished for him to be marginally more sensitive, since he possessed that peculiarly male talent for failing to recognize when she was unhappy, or ignoring her in the hope that she'd get over it in time without his having to involve himself. Now the cries of a dead girl were keeping him from his sleep, and when he was away from the house she knew he was thinking only of the child.

So Harriet was jealous but also frightened. The disfigured boy was to have been the crowning glory of their collection—part payment for advice, contacts, and storage—but now she wished they had never entered into the bargain. The corpse was a ruin, interesting only as a curio, the kind that might have been placed in the second row of a traveling freak show alongside some taxidermied fusion of mammal and fish, the stitches visible if one looked closely enough. The boy wasn't as desirable as his sister—well, Harriet called her that, but who could say they were even related? Nevertheless, they'd been together so long that it seemed easiest to regard them as siblings and have done with it. Whatever the truth, Harriet had decided she could do without the boy. Devin Vaughn had promised to compensate them for the loss; if it came to a choice between a preserved corpse and a marginally more comfortable old age, she'd accept the latter without blinking. More to the point, the boy didn't speak to Hul in the same way as the girl. The boy didn't speak at all. His soul, his spirit, whatever one chose to call it, might have been muted by the painful manner of his dying. If it was still in there, somewhere, it was a stunted, fluttering thing. Hul might have felt pity for him, but not love. The girl was different. Something inside that husk endured. Still, Hul had been prepared to settle for the boy—not that he had a whole lot of choice, not with wealthier men putting up the seed money, but the boy was more than he could ever have hoped to acquire by his own devices. This misshapen figure would be the culmination of a lifetime of acquisition, and all they'd had to do in return was provide advice before the raid and stash the four children in the months after.

But now the boy was to be burned, and Harriet could do as she wished with his ashes. Vaughn was interested only in what might follow the burning. Like Hul, he believed that some aspect of the children might have survived, an echo of what they once had been contained in their mummified corpses. It was a faith shared by Blas Urrea, although Harriet did not know if Urrea, like Hul, heard their voices or merely attributed his good fortune to the presence of the children in his life. Harriet very much hoped she never had the opportunity to inquire of him in person. If she found herself in Blas Urrea's company, it would mean she was not long for this earth.

Of course, Harriet could simply have dumped the boy in the woods and he'd have begun to decay. She had no idea how long the process might take, but it was longer than Devin Vaughn wanted to wait. Vaughn's orders were that the destruction should be rapid, and Harriet was to record it. She was to do this at 11 p.m. precisely: at that time, Vaughn would be seated in the presence of *his* child. Harriet didn't know if whoever possessed the fourth child would be near those remains and listening also. Some questions were better kept to oneself.

Harriet was carrying the spare gas can from the car, but she didn't think she'd require more than a sprinkle to set the boy alight. She knew from experience that the dark brown skin would be hard and leathery, yet capable of being bent under pressure and igniting rapidly. In her other hand, she held a crowbar. She didn't want to waste time dismantling the equipment and trying to open the anoxic case. She'd shatter the top pane, pour in the gasoline, and let a match do the rest.

"You need to get back up here."

It was Hul. He was standing at the top of the basement stairs, where he very much wasn't supposed to be. She'd left him sleeping soundly, the plan being that he would wake to find the deed done and the boy reduced to ash and blackened bone.

"I said—"

"I heard you the first time," Harriet replied, "and I didn't like your tone, not one bit."

When he spoke again, he was more conciliatory.

"Harriet," he said, "please leave the boy alone and come upstairs."

"I can't. *We* can't. Vaughn has ordered the body to be destroyed."

"That's not going to happen."

"I have to make a FaceTime call to him," said Harriet. "Vaughn wants to watch it happen. If we don't do it, he'll be angry. He'll send his people, and they won't just set fire to the boy's remains. They'll burn our house down around our ears to teach us a lesson in obedience."

"I won't let them do that."

"How? What will you do? You're an old man who has never fired a shot in anger in his life. Vaughn has stone-cold killers working for him. If we force them to come here because we refuse to do what we're told, they'll hurt us. Jesus, Hul, we should never have agreed to involve ourselves in this, never!"

She returned her gaze to the boy. She hated him. She wanted him gone, him and his sister both.

"It's too late for that." He started descending. "We're part of it. We have obligations."

"Yes, to Devin Vaughn."

"No, to the children. We can't let injury befall them."

Hul was already halfway down the stairs. Harriet backed away.

"These aren't children," she said. "They're exhibits. Let Vaughn have his pyre."

"The boy is more than an exhibit," said Hul. "They all are. But even if they weren't, I still couldn't stand by and let you burn one of them, so put down the can and move away. You're distressing him, Harriet. He senses what you intend. They both do, but it was he who woke me. I hadn't heard his voice before, but I knew it was him. He cried out because he needed me, and that's as good as love."

"Listen to yourself!" she said. "Listen to what you're saying. This has to stop. It's affecting your mind. We're talking about mummified children that have been dead for hundreds of years. They don't know anything. They *can't* know anything."

"Yet they do," said Hul. "They're blind, but they can hear voices and have a rudimentary perception of what goes on around them. The reasonable conclusion would be that they pick up on emotions."

"Reason doesn't enter into this," said Harriet. "There's nothing 'reasonable' about it." She was standing by the case now. "This has to end, honey. It's for the best."

She hefted the crowbar, ready to strike its rounded heel against the glass.

"I suppose you're right," said Hul.

He drew a Colt pistol from behind his back and shot his wife through the heart.

CHAPTER LVII

With Blue Tweed departed, Little Lyman became the new owner of an 1854 copy of the New Testament. Only when he picked it up from behind the bar the following morning, still uncertain of what to do with it, would he find his $80 folded inside the back cover. Alongside it would be a card from a casino in Reno, Nevada, that read THANK YOU FOR PLAYING. Out of curiosity, Little Lyman would google the name and learn that it had burned to the ground in 1975.

But that was for another day. For now, from somewhere outside the bar, Little Lyman heard the sound of music playing on a radio. He went to the front window of the Old Hatch and glimpsed an interior light shining in a black Mercury Marauder. It was now one of just two vehicles parked in the lot, the other being Little Lyman's Accord. Little Lyman could see a newspaper spread across the steering wheel of the Marauder. Blue Tweed was working on a crossword. Even though the interior of the Old Hatch was now almost entirely dark, and the blinds on the window should have concealed him from view, Little Lyman saw Blue Tweed turn in his direction and thought the man might have tilted his head in acknowledgment.

Little Lyman came from a long line of men who weren't dumb.

He wants to be seen. He wants to be remembered.

And Little Lyman was convinced that somewhere not too far from the Old Hatch, bad business was going down, business in which Mr. Blue Tweed had a vested interest.

CHAPTER

LVIII

Hul Swisher sat on the basement floor, cradling his wife's body in his arms. His life as it was had come to an end. Friends would quickly begin to wonder where Harriet might have gotten to. He supposed he could lie and claim she'd gone to visit her sister in Manhattan Beach, California, but that story would hold for only so long; or, he could report her missing once he'd disposed of the body, but he knew that would cause the police to search the house. Even if he managed to clean up the blood enough to fool their forensics people, the fate of the children had to be considered.

The silence in the basement was unnerving. Hul could no longer hear the boy or the girl. It could be they were waiting to see what he'd do next. First things first: He might have been torn up over Harriet, but he had to quit crying and let Donnie Ray Dolfe know that the children needed to be moved. Hul doubted Donnie Ray would approve of Devin Vaughn's order to obliterate one of them. Like Hul, Donnie Ray believed in preserving the old, not destroying it. Donnie Ray might help Hul get rid of Harriet's remains, the Dolfes having some experience in that regard, or he could decide to get rid of Hul as well as Harriet, leaving Donnie Ray with two children instead of one.

Upstairs, Hul's cell phone began to ring. It was soon joined by the sound of his wife's phone next to it, the pair of devices calling out in unison. Both phones were set to ring for the maximum of thirty seconds—being older folk, the Swishers required extra time to get to them—but Hul's suddenly stopped mid-ring after about ten seconds and his wife's ceased immediately after. They did not ring again. Either the callers had decided not to bother, or the phones had been silenced.

"Hello?" Hul called out, before realizing that if someone else was in his home, they had no right to be there. Hul did have a gun, so he wasn't helpless. Then again, he was sitting with his wife's body in his lap, and his hands and clothing were red with her blood. If it was the police up there, he was done for. But wouldn't the police have identified themselves?

Hul calmed himself. He and Harriet always charged their phones in the morning, gradually letting them run down. Sometimes, they even got the best part of two days out of a charge, so little use did the phones receive. Hul tried to remember if they'd charged the phones that day. If they hadn't, both could have lost their juice at more or less the same time.

He eased Harriet's corpse to the floor and moved to the stairs. One thing about the house, Hul had put serious work into it. He didn't hold with stuck doors or boards that creaked, and those basement steps were solid and soundless, especially in his stocking feet. Using the rail for support, he made his way upstairs with the barest whisper of cotton against wood.

The hallway was quiet when he reached the door. He held the Colt close to his side in a two-handed grip, the former so that nobody could knock it from his hands and the latter for stability: he wanted to be sure he hit whatever he was aiming at. The 1911 had a pretty gentle recoil, but Hul wasn't as strong as he used to be and had developed a pronounced tremor in his hands in recent years.

But you managed to hit Harriet without any trouble, didn't you? Right through the old ticker, no doubt there. Bull's-eye, sir. Pick a prize from the top shelf.

"Fuck you," said Hul aloud.

The torment came suddenly, starting at his back, worming its way through his insides, and exploding in a crescendo by his left breast. He felt something hard and sharp being withdrawn from his body, and then Hul Swisher was falling. He landed facedown and tried to raise the Colt, but his arm wouldn't respond and he couldn't feel his legs.

The gun was kicked from his hand before he was pushed onto his back, the pain of it causing Hul to shriek. He was staring up at a woman, and the moonlight caught the weapon in her hand. It was a bronze tumi, an ornamental Chimu dagger, but unlike any in the Swishers' collection. This one was twin-bladed: the first blade six inches long, stiletto-thin, and currently wet with Hul's blood, and the second semicircular and very sharp. The blades were connected by the effigy of a high priest, which served as the hilt. Under better circumstances, Hul might have been tempted to make an offer for it.

The woman moved to straddle him, her knees pinning his arms to the floor. With the tumi's curved blade, she sliced through Hul's pajama top and the layers of skin beneath. He was dying. He could feel it. He willed it to come quickly, before the woman commenced her labors in earnest. But it didn't, and Hul Swisher was still alive when her fingers touched his heart.

CHAPTER

LIX

Clemmie Dolfe joined her father in the kitchen, where he was brewing mint tea to help him sleep. Alcohol might have done the trick better, but Donnie Ray Dolfe had never been a drinker. He'd seen the damage caused to generations of his family by alcohol and had resolved not to perpetuate it.

"I'm not getting an answer from either of the Swishers," said Clemmie.

"It's late. Maybe they don't answer their phones past a certain hour so long as they're together."

"Should I send one of our people over?"

Donnie Ray tasted his tea and worked through various options and outcomes. He'd killed people—fewer than rumor had it but more than many knew—and it was draining, even without inflicting the kind of additional suffering Emmett Lucas had endured. Whoever dispatched him must have been tired out after; they wouldn't be human otherwise. Nobody went around murdering folk that way on a nightly basis. It got to resemble hard work.

Also, Clemmie was right: Lucas's body had been left as a message, an ultimatum just short of dumping the remains on Donnie Ray's doorstep. Somewhere, Blas Urrea's agents were waiting to see how he would respond, hoping the murder would induce him to hand over his prize without a fight. If they were watching the Dolfes, sending a search party to the Swisher house would only lead them to the children.

"I find it's always best to sleep on a problem," said Donnie Ray. "Let's wait until morning, see what the dawn brings."

CHAPTER LX

Seeley made the call from the Swishers' back porch, and within minutes a van was pulling into the Swishers' yard. Seeley and the driver, Harry Acrement, were old associates. The two men had familiarized themselves with the storage equipment, but this was the first opportunity they'd had to put that knowledge to use. The cases were lighter than anticipated, as the children didn't weigh very much. La Señora shadowed them every step of the way: from the basement to the van with the boy, then again with the girl, all the time whispering to them in a language unknown to Seeley, though he didn't have to understand it to know what she was saying.

"You're safe now. I'm here."

AFTER THE VAN WAS loaded, now carrying two children in addition to a pair of mutilated human hearts in Ziploc bags, Seeley returned to the Marauder, la Señora beside him. He was tired but could get by on a few hours of sleep, and la Señora's work wasn't yet done. Also, it made sense to finish this part before Donnie Ray Dolfe became aware that the children had been seized.

They drove for twenty minutes—giving a wide berth to the roads around the barn, which were crawling with police—and arrived at a point a mile northeast of the Dolfe house. La Señora got out of the car, the tumi wrapped in an oilcloth, and started walking. Seeley lowered his seatback and prepared to close his eyes. Should the police stop to investigate, he was a businessman taking a nap to avoid crashing from tiredness, his car filled only with religious publications. If the Dolfes came knocking, he'd bluff them. If that didn't work, he'd kill them.

Seeley tried to descry the woman, but she was already lost from sight.

Seeley dozed.

HE WAS WOKEN BY a tapping at the glass. Beneath his coat, his right hand rested on the butt of a Heckler & Koch .45. Seeley rarely had cause to use a gun; when he did, he liked to be sure that whatever he hit was, unlike Christ, destined not to rise again. In addition, the H&K had suppressor-height factory sights, making it an ideal weapon to be fitted with a can, as now. If there was anything better than killing someone quickly, it was killing them quickly and quietly.

But he had no need of the gun, because it was la Señora returned. Even in the gloom, Seeley could see that her mouth was stained. He unlocked the door to admit her. In her left hand she carried one of the ever-useful Ziploc bags, this one containing a chunk of flesh. The heart, Seeley noted, appeared to have been gnawed, and the Marauder's interior light revealed that the smudging on la Señora's face was dark red. Seeley handed her a wet wipe and invited her to use the rearview mirror to clean herself. What was left of the heart he placed in a cooler box behind the passenger seat.

"How many did you have to kill?" he asked.

"Only him."

Seeley was impressed. The Dolfes would have been on high alert after what had been done to Lucas, yet the woman had managed to enter and exit the house unseen, killing Donnie Ray Dolfe in the interim and extracting his heart. On the downside, they were leaving a chain of corpses in different states linked by the excision of an organ, and were about to add more to the tally. It wouldn't just be Devin Vaughn and his associates trying to track them, or the police either, because the feds would soon become involved. It was too late to do anything about the remains of Emmett Lucas and Donnie Ray Dolfe, but Seeley decided it might still be wise to throw some smoke across the trail, both literally and metaphorically.

"We have to revisit the Swisher property," he told the woman.

"Why?"

Seeley started the car.

"I want to burn their bodies."

CHAPTER

LXI

Moxie Castin called me at 8:30 a.m., which counted as early for me and late for him, Moxie regarding as a poor day one that did not involve greeting the dawn. I found Moxie, like the peace of God, beyond all understanding.

"You ever hear of a guy named Lucius Bleddyn?" he asked without preamble.

"No."

"You want me to spell it for you? It's Bleddyn with—"

"I don't want you to spell it for me. If you do, I'll just know how to spell the name of someone I've never met, because I'm sure I'd recall meeting a man called Lucius Bleddyn."

"You know, you're very grumpy in the morning," said Moxie. "It's the best part of the day."

"Only if it doesn't involve you."

Moxie tut-tutted. I'd have tried to glower him into silence if he'd been in sight. Instead, I could only glower at the phone.

"A little bird told me that you might still be nosing around that business of Zetta Nadeau's missing boyfriend despite being fired by her," he said.

"Which little bird would that be?"

"Her mother."

"Jerusha's not one of your clients, is she? If you need money that badly, sell yourself on the street."

"Amen," said Moxie. "I'd rather lose a finger than work for that woman. More correctly, I heard it by way of a third party, who heard it from Jerusha. It seems Jerusha was renting a room in her home to Bleddyn's on-again, off-again girlfriend, whom he'd met while they were both working in the same bar in Norridgewock. Bleddyn is now an ex-employee of the establishment. There was an argument over free shots for Bleddyn's buddies, in addition to a lightness to the register, and Bleddyn got fired—or quit, depending on whose version you choose to believe. He handed back the keys to the bar, as instructed, but he'd had a second set made, and the owner neglected to change the locks. Bleddyn was arrested while loading a truck with cases of beer, vodka, and bourbon, as well as ten boxes of Red Snapper hot dogs, and is now cooling his heels in the Somerset County lockup in the absence of sufficient shekels to cover his bail bond."

"And?"

"His girlfriend learned about Zetta's missing boyfriend from Jerusha, who has always kept tabs on her daughter—not out of any desire to protect her, but more to foul Zetta's lines should the opportunity arise. Bleddyn says he filed the information away in case it might prove useful, and now it has. He wants me to get his bail reduced and cut a deal with the Somerset County DA for probation, on the grounds that the bar refused to give him his back pay and he was only trying to cover what was owed. If he gets the wrong judge, he could be looking at three years, even the full five."

"If he's struggling to make bail, he doesn't sound like he's going to be able to put much food on your table."

"There's always garnishment, or I could just file it in the drawer marked 'Favors Folks Owe Me.' At any rate, Bleddyn says that Jerusha gave his girlfriend the bum's rush a couple of days ago and refunded her the rent she'd prepaid, which is so out of character for Jerusha as to make one wonder if aliens might not have replaced the original with one of their own. Jerusha told the girl that she needed the room for someone who'd pay better, and if the girlfriend had a problem with that, she could go screw a moose, or words to that effect. The girlfriend was a tenant at will, so no lease, but she still had the right to a seven-day minimum notice. The room was a dump anyway, and Jerusha is nobody's idea of the perfect landlady, so the girlfriend elected not to kick up."

"Do we know who the new renter is?"

"No, but here's the clincher," said Moxie. "The girlfriend claims it was Zetta who asked her mother to do her a solid and provide the room. She overheard their phone conversation, with Jerusha haggling over the price, because that lady never does something for nothing, not even for her own blood. Now, it may be that Zetta has friends she doesn't like anymore and wants to enrage them by having them stay awhile with her parents, or alternatively, desperate times have called for desperate measures where Wyatt Riggins is concerned."

"If it is Riggins," I said, "I don't understand why he hasn't left the state. Why stay close to Zetta?"

"A misplaced urge to protect?"

"If he cared that much, he shouldn't have been dating her."

"What is that sound I hear?" asked Moxie. "Hark, it's alarm bells ringing. As your lawyer, if not your accountant, I feel obliged to remind you that you're not being paid to find Riggins, and the circles in which he's been operating—Devin Vaughn, Blas Urrea—are unsavory, to put it mildly."

"Those circles may be drifting this way," I said.

"Hand it over to the police."

"I've nothing to hand over, only hearsay."

"Talk to Macy."

"I have," I said, before qualifying that with "some."

"I'm trying to help here," said Moxie.

"I know," I replied. "So am I."

I thanked Moxie and hung up, but not before reminding him that I regarded 8:30 a.m. calls as a severe test of our friendship. Though I wasn't about to let Moxie know, I'd already been up for an hour because I had a gym session scheduled for ten. I had recently begun working out with a personal trainer named Valentin, which might have counted as a luxury if I hadn't been in pain so much of the time. It came from being shot and punched more than was advisable—that is, at all. When I went to the gym alone, my instinct was to take it easy for fear of making a bad condition worse, with the result that I was doing less and less, which caused me to stiffen up more and more. Eventually, I began to worry that I would wake up one morning and find myself barely able to move, hence Valentin.

It was possible that Valentin might once have been teased about his name, but only by someone with a death wish. If Valentin stood still for long enough, he'd be forced to apply for a building permit. Even the Fulcis, known to block out sunlight, openly confessed their admiration for the man's physique. But Valentin, Slovenian by birth, was also clever and patient, the former evinced by a handful of college degrees and the latter by his never growing irritated by repeatedly being forced to explain where Slovenia was. So I got in the car and drove to Valentin's private gym, all the while wondering if my decision to train with him was a facet of the same masochistic streak preventing me from allowing Wyatt Riggins and Zetta Nadeau to sink to the bottom and drown.

CHAPTER

LXII

Aldo Bern had assumed personal responsibility for tracking down Eugene Seeley, which was why Bern was currently in Nashville, Tennessee, a place that already appeared as alien to him as the moon. An additional element of urgency had been added to Bern's quest by the death of Donnie Ray Dolfe, whose heart had been removed the previous night without a small army of yokels becoming aware of it until someone tried to wake Donnie Ray for breakfast.

In addition, the Swishers, who had been keeping two of the children on their property, had died in a fire at their home. According to Donnie Ray's grieving daughter Clemmie, there was no sign in the smoldering ruin of the cases in which the children were being kept, suggesting that whoever killed Donnie Ray had also dispatched the Swishers, recovering the kids along the way. The remaining two children were in the possession of Devin Vaughn and Mark Triton, and both men were understandably anxious that the Seeley difficulty should be resolved as quickly as possible.

But Aldo Bern was very weary.

BERN UNDERSTOOD THAT TROUBLES, when they came, had a habit of arriving not individually but in numbers. That was life, as Frank sang—

or maybe it was Marion Montgomery first; Bern couldn't say for sure—but sometimes those troubles were cumulative, caused by a failure to pay attention to details. A pebble dislodged on a hillside by a careless step caused a stone to shift, followed by a rock, then a boulder, until finally everybody was lying under a ton of rubble.

Bern tried to locate the moment when that first pebble had come loose. It might have been when Blas Urrea offered Devin Vaughn a seat on the cryptocurrency carousel, a ride on which Urrea himself had opted to pass. Then again, it might have been the gold or the scrap metal, and before that the coke and the fentanyl. It might even have been their initial meeting, when nothing more than a handshake had been exchanged. Bern wasn't prepared to go so far as to describe Blas Urrea as the author of their misfortune, but he'd helped underwrite it. Devin Vaughn had done the rest himself.

Bern couldn't recall the last day that had gone by without some contact from Devin: a fire that needed to be extinguished, or a decision that required Bern's input. Bern had grown to accept that he'd cease to be bothered by others only when he was dead, although even then, given the life he'd led, his problems might only be starting. Nonetheless, the days when he would have preferred not to turn on his phone were becoming more frequent, as were those when he elected not to pick up a newspaper or watch BBC News first thing. Bern wondered whether it was a function of age: that at some point a person had seen and heard enough, so that even the seemingly infinite variations on human suffering grew monotonous.

I should have walked away long before now, he reflected. *I ought to have left Devin to navigate this world's obstacles unaided.*

I stayed too long.

I am a dead man.

BERN COULD HAVE ASSIGNED the task of tracking down and neutralizing Eugene Seeley to an underling or independent operator, but he didn't like farming out scut work to others, notably when it might involve taking a life. It wasn't that Bern cared to spare someone else from guilt, because he knew plenty of men, and a few women, who had a better chance of spelling *guilt* than feeling it. However, all those movies featuring intelligent, ruthless, highly paid professional assassins charging seven-figure fees for hits were, in Bern's experience, largely horseshit—Reapers being among the few exceptions, and even they had been relatively affordable. A modest four-figure sum would buy you a disposable chump with a gun and no conscience. Five figures would secure you someone who might actually do the job without getting caught, or slipping on the blood and knocking themselves unconscious. No, it was more that murder was a solemn endeavor, and the fewer trailing hooks and loose ends left after the act, the better. That was why, in all his years of lawbreaking, Aldo Bern had sanctioned only a handful of killings. In Bern's view, executing someone wasn't just a last resort but an admission of failure.

And while competent individuals capable of murdering for money were rare, rarer still were the ones who could be relied on not to give up their paymasters under pressure. Offer them the choice of a needle or life with or without the possibility of parole and most would bite your hand off for a clean cell and three squares a day. That went double for somewhere like Tennessee, a state that always did have a taste for execution. Back in the thirties and forties, Tennessee was executing up to three prisoners a day. Now it was down to about three a year, but the executioners had a reputation for being half-assed by botching the lethal injection, and the electric chair would strike only the most desperate as a more favorable option. Hell, Tennessee liked judicial killings so much that if it couldn't buy poison and the power went out, some hillbilly would beat you to death with a rock and invoice the state for his efforts. In Bern's view, the perfect assassination would conclude with the suicide of the assassin, but it being difficult to find a triggerman who might consent to such an arrangement, he had now been forced to take action personally. After all, if you couldn't trust yourself, who could you trust? So Bern would find Eugene Seeley, and the woman from Mexico too, and kill them both.

INITIALLY, BERN HAD FEARED that the Nashville Codex Corporation might be nothing more than a front—a bare-bones website, a private commercial mailbox, and a telephone number that went to an answering service in India or Pakistan—but someone, somewhere, was producing ornately restored and reworked Bibles and religious books in the name of the NCC and accepting money in return. A little digging came up with an address that was now the site of a housing development, with no connection to the NCC. But thanks to the banker Elena Díaz, Bern knew of the various financial institutions with which the NCC did business and the account from which monthly payments were made to Shining Stone Senior Living in Murfreesboro to ensure that the NCC's nominal president, Varick Howlett, didn't expire facedown in his soup.

Meanwhile, a visit to Shining Stone confirmed that Howlett remained alive, because Bern was admitted to his company, or what passed for it, Howlett now consisting of barely more than a wrinkled bag of fragile bones that spoke little and remembered less. As if to prove the point, Howlett opened his eyes, regarded Bern blearily, mumbled something unintelligible, and immediately nodded off again.

Bern had brought a bunch of flowers, some premium marshmallows, and a refurbished iPod Nano onto which he had downloaded a selection of songs from the fifties. He sat next to Howlett as one of the orderlies hovered watchfully nearby, just in case Bern took it into his head to begin beating up on the old man. The dayroom felt uncomfortably hot to Bern, but was barely warm enough for Howlett and the other residents, who were all wrapped in layers of clothing and blankets.

"Varick doesn't get many visitors," said the orderly, "or not beyond the usual one, and even she don't come by more than once or twice a year."

The orderly's badge identified her as Loucilla, one of those older Southern Black names passed down from generation to generation, and not always to be embraced with gratitude. Loucilla must have been content enough with hers; she could easily have shortened it otherwise.

"I worked for the Nashville Codex Corporation until I retired a few years ago," said Bern. "I live in the Northeast now and don't get back here very often, but I remain invested in Mr. Howlett's care." He smiled apologetically. "I'm glad to hear you calling him Varick so fondly, but to me, he was always 'Mr. Howlett.' Funny how these habits linger, no matter how many years go by or how old we get. The boss remains the boss."

Bern saw Loucilla begin to relax. He'd talked his way past the front desk while her superior, Brent Cutler, was tied up on a call, Bern arguing politely that he'd traveled far and had only so much time to spare. Loucilla must have been worried that Bern might get her fired. It was important that he set her mind at ease. If she was relaxed, she might reveal more.

A middle-aged man, wearing a cream short-sleeve shirt and a red, white, and blue tie held in place by a gold Jesus fish clip, entered the dayroom. Bern, who had never owned a short-sleeve shirt and wouldn't have accessorized it with a tie if he had, summoned up all his reserves of patience and diplomacy. He recognized Cutler from his profile on Shining Stone's website. Cutler, not Loucilla, was the person whom Bern really needed to bring onside.

"You must be Mr. Cutler," Bern said, rising to extend a hand. "My name is Whittier. I've known Mr. Howlett for many years, since back when I worked for the Nashville Codex Corporation. Best job I ever had. I even retain business cards as mementoes."

From a cheap steel case purchased in a discount tobacco outlet on Lebanon Pike, Bern produced one of a batch of cards he'd had run off in a print store. According to the card, he was George Whittier, Northeast Director of Sales (Retired)—or George *Whitefield* Whittier, named after one of the founders of Methodism.

"I believe that was why Mr. Howlett hired me," said Bern, "even if I have to admit I got off lightly compared to him, Whitefield being less of a mouthful than Pantycelyn Strawbridge, fine compellations though they are."

Just as Loucilla had done earlier, Cutler commented on Howlett's general lack of visitors, and Bern offered the same explanation for his failure to present himself previously, adding that he couldn't speak for the absence of any other current or former employees of the company.

"But Mr. Seeley comes by personally, doesn't he?" asked Bern.

"We haven't seen Mr. Seeley in years," Cutler replied.

Cutler kept his tone neutral, avoiding any suggestion of judgment being passed, but it wasn't hard to see that he regarded this lack of in-person contact as a failing on Seeley's part, if not one to be criticized openly so long as the monthly payments continued to be made.

"I'm sorry to hear that," said Bern. "It may be that I should have a word with him. But someone does come by to check that Mr. Howlett's needs are being met, right? Ms. Loucilla here alluded to a visitor."

Cutler indicated that Loucilla should feel free to respond.

"Miss Mertie," said Loucilla. "But she ain't been in since Thanksgiving."

"That would be Mertie Udine," Cutler clarified. "I believe she's Mr. Seeley's personal assistant."

"Of course," said Bern. "Mertie knows what she's doing. Nevertheless . . ."

He let his concern at Seeley's lack of involvement hang unspoken yet audible to him that hath ears to hear. He moved on to discuss the playlist of songs on the iPod, which he said he'd assembled because he'd heard that music could be helpful or comforting to those tested by God in the manner of Mr. Howlett. After more polite chitchat, Cutler gave signs of wanting to be on his way, George Whitefield Whittier having delighted him long enough.

"Actually," Bern added, "I'm not here solely to pay my respects to Mr. Howlett. As I was explaining to this kind young woman here, I'm also one of those responsible for ensuring that Mr. Howlett is well looked after, and for signing off on the relevant expenses."

At this Cutler shifted into more obviously obsequious mode, allied to a defensiveness now that the subject of money was out in the open. Seven thousand dollars a month wasn't chump change and Cutler wouldn't want to lose residents—not even to death, if that could be postponed for as long as possible.

"I can assure you that Mr. Howlett's care is second to none," he said.

"Oh, I don't doubt that," said Bern, "especially now that I've seen this place for myself. But if you have a moment before I leave, I'd like a quick conversation about how those of us who knew him in his prime might be of greater assistance. It may even be appropriate to increase the payments, if that would help."

Again, Bern lowered his voice. He placed a hand on Cutler's shoulder.

"I'm distressed to learn that Mr. Howlett has been wanting for visitors," said Bern. "He deserves better. It doesn't say much for the Christianity of those responsible, and I'm not sparing myself in that regard. The only consolation is that he's in the right facility and being watched over by the right people—and at the right price," he added.

Bern figured he had pushed the correct buttons, but was assured of it when Cutler replied "Amen," either instinctively or calculatedly, it didn't matter which.

"Amen," Bern echoed.

"Amen," added Howlett, who was awake again, and Bern was

surprised by the strength of his voice. On that word, at least, it barely faltered. Bern beamed down at him, and Howlett beamed back vacantly. Bern took Howlett's right hand in his and squeezed it gently. Howlett's skin was cold and slightly moist, the bones, unencumbered by spare flesh, palpable beneath. It reminded Bern of holding an uncooked chicken leg.

"Looks like he recalls you," said Loucilla.

"Then I'll sit with him, if I won't be in the way."

Loucilla positively glowed.

"I'm sure he'd like that very much."

LOUCILLA, AIDED BY A male orderly, commenced checking on the other residents, some of whom had their attention focused on the big-screen television on the wall, where TV Land was showing the first of that afternoon's episodes of *Gunsmoke*. Cutler returned to his office, promising that all Howlett's records would be available for scrutiny at Bern's convenience.

"Printed, please," said Bern. "I'm old-fashioned that way."

Bern took a seat in the armchair beside Howlett. He wished the dotard no injury, and even felt a degree of resentment toward Seeley on Howlett's behalf. Whatever corporate structure Seeley had instituted required Howlett as a figurehead, which probably meant that, every so often, Howlett might have to make his mark on a document, perhaps witnessed by Cutler or a tame lawyer, everyone pretending that this stooped little bird of a man was somehow compos mentis enough to comprehend what he was signing. Then again, Seeley could have consigned Howlett to somewhere far worse than Shining Stone, which implied some residual affection. It made Bern more curious to meet Seeley, even if he would be forced to kill him soon after.

Bern placed a pair of padded headphones over Howlett's ears and pressed the iPod's play button, keeping the volume low at first so as not to cause any alarm. Only when he saw Howlett grin and heard him hum along tunelessly did he increase the sound. He stayed with Howlett for an hour and pretended not to notice when the old man cried.

LATER, IN CUTLER'S OFFICE, Bern used the information supplied to him by Elena Díaz to assuage any remaining reservations Cutler might have had about his bona fides. Since Bern was already familiar with account details and dates of payment, Cutler saw no difficulty in allowing him access to everything else, going back to Howlett's admission fifteen years earlier. At that time, according to the paperwork, the Nashville Codex Corporation was based in Belle Meade, but those premises were sold shortly after Howlett arrived at Shining Stone. All this Bern had discovered through his own efforts. What he still didn't know, and what Cutler's documentation failed to reveal, was where the NCC might currently be based.

The contact number supplied by Seeley to Shining Stone was the same as the one on the NCC's website. It wasn't linked to any billing address, so was virtually guaranteed to be a prepaid account and contract-free; it was one thing for a man like Seeley to be contactable, but another to be locatable. The cost of Howlett's care was covered by a shell company based in the Bahamas but paid for from a U.S. bank account. The company would have been required to provide proof of a physical address in the United States to open that account, though a mailbox might have sufficed. But a firm couldn't produce ornate Bibles from a mailbox, not unless it was farming the work out to angels who could also dance on the head of a pin. Bern took in the shelves behind Cutler. Alongside the file boxes, folders, and books on elder care was a leather-bound Bible with fresh gold stamping on the spine. A thought struck Bern.

"Has Mr. Seeley donated Bibles to Shining Stone?" he asked.

"Not to Shining Stone," Cutler replied, "but he was kind enough to offer some to my church."

"I'm glad to hear it. Did you collect them, or did he drop them off himself?"

"Oh, there were too many for him to deliver unaided. Our church is one of a number involved in missionary work across Tennessee and the contiguous states. We hand out Bibles to the poor and the homeless. We also provide clothing and food, but man cannot live by bread alone."

"So how did the Bibles get to you?"

"We collected them," said Cutler. "From the house in Madison."

CHAPTER

LXIII

Madison wasn't necessarily the first suburb in which one might have expected to find a business specializing in religious publishing, fine editions or otherwise, although it could be argued that, if one wanted to spread the word of the Lord, it made sense to lodge oneself among the less privileged of His children. To Bern, Madison possessed all that was required to distract the poor from their lot: pawnshops, liquor stores, smoke stores, payday loan companies—the routine trappings of poverty, or its nearest neighbor, want. Who could blame these people for spending their money, what little they had of it, on lottery tickets and in casinos, because sure as death and taxes, they weren't going to be able to dig themselves out of the holes they were in by working minimum-wage jobs. Even the winnings advertised by the out-of-state casinos on the highway billboards were deliberately modest: $13,320 here, $11,053 there, sums designed to appeal to those for whom $13,320 sounded life-changing, and might actually be so when $1,000 would make a difference. These were imaginable amounts, seemingly attainable even if they weren't, not really, because the odds always favored the house, in casinos as in life. The sooner one became reconciled to this reality, the sooner the pain of existence began to dull—and in places like Madison, there was a lot of pain to be dulled. Even in a city with a crime rate as high as Nashville's, Madison's incidence of violent crime was still multiples of the national average, but its long-term residents watched out for one another, and sections looked to Bern as though they might be on the upswing. He thought it could have done with a few more places to walk, but that hardly made it unique among suburban neighborhoods. In other words, he'd seen worse—which was true of most things, until you were dead.

The Nashville Codex Corporation wasn't advertising its presence, not even with an unobtrusive sign. It occupied a run-down cottage off Sandhurst Drive, with a covered, stone-framed front porch and a big two-car garage at the rear. No fence divided it from the adjoining properties, and only bulky security cameras at the front porch and above the garage doors distinguished it from the rest.

Bern had driven by the property just once, the tinted glass of the Explorer allowing Darold Doak, sitting beside him, to film it with his phone as they passed. Bern then turned back onto Sandhurst, parked, and waited for Doak to play the clip. Bern didn't own a smartphone. None of the older crooks did; they were too sharp, too vigilant.

"I'd bet on a camera at the back door as well," said Doak. "No way to get closer without being seen. But someone is home. See, second window on the left side."

He played the clip again, faster this time, slowing it down only about twenty seconds from the end, where Bern clearly saw a shape move behind the glass.

"You have good eyes," he told Doak. Bern had chosen Doak from the local talent pool because he was reliable and knew how to keep his mouth shut. Bern had made it clear to Doak that they would be removing Eugene Seeley from the board. Doak had replied that not knowing the guy would make it easier, but knowing him wouldn't have made it a lot harder.

Bern was glad that the house wasn't unoccupied. It meant that even if Seeley wasn't home, whoever was inside might be able to provide them with information. If the occupant was a person Seeley cared about, they might also offer Bern leverage to use against him.

"Looks like a woman," said Doak, running the clip one more time.

"It does, doesn't it?"

"Wife?"

"If he's married, he's managed to keep it quiet," said Bern. "Could be a girlfriend, or a secretary to look after paperwork and deliveries. It is a legitimate business, even if it is a front. My guess is it's the Udine woman."

"So what do you want to do?"

"We ring the doorbell," said Bern, "and ask about Bibles."

THE WOMAN WHO ANSWERED the door was in her late fifties or early sixties, her silver-gray hair styled in a bowl cut secured with so much spray that it might have been mistaken for a wig were it not for the patches of pink scalp showing through. She wore a vast blue-and-white flowered dress that ended below the knees, and white support stockings. Her feet were tiny, like a dancer's, and encased in blue satin slippers. Strangely, her lipstick, the only trace of cosmetics Bern could make out, was also blue. Since she was otherwise pale, it made her look like she was freezing to death.

"Can I help you?" she asked.

"We're seeking the offices of the Nashville Codex Corporation," said Bern.

"You found them, but we're not open to the public." She had the singsong voice of a little girl. "We prefer all contact to be made through our website."

"I understand, but I had hoped to speak with Mr. Seeley personally. It concerns a potentially lucrative contract. He wouldn't be around, would he?"

"I'm afraid he's not available right now." She glanced at her watch. "But he shouldn't be too long, if you don't mind waiting. I've just made a fresh pot of coffee, and there might be leftover Bundt cake."

"We don't mind waiting at all," said Bern, "as long as we're not imposing. And I love Bundt cake."

The woman stepped aside to let them enter. The door opened directly into a large living area repurposed as an office, with filing cabinets against the walls and an electric typewriter on a banker's desk. An archway provided access to a small kitchen, with a hallway to the left leading to the bathroom and bedrooms.

"I take it Mr. Seeley does most of his work in the garage out back," said Bern.

"If you ask nicely," said the woman, "he may show it to you. He's got a lovely old Chandler and Price printing press dating from the turn of the last century, and an Albion hand press that's even older. Cream and sugar?"

She progressed into the kitchen, and Bern and Doak heard the rattle of cups.

"Black is fine," said Bern, as Doak slipped past him, moving quietly for a big man.

The woman reappeared, but carrying neither coffee nor Bundt cake. Instead, she was pointing a silver semiautomatic directly at Bern. Before she could pull the trigger, Doak shot her in the head. She dropped to the floor and blood flowed from the hole in her skull like wine from a fractured jar. Even with the suppressor, the noise was loud enough to have drawn the attention of anyone passing by, but when Bern peered out the window, the street was empty. He drew his gun, locked the front door, and shadowed Doak to make sure the cottage was clear. Then, exiting through the kitchen, they checked out the garage workshop. The side door was locked and no one was inside. Bern decided a search of it could wait until later, so he and Doak returned to the cottage.

With Doak on sentinel duty, Bern turned the place over, looking for anything that might give them an advantage over Seeley or an insight into how his shadow vocation operated. He found nothing that did not relate to the work of the Nashville Codex Corporation, including yellowing invoices going back a decade or more, carbon copies of typed letters and receipts, some dated for the current year, and hardback account books, the entries written in blue fountain pen by two different hands—Seeley's and the woman's, Bern supposed. The driver's license in her purse confirmed her identity as Mertie Udine.

Bern's search of the house revealed no further trace of a woman's presence: no clothes, makeup, toiletries. If Seeley was screwing Udine—in which case, Bern reflected, he was either very desperate or very charitable—she didn't stay the night. Then again, even the evidence of male habitation was scant, which meant the Madison property might not be Seeley's principal residence. The closets contained men's clothing, but only sufficient for a couple of changes, and the toiletries in the bathroom cabinet were travel size. Even the toothbrush was barely used.

Bern returned to the garage studio. The trees on the adjoining lots offered cover for him to work on the lock without being observed. He saw no sign of an alarm system, perhaps because whatever the garage contained—paper, old books, and heavy printing presses—would be of little value to a thief. Bern also reckoned that the local junkies, creeps, and vandals knew better than to cross Seeley. Men like him had ways of making themselves untouchable.

Bern had the lock picked in under a minute. The garage interior smelled of oil, ink, leather, and old paper. He ran his fingers over Bibles and religious tracts in varying stages of dismantlement, reassembly, and restoration. Between two windows stood the Chandler & Price platen press, which looked to Bern like a sewing machine crossed with a wheelchair. He could see it was conscientiously maintained, with fresh varnish applied to the wood parts and lubricant to the metal. Swatches of leather, predominantly red and black, were stored in rolls on a dedicated shelf beside a vintage printer's tray in dark wood, its alcoves filled with neatly arranged metal letter blocks. The whole layout communicated neatness and precision. Once again, Bern felt admiration for Seeley even as his disquiet grew. Whatever the range of Seeley's more singular expertise sets, he had managed to keep it concealed from all but those who might have need of them. This was no garden-variety troubleshooter, no blunt instrument for hire to the highest bidder. No, this was a craftsman, perhaps even an artist.

In a closet at the back of the workshop, Bern discovered a fireproof document box. Inside was paperwork relating to a self-storage unit on Welshwood Drive and, more intriguingly, the ownership of a farmhouse in Blountville, including utility bills and a warranty for roof repairs dating from 2022. Blountville was close to the Tennessee-Virginia border, within easy reach of North Carolina, Kentucky, and even West Virginia if one was familiar with the roads. The farmhouse would make sense as a base or refuge, a location from which a man like Seeley could dart with ease across state lines should difficulties arise. He wondered if Seeley had chosen Nashville for a similar reason; it was central enough to make cities like Dallas, Chicago, New Orleans, and parts of the East Coast accessible by road in eight or nine hours, if that. For someone in Seeley's line of work, it wouldn't pay to be too remote.

Bern made a note of the address, along with the particulars of the self-storage unit. He then restored the paperwork to the box and replaced it where he'd found it. Bern left the workshop and pulled the door closed behind him. In the cottage, he and Doak rolled the dead woman in a rug and deposited her in one of the bedrooms before Doak used a mop and bucket to clean up the blood. They didn't want a mailman or curious neighbor spotting either the body or the redness and calling the police.

"Her phone beeped once while you were outside, then rang once as well," said Doak. "The screen flashed, like it was malfunctioning. When

I picked it up, it went dark. I tried using facial recognition and her finger- and thumbprints to open it, but no dice."

Udine's cell phone was sitting on the breakfast bar. It wasn't any make that Bern recognized and was unusually solidly built. Bern tapped at the screen with a gloved finger. As Doak had said, it remained dark. Bern tried hitting buttons on the side and activated only a request for an eight-digit security code. He set the phone down again, saying nothing, but his anxiety crept up another notch. He tried to calculate how long it might be before Seeley realized there was a difficulty in Madison: close of business that day, he decided, at best. It would take them about four hours to get to Blountville. If Seeley was there, they'd deal with him immediately. If he wasn't, Bern would leave Doak to wait in case Seeley returned.

The fact that the Udine woman had come at them with a gun confirmed that Seeley wasn't only a fixer but a killer too: secretaries didn't normally go pulling guns on strangers without the approval of their bosses. Someone at Shining Stone Senior Living could have alerted Udine to questions being asked by a stranger. Despite his religious tie clip, the facility manager struck Bern as slippery as an eel in a bucket of Vaseline, and he could well have been under orders to make a call should anyone come inquiring after Howlett. Also, if Seeley was aware of Devin Vaughn's involvement in the theft of the children, he would have gone to the trouble of familiarizing himself with Vaughn's associates and shared that information with his factotum, Udine.

Bern took a last look around. The activation of Udine's odd cell phone nagged at him. Had he been a betting man, he'd have laid good money on his having missed an alarm at Seeley's workshop. All the more reason, then, to get moving.

Bern and Doak left through the kitchen, making sure the front and back doors were locked behind them, before walking a block to where the Explorer was parked. They stopped at a gas station near Lakewood to buy supplies and use the bathroom because committing a crime, especially murder, did things to the bowels; it had been all Doak could do to hold it in until they'd left the house. Amateurs sometimes couldn't manage this and ended up defecating where they'd robbed or killed, leaving behind a sample rich in DNA for the police to work with. His stomach settled, Doak took the wheel and they drove northeast toward Blountville.

CHAPTER

LXIV

Seeley had been following news reports of the previous night's events in Loudoun County when his phone beeped, indicating that persons unknown had entered the Madison workshop without first deactivating the alarm, the keypad for which was concealed behind a sliding wood panel by the door. Mertie Udine had been by Seeley's side for so long that she would never have set off the alarm accidentally, and she rarely had cause to enter the workshop. If someone else had done so, Udine would immediately have been in touch with Seeley because her cell phone would have received the same notification. The procedure had been in place for years.

When Udine didn't call, Seeley sent a coded message to her secure phone. He gave it five minutes, and when Udine still hadn't responded, Seeley reached out for assistance. While the Nashville property had cameras in place, the system was relatively primitive, linked to a hard drive in a bedroom closet: another demonstration of Seeley's reluctance to live any aspect of his life online. But Seeley's IT expert—the same young man recently responsible for supporting *The Tennessean* by buying two copies—had gained access to the Blink cameras on two nearby houses, one of them directly opposite Seeley's own.

"What do you have?" Seeley asked him.

"Two men approaching from the street. The door is opened. The men enter. They exit from the back twenty-eight minutes later and head east. One looks to be in his thirties, the other twice as old. No vehicle that I can see."

"Isolate as clear an image as you can, then fax it," said Seeley.

"Doing it now."

The fax came through shortly after. The younger man was unknown to Seeley, but the other's face was familiar: Aldo Bern.

Seeley went to the farmhouse's guest bedroom. La Señora was sitting on the side of the bed, staring out at the trees beyond. The bed had not been slept in, just as the adjoining bathroom had not been used, nor had his guest consumed any of the food in the kitchen. He had witnessed her drink some water, but so little that it must barely have moistened her mouth.

"I think we ought to leave," said Seeley.

They had driven through the night from Virginia to Blountville, after which Seeley had gone to bed for a few hours. He was somewhat refreshed but not so much so that he wanted to get in a car again so soon. Harry Acrement was in Manassas, preparing for the move against Devin Vaughn. Seeley had persuaded la Señora that it would be wiser if they retreated to Blountville in the interim, just in case they had tripped a wire in Virginia. The woman had consented, if reluctantly; she wanted to be closer to the third child, not farther away.

From the bed, la Señora stared at him. Even after the time he'd spent with her and the devastation they'd visited on others together, he still found being the focus of her attention deeply unsettling. Hers was an inhuman regard.

"Why?"

The word was barely a whisper. Had the house not been so quiet, he might have missed it entirely.

"There's been a break-in at my workshop," said Seeley, "and Miss Udine isn't answering her phone." He felt sorrow rise like bile, but swallowed it down. "The security of the Madison office has been compromised, which means this property may also be at risk."

"From the ones who took my children?"

"By those they've sent after us, yes."

"Then we will wait for them," she said in her slow, accented English, which seemed to improve with each day. "We will find out what they know."

She turned away from Seeley, back to the light, signaling an end to the discussion. She liked the sun, even at this time of year. She relished it as one who had been deprived of it for too long: a prisoner, maybe, or—

A corpse.

The thought had been lurking at the back of Seeley's mind for a while, but this was the first time he'd acknowledged it. The idea made no sense, of course: la Señora walked and talked—well, not so much the latter, though certainly the former—but she didn't seek much rest or sustenance and there was a dryness to her tegument, a hint of desiccation. She rustled when she moved, like dead leaves brushing against one another.

Blas Urrea had advised Seeley that he was to be guided by the woman in all matters relating to the children, but Seeley hadn't survived this long by surrendering authority and judgment to another.

"I have my methods, just as you do yours," he said. "If enemies come, they should discover only an empty house. Outright confrontation would be better avoided."

What happened next would haunt Seeley's dreams. He caught a blur of motion, like the leap of a predatory insect or spider. One moment, la Señora was seated, the next, she was inches from him, so close that he could glimpse the staining at the exposed roots of her teeth and inspect for himself the reddish purple of her gums. He noticed for the first time that the teeth, which he had taken to be gapped and uneven, were regularly spaced but filed down almost to points. Her eyeballs were yellowed and without visible blood vessels, so they might have been made of glass, and her pupils, which he had thought to be a deep brown, now looked closer to red. Her skin had the texture of paper crumpled and unfolded before being pasted over a skull. Seeley felt breath on his face, but only barely. It smelled musty, like a room that had not been opened in many years.

La Señora's hand caressed his cheek—once, twice—before freezing. She glanced down at the gun in Seeley's hand, its muzzle a hairsbreadth from her belly. It was a little two-shot Bond Arms Roughneck .357 Mag that never left his person. Seeley had only ever fired it once in self-defense. He'd been shocked by the mess it made.

"Old habit," said Seeley. "Comes without thinking. Now, back away."

She tilted her head, reassessing him, but gave no sign of being frightened by the gun.

"Remember who you work for," she said.

"I can't work for anyone if I'm dead."

"Why not? I can."

Seeley waited for her to smile. She didn't.

"You have an odd sense of humor," he told her.

"I have no sense of humor at all," she replied.

"We'll soon have that in common, because mine is rapidly running out. I'll tell you once more: back away."

"Your weapon won't do any good," she said. "It's been tried before."

Seeley cocked the hammer on the Roughneck.

"Not like this," he said, "and not by me."

Slowly, La Señora retreated until she came to a standstill against the bedroom wall. She wore the same dress she'd had on since her arrival: a shapeless shift of tan linen, buttoned down the front and falling to her shins. Over it was a green wool cardigan, hand-knitted. Her plain brown sandals had been set aside, and her feet were bare. The toes curled in on themselves, as if from lengthy constriction. She touched the fingers of her right hand to her groin.

"Do you want to see where they came from?" she asked. "My children, all my children?"

There was nothing lascivious about the gesture or the offer. She might have been asking him if he wished to look at a photograph of her in the cradle.

"I do not."

"I think you should. I think you need to understand."

La Señora began unfastening the buttons of the dress. Seeley tried to tell her to stop, but no words would come, just as he could not make himself look away. She had fixed him with her eyes as assuredly as she had silenced him. When all the buttons were undone, she put a hand to each side of the dress and exposed herself to him. A scar ran from her vulva to just below her neck, as though she had been opened from her groin to where her breasts formerly were, even if all that remained of them was a second scar running perpendicular to the first, carving a cross in her flesh. The incisions, though partly open, were completely dry.

Seeley found his tongue.

"My god."

"If you wish," said la Señora.

CHAPTER LXV

Bern and Doak arrived in Blountville with the sky burning crimson and orange, the last of the clouds like smoke drifting above the conflagration, the trees against it reduced to their lineaments so that they appeared to Bern already charred, lifeless.

Bern had spoken with Devin Vaughn on the ride east, but only after the latter texted Bern to advise that he and Doak ditch their cell phones in favor of fresh burners. The new numbers were to be shared the old way, which meant calling an electrical repair store in Richmond's Jackson Ward and relaying them to the owner. Doak bought the cheap phones at a gas station, along with some jerky and a couple of energy drinks that tasted vile to Bern but did perk him up some.

"What's with the extra precautions?" Bern asked, once he and Vaughn were in voice contact again.

"There's a problem with an apartment near the house. We think it's federal. A delivery guy spotted activity and made a call. If it is the feds, they'll have been listening to calls, picking up emails, who knows what else."

"We don't put anything in emails," said Bern, "and we change phones more often than my wife changes her mind."

"Minjun says that may not be enough if we're under surveillance." Minjun looked after Vaughn's tech. Bern thought Minjun might be

Korean, or half-Korean; honestly, he'd never cared enough to check. "He says they may be sweeping up every phone in the area. Whenever a new device is activated, it's added to the list."

"So where are you now?"

"Driving around, trying not to be overheard," said Vaughn.

"You have someone with you?"

"Redcross and Arturas."

Two of Vaughn's people out of Maryland. Hard men.

"You could leave the city," said Bern.

"You know, until you deal with Seeley, I figure I'm safer where I am. I now have federal bodyguards. They have a vested interest in not seeing me butchered."

More was now known about the catastrophe in Loudoun County. The bodies of Hul and Harriet Swisher had been recovered from what was left of their home, the latter's body less ravaged by flames thanks to the protection offered by the basement.

"Clemmie Dolfe says Harriet Swisher's heart was cut from her body, just like Emmett Lucas's," Vaughn told Bern. "Hul was too badly burned to tell for sure. You think this Seeley is the cutter?"

"Could be."

"You sound unsure."

"If he's doing the carving, it's on Blas Urrea's orders. But from what I've learned about Seeley, I don't believe he goes in for showmanship."

"Then it's the woman," said Vaughn. "When you find them, have both their fucking hearts cut out, and we'll ship them to Mexico."

"You want me to call when it's done?"

"It would help me sleep better," said Vaughn. "But keep it short, bearing in mind who might be listening."

BERN AND DOAK LEFT the main road and headed into countryside dotted with community churches—Baptist for the main part, with some

Methodists thrown in for variety—and family homes, the grass neatly cut and the yards tended, even when the houses themselves looked run-down. God's country, reflected Bern, as long as God's idea of a good time was dinner at Olive Garden or Texas Roadhouse, and a round of golf at Crockett Ridge on weekends.

Seeley's place was way out on Boozy Creek Road, the creek itself running alongside at intervals, the land hilly and wooded. Passing motorists waved greetings, and Doak raised a hand in return because to do otherwise might have caused them to lodge in someone's mind. Meanwhile, the road was partly sponsored by the Boozy Creek Chapter of the Peacemakers Motorcycle Club, which didn't make Bern any happier. He didn't want bikers getting in his way or taking a proprietorial interest in traffic crossing through their territory. He was grateful that, once they were done, Doak's vehicle would be returned to the dealership from which it had been borrowed and the original plates restored.

They stopped in the empty parking lot of Gardner's Memorial Primitive Baptist Church, where Boozy Creek Road intersected with Tri State Lime Road. Bern didn't know any Primitive Baptists, but if regular Baptists were anything to go by, these ones would be no fun at all.

"I went to a church like that when I was a boy," said Doak. "In summer, we had Black Flag spray guns and fly swatters to deal with the insects. You have flies in your church?"

"I don't recall many flies," said Bern. "But I'm Catholic, so maybe flies are strictly a Protestant scourge, on account of that wrong turn you took at the Reformation."

But Doak wasn't paying attention. He was lost in the past.

"In winter, we tried to stay as close as we could to the potbellied heaters," he continued. "Whenever I sweat or freeze, I think of God."

"Given the things you've done since then," said Bern, "you'd better hope God has forgotten you ever existed. Head on up a ways. I think we're nearly there."

Farther along Boozy Creek Road, they arrived at a cut on the left marked PRIVATE and DEAD END. The gradient made it hard to see what lay ahead. Bern checked the Google Maps screen grabs he'd saved on his now SIM-less smartphone.

"This is the one," he said, and Doak made the turn.

"I don't reckon any of these houses are occupied," Doak observed as they drove down the patched blacktop toward Seeley's farmhouse, and Bern thought he might have been right. The homes that weren't boarded up were gone to seed, with filthy glass in the windowpanes and slates dislodged from the rooftops. No flags fluttered from porches and no vehicles were parked in sight. In one of the yards stood a metal post with a chain extending from it, where a dog might once have been secured. It wasn't as though Bern had never encountered similar signs of abandonment in his travels—poverty was more noticeable the farther south one ventured—but this neglect had an air of contrivance about it. He wondered how much a property along this road might cost a person, and supposed it depended upon the value they placed on their privacy. He had an idea that with committed digging, the ownership of the houses and their surrounding acres might be traced back to businesses and accounts linked to the Nashville Codex Company, or even Eugene Seeley himself.

Now here was the farmhouse, the last on the road, where blacktop turned to dirt before the whole was swallowed by undergrowth and the waiting woods beyond. The original single-story dwelling had been augmented over the years, with no great care taken to blend old and new. A second floor had been added the way a child might have worked with LEGO: by sticking a square on top of the existing rectangle, not even bothering to match the windows, before sourcing an overornate gable from the bottom of the box and jamming it into place in some misguided nod to architectural niceties. This was a building to be lived in, not admired. It was also shielded by glades of mature trees—another manifestation, perhaps, of the care taken by Seeley to guard against unwanted attention, though there was no longer a call for such vigilance. The neighbors were all gone, leaving Seeley to reside unmonitored and unmolested.

Doak pulled directly into the driveway, the two men having decided that if Seeley suspected they were coming, he would either be waiting for them or already gone. If the second, they had nothing to fear. If the first, a cautious approach wouldn't do them any good, just as there would be no advantage to waiting until dark, Seeley being more familiar with the lay of the land, night or day, than they were. Both men had taken the precaution of adopting body armor, especially after their brief encounter with the late Mertie Udine. Beneath their casual jackets, they wore EnGarde vests, though without the additional hard plates because Bern didn't picture Seeley as the assault-rifle type. He did make him for a practical man, which meant Seeley wouldn't be trying for head shots; that nonsense was only for video games. In real life and up close, you aimed for the largest target: the torso. Even then, amid the noise and terror of a gunfight, there was a good chance of missing entirely, which was why numerical advantage counted.

Just to further improve the odds, Bern had broken out a tactical shotgun, the ever-reliable Benelli M4, while Doak had added a shoulder stock to his Glock 18 along with a thirty-three-round magazine. Bern thought the shoulder stock was showy and thirty-three rounds counted as overkill, but there was no reasoning with younger people. Anyway, it wasn't as though they planned to sit Seeley down and discuss the error of his ways. No, the intention was to leave Eugene Seeley so ripped apart that anyone else who might be tempted to assist Blas Urrea in his endeavors would first seek alternative ways of dying. To reinforce the point, pictures of what was left of Seeley would be circulated, a reminder that Devin Vaughn might have taken some punches but was far from out. Vaughn's gag about Seeley's heart might not be so far from the mark, either, though they'd have to include his head as well, just to eliminate any doubt.

Bern and Doak broke right and left from the Explorer. Theirs was the only vehicle in the drive and the property had no garage. Thin linen drapes hung behind the front windows and the blackout rollers were only partly drawn, enabling Bern to see into the living room. The interior walls were painted an off-white and hanging on them was art that didn't look to Bern like anything at all, and was therefore probably expensive. The furniture was surprisingly modern, with an Eames-style lounger and ottoman facing a TV in the corner, and a pair of open double doors led into the bright kitchen. Bern picked up no signs of occupation, but that didn't mean anything. If Seeley was watching for them, he was hardly going to do it while sitting in that Eames chair with a target pinned to his chest, just as they weren't about to announce themselves by ringing the doorbell.

Bern and Doak met at opposite sides of the front door, where Bern took a step back to blow away the upper and lower locks at the jamb, leaving the door standing ajar. Doak kicked it fully open with his right foot. He was already halfway into the hall when he spotted the draft excluder on the floor, and behind it, a convex plastic rectangle on scissor legs. Doak had enough time to say only "Ah" before the Claymore detonated, distributing seven hundred deformed steel ball bearings in an arc that tore through wood, glass, and—most ruinously—flesh. Doak took the brunt of the blast, his body instantly shredded from the stomach down and his left hand amputated an inch above the wrist. He collapsed to the floor and commenced screaming. Bern, who was close behind, had Doak to thank for not being more grievously injured, but he still took a storm of shrapnel to his left leg, some of which shattered his ankle.

Seeley emerged from the closet under the stairs. A gap in the wood had permitted him to watch the door and judge the perfect moment to trigger the Claymore with the electrical clacker. A second Claymore had been set up by the back door, with another closet spyhole giving

Seeley a view of the kitchen. It would have been complicated to activate both Claymores had the intruders split up and taken a door each. Thankfully, the need hadn't arisen.

Seeley shot the man on the floor twice as he passed, taking care to step around the blood. The screams were a distraction, and one never knew who might take it into their mind to drive down a quiet road at sundown, the local law not being averse to occasional checks. Silence was preferable on all counts.

Aldo Bern had stumbled onto the lawn and was lying on his back. As Seeley approached, Bern made a half-hearted effort to reach the shotgun. Before he could touch it, a woman appeared beside him and put an ornamented blade to his neck.

"No," she said, and Bern left the shotgun where it was.

Seeley saw the western sky was now fully red. The light of the setting sun was reflected in the windows of the house, so the whole might have been the backdrop for a revenge tragedy. If so, it was not yet the final scene, and neither was it Seeley's tragedy, nor the woman's.

There would be more blood to come.

BERN HAD NEVER KNOWN pain like it, and he'd endured two heart attacks. Through the tattered material of his trousers, he could see what remained of his leg, rich with colors of which he had never wished to be cognizant. He could no longer speak, only sob.

He wanted to die. He did not want to die.

Bern's shotgun was now elsewhere, and the woman's strange weapon had been set aside. She had no need of it, not out here.

"We have to get him inside," Seeley told the woman.

He squatted beside Bern. "Turn to your right," Seeley instructed, "hands behind your back."

"I can't move," said Bern. "It hurts too much."

Seeley dipped an index finger into the nearest hole in Bern's leg. Bern shrieked and flailed at Seeley, who struck him across the face before forcing him onto his side and yanking his arms behind his back. Bern felt the bite of a cable tie as his wrists were cinched tight before a handkerchief was jammed deep into his mouth.

"This is going to hurt," said Seeley, "but not as much as what will come next."

With that, he dragged Bern into the house.

CHAPTER LXVI

I had assembled a file on Blas Urrea, but it made for grim reading over morning coffee. Urrea might have qualified as cultivated by the general standard of Mexican cartel bosses, but that was a low bar when it came to men whose brutality had altered language itself. In Mexico, a *zacahuil* was a tamale up to six feet long. Thanks to the activities of the Los Zetas cartel, to *zacahuil* meant to roast another human being alive in an oven. Urrea hadn't cooked anyone, not as far as I could tell, but he wasn't above acts of beheading, burning, and dismemberment when pushed too far, in addition to his fondness for the sledgehammer as a speedy method of execution. I even had the pictures to prove it.

Zetta Nadeau was really beginning to irritate me. I couldn't be sure she was trying to protect her boyfriend by stashing him with her parents, but I couldn't think of a better reason for her to reach out to her mother. It looked like I'd have to visit Anson, though I was still trying to find excuses not to. Negotiating with Ammon and Jerusha Nadeau was guaranteed to leave me with a headache. Unfortunately, the telephone rang, and the ensuing conversation made a trip to Anson unavoidable.

"Doing anything interesting?" Carrie Saunders asked, as I closed an image of five heads placed side by side on an overpass in Coahuila.

"Putting myself off breakfast. I may be in the market should you have a vacancy for a one-off therapy session. I can pay cash, but I'll expect a discount."

"If you're serious, I can refer you to someone I don't like, but only out of pity."

"I suppose I'll just have to cope alone," I said. "Are you very lonely, or did you have something you wanted to share?"

"I spoke to Noah Harrow, Wyatt Riggins's clinician," said Saunders. "He was, needless to say, reluctant to disclose very much, but he did confirm that Riggins had been in touch."

"Recently?"

"About three days ago. Riggins said he'd misplaced his medication and wanted a new script. Noah said he thought Riggins sounded antsy, but that wasn't a surprise if he was struggling without his meds. Noah asked him if he wanted to come in for a talk, but Riggins said that wouldn't be possible for a while. A phone consultation followed, because Noah's by the book about these things. Ultimately, it ended with Noah agreeing to email a script to a pharmacy and Riggins promising to arrange an appointment down in Saugus as soon as circumstances permitted."

"Did Harrow tell you which pharmacy?"

"He hemmed and hawed, but eventually decided that identifying it wouldn't break any oaths. The script went to a Walmart up in Skowhegan."

"Huh."

"Does that mean something to you?"

Skowhegan was about eleven miles from Anson, home to Ammon and Jerusha Nadeau.

"It might."

"Then I want you to listen carefully. Like Noah Harrow, I can square what I've told you with my conscience. Right now, there's no proof that Wyatt Riggins has committed any crime, and if it turns out he has, the law can deal with him, not you. Are we clear?"

"We're clear."

"And that goes for those two thugs who travel with you—in fact, double for them."

"I'll be sure to let the thugs know."

"Don't screw me on this," said Saunders. "You can't afford to lose friends."

"Wow, are we friends now?"

"No, that was just a general observation. I'm going to give you Noah's cell phone number, with his consent. I've advised him that Riggins may have managed to get himself into a serious quagmire, but I spared him the part about the missing children. If you think Noah can be of assistance, you're free to contact him, day or night. If you need me, I'm also available, but Riggins isn't my patient so there are limits to my assistance. Still, I can try."

Saunders and I parted on reasonably good terms. As she said, I couldn't afford to lose friends, or even acquaintances. On enemies, I was running an unhealthy surfeit. What Saunders had told me supported the view that Wyatt Riggins had found sanctuary at or near the childhood home of Zetta Nadeau.

But once again, why had Riggins stayed in Maine if he knew that Blas Urrea's people might be looking for him and could track him to the state? Perhaps he liked Zetta as much as she did him. As Moxie had suggested, Riggins might even have been concerned that Urrea would find out about her. Anson was roughly ninety minutes from Falmouth—fewer, if you put your foot down, which struck some balance between accessibility and remoteness, however imperfect. Then again, if Wyatt Riggins was sharing living space with Ammon and Jerusha Nadeau, he had my sympathies. He might even have been tempted to take his chances with the Mexicans.

I shut down my computer and armed myself with pepper spray, a telescopic baton, and, as a last resort, my gun. I hoped Wyatt Riggins wouldn't make me use any of them. I wanted to help, if only to do the right thing where the children were concerned. More than that, I still wanted to protect Zetta. I debated asking Angel and Louis to come along for the ride, but decided against it. I believed I had a better chance of making Riggins see reason if he didn't feel threatened.

In retrospect, that was a mistake.

CHAPTER LXVII

From the road, the home of Zetta Nadeau's parents didn't look appreciably better or worse than any of its neighbors. It was a half Cape Cod with an off-center door and covered porch to the left, the whitewash needing freshening up and exposed wood showing through the blue trim. There was no junk in the yard and the tan Subaru Outback parked in front of the garage had four wheels, all its glass, and might have started without too much trouble on a warm day.

But viewed up close, the property struggled to hide signs of deeper neglect. The wood beneath the trim was rotten, and the paintwork left as it was out of fear of what stripping it back might reveal. The windows hadn't been cleaned since before winter, if then, and the screens served as a storehouse for leaves, cobwebs, and the corpses of insects. The lawn was pockmarked with bare patches, and keeping it short disguised the fact that the greenery was as much weed as grass, while the Subaru was filthy, inside and out.

My cell phone rang. It was Carrie Saunders again. I picked up as I approached the Nadeaus' front door.

"Carrie," I said.

"Emmett Lucas is dead."

"How?"

"He was murdered down in Loudoun County, Virginia, and he wasn't the only one. There are four victims, all possibly—probably—linked, at least according to the reports. I have someone at the local VA trying to find out more."

"Who were the others?"

"A local couple, the Swishers, and a man named Donnie Ray Dolfe who was embedded in the DMV narcotics trade." The DMV referred to the District of Columbia, Maryland, and Virginia region. "Look, unlikely as it may seem, this could be unconnected to your investigation, but if it is connected—"

"I can use it to pressure Riggins," I said. "Thank you."

"Right now, he's going to be scared, especially if he's aware of what happened to Emmett Lucas. Convince him to contact Noah or me if he's reluctant to talk to the police. We'll do what we can to protect him. Parker, don't hurt him."

"I'll try not to," I said.

Famous last words.

I SMELLED OLD GARBAGE and dank kitchen grease as I rang the doorbell. The lid on one of the cans by the porch had been knocked off, possibly by an animal. I peered inside and saw an empty bottle of Fifty Stone single malt and fresh bags from Macy's. Fifty Stone retailed for $50 before tax. I might have been wrong, but I'd always taken the Nadeaus for Caliber Premium Canadian folk: $14, give or take, for 1.75 liters of 80-proof prime hooch, the kind that left you with a hangover you could bequeath to your descendants without any noticeable diminution of its effects. If the Nadeaus were buying craft whiskeys from small Maine distillers, they were celebrating on someone else's dime. I checked the Macy's bags and emerged with a receipt for men's and women's clothing totaling just under $350.

"What are you doing there?"

Actually, what I heard was closer to "watcha dun dere?" because

Ammon Nadeau was old Maine through and through. He was wearing what might have been some of the purchases from Macy's: very blue jeans, box-fresh sneakers, and a new Red Sox hoodie that already had a stain on the front. His hair and beard were newly trimmed and he smelled of Old Spice. All told, Ammon looked fairly respectable as he peered at me from the doorway.

I let the receipt fall back into the garbage can.

"We've met before, Mr. Nadeau. My name is Parker. I'm a private investigator."

"You investigating trash now?"

"Natural curiosity."

"That's private property. It's not on the street, so you got no right to go poking in it."

"I thought I might have seen a rat," I said.

"All the more reason to keep your hands to yourself. What do you want?"

"I've been working for your daughter," I said.

"Not anymore, was what I was told."

"Have you heard from Zetta?"

"She's my child. Why wouldn't I?"

"My impression was that you and she were estranged."

"Fences can be mended. Zetta's a good girl."

"You won't get any argument from me."

Ammon Nadeau had thrust his hands into the front pockets of his jeans and was rocking back and forth in his fresh sneakers.

"I asked you what you wanted," he said.

"I'm looking for a man named Wyatt Riggins. I have reason to believe he may be spending time in these parts."

"I don't know the individual."

"I'm surprised," I said. "Seeing as he's dating Zetta, and you and she have mended your fences, I thought she might have mentioned him."

"Well, she hasn't, so you can be about your business."

"Riggins wouldn't be living here with you, would he, Mr. Nadeau?"

Ammon tried hard to keep a poker face but couldn't manage it.

"I told you: I don't know the man."

"Has he shared with you why he's hiding?"

"He hasn't told me—" Nadeau stumbled, recovered. "He hasn't told me anything because I don't know him. How can a man I don't know take me into his confidence? Now, I'm telling you to get off my property. Don't make me go find my pistol."

I raised my hands in surrender.

"I don't want to overstay my welcome," I said. "But it's a shame, that's all."

"What is?"

"That now I'm going to have to waste time hiring people to hang around up here, waiting for Wyatt Riggins to show his face, all because he's put your daughter in danger by his actions—you and your wife too, I'd venture, seeing as how Riggins may be staying in the neighborhood. The people looking for him have probably already established his relationship with Zetta, so you'll be next on their list. After all, if I can find my way up here, so can they, and they play a lot rougher than I do. With that in mind, you might also want to inform Wyatt that his buddy Emmett Lucas has been murdered. Tell him I'm sorry for his loss."

I took out a business card and jammed it into a crack in the porch rail.

"When you've had time to reconsider," I said, "give me a call. You may even be able to spot me in the distance, in which case just holler."

A drape twitched at one of the windows. Through the gap, I saw Jerusha Nadeau scowling at me. I nodded politely. She raised a middle finger and mouthed, *Fuck you*. All things considered, it was a miracle that Zetta had turned out as well as she had, but there was much to be said for having something to rebel against, even if it was only ignorance.

I paused at the Subaru. The car was encrusted with dirt but not dusty, which meant it was usually garaged. Now it was sitting outside while the garage remained shuttered. Perhaps there was currently another vehicle inside, or even another person. I thought I'd stick close for a while, long enough to get one or both of the Fulcis up to Anson. That way, if Riggins was in the vicinity, he wouldn't be able to leave without being seen. I could even try to find a way through the woods at the back of the Nadeau property and take a look in the garage.

The front door of the house was now closed. Ammon Nadeau was gone, and his wife had similarly vanished. Beyond the yard, all was silent. There was no sound of cars, no birdsong, nothing to distract me, so I should have heard the approach from behind. I should have, but I didn't.

The first blow hit me across the shoulders, sending me to my knees. The second broke my nose, but not before I caught sight of a length of two-by-four heading for my face, with Wyatt Riggins's features hovering fuzzily behind it like a bad moon. I glimpsed redness lit by white flares, as though I had flown too close to the sun. I tried to reach for my gun—the time for pepper spray and batons was already past—but Riggins was too quick. He stood on my hand while the block of wood took a sharp jab at my ruined nose. The red sun flared alarmingly.

"Quit looking for me," said Riggins, "you hear? Quit this, period."

I bowed my head and watched my blood pool on the grass, which meant I didn't see the fourth blow coming. I felt it, though, felt it good.

Lights out.

Gone.

CHAPTER LXVIII

Seeley was angry at being forced to abandon his life in Tennessee, though it was not the first time he would be required to reinvent himself. Eugene Seeley would cease to exist, but then Eugene Seeley had never really existed, just as Vernon Barnett had not existed, or Howard Lindikoff, or—briefly—Leonard Dolan. The man who called himself Seeley had always been capable of shedding identities like skin, and sometimes he struggled to recall his birth name, so long had it been since he'd had cause to use it.

The rub this time was that he had grown comfortable as Eugene Seeley, so much so that he had become the Seeley persona, the character fitting so snugly that his existence had ceased to count as imposture. Seeley wondered if it was a function of aging, so that building a new self in later years was akin to trying to learn a new tongue, the rules and constructions of the primary language becoming so fixed that they impaired one's ability to add another idiom. The specters of previous selfhoods haunted Seeley, manifesting as half-remembered tastes or opinions, rusted skill sets that he could still draw on by instinct when required, even flickers in his signature when one name briefly threatened to become another. It was among the curses of a life built on impersonation: behind one, many.

In the case of Eugene Seeley, he had also grown to love working with books. Calligraphy and lettering had fascinated him since he was a boy, but the Seeley persona represented the first opportunity to turn that interest into a profession. Then there was Mertie Udine, who had formerly shared his bed and—until recently—his life. Over time, he had revealed much of his past to her. He trusted her, which was as close to love as he had ever felt for another person. Now she was dead, which added to his rage, even as a colder part of him recognized that in dying she had left him compromised.

Mertie lived alone, but she had relatives with whom she was still in contact, and a small circle of friends. Seeley had considered having her body removed from the house in Madison, before deciding that it might cause more problems than it solved. If he left her to be found, the police would access the same Blink footage as Seeley's expert, which would pin the blame for her murder on Aldo Bern and his associate. The police might investigate the Nashville Codex Corporation, if only to establish the circumstances through which two men known to be involved in organized crime had arrived on its doorstep, but they would delve in vain. Inquiries into the NCC would lead them to Varick Howlett at Shining Stone Senior Living, where the trail would peter out. As far as the NCC was concerned, Eugene Seeley was barely more than a signature in a checkbook. Already, he was melting away, and a new identity would accrete around a man of below-average height who might, as a hobby, engage in the conservation and restoration of books. Three clean passports were immediately available for his use: one Maltese (by investment), one Israeli (by the Law of Return), and one Belgian (by theft from a safe in Tongeren town hall in 1998, during a run on blank Belgian passports). There was also a U.S. document, but he was reluctant to bring it into play until the fuss had died down.

La Señora sat in the back of the car, leading Seeley to feel like her chauffeur. She made sure not to sit directly behind him because she knew it made him nervous. Whoever or whatever she really was, Seeley wasn't convinced that la Señora was operating under Blas Urrea's instructions or control. In fact, Seeley was beginning to fear that, rather than being Urrea's creature, Urrea might be hers. Regardless, the remaining children had to be recovered, and the last of the thieves punished. That was the deal Seeley had agreed.

According to the now-deceased Aldo Bern, the third child was being kept at Devin Vaughn's Manassas home. The antiquities dealer Mark Triton had the fourth, but Bern didn't know where. Triton had galleries and warehouses scattered across the country, and the child could be in any of them. But Triton owned both a house and a gallery in Maine, and Vaughn was in the cannabis business there. Wyatt Riggins, too, had briefly surfaced in Maine. Were Seeley in Triton's position—holding treasure stolen from Blas Urrea, in the knowledge that Urrea would do all in his power to retrieve it—he might have sought to keep someone like Riggins nearby.

Seeley and the woman were within striking distance of Manassas. Seeley considered it mildly amusing that Devin Vaughn had built his primary residence barely twenty miles from the FBI Academy near Quantico. Had they chosen to do so, the feds could have organized field trips for trainees with Vaughn as their subject.

Later, when the shooting was over, Seeley would reflect on how a man could inadvertently and simultaneously be so right about something—and also so wrong.

CHAPTER

LXIX

I regained consciousness shortly before the ambulance arrived, but only because Ammon Nadeau was trying to put something under my head to cushion it, which wasn't helping at all.

"Get away from me," I said, or something like it. I didn't want Ammon causing any more damage than had already been done, but I also didn't care to have his hands on me.

Ammon looked hurt by the rejection.

"I called nine-one-one," he said, as I heard a siren in the distance, even as it struggled to make itself heard over the ringing in my head. I threw up on what passed for the Nadeau lawn and my blurred vision picked out blood. I wasn't surprised. My mouth tasted of it, and I could feel it leaking from whatever was left of my nose.

"I didn't think he'd beat up on you," said Ammon.

That wasn't worthy of a response so I didn't offer one. I felt like I wanted to die and the only thing stopping me was wanting Wyatt Riggins to die more. Plus, the ambulance pulled up, accompanied by a patrol car from the Somerset County Sheriff's Office, and both the medics and the deputy were reluctant to let me expire peacefully. I was taken to Redington-Fairview General, where the emergency room doctor asked about next of kin and I gave her Angel's number before immediately throwing up again. I was X-rayed, scanned, and sedated—

or maybe it was the other way around—before the blood was cleaned from my face and head, a scalp wound was stitched, my nose was reset, and I was told I'd be kept overnight for observation. I spotted Angel in the distance, but by then I was very woozy and wished everything would stop hurting.

Finally, I was wheeled into a private room by a pair of male nurses.

"Why couldn't the last faces I see have been female?"

"I guess it just hasn't been your day," one of them replied.

"When is it ever?" I asked, and closed my eyes.

CHAPTER

LXX

That night, Zetta Nadeau returned to her studio after a bathroom break to find Louis circling her work in progress. To him it resembled a giant hand, its vertical fingers constructed from car fenders. The ends of the fenders had been sharpened to points by an angle grinder, transforming them into claws, and the palm was cupped. It was a throne fit for a demon ruler.

"How did you get in here?" Zetta asked.

"The gate was open."

"No, it wasn't."

"It was after I unlocked it."

Zetta picked up a length of pipe. She wasn't sure what to do with it, only that she felt safer with it in her hand.

"I recognize you," she said. "You were at the Triton Gallery with Parker."

"That's right. Aren't you going to ask how he is?"

Zetta might have preferred not to, but didn't hold out for long.

"How is he?"

"Not good," said Louis. "Your boyfriend attacked him at your parents' house. He's in the hospital up in Skowhegan—Parker, that is, not your boyfriend, though there are those of us who would prefer to see the positions reversed. For that reason, I'm here to ask you some questions."

"And if I don't want to answer them?"

"That isn't an option."

Zetta laughed.

"What are you going to do, beat me until I cooperate?"

Louis didn't reply. Zetta stopped laughing.

"Big man, threatening a woman," she said.

"Don't mistake me for someone with scruples," said Louis. "By the time I leave your body behind, I'll already have forgotten your name."

Zetta Nadeau had grown up the hard way and, as an adult, had shared her bed with lovers better avoided, but she'd never stared into eyes like this man's.

"Nobody was even supposed to know Wyatt was up there," she said, "except my folks."

Louis indicated a pair of folding chairs by the studio wall. "Why don't we take a seat. I have plenty of time. Not a great deal of patience, but plenty of time."

CHAPTER

LXXI

I slept fitfully, even with the aid of whatever drugs I'd been given, before being woken by a nurse at some god-awful hour, presumably to make sure I wasn't dead. I dozed after eating breakfast and throwing up, then made the mistake of trying to get out of bed. I fell, landed on my busted ribs, hit my head, and blacked out.

So another day passed.

CHAPTER

LXXII

In the laboratory version of the observer effect, studying an electron requires a photonic interaction, one that alters the electron's path. Similarly, in the social sciences, an awareness of observation may cause the subject to change their behavior, while observer bias can lead those watching to interpret what they see according to their expectations and miss or ignore what does not match those preconceptions.

The federal agents conducting surveillance on Devin Vaughn suspected he might have become aware of them. It was a feeling as much as anything else, though one based on what the more experienced among them saw as identifiable changes in his habits, including leading them on a merry urban dance while they'd attempted to lock on to his latest burner. Vaughn had also ceased communication with Aldo Bern, or at least contact by any traceable means. Vaughn and Bern might well have reverted to old-school methods, which was why additional wiretaps were being sought for landlines in three business establishments frequented by some of Vaughn's known associates.

Bern's continued absence was a matter of concern to the agents. Devin Vaughn had been prone to rashness in his youth until Bern took him under his wing. Subsequently, Vaughn and Bern had developed a successful working relationship based on mutual respect and Bern's near-constant presence at Vaughn's side. They were two faces of the same coin. Bern was believed by the FBI to have traveled to Tennessee, an undertaking related to the ongoing tensions between Vaughn and Blas Urrea. Now Bern had gone quiet, though not before gifting the FBI a name, Eugene Seeley. Digging had revealed Seeley to be linked to the Nashville Codex Corporation, which, for a company dealing in Bibles and restored religious tracts, had a complicated, even byzantine, financial setup. The FBI was prepared to set aside the NCC for the present, but they'd return to it in their own good time.

A more immediate problem involved the specific application of a general issue in surveillance, namely how beneficial it continued to be after its existence was noted by the subject. If that subject was a criminal or spy, surveillance temporarily removed them from the game, the downside for the observers being that the operation continued to consume valuable resources of time and manpower while potentially leaving the subject's confederates to go about their business unhindered. In very sophisticated operations, awareness of surveillance could be used to influence a subject, a variation on photonic interaction, so that conscious changes in behavior revealed the existence of patterns by deviation. Eventually, the sensation of being watched, or the fear of it, might even break the subject, leading them to seek an accommodation to bring it to an end.

In the case of Devin Vaughn, no definitive proof existed that he knew he was under the eye of law enforcement, and the threat from Blas Urrea remained real and imminent. It was decided that the surveillance should continue across all platforms, but as a precaution, the two fixed locations were abandoned, and alternatives secured at considerable expense.

WHEN SEELEY AND THE woman arrived in Manassas, the exterior of Vaughn's home was being monitored by infrared and night vision cameras. The FBI had one electronic ear inside the house—a new recruit to Vaughn's security detail, careless with his cell phone—aided by horn antennae, which blasted radio beams at the building from outside. The beams were modulated by the minute surface vibrations caused by speech, and the results then amplified and analyzed. So far, all the agents had picked up were discussions of women, pizza, and YouTube videos. Vaughn might have swept the house for devices, but he was still reluctant to say anything aloud that might be used against him in a court of law. Mostly, the FBI was relying on the fact that no living creature of any size could approach or leave the house without being picked up by a camera.

THE AGENTS AT THE eastern fixed-surveillance point—the top floor of a derelict office building, accessible only by a ladder as the stairs had collapsed—were watching two guards patrolling Vaughn's yard, the thermal imaging revealing them as healthy blurs of red, orange, and yellow. The agents were sipping fortified water and thinking of the overtime when one of the guards slumped against a tree and slid slowly down the trunk.

"Wait," said the first agent. "Is he—?"

A match flared, followed by the incendiary glow of a cigarette.

"No," said the second, "he's taking five."

"If Vaughn catches him, he'll take five in the ass."

They returned to drinking their water and ranking the worst college football teams, which was easy until you got beyond Hawaii and UMass, maybe Colorado. It passed the time.

LA SEÑORA MOVED THROUGH Devin Vaughn's house. Her feet were bare and made no sound as she climbed the stairs. The child, sensing her proximity, called out, but la Señora ignored her for the present.

Seeley had tried reasoning with la Señora as they sat parked near the property. The child was the priority, he reminded her. Vaughn could be left until later. Seeley even offered to kill Vaughn for her before couriering his heart to Urrea. He wouldn't even charge extra for the job.

"But the hearts are not for him alone," the woman replied. "The hearts are also for me. You should know that by now."

"Then I'll deliver Vaughn's heart to you in person."

"Where?" asked the woman. "Where will you deliver it?"

To which Seeley had no reply, recognizing that, once they were done with this and the children were recovered, la Señora would not be seen again. She would vanish as surely as Seeley was set to vanish—except that while a man who resembled Eugene Seeley would continue to walk the earth under a new name, the woman would evanesce. He had a vision of her disintegrating, her integument fragmenting to be carried away like so much dust upon the breeze.

La Señora arrived at the master bedroom. She could hear water flowing and a female voice humming a tune. La Señora entered and saw a girl, not yet into her twenties, brushing her long fair hair in front of a mirror. The girl was naked from the waist up, her lower half concealed by a cream slip. To her right was the master bath, its door open and the faucet running inside.

The girl paused in her brushing. La Señora was already close enough to be able to make out the goose bumps forming on her skin. The girl turned, the tumi flashed, and a spray of blood washed over la Señora, the carpet, the bed. The girl staggered back but made no sound, so keenly did the blade cut. La Señora gazed at her dispassionately. There were no innocents here; the girl ought to have kept better company. The back of her thighs hit the bed and she collapsed backward on the mattress. La Señora did not stay to watch her die.

She was already moving toward the bathroom when Devin Vaughn emerged with a towel wrapped around his waist and a gun in his right hand. Again, the tumi gleamed, its edge almost severing the hand from its wrist before Vaughn's finger could pull the trigger. Instinctively, he lashed out with his left, scratching the woman's face but drawing no blood, though his nails dug deep. The tumi sliced Vaughn's belly, and he cried out for help even as la Señora twisted the weapon, the spike entering Vaughn from below, gouging its way toward his heart. She gripped his chin with her left hand, jamming his mouth shut so that he made no further utterance as the life left him. Finally, she yanked free the tumi, shifted her grip once more, and commenced a more exquisite excavation of Devin Vaughn.

THE COLLEGE FOOTBALL DEBATE had run its course.

"Has he even smoked that cigarette?" asked the first agent. "It doesn't look like it's shifted from his hand."

"It doesn't look like he's moved, either." The second agent leaned forward. "Could be he's asleep."

They'd lost sight of the second guard, who was now at the rear of the property. The first agent got on his Sonim and called the team on that side of the house.

"Do you have eyes on a guard?"

"Yeah, he's sitting in a lawn chair with a cigarette."

"How long?"

"Ten minutes, could be a little more."

"Has he smoked the cigarette?"

"What? I guess. I mean, we haven't had much motion. Ah, jeez—"

"We've got the same here. No movement."

"Shit."

The first agent took a few seconds to think. He didn't want to go sounding the alarm unnecessarily. That kind of overreaction gained a person an unwanted reputation for flightiness.

"Let's give it two more—"

The shape against the tree tipped over on its side to lie still on the ground, and the first agent ditched the Sonim for the general radio.

"We have one guard down, possibly two. Advise."

There was no way of knowing if the guards were dead or simply incapacitated. A dead body cooled at about 1.5 degrees per hour, so it would be a while before any change registered on the thermal imaging.

"Do you have motion?"

"Nothing. If he was shot, it came from outside."

"Hold."

They held. The voice returned.

"Wait."

They waited.

LA SEÑORA WAS ALMOST at the bottom of the stairs when one of Vaughn's men ambled from the kitchen, a glass of milk in hand, to be confronted by a vision from an abattoir, trailing bloodied footprints across the carpet. He dropped the glass and reached for his gun, but she was on him before his hand could pull it from its belt, the impact of the blade driving him back into the kitchen, where he died as easily or as hard as the rest.

Now the woman had no choice but to finish off the last of them before retrieving the child. She picked up the fallen glass. Beside her, by the door leading to the living room, was a console table. She climbed on top of it before throwing the glass against the wall.

"Marek?" a man's voice called.

La Señora heard him approach the door. He was being cautious, but not enough to escape her notice. He made his final move quickly, the compact Bushman submachine gun held close to his body. Wherever he might have been expecting the threat to come from, it was not from above, as La Señora drove the blade into the side of his neck. It sank to the hilt and the man went down, La Señora on top of him. He hit the floor, a finger spasmed, and shots were fired.

BOTH FIXED SURVEILLANCE TEAMS heard the gunfire from Vaughn's house. Within seconds, agents were descending on the property. Seeley watched them go. Bern had revealed that Devin Vaughn might be under surveillance. Whether true or not, Seeley, aided by Acrement, had taken precautions.

The first device exploded inside a car parked at the eastern perimeter of the house, and the second, moments later, in a stolen SUV not far from the rear entrance to the south. The latter was the larger of the two blasts, the SUV packed with a mixture of fertilizer and fuel oil. It was, on reflection, a miracle no one died, not that Seeley bothered to check the surrounding area before activating the device. The explosion shattered windows, set off alarms, and scattered debris across the street, as well as demolishing a section of the late Devin Vaughn's back wall. La Señora stepped through the gap shortly after, a bundle at her breast, her departure wreathed by smoke and fire. By the time the agents managed to get past the bomb site, the woman, the child, and Seeley were gone.

CHAPTER LXXIII

On my second morning at the hospital, I woke to find Angel and Louis standing over me.

"Is this where you tell us we should see the other guy?" asked Angel.

"I am the other guy," I said.

I made some tentative movements to test my ribs. Breathing in was like having someone bang nails into my side.

"I picked up some fresh clothes from your house," said Angel. "Also, a detective is waiting in the lobby to take your statement."

I'd told the officers at the scene that it was Wyatt Riggins who had attacked me, but I wasn't in a position to go into more detail. I'd have to be careful about what I shared with the law until I'd had a chance to confront Zetta Nadeau, who had used up any remaining quota of goodwill.

"I'll talk to the detective," I said. "In the meantime, one of you could look for a doctor to give me the all-clear to leave. After that, I'll need some help getting dressed."

"Be still, my beating heart," said Angel.

"I meant find a nurse."

"Thank God."

They both left. A minute later, a Somerset County detective named

Porter Hammond, known in law enforcement circles as Portly Hammond, arrived to take my statement. I told him I'd been hired by Zetta Nadeau to locate her boyfriend, Wyatt Riggins. When she dispensed with my services, I kept looking for Riggins because I'd never managed to overcome my adolescent OCD. Unfortunately, Riggins didn't want to be found, or certainly not by me. Ammon and Jerusha Nadeau had done nothing wrong beyond providing refuge for a man who preferred to do his talking with a big stick. Hammond dutifully recorded everything I said, but was too experienced not to spot when he was being fed scraps from the table.

"There are gaps in this story I could fall through and hurt myself," he said, which was quite the claim, given his girth.

"I won't be filing for assault," I said. "Not yet."

"Come again?"

"It may have been a misunderstanding."

"That's quite the misunderstanding. Have you looked in a mirror?"

"I'm saving the pleasure."

"Well, have someone take a video when you cave in, and be sure to send it to me. I can make money selling it as a misery meme." He tapped his pen on his thigh. "I'm reluctant to let this slide. If Riggins had hit you any harder, you'd be in a coma—or dead. I don't want him developing a taste for violent discouragement. Not everyone out there has a skull as hard as yours."

"I intend to speak with him again," I said, "and I don't want to compete with the police for the privilege."

"Just speak?"

"I may be forced to use strong language."

Hammond scratched his belly. He looked like he'd struggle to chase a suspect for more than half a block, which was probably the case, except he wouldn't let a suspect get away to begin with. The list of people who'd underestimated Porter Hammond and lived to regret it was long, and most could compare notes in prison.

"How much of a pickle is Riggins in?" Hammond asked.

"What do you mean?"

"If you're looking for him, either he's done something bad or someone wants to do something bad to him—and that was before he whaled on you, which means you and your buddies will be happy to whale right back on him."

"I don't think he's killed anyone, if that's what you mean."

"That's aiming low," said Hammond. "Scale of one to ten?"

"Nine."

"And that's without killing someone? Christ. What would we get from his girlfriend if we talked to her?"

"The bum's rush."

Hammond put away his notebook and pen.

"This is making me very unhappy," he said, "and when I'm unhappy, I feel the urge to spread the load. I'd accuse you of having wasted police time, but you weren't the one who called nine-one-one so it wouldn't be fair. Regardless of your reluctance to press charges, I'd prefer not to have ex-soldiers taking it into their heads to deliver rough justice in our jurisdiction. If we stumble across Riggins, I'll let you know—eventually."

"You may struggle to find him," I said. "I'm surprised he broke cover to attack me. He panicked."

"He must have rated your investigative skills more highly than you rate ours," said Hammond, easing himself from his chair and heading for the door. "Should you ever consider relocating to a different state, I'll be available to help you move your stuff."

ANGEL RETURNED WITH A doctor in tow. She did what doctors do in these situations, which was poke, prod, and shine lights.

"Any blurring of eyesight?" she asked.

"No more than usual."

"Double vision."

"Likewise."

"And it's probably pointless to ask about pain, since I've seen your scars." She put away her flashlight. "The CT scan showed no signs of hemorrhaging or hematoma, so you got away with a concussion and a busted nose. The reset on your nose went okay—we were able to manually realign—and it should be healed after three weeks. You have a pair of fractured ribs, but there's not much that can be done with them. I'm advising you to take it easy, especially for the next day or two—though I've been told all about you by Detective Hammond, so I doubt you'll listen. Use Tylenol for pain relief, but not ibuprofen or aspirin. If you live alone, you should have someone stay with you for the next twenty-four hours."

I pointed at Angel and Louis.

"I'm sure my friends will oblige."

"Will he need to be bathed?" asked Angel. "Because there are limits."

"I won't do anything that requires the wearing of rubber gloves," added Louis.

The doctor stared at them before returning her attention to me.

"Do you have any other friends?" she asked. "Any at all?"

I was left alone to freshen up. I took the opportunity to examine my face. Both my eyes were blackened, my nostrils were packed with gauze, and a dressing covered my nose. I was sure I'd looked worse. I just couldn't remember when.

My phone rang. I was tempted not to answer until I saw the caller ID: SAC Edgar Ross of the Federal Bureau of Investigation.

"I heard you took a beating," he said when I picked up. "Another one, I mean."

"Good news travels fast. If you're calling to commiserate, I'll have to work hard to pick up on the sincerity."

"How bad is it?"

"A busted nose, a sore head, a couple of fractured ribs. I'll live."

"I never doubted it."

"What do you want? I already have a headache. Don't add to it."

"You were mentioned in dispatches."

"Whose dispatches?"

"Devin Vaughn's. An overheard conversation."

"Careless of him."

"Hardly, not with all the eyes and ears we had on him. He was heard to suggest that if some harm befell you, it would be no more than you deserved. It sounds as though his wish came true. He also mentioned someone named Wyatt who, unless there's a sale on coincidences this week, is the same Wyatt responsible for putting you in the hospital."

"That's him."

"We were interested in Devin Vaughn. Now it seems that you were interested in him too, and look what's happened as a consequence."

"Riggins worked for one of Vaughn's companies up here, a cannabis farm and dispensary called BrightBlown. That's as far as my interest in Devin Vaughn's business activities goes. Wait a minute: Why do you keep referring to Vaughn in the past tense?"

"Because," said Ross, "someone broke into his house last night, under the eyes of any number of federal agents, and killed him, his girlfriend, and four of his men. Oh, and they cut out Vaughn's heart for good measure, probably with the same blade that was recently used to eviscerate a Virginia narcotics dealer named Donnie Ray Dolfe and two collectors of ancient artifacts in Loudoun County—and perhaps an antiquities smuggler called Roland Bilas in Los Angeles a while before that, not to mention an ex-soldier named Emmett Lucas who also ended up with his balls in his mouth. I'm just a lowly government employee, but even I can discern a pattern. We're now of the opinion that Vaughn, Dolfe, Bilas, Hul and Harriet Swisher, Emmett Lucas, and your target Wyatt Riggins were involved in some mischief involving one Blas Urrea, a Mexican cartel boss. You wouldn't know what mischief that might be, would you?"

"I'm still piecing it together."

"And there I was, trying to look after your welfare. This may be why misfortune keeps befalling you. You can't accept a helping hand."

"Are we done?" I asked.

"For now."

"Good, because talking hurts. I just want another day. After that, I'll share what I have with anyone who cares to listen."

"Share?" said Ross. "Without being forced? That is out of character."

"Now who can't accept a helping hand?"

"Call it justifiable skepticism. But as an advance gesture of goodwill, here's a name for you: Seeley. Eugene Seeley."

I gave no indication that I'd heard the name before.

"And who is Eugene Seeley?"

"The man who had Devin Vaughn so unnerved before he died. Also, by extension, the man who may be looking for Riggins, and should, therefore, be of interest to you. Be wary of this one, any skill with a blade aside."

"Because you know who he is?"

"No," said Ross, "because we don't."

WITH SOME EFFORT, I managed to pull on my underwear and trousers unaided. Angel helped with the shirt. He'd bought me a pair of slip-on sneakers, meaning I didn't have to bend down to tie laces or pull on boots.

"So," said Angel, when we were done, "home to put your feet up, like the doctor ordered? If we hurry, you can still catch *The Young and the Restless*."

Behind him, Louis was amusing himself by leaning against the door and making passing strangers nervous.

"Let's pay a call on Zetta Nadeau," I said.

Louis gave up on intimidating patients and staff alike.

"I already did," he said.

"Was she forthcoming?"

"Eventually."

"And?"

"I have good news and bad."

"I'll take the bad news first."

"Those children Riggins stole from Mexico are already dead," said Louis.

I felt like crawling back under the sheets and never coming out again.

"And the good news?"

"They've been dead for a long, long time."

5

The modern artist must live by craft and violence . . .
Those artists, so called, whose work does not
show this strife, are uninteresting.

Ezra Pound, "The New Sculpture"

CHAPTER LXXIV

They had no names, for their names were not recorded. Three girls, one boy: the girls aged approximately six, eight, and eleven, the boy fourteen. They were children not of the poor but of nobles, each selected for their beauty; the offerings had to be as close to perfection as human frailty allowed. They would have been brought to the Incan capital, Cusco, along with tens, even hundreds of others, from there to be dispatched across Tawantinsuyu, the empire, all destined to end their lives in a pit.

Sometime in the late fifteenth century, these four were sent to the southern reaches of Tawantinsuyu, near the volcano called Nevados Casiri, or Paugarani, close to what is now the Peruvian-Chilean border. There they were dressed in finery, their hair braided, and their faces marked with pigment. In a cave within sight of the volcano, on high arid ground, they were fed corn alcohol, or *chicha*, to put them to sleep, and their mouths were stuffed with coca leaves before their bodies were placed in the ground—though not covered. The winds passing through the chamber desiccated their skin and internal organs, the cold slowed bacterial decay, and thus a process of natural preservation occurred.

The children were not sacrifices. A sacrifice would not have been treated so tenderly, but would instead have been burned, beheaded, pierced with arrows, and their heart torn out. These children were mediators, destined to act as intermediaries between men and gods—or *a* god, for the Andean cave in which they were discovered contained, along with some food, fabrics, and small items of gold and silver, likenesses of only one deity: Supay, the god of death, ruler of Ukhu Pacha, the underworld.

Before the Inca, the Wari and Tiwanaku had also journeyed to that place to leave their offerings. It was not a cave but a gateway, and Supay had many cognomens. What mattered was that the children were not alone in the dark.

They had a mother.

CHAPTER LXXV

We crossed the Kennebec to the Bankery in the Flat Iron District because I wanted a good cup of coffee. I thought it might make my head stop hurting; if it didn't, it couldn't make it hurt any worse. The Bankery combined a coffee shop and a florist, which was unusual.

"Did you pick this place because we're gay?" Angel asked, as we sat down to coffee and a mix of morning buns and Danish pastries.

"Do you have an objection?"

"Not at all. I just didn't credit you with so much sophistication."

I drank my coffee and instantly felt better. The same couldn't be said for anyone seated within sight of me. If I'd owned the Bankery, I'd have asked me to eat with a bag over my head or have me hidden away behind some bouquets. That nobody did either was a testament to the kind nature of the staff. Now, at the Bankery's most secluded table, Louis shared with me all he had learned from Zetta Nadeau.

"She confirmed that Riggins and Emmett Lucas did the grunt work," he said, "helped by some local talent and a pair of antiquities dealers—a Mexican and an American out of Palm Desert, California. On this side of the border, a couple called the Swishers provided contacts and advice on transportation and preservation. They also stored the children for a while, and performed repairs and restoration. Funding came from multiple sources, but Devin Vaughn was the instigator, and one of the principal investors. His mentor, Donnie Ray Dolfe, was another."

"And the rest?"

Louis shrugged. "I think Zetta would have told me if she knew."

Riggins and Lucas had traveled to Blas Urrea's stronghold of Guerrero in late fall to scout the terrain, before returning to the United States to prepare for the extraction, where they stayed for a few days with Hul and Harriet Swisher in Virginia. The Swishers schooled them on the proper care, handling, transportation, and storage of delicate human remains. Zetta, said Louis, had found the mechanics of the process familiar, being not dissimilar to how fragile artworks are handled. The two men had then flown to Morelia in Michoacán, the neighboring state to Guerrero, where the equipment they would require was shipped to them from a number of unconnected suppliers. The cache included aluminum-coated Cellite boards fitted with a layer of Plastazote covered with calico, with an additional tier of Melinex to act as a cushion between the calico and the children's clothing; five plywood and timber crates treated with waterproof paint; and Tyvek-covered foam pads to fill the negative space. The children were to be placed horizontally on the Cellite boards and packed singly into the crates, with those crates to then be strapped into the back of an air-ride truck to dampen vibration.

Riggins had settled on Michoacán as a base since they would be less likely to attract attention from Urrea loyalists, and he retained reliable contacts in Morelia from previous employment. Michoacán was also within striking distance of the *municipio* of Zirándaro, where Urrea was storing the children. In Morelia, Riggins and Lucas were joined by two of the former's contacts, whose names Zetta did not know, and in a warehouse the four men practiced assembling the material, carrying plaster models on the handling boards, packing them into crates, and doing dry runs for the raid.

They drove into Zirándaro as Mexican/American duos, each in separate vehicles. One additional member of the team was already in Zirándaro, watching the old church that served as the shrine for the children. He confirmed the presence of only three guards, all casual to the point of somnolence because Urrea considered himself untouchable in Guerrero. The two trucks came to a halt within sight of the church, and Riggins and his colleague, assisted by the sentinel, took care of the guards after a brief scuffle.

"But Riggins didn't want to eliminate them, right?" I said.

"Zetta claims Riggins isn't a stone killer," said Louis. "Neither was Lucas. Call it professional ethics. Special forces soldiers don't kill anyone without a gun in their hands, not unless they have to. But Vaughn also liked the idea of avoiding casualties. He thought it would add to Urrea's humiliation. The whole operation took less than an hour, from the moment the first guard went down to the time the trucks drove away with the bodies. They crossed back into Michoacán, switched the crates to a larger single truck in case the others had been noticed, and Riggins and Lucas took it to the Port of Lázaro Cárdenas. The Mexican dealer had the connections to get the crates safely on a ship to San Diego and off again at the other end, and the Palm Desert guy took care of getting them from San Diego to the Swishers in Virginia. And that was it, until Urrea tracked down the first of the Mexicans from Michoacán."

I went over the tale again in my mind, or the region of it unaffected by misery and medication.

"You mentioned five crates," I said, "but only four children. So one crate was a spare?"

"There was an additional corpse in the church."

"A fifth child?"

"No, a woman: centuries older than the rest, and discovered in the same cave. Riggins and Lucas were ordered to bring her along if they could, but she wasn't as desirable as the children. According to Riggins, it was hard to tell that the body was even female because it was curled up in a ball. Only the long hair gave it away. Anyway, there was a problem with securing her crate, and Riggins was worried that it might come loose and damage the rest, so they dumped the woman and left her to rot. She wasn't important. The kids were Urrea's real good-luck charms, and he'd paid a lot of money for them. But more than that, they were his responsibility. They'd once been offered to a god, who had presumably accepted them. Maybe they should never have been removed from the cave, just left to be buried when it collapsed, as it was set to do within a few years. But once the decision was made to retrieve them, a duty of care was implied, regardless of any payment involved, and that duty was Urrea's. Losing them was bad for business, bad karma, bad everything, and most of all, it made him look weak. Now, not only does he want them back, he needs them, which is why the locals who helped steal them are dead, Bilas is dead, Emmett Lucas is dead, and who knows how many others. Urrea is on the warpath through his proxy, Eugene Seeley."

"Given the corpses he's left behind, Seeley's quite the proxy," I said, "but he can't be working alone."

"Urrea must have men on this side of the border," said Angel.

"But would they defer to Seeley?" I asked Louis.

"They'd do what Urrea told them," he replied. "But if I were Seeley, I'd use my own crew—except for seriously dirty work, which I'd leave to Urrea's gunmen. Urrea might have placed a lieutenant alongside Seeley, though, someone whose loyalty goes beyond money."

"Loyalty to Urrea or the children?"

Louis shrugged. "How about both?"

"So, again, who now has the children?"

"Zetta claimed not to know, only that Vaughn definitely had one and Dolfe another. It was Dolfe, not Vaughn, who suggested using Riggins and Lucas. They were all from the same area, more or less, and Riggins and Lucas ran with Dolfe's kids. Dolfe is also dead, by the way, and the Swishers too."

"I heard," I said. "Carrie Saunders told me before I got knocked on the head."

"Someone stole into his home a few nights back and cut out his heart," said Louis. "The death was covered in the newspapers, but the particular about the heart is being held back for now because the law is also looking at a link to the killing of the Swishers, who died in a fire in Loudoun County the same night. The husband's body was badly burned, but the wife's remains were less damaged—aside from being dead, that is, and missing a heart."

"Might they still have been holding on to one or more of the children?"

"Like I told you, Zetta couldn't say."

"Couldn't?"

"I stopped short of hurting her," said Louis. "I kept hearing your voice, objecting. I can go back. I don't like her art very much, so I'd be acting as much out of an aesthetic motive as any other."

"Did she tell you who advised Riggins to run, and why he stayed in Maine even after he received the warning?"

"Emmett Lucas sent the message. He and Riggins had set up trip-wires in Mexico for their own protection, an additional precaution they chose not to share with Vaughn or anyone else. When Urrea succeeded in tracking down the first of the locals, the alarm was triggered, giving Lucas and Riggins time to go to ground."

"Except Lucas didn't manage it as well as his pal."

"He might have been unlucky. It happens. As for why Riggins

remained in Maine, Zetta said he was worried about her. But we also know that Vaughn was the one who secured Riggins the job at BrightBlown, at an inflated salary, which was in addition to his payment for what went on in Mexico. It would make sense for him to remain close to BrightBlown and his paymaster."

"Except it doesn't," I said.

"Why?"

"It sounds as though Riggins was being paid to keep watch over someone up here in case things went bad, but that person can't have been Devin Vaughn."

"Zetta Nadeau?" Angel suggested.

"That would hold true only if she had one of the children," I said, "and I went through her place with her consent. It's not that big. Whatever she's hiding, it isn't a child."

"But she's hiding something," said Angel, "even if it's just knowledge."

We'd have to talk to Zetta again. We could do it on the way back to Scarborough. After that, I was unsure how to proceed. Mostly, I wanted to lie down and sleep for two weeks, and when I woke up, my head wouldn't ache and my face wouldn't be in danger of turning milk sour. But Zetta might yet be persuaded to see reason and sway her boyfriend into doing the same, because reports of people being eviscerated had a way of focusing the mind, and Eugene Seeley was coming for Wyatt Riggins.

"Either Seeley's no good, or he's very good," said Louis. "I'm leaning toward the latter."

I sneezed, and the pain was like being hit in the nose again. Blood sprayed across what was left of my morning bun—and I'd been enjoying it.

"The hell with this," I said. "We take one more run at Zetta and see what she has to say once she gets a look at my face. If I'm not happy with her, I'll sit down with the Falmouth PD and the FBI resident, with Macy as the go-between, give them everything I have, and wash my hands of it all. Zetta can take her chances with the law."

Louis patted my arm.

"Don't feel sore about it," he said. "The art world will get over the loss."

CHAPTER

LXXVI

When we arrived at Zetta Nadeau's studio, the gate was locked, her truck was absent, and the house looked deserted. Locking up hadn't saved her from an encounter with Louis before, but it didn't seem worth the trouble of breaking in just to confirm no one was home. I called Zetta, but the number rang out without going to voicemail. She either couldn't get to her phone or she'd made herself scarce.

On the other hand, two SUVs and a pair of panel vans were parked in front of Mark Triton's cottage, while a trio of men who didn't resemble art aficionados were watching us with the kind of interest that might have caused less hardy souls to quail. Triton's front gate was closed. I hit the intercom set into the pillar. A woman's voice answered, and I identified myself and asked if it might be possible to speak with Mr. Triton. The gate opened, and after a moment's pause for reflection, I asked Louis to drive us up to the cottage.

"In case we have to bust our way out later?"

"No," I replied. "Because my falling over while walking would make an abject first impression."

We pulled up outside the front door and got out. Two of the art non-lovers were keeping a marginally less close eye on us than a third, who had shadowed us on foot from the front gate. He was short and stocky and, in common with his colleagues, didn't carry himself like regular private security. He was too relaxed—even down to his clothing, which could have done with a wash and an iron—but the casualness didn't quite tip into cockiness. He was relaxed because he knew what he was doing and had carried out more difficult tasks elsewhere. I couldn't see a gun, but one would be concealed beneath his black Alpha Industries jacket, the weapon likely to be as worn but well maintained as the jacket itself.

"You think we should thank him for his service?" asked Angel quietly.

"While we're at it, we can ask him if Wyatt Riggins snores," I replied, "because I'll bet he has personal knowledge."

The front door opened and Mark Triton stepped outside, which saved having to invite us in. Behind him hovered a younger Native American woman. She appeared unhappy to see us, but that might just have been my face.

"Mr. Parker," said Triton. "It seems you've been in the wars."

I'd met Triton once before, when Zetta was having dinner with him at Boda on Congress. I wondered whether he'd have remembered me had I not first identified myself at the gate. I thought he might, because I was beginning to put together a picture that included him, Zetta, and Wyatt Riggins.

"Stepped on a rake," I said. "It might have been funny had it been caught on camera. I was looking for Zetta Nadeau."

"She's gone away, I believe." He peered past me to where Louis was standing. "An intruder made her concerned for her safety."

I gestured at the ex-military goon who had taken up a position to our left, giving him an uninterrupted field of fire. We weren't the threat, but no one had informed him.

"She doesn't strike me as the only one with safety concerns," I said.

"I'm planning a sale of items from my collection," said Triton. "Some of them are very valuable. These men will guarantee that all goes off without a hitch."

The Native American woman had quickly left us to our conversation; at least, I could no longer see her. If she was listening, she wouldn't learn anything because nobody here was telling the truth, or not all of it.

I turned my attention to the goon in the Alpha Industries jacket.

"Did you serve with Wyatt Riggins?" I asked.

His expression didn't alter. He had the fixed smile of a dead clown.

"Did Riggins own the rake you stepped on, Mr. Parker?" Triton asked. "Through Zetta, I'm aware that you've been searching for him."

"He was reluctant to be found," I said. "Emphatically so."

"Then perhaps you should leave him be, and Zetta too."

"A lot of the people I look for don't want to be found," I said. "If I followed your advice, I'd never leave the house."

"Given your current condition, that might be for the best," said Triton. "When I see Zetta, I'll tell her you were asking after her, but I really must be getting back to work."

I'd kept my right hand in my trouser pocket throughout. It wasn't as though I'd be much use anyway if Triton decided to have us thrown out. I had my finger on the call button of my cell phone, and now I pressed it. From somewhere inside the house, just before the door closed behind Mark Triton, I heard another cell phone ringing.

Zetta Nadeau's cell phone.

CHAPTER

LXXVII

The third of the recovered children, the girl taken from Devin Vaughn's home, was consigned to the care of Blas Urrea's people at a rendezvous point in Marriottsville, some twenty-eight miles west of Baltimore. La Señora had held the body in her arms, crooning to her in their common tongue, before surrendering her to a pair of Urrea's underlings. They would reunite the girl with two of her siblings at a private terminal on the Patapsco River, there to await the arrival of the last of them before all four were returned to Mexico by sea. Seeley noted how the Mexicans deferred to la Señora and did their damnedest not to look at her directly. If they weren't sure of who she was, they knew enough to be frightened of her.

Seeley had spoken with Urrea following Devin Vaughn's death, and was now aware of certain facts that had been concealed from him. Urrea had called to congratulate Seeley on what he had achieved so far, and to confirm that a bonus payment would be made to his account.

"I need to know," said Seeley.

"Know what?"

"About the woman."

"Why?"

"Because if I know about her, I can quantify her, and if I can quantify her, she won't disturb my dreams."

"She came out of the mountain," said Urrea. "With something inside her."

SEELEY AND ACREMENT WATCHED the van containing the child drive away. La Señora did not follow its progress but kept her head lowered. Had she not been so withered, so parched within, Seeley might have thought she was crying.

"We may soon have to part ways," said Acrement.

"Are you troubled?" Seeley asked.

"Troubled doesn't even begin to cover it."

"You aren't alone. When the children are safe, I may be forced to make new arrangements. I feel the call of foreign climes."

Behind them, the woman slid into the back of Seeley's car and lay down.

"She acts like she's their mother," said Acrement, "but their mother must be long dead. Like them." He tugged at his bottom lip. "Like—"

"Better not to reflect too hard on it," said Seeley.

"Did Urrea tell you who she is?"

"He said she was a god, or carried a god within her."

"Not a goddess?"

"He wasn't prepared to commit."

"Fucking woke is everywhere. So which god?"

"Urrea wasn't sure."

"Jesus Christ," said Acrement.

"But not that one, I'll wager."

Acrement glanced back at the car.

"What will she do when this is over?" he asked.

"Sleep, I imagine."

"No," said Acrement, "I think she'll decay."

"Let's call it 'resting,'" said Seeley. "It sounds less disconcerting."

THEY SWITCHED VEHICLES FOR what Seeley hoped would be the final time. He and la Señora picked up I-66, then 495 North to cross the Potomac into Maryland. Seeley would have preferred to avoid the highways, but the paucity of bridges restricted his options and he wanted to leave Virginia behind as quickly as possible. They entered Pennsylvania, where they stopped at a hotel for the night. Seeley booked two adjoining rooms, unlocked the door between them, and slept soundly, knowing the woman would not close her eyes. He woke refreshed to the noise of late-night traffic and considered finding a convenience store or fast-food restaurant. He knocked at the connecting door out of politeness and opened it without being invited to enter.

La Señora was sitting in a chair by the window, the blackout blinds raised but the thin drapes kept in place so she could observe without being observed in turn. Seeley tried to keep his expression neutral. La Señora had aged visibly during the time he'd been asleep. There were more lines on her skin, which was now little more than a pellucid membrane over bone. Her hair was finer, her body frailer, and her eyes were rheumy. Perhaps consuming pieces of her victims' hearts was an effort to sustain herself—Seeley hadn't cared to ask—but if so, it was failing.

"We are almost at an end," she said, and Seeley knew that she was referring both to their mission and herself.

"What can I do?" Seeley asked.

"Help me finish it. Take me to the last of my children."

CHAPTER

LXXVIII

Angel, Louis, and I sat in my kitchen, where I popped two more painkillers and waited for Macy to join us. While Wyatt Riggins had been practicing his swing on me, she'd been in Houston, Texas, bringing a northern perspective to a multi-agency panel on border security. She'd kept in touch with the hospital—Angel had told her what happened—but she hadn't been able to get back to Maine until that evening. She arrived at my home just as the Tylenol began to kick in—which was fortunate because she immediately commenced shouting, causing my head to start hurting again, though not as much as it might have done without the pills.

"What were you thinking? You knew Riggins might be dangerous, and still you tried to beard him without backup. Were you even armed?"

"I wanted to reason with him," I replied, "not kill him."

"And how did that work out for both of you?"

"Better for him than me," I admitted.

Macy transferred her ire to Angel and Louis.

"Where were you two while all this was going on?"

Louis looked at Angel, who shrugged.

"I think we were eating lunch," said Louis. "I had the fish."

"He definitely had the fish," said Angel.

I thought Macy might be about to flatten both of them, but the urge passed and she took a seat at the table. Louis poured her a mug of coffee and Angel slipped her a Two Fat Cats cookie he'd found at the back of the bread basket.

"Tell me all of it," she said.

CHAPTER

LXXIX

Early the next morning, Seeley and la Señora were on the move again: north through New York, New Haven, Hartford, Worcester, and circling Boston to end up on 295. They stopped only so that Seeley could use a restroom and buy some snacks. The woman consumed desultorily, mainly sweet things: candy, fragments of doughnut, even the unused sachets of sweetener bagged with Seeley's takeout coffee. Eating might simply have been a distraction for her, but he didn't doubt that she liked the taste of sugar.

They crossed the Piscataqua River Bridge into Maine, after which Seeley drove for another half hour until they reached the Kennebunk Service Plaza, where they waited for Acrement to catch up in the van. He did not arrive alone, because three men pulled up behind him in a dark Toyota RAV 4: Blas Urrea's killers, called into service by Seeley. Triton's property had been scouted, revealing that the collector might be prepared to fight to keep what was not his, and Seeley was not willing to die for the last child. Urrea's gunmen got out to stretch their legs and smoke but otherwise kept their distance.

Seeley made the call just as the afternoon sky brightened briefly in a token stand against the darkness to come.

"I count five armed men," said the woman who answered, "including Riggins. If they aren't all ex-military, I need my eyesight tested."

"Riggins is there?"

Seeley was surprised. Riggins must have known that he was as much a target as Triton. Perhaps he believed there was safety in numbers. If so, that illusion was about to be shattered.

"And Riggins's woman, the artist. She rents an onsite property from Triton, but she's retreated to the main house. I've seen another woman moving around as well. She looks Native American. Triton's girlfriend was here earlier, but she left before noon and didn't return."

"Have they tried to move the child?" asked Seeley.

"Not that I can tell, assuming Triton is keeping it at the house."

If the child was elsewhere, La Señora would make Triton tell.

"It's odd," said Seeley's contact.

"What is?"

"That they're waiting for you to descend on them."

"What would you do in their place?"

"I'd bug out."

"Really? How far do you think you'd get?"

The contact went quiet.

"I take your point," she said.

But Seeley's thoughts had already moved on. Triton, probably guided by Wyatt Riggins, had decided that he didn't want to pass the rest of his short life in fear, but appreciated that surrendering the child wasn't an option. He was calculating that if Urrea lost enough men, he might be forced to back off, even as he continued to be weakened by the theft of his talismans. But Triton, like the rest, had no idea of the forces Urrea had unleashed against him. Seeley and a trio of gunmen were the least of them: La Señora was the principal agent of vengeance. But time was against her, just as it was against Urrea, their fates being linked.

Seeley had no illusions about Blas Urrea, and no obligations to him beyond the task he was being paid to perform, but he was experiencing an uncomfortable sense of vocation when it came to La Señora. For her, this was not about money, pride, or the survival of a criminal enterprise. When those four children were laid in the dirt, they had passed into her care, and she would not forsake them. Their offering had been a bargain, a covenant between the weak and the strong. If either party failed to adhere to their side of the agreement, there would be consequences. La Señora's potency was predicated on belief, and that belief would be weakened if she was deemed to have failed to protect the children. If she couldn't watch over them, how could she be relied on to safeguard the faithful?

Seeley didn't bother telling his contact to stay in touch; she knew what was required of her. He hung up and shared the intel with Acrement and the Mexicans, who listened without comment. Only at the end did one of Urrea's men speak.

"They're expecting us?" he said. He didn't display fear. It was purely another variable to be factored into the equation.

"They're expecting someone," said Seeley. He gestured toward his car, where La Señora waited. "But not her."

CHAPTER
LXXX

On Cousins Island, two shapes resembling bears in green leisure suits were monitoring the Triton compound.

"What's that name they give to birdwatchers?" Tony Fulci asked his brother.

"Poindexters," Paulie replied.

"No, the other name."

Paulie mulled, gears turning slowly in his mind, the machinery grinding out an answer.

"Chasers," he said.

"That's it."

"Why?"

"The old lady down there, the one with the binoculars, she's got a bird book and a pencil, but she don't show no interest in birds."

"So what's she looking at?"

"Same thing we are: Triton's house."

"You want I should go talk to her?"

"What would you say?"

"I could ask her about birds."

"You don't know nothing about birds."

"If you're right, she don't either."

"Then what would be the point?"

Paulie figured his brother was right. Tony often was. Nevertheless, and without consulting him further, Paulie took out his cell phone, thumbed through his contacts, and stabbed the call button. This was what Paulie understood as "showing initiative," and was generally considered a good thing, so long as only the right people got hurt.

"Mr. Parker? Oh, sorry." Paulie paused. "We thought you should know we're not the only ones watching the house."

He explained about the woman by the water, listened for a while, said thank you, and hung up.

"What did Mr. Parker say?" asked Tony.

"It wasn't him. It was Mr. Louis. Mr. Parker's resting."

"So what did Mr. Louis say?"

"He told us we should feel free to drown her."

Tony took this in.

"Not unless we have to," he said.

And they returned to observing the house and the old poindexter. Chaser. Whatever.

CHAPTER LXXXI

Seeley's preparations for disappearing were virtually complete. Soon, funds would be transferred, old accounts closed and new ones opened, companies shuttered and assets disposed of. A clean identity would be activated, one known only to a handful of financial advisors, their discretion assured by relationships stretching back decades and generous commissions, because nothing said "I care" like a little douceur.

They would strike at Triton that night. Seeley would have preferred to wait, giving them more time to establish the routines at the property and assess the capabilities of Triton's security team, but retrieving the final child had become a matter of terminal urgency for la Señora.

In a vacant Freeport condo building rented for them by Seeley's Maine contact, Urrea's men were suiting up in full-body bulletproof armor: Level 3A+ equipment that covered the chest, shoulders, upper legs, groin, and neck. Seeley reflected that had Aldo Bern and his colleague invested in protection a grade or two higher, they might have suffered fewer injuries from the Claymore. They'd still be dead, of course—Seeley was always going to be better than them—but their suffering would have been lessened.

Urrea's Mexicans had prepared a big jug of *michelada*—beer mixed with tomato juice, lime, and hot sauce—and were consuming it from disposable cups while they worked. On the same table lay cold cuts, cheap sliced bread, and a selection of salads and fruit. Whatever the men discarded was placed in a black garbage bag, and they wore lightweight full-finger gloves that allowed a touchscreen to be operated without their removal. They had also brought a handheld vacuum fitted with a dust bag. Before they left the condo, one of them would don a surgical hair cap and clean the rooms, leaving as few traces of their occupancy as possible.

La Señora was sitting alone on the patio. Seeley thought she might be conserving what was left of her strength. He was reluctant to disturb her, but he had a final question he wanted answered before they went after Triton. It might have been attributable to curiosity had la Señora's impact on Seeley's beliefs not been so overpowering. He had caught a glimpse of the numinous, had entered its presence, and now required more: a confirmation, a revelation.

Seeley pulled up a chair beside her, in front of an empty swimming pool hardly big enough for a small child to complete more than a dozen strokes. The pool covering had come away to reveal dead leaves and the corpse of a bird. La Señora did not look at him, he did not look at her, and the afternoon sun barely warmed them both.

"Do you have something to say?"

"A question to ask," Seeley replied.

"Then ask it."

"Who are you?"

"Didn't Urrea tell you?"

"He told me a story: of children, a mountain, and a deity."

The woman laughed. It was a strange, rasping sound, and when she stopped, her breathing was more labored. A breeze arose, setting the leaves dancing and causing the dead bird's feathers to flutter.

"Urrea said that the children were taken from a cave that was about to collapse," continued Seeley. "It was assumed they'd been sacrificed to an *apu* linked to that place, but Urrea's researches revealed this was an error. The cave wasn't the home of a spirit, but a god."

La Señora's face bore a trace of amusement.

"Go on. I'm interested to hear where your reasoning leads you."

"You were there from before, long before. You watched over the children, like a mother."

"Like the First Mother."

Seeley heard regret—and love.

"Were there other children?" he asked.

"Yes, but not like them."

"Why were they different?"

"They did not fall silent like the rest, so I was not lonely." Lost to memories, eyes closed, she stroked her hair with her left hand. Seeley noticed that with each caress, strands came away from her scalp, falling to her shoulder.

"Name me, Seeley," she said. "We have come to it. That's what you want, isn't it? To speak, and in speaking, to bear witness?"

"Mama Sara?" he offered.

"A goddess of corn and crops? *¿Neta?* Try harder."

"Mama Quilla, then."

"The moon goddess, protector of women? Don't insult me, Seeley."

Her eyes flicked open and she bared her teeth. Seeley had pretended ignorance but she—they, *it*—had seen through him. He realized his error: men should not play games with gods. She turned to face him, and those teeth, now further exposed by the accelerating recession of her gums, seemed to him impossibly long and sharp.

"It was an error on my part," said Seeley. "I take it back. I should not have asked."

"Too late. The error is made."

"I don't—"

"It was not just a cave, but a doorway," she said, "an entrance to Ukhu Pacha. Do you understand? Are you beginning to see?"

Yes, Seeley was beginning to see, though he wished it were otherwise. Urrea had not been mistaken. This was no mere *apu*, but nor was it a mere god.

La Señora's voice altered, and Seeley heard both the male and female in it, the former now dominant. Seeley, who had been exposed to the worst in men, was confronted with a greater darkness, a convergence of shadows at the heart of existence from which emerged an intersex being of male and female aspect, and for the first time he feared, not the pain of dying, but what might come after. He had predicated his life on a promise of oblivion when it ended, a peace without end. Now that was taken from him, and what replaced it would haunt him until it became his reality after death. Behind the glass of the patio window, Urrea's men gathered. The gringo might have been a *chingon*, a badass, but even a *chingon* was capable of folly.

"You asked the question," said the voice, quieter now. "Speak the answer. Say my name."

"Supay," said Seeley at last. "I think you are Supay."

Inside, the Mexicans dispersed, returning to their tasks. La Señora's dry fingers stroked Seeley's face, the right index coming to rest against his lips. When she spoke again, it was in her usual register.

"How much longer?" she asked.

"As soon as night falls," said Seeley to the god of the underworld, the god of the dead and dying.

La Señora nodded. Seeley stood. He re-entered the building, went to the bathroom, locked the door, and tried to scrub away the memory of her touch.

CHAPTER

LXXXII

Macy agreed that the police lacked probable cause for a warrant to search Triton's property, and Yarmouth PD, with fewer than twenty officers, didn't have the resources to mount a major surveillance operation. The FBI's Art Theft Program would be able to do it, assuming they were interested, but they'd need time to set up. Their resources weren't as limited as Yarmouth's, but they were as stretched as any other branch of law enforcement. Macy thought it might take them between two and three days to get moving, though Ross might be able to help accelerate the process.

"You contact him," she said. "I'll alert Falmouth to what's happening, detailing the source of my information. Even if they can't do much, the machinery will have been set in motion, and both of us will be unsullied. I know you were trying to help Zetta, and save Wyatt Riggins too, but if you're right about everything, the best way to do that is to bring in Ross and the feds."

Sometimes, that's the way cases peter out: without a satisfactory resolution and with only a semblance of order restored. Anyway, order, justice, and reason were myths. Underlying all was chaos. The natural order was disorder.

"Until the feds or the local law get involved," I said, "we'll keep Tony and Paulie where they are—with assistance."

Macy glared at me.

"You're going to join them, aren't you?"

"The fresh air will do me good."

"If anything happens—"

"Nine-one-one, I promise."

She kissed me, carefully avoiding my ruined nose.

"I want this relationship to work," she said.

"So do I."

"It can't work if you're dead."

She kissed me again.

"I'll stay out of trouble," I said.

"Liar."

"But one with the best of intentions."

I was tired of being alone. I hadn't realized just how tired until I wasn't alone anymore.

MACY CONTACTED YARMOUTH PD. She informed them that I continued to regard Zetta Nadeau as a client and, in line with my commitment to her, had arranged to watch her place of residence, and by extension that of her landlord, Mark Triton. I called Ross from Louis's car, as he, Angel, and I drove north to join the Fulcis. I put Ross on speaker and gave him everything I had, holding nothing back.

"Why didn't you just bring in the Portland resident?" he asked.

"Because he'd call his boss, who'd call his boss, who'd call you. This way, I'm saving the taxpayer money."

"You're sure about Triton?"

"Close enough. Do some digging, and you should find the tie to Devin Vaughn. Triton's an art dealer, not a criminal—though given some of the prices he charges, that may be a moot point. But somewhere, he's been careless."

"I'll talk to Boston," said Ross. "If I can bring them around, we could have people on this by tomorrow morning. If I can't, you'll have to rely on the natives. I was about to add 'and your own discretion,' but you don't have any."

He hung up. Louis peered at me from the rearview mirror.

"How did it come to this?" he asked.

"Specifically, or in general?"

"I mean us and Ross."

"Bad luck. Poor judgment. Take your pick."

"I blame you," said Louis.

"Rightly so," I replied. "I blame me too."

CHAPTER LXXXIII

Night fell. In the woods, and now with us for company, the Fulcis had made themselves comfortable with a flask of fresh coffee, some candy, and a variety pack of Reese's Puffs and Cinnamon Toast Crunch Treats. The elderly birdwatcher was still seated in her car with the Triton compound in sight.

"How long do we stay here?" asked Angel, who had always regarded the great outdoors as unpromising, if only because there was traditionally nothing in it worth stealing.

"Until they come for Triton," I said, "or the feds take over, whichever is first."

I could just make out the shape of the birdwatcher, real or pretend, behind the windshield of her car. The interior light was off but the dashboard radio was glowing. My nose was hurting again, and my ribs too. I swallowed more painkillers and leaned against a tree, because standing was more comfortable than sitting. Perhaps whatever was going to happen wouldn't occur tonight, but the figure in the car said otherwise. If Triton had intended to move the child, he'd have done so already, and the woman would have been elsewhere. She wasn't just watching; she was waiting.

An hour passed, then two, then three. The lights were on in the Triton house. Through my Bresser night vision binoculars, I could see three people by the front door, one of them the small, silent man in the

Alpha Industries jacket. Two more joined them, a man and a woman. The woman was Zetta Nadeau, and the man, unless I was mistaken, was Wyatt Riggins. He lit a cigarette and said something to Zetta, who left him to walk down the driveway toward her home, entering through the back gate. I tracked her until she was lost from sight. No lights went on in the cottage so she must have been going to her studio. A few minutes later she returned to the main house and went inside. Riggins and the others didn't pay her any further attention.

Below us, a car started up. The birdwatcher was leaving, but instead of heading toward the main road, she stopped at the front gate of the compound and flashed her headlights. One of the guards began walking in her direction.

"You see that?" I asked Louis.

"Maybe we were mistaken, and she was one of Triton's people all along," said Angel.

But I didn't think so. I shifted the binoculars back to the house. Riggins and Alpha Industries were no longer in sight, but the guard approaching the gate was keeping his body turned slightly to hide his gun and make himself a smaller target. Whoever the woman might be, she wasn't known to them. Another guard descended to a spot halfway down, where a stone bench offered a modicum of cover.

The first guard was almost at the gate when the car suddenly reversed and shot left, speeding away from the property. The guard paused, staring after it in puzzlement, before spotting an object on the ground in front of him. He bent down to peer more closely at it.

When it came, the explosion caused a flare in my lenses that left me blinking away stars, even as the sound of the blast was oddly muffled. When my vision cleared, I didn't need the binoculars to see that the guard by the gate was down, and within seconds, we heard the first of the gunfire. I remembered my promise to Macy.

"Give us time to get down there and find Zetta," I shouted to Tony Fulci, "then call nine-one-one."

Angel and Louis were already on the move. Despite my busted ribs warning me against it, I went after them.

THREE OF TRITON'S MEN were already lying dead by the time Seeley approached the house. Two of Urrea's gunmen walked ahead of him, another alongside. The Mexicans on point had taken hits to the torso—Seeley saw them buck at the impacts—but the body armor had held up as they returned fire. Of la Señora, there was no sign. As soon as the device at the gate had gone off, she'd slipped over the low boundary wall and vanished into the shadows. Now, as Seeley reached the first of the dead guards, he saw he had been gutted. Urrea's gunmen might have killed the others, but this was the woman's work.

A pair of patio doors stood open before Seeley. The first of Urrea's men entered, the second close behind. The third was about to follow when a fragment of his skull separated from the rest and he dropped to the patio, taking a chair with him. Nearby, Seeley saw a black-jacketed man only a few inches taller than himself pointing a pistol in his direction. Seeley had just enough time to reflect that this was not how he would have wanted things to end when he heard a click but no discharge. The guard didn't panic at the misfire, just tossed the gun and reached behind him for a second, but by then Seeley was advancing. He fired and fired until the guard went down, and kept firing until his own weapon clicked empty and he had brought himself back under control.

Seeley followed the others, reloading as he moved into the house, but there was no more gunfire to be heard. Of Urrea's surviving men, Matías was positioned by the front door, while the second, Rubén, held a Native American woman by the hair. The woman was on her knees and bleeding from a cut to her forehead.

"Who are you?" Seeley asked.

"My name is Madeline Rainbird."

"Why are you here?"

"I'm a conservator. I'm advising Mr. Triton."

"Where's the child?"

"I don't know." Rainbird was scared, but she wasn't crying. Seeley regarded this as admirable under the circumstances. "She was there earlier."

Rainbird pointed to the living room, where Seeley saw an empty display case on a heavy console table. The glass front of the case had been shattered. "I swear she was, and now she's gone."

Seeley spoke to Rubén.

"*¿Dónde está la Señora?*"

"*Arriba. ¿Y esta chica?*"

Rubén tugged harder on Rainbird's hair.

"*Mantenla viva*," Seeley told him, "*por ahora*."

Seeley ascended. In the first bedroom, he found la Señora. She was kneeling over Triton, who lay spread-eagled on the bed. La Señora's face was red with blood, most of it probably Triton's, a stream still bubbling from the gash in his neck. La Señora was working at his chest with the curved blade of the tumi, but Seeley could tell that she was struggling. Her strength was almost gone.

"The child," Seeley asked her, "do you have it?"

She shook her head. With a final effort, she pushed the blade down, twisted, then pulled it free. Triton shuddered as she reached into the hole she had made.

"Find her," said la Señora. "Don't make me return."

Seeley heard both a plea and a warning, and knew la Señora would not be leaving this house. He turned away as her right hand arose from Triton's concavity clutching a reddish-black mass.

Seeley hurried downstairs, where Madeline Rainbird remained on her knees before Rubén.

"Riggins and Nadeau," he said, "where are they?"

"At the cottage, maybe," Rainbird replied. "That's where Nadeau lives. Don't hurt me, please. I've told you all I know."

"I believe you."

Seeley looked at Urrea's men. If he walked away now, the Mexicans would kill her. It would solve the problem she presented, but not in a way that sat comfortably with him. Seeley ordered Rainbird to be secured, hand and foot, and dumped on the lawn. There might yet be more killing, but he saw no reason to add her to the number. Acrement was parked on the road, ready to receive the final child. Seeley ordered Rubén to retrieve his fallen comrade's body and join Acrement in the van.

"*¿Qué pasa con la Señora?*" asked Matías.

"*Ella no va a volver con nosotros.*"

Matías accepted this without comment.

"*Venga conmigo,*" said Seeley.

Together, he and Matías descended toward Zetta Nadeau's home.

CHAPTER LXXXIV

Wyatt Riggins emerged from hiding once the attackers had left. He had been in the basement when the assault commenced, looking for a bottle of good wine with which to pass the time. As soon as he heard the shooting, he decided to stay where he was. Riggins wasn't a coward, but he wasn't suicidal either. If he left, he'd be entering a crisis situation in which he lacked knowledge of the threat and the disposition of the opposing forces. He'd also be doing it unarmed since he'd left his gun on the kitchen table, so he stayed quiet and listened to what he could make out from the exchanges above.

Riggins hoped that Zetta had managed to get as far away as possible. As for the final child, Riggins had heard something about its being missing, which meant Triton might have found somewhere to conceal it as soon as the attack commenced. Riggins wondered if Triton was dead. If so, the absence of the child was the only obstacle to the whole sorry affair being over and done with.

Carefully, Riggins ascended. If he couldn't find Zetta, he'd leave without her and make contact again once he'd found them somewhere safe to stay. She wouldn't have to worry about the police. She'd done nothing wrong. Neither had he, or nothing that could be proven, but it would be better if he was gone before they arrived.

He was two steps from the basement door when he smelled the

smoke and heard the crackle of flames. The house was burning. Urrea's people must have set it ablaze in a final act of spite before they left. The door was ajar. Through the gap, Riggins could see the open front entrance and the night beyond. Wherever the fire had started, it had not yet reached the hallway.

Riggins lay flat on the stairs before easing the door wider, giving him a clearer view of his escape route while making himself difficult to hit, but he saw no one, and no shots followed. He risked a glance around the doorframe, again to no response. To his right, the stairs leading to the second floor were half-obscured by smoke, and heat was coming from above. The fire must have been set upstairs, which was good news for him. More smoke was seeping from around the fittings of the hallway chandelier and billowing from the open coat closet by the front door. It looked like something in there had already caught fire as the flames ate through the floorboards above, but his attention was fixed on the rectangle of star-filled sky. It represented life.

Riggins made his move, his sweater pulled up over his nose and mouth to shield him from the smoke. He was just passing the closet when the pall inside assumed human form. Riggins reacted too late to the threat, and the blade entered beneath his left arm before punching straight through to his heart.

Riggins stumbled back, the blade still embedded in his torso, as a rush of blood filled his mouth. He bounced off the wall and slid to the floor, his head coming to rest against a mahogany table. The last sight to which he was privy before he died was a withered face in the process of disintegration, the features flaking scraps of skin like pale moths taking flight, and beneath the skin was—

Nothing, nothing at all.

CHAPTER
LXXXV

The vertical roller door of Zetta Nadeau's studio was closed to within a foot of the ground as Seeley and Matías reached it. Soft light spilled through the gap but no noise came from inside. The two men stayed back, because to step into the light would risk being shot in the lower legs by whoever was in the studio, whether that was the woman alone or she and Riggins both.

"Ms. Nadeau," said Seeley. "We only want the child. If you have it, give it to us and we'll be gone. We have no quarrel with you."

The only voice that responded came from the shadows nearby.

"But you may have a quarrel with us."

Seeley turned his gun toward the sound, searching for movement.

"And who are you?" he asked.

"My name is Parker. I'm a private investigator. Ms. Nadeau is my client."

"I repeat: we want the child. We won't leave without it."

"You have three guns on you," I said. "If we tell you to leave, you'll leave."

"But only to return, Mr. Parker. This can't end until the child is surrendered. I think you know that."

The sound of the garage mechanism broke the standoff. Gradually the door rose to reveal the studio and what it contained: Zetta Nadeau, standing by the clawed throne she'd created, and seated upon it, the hunched, mummified body of a female child.

Zetta's eyes shone unnaturally bright but lifeless, like glass.

"See," said Zetta, "I've humanized my art."

And for a time, the only sound was her laughter.

CHAPTER LXXXVI

Seeley took the child. We didn't try to stop him. Neither did Zetta. By then, something had broken inside her that would never be repaired. The last we saw of Seeley was his shape silhouetted against the burning house, cradling the child, a gunman trailing behind. They paused only to stare into the flames, and we, like them, glimpsed the figure of a woman standing unmoving in the doorway, though her whole body was afire. Then the ceiling came down on her and she was gone.

I FACED NO INTERROGATION in the aftermath, or none that presented any legal difficulties. It was an unusual position in which to find myself, and I might have grown to like it had I not recognized that it was unlikely to be repeated often.

Zetta Nadeau left the state of Maine. It was rumored that she lived in New Mexico for a month before crossing the border and journeying south through Colombia, Ecuador, Peru, Bolivia, Chile, and Argentina—the former territories of the Inca Empire.

Whatever she's searching for, I hope she never finds it.

6

Consider, brethren, what a wonderful honour this is. We men are cared for by angels . . .. we who are so full of the miseries of the flesh that we cannot bear at times to be in each other's presence are watched without ceasing by these glorious beings.

Gerard Manley Hopkins, "On Divine Providence and the Guardian Angels"

CHAPTER LXXXVII

A week later, Sam phoned to say she had spoken to her mother about her revised plans for college.

"How did she take it?" I asked.

"She told me she was going to talk to you."

"Did she look happy when she said this?"

"I'm hoping she was smiling on the inside."

"Great," I said. "Just great."

THAT SAME EVENING, RACHEL arrived at the house. I made a pot of coffee and we sat together in the kitchen we had once shared.

"I hear you have a girlfriend," said Rachel.

"Did Sam tell you?"

"Yes. Sam says she's a police officer."

"That's right."

"Do you love her?"

"I think so."

"Good."

"And you?"

"Jeff and I are back together, kind of."

Jefferson Reid; I'd never much cared for him. He was a rich fool—if that wasn't a contradiction, given that he'd made all his money himself—and I was sorry he was back in Rachel's life. At least Sam wouldn't have to put up with him, not if she was going to college.

"Do you love him?"

"No, but I enjoy his company and that's enough. He's nicer than you give him credit for, which wouldn't be hard." She stared at her feet. "But Sam doesn't like him. She gets that from you."

"I've never spoken badly of him in front of her," I said, or I was pretty sure I hadn't. Seventy-five percent sure. Say sixty and call it quits.

"You didn't have to. Sam picks up on things that remain unsaid. She always has."

"She gets her perception from you."

"Not all of it. Not the stranger part."

I didn't reply.

"She told me she wants to be a private investigator, like her father," Rachel continued.

"Not like me. Better."

"Would you take my side if I tried to stop her?"

"No," I said. "But I doubt you will."

Rachel set down her coffee cup.

"It wasn't what I wanted for her," she said.

"What did you want?"

"Conventionality. A normal life. I think it was only ever a dream. Because of you."

"I'm sorry," I said, and I was.

"You can't help what you are."

"Says the psychologist. I hope that's not your guiding professional principle or you'll die poor."

"Others can help themselves," said Rachel, "but not you. I don't know what you are. I don't believe I ever did. But I loved you. I still love you, though I never want to be with you again. You frighten me."

The room was quiet for a long time. I heard a bird cry in the marshes.

"Sam told me something else," said Rachel. "She said she could see Jennifer, or used to."

"Yes."

"And you never thought to share that with me?"

"Are you saying you suspected nothing? If so, I'm not sure it would be the truth."

Rachel opened her mouth to speak, only to close it again without saying anything more. She drank her coffee, just to give herself something to do.

"No," she said at last, "it wouldn't be. Do you know why Jennifer came to Sam?"

"I'm not sure. It may have been to protect her."

"That's not what Sam thinks, or it's not the only reason. She thinks Jennifer was trying to protect both of you, but you more than her. You must know why that was, or is."

"I don't."

"Do *you* still see Jennifer?"

"Not for a long time," I said. "I've felt her close. She watches me while I sleep."

Rachel buried her face in her hands.

"Oh God," she said. "Oh God, oh God, oh God . . ."

I went to her. I held her close as she shook her head against me.

"What are you hiding?" she asked.

"Nothing."

She pulled away from me.

"No, what are you hiding from yourself? What have you buried so deep that it's been lost even to you?"

But I had no answer to give.

Rachel stood to leave.

"Sam will do whatever she wants," said Rachel. "But I expect you,

Angel, and Louis to guide her as best you can, to educate and train her so that if she follows this path, she'll have all the skills she needs to survive. I want her kept safe. Do you understand?"

"Yes."

"In the meantime, you need to uncover what's hidden. Until you do, we're all vulnerable."

I followed her to the door. I didn't offer her a bed for the night. I knew she wouldn't want to stay, not after this, not ever.

"Rachel."

She paused. Around the porch light, early insects flitted, newly hatched and drawn by the radiance.

"What if it's better that it should stay unknown?" I asked.

"Why? What do you think might happen?"

A beacon revealed itself, cutting through the dark. A signal pulsing in the abyss.

"I think they'll realize," I said. "I think they'll come."

CHAPTER LXXXVIII

From the woods, Jennifer Parker watched the angels: three of them, the two from before and another, taller and more attenuated, its configuration less fixed, like a bare winter tree glimpsed through gray-black smoke. It was sexless, featureless, and trailed long shreds of darkness behind it, as of a tattered cloak caught by the wind—or vast wings unfurled, except this was an illusion, one that might have given rise to the concept of flighted angels. What Jennifer was seeing were shreds of reality, the fractured aftermath of the sundering of dimensions.

Such power, even if it is borrowed from another . . .

It hurt Jennifer's eyes to look at the third angel, but not because of any beatific luminosity. This one was beyond light or dark and held only the void within. For the first time, Jennifer understood why the shepherds in the Bible were so afraid when God's messenger appeared to them. Terror was the only appropriate response to such an entity.

"Keep very still." It was Martin's voice, whispering behind her.

"It's not like the others."

"No, it's not. It's much worse. They've been telling tales, those two."

"To who?"

"A higher authority. I'd say that was what the firstborn of Egypt glimpsed before they were put to the sword, and the Israelites who were judged because of David's numbering of them, and the Assyrians who attacked Jerusalem. They saw a *malakh ha-mashhit*: a dark angel, a destroyer of men."

The dark angel took a single step toward the woods. At the same time, its companions disappeared, leaving Jennifer and Martin alone with it. Beyond, the dead kept their eyes fixed on the water, the horizon, anywhere but on the being by the shore. Jennifer doubted they knew what was there, only that something was, its existence better left unacknowledged.

"Can it hear us?" Jennifer asked.

"I don't think so, but it knows we're in here—or that you are, more to the point. It's trying to decide whether it's worth the effort of hunting you, because even it doesn't care for these woods. It's also probably beneath its dignity to tangle with a child."

No eyes were visible in the angel's face, but Jennifer could see its head moving as it scanned the trees until, finally, it fixed its attention on where she and Martin lay. The next moment, Jennifer felt it probing at her, and less gently than the others had done. Where they had left doors unforced and locks unbroken, this one tried to rip apart the barriers she had erected to protect herself. She reached for Martin's hand and gripped it tightly.

"Fight it," he said. "Don't let it in."

"I won't," she said, and she didn't, but the effort cost her. By the time the angel abandoned its attack, she was in pain, and she could not remember when last she had known pain.

The archangel folded around itself what passed for its wings, its aspect growing ever narrower until, at last, it was gone. Only then did Jennifer release Martin's hand.

"What happens next?" she asked him, as the pain eased.

"It will inquire into you."

"And then?"

"That depends."

"On what?"

"On what it discovers."

"But they still can't force me to go with them. You said so."

"They can't force you, but I told you: They can wear you down until you'll be doubting your own name and fearful of everything but the water and the release it promises."

"So what should I do?"

"Keep to the woods. Stay out of sight. They think time is on their side, because they have eternity. But they're wrong."

Jennifer turned to look at him. Even in the dimness, she could see doubt on his face.

"Or," he added, "I hope so."

CHAPTER LXXXIX

In the place between sleeping and waking, Jennifer came to me. I heard her voice as surely as I had in those days when, unable to sleep or frightened by a bad dream, she would trek from her room to stand by my side and wake me from sleep with the touch of her hand.

daddy, she said, *i made a mistake*

I felt her fingers brush mine, in death as once in life. I saw the shoreline, and the waters in which the departed immersed themselves. Where Jennifer would sometimes sit, waiting for the day when I might join her, I glimpsed three figures, one taller and darker than the rest, its form indistinct, shimmering, threatening. This was what Jennifer had witnessed from her place of concealment, and she wanted me to witness it too.

i should have hidden myself better

The tallest of the three stepped forward, its features transforming from the indistinct to the defined without remaining fixed on any one aspect, as though a multiplicity of identities resided within a single being, each seeking precedence and each failing. Some I knew by name or sight, while others seemed familiar without my being able to recall precisely why. But what they had in common, either remembered or sensed, was that all had caused me harm. Briefly, the features became those of the Traveling Man, he who had taken Jennifer and her mother from me, before finally settling on one face.

My face.

Jennifer's voice broke in sorrow.

i should have hidden us both

ACKNOWLEDGMENTS

Writers are magpies by nature, always keeping an eye out for shiny things they can use. My office is full of books marked with pieces of card, clippings from newspapers and magazines, and scribbled notes to self that, even if they were legible, would probably make no sense, though they must have seemed very important at the time. In the past, I would sometimes take photos of articles or book pages on my phone and never look at them again, so I've reverted to keeping a notebook, which is far more useful.

But memories are also shiny things, and *The Children of Eve* comes freighted with them: of my first visit to Argentina more than a decade ago, and making the mistake of trying to drive the scenic route from Salta to Cafayete in a vehicle unsuited to the rough terrain. Darkness descended on the unlit road, and suddenly the car lurched and dropped on one side. Sparks flew into the night as the rear right tire parted company with its wheel, leaving me stranded.

Then, miraculously, a car filled with Argentinian policemen appeared out of nowhere, perhaps drawn by the flashes in the dark. They changed my wheel, tipped their caps to me, and vanished into the night, enabling me to drive the remaining ten miles or so to Cafayete. Unfortunately, the experience left me so shaken that the appeal of Cafayete and its surrounding landscape was rather spoiled. I returned instead to spend my remaining few days in Salta—this time via the main road—where I visited the Museo de Arqueología de Alta Montaña, the Museum of High Altitude Archaeology, which contains the mummified bodies of a female adolescent and two children left on the Llullaillaco volcano as an offering to gods, probably in the fifteenth century. The display is macabre, unsettling, and strangely moving; I feel pity for those children to this day.

Yet, as Graham Greene observed, every writer has a "splinter of ice" in their heart that allows them to file away even the most awful of experiences—their own or, better yet, someone else's—for future use. So, despite all I might have felt for them, the Children of Llullaillaco were hoarded, three shiny things among the rest, until they found a place in this novel.

My thanks to Sue Fletcher and Jo Dickinson, my editors at Hodder & Stoughton, and Emily Bestler, my editor at Atria/Emily Bestler Books, for continuing to support and improve my work after more than twenty-five years. Thanks, too, to the staff at Hachette and Atria: at Hachette, Katie Espiner, Swati Gamble, Alice Morley, Catherine Worsley, Rebecca Mundy, Eleni Lawrence, Oliver Martin, Lewis Czizmazia, Dominic Smith and his sales force, Jim Binchy, Breda Purdue, Ciara Doorley, Ruth Shern, Siobhan Tierney, and Elaine Egan; and, at Atria, Lara Jones, Gena Lanzi, Hydia Scott-Riley, Dayna Johnson, Sarah Wright, and David Brown. My agent, Darley Anderson, and his team are as professional as they are considerate. Steve Fisher, my film and TV agent at APA, and his assistant, Chip Draper, are proof—if proof were needed—that the movie business can be a kind and decent one.

Regarding the Dead: Human Remains in the British Museum, edited by Alexandra Fletcher, Daniel Antoine, and J. D. Hill (British Museum, 2014), was a useful source of ethical and practical information on the retrieval, transportation, and storage of ancient bodies. *The Ancient Kingdoms of Mexico* by Nigel Davies (Penguin, 1990) and *Art of the Andes: From Chavín to Inca* by Rebecca R. Stone (Thames & Hudson, 2016) provided background on sacrifices and art. "The Bone Collector" by Josh Sanburn (*Vanity Fair*, November 2021) opened my eyes to the lengths some collectors will go to in order to feed their obsession with antiquities, and "Commentary: Tribes in Maine Left Out of Native American Resurgence" by Joseph Kait, Amy Besaw Medford, and Jonathan B. Taylor (*Maine Sunday Telegram*, February 19, 2023) enhanced my understanding of the situation of Native Americans in Maine. In addition, Brian Woodbury, former bookseller and continuing decent person, cast an expert eye over some of the cannabis sections, aided by the kind folk at Firefly Organics in Maine, who bear no resemblance at all to Devin Vaughn and his associates, Firefly being thoroughly good sorts. It was then left to Dominick Montalto and John McGhee to correct all the stuff I still managed to get wrong. Whatever errors remain, I ashamedly claim as my own.

Finally, my gratitude to Laura Sherlock and Becky Hunter for publicizing my books in the UK; Ellen Clair Lamb for assisting, proofreading, and promoting; Cliona O'Neill for her keen eye; Cameron Ridyard for my website; and Jennie, Cameron, and Megan, and Alastair and Alannah for being on my side. Love to you all.

John Connolly
Spring 2025